AUG 20

D1374867

Two Times
Twenty

60000 0000 09307

Also by

Bethan Darwin

Back Home

Two Times Twenty

Bethan Darwin

HONNO MODERN FICTION

Published by Honno
'Ailsa Craig', Heol y Cawl, Dinas Powys,
South Glamorgan, Wales, CF64 4AH

© Bethan Darwin, 2010

The right of Bethan Darwin to be identified as the author of this
work has been asserted in accordance with the Copyright, Designs and
Patents Act 1988.

The author would like to stress that this is a work of fiction and
no resemblance to any actual individual or institution is intended or
implied.

ISBN: 978-1-906784-23-2

All rights reserved. No part of this book may be reproduced, stored
in retrieval system, or transmitted, in any form or by any means,
electronic, mechanical, photocopying, recording or otherwise, without
clearance from the publishers.

Published with the financial support of the Welsh Books Council.

Cover design: G Preston
Cover photograph: ©Baoba Images/Getty Images
Printed in Wales by Gomer

**Peterborough
City Council**

60000 0000 09307 ✓	
Askews	Oct-2010
	£8.99

*This book is dedicated to my parents
Doreen and Eric Darwin who fell in love in 1960
and have stayed that way ever since.*

I thought getting a first book written was difficult; getting a second one done seemed almost impossible. My thanks go to everyone who helped me get there; my partners and colleagues at Darwin Gray Solicitors, Shelley Murray, Patricia Clayton, Suzanne Bartch, Caroline Oakley, Helena Earnshaw, Denice Cummings-Jones, Anna Chalkley, Rhianydd Darwin and all the super women and men who read the first book and took the time to tell me they enjoyed it and were looking forward to the second. And to David, Caleb and Megan I love you three so much, I'll even go to Disney World (and back) again.

Chapter 1

The thing about being forty is that I don't feel that much different from the way I felt at twenty. Really I don't. I still like the same food I liked when I was twenty and I still have the same lefty views, more or less. OK, admittedly a bit less nowadays. I still drink too much of a Saturday evening and when I'm with my parents I still feel that they're the grown-ups really. Even though I've got kids of my own now, I'm still the me I was when I was twenty. Except, of course, when I look in the mirror and see the size of my arse and the bags under my eyes. The mirror tells me for a fact that I'm not the same me I was when I was twenty. I might feel like I did back then but I've lived a whole lot longer and a whole lot harder since and it shows. Boy does it show.

Turning forty is a big deal. Forty is a birthday that forces you to climb up on the shoulders of your life and from that steep and craggy vantage point look back over your past. And if when you get up there you find you don't like what you see, you'd damn well better choose where you go next more carefully.

Perhaps that's why my fortieth birthday was so important to me. Because, my children aside, I was distinctly underwhelmed with what I had to show for my first thirty-nine years on the planet. Or perhaps it was because it was dawning on me that forty was halfway to eighty and that made me officially middle-aged, with the best half already lived. Whatever the reason, I decided that what I needed for my fortieth was a party. A cheesy party, with a disco and flashing lights and a cake with candles, to which I could invite just about every person in my life who mattered to me and quite a lot of people besides who didn't matter at all. The kind of party at which I could shake my fist in the face of death while I still had the chance.

Persuading the publican at my local to let me take over his entire pub for the night of my birthday was not easy. He was worried about his regulars.

'That's a Saturday night Anna. I can't close for a private party on a Saturday. How about a night in the week instead? Thursday night is the new Friday night, apparently.'

'I want people to have fun Steve.' I did a little step to the left, another to the right. 'You know, do a little dance, get down tonight, that sort of thing. Not sip a pineapple juice and slope off home for the 10 o'clock news because they've got to go to work the next day. And parties just aren't the same if they're not on the actual day.'

'But you know how it is round here Anna. People take offence easily. If they turn up on a Saturday night and get turned away they'll be off down the Royal Oak and the next thing you know I'm out of business. I couldn't risk it love. Commercial suicide.' Steve tugged his shirt nervously over his beer belly. Even with a bit of a gut, Steve's a nice-looking bloke with kind eyes and long legs but he will insist on wearing black shirts because he thinks they make him look thinner when in fact they make him look like a darts player.

'Oh come on Steve! My birthday's not till July. You've got the best part of three months to warn your customers you'll be closed for a private party that Saturday night. Half of them will be invited anyway. I'm going to put a stash of money behind the bar so you're bound to take more than you would do normally. And I hope you'll be there? As a guest that is, not working the bar. I tell you what, if a real regular turns up for a drink we'll just let them come in and join the party. How's that?'

'I don't know Anna.'

I played my trump card. 'All the girls from the aerobics class will be there.'

There hadn't been a Mrs Steve for quite some time.

'All of them?' he smiled at me.

'Every single one.'

Got him!

It was hardly a high-society venue I was negotiating for. It's a local pub, like thousands of other local pubs across the country. It has a snug where the old boys drink and a lounge bar, where the rest of us go, with a flowery maroon carpet and wooden tables and chairs sticky with dark-brown varnish. There's a gambler, a juke box and a fag machine. There's a small kitchen and, strictly between 12.30pm and 2pm only, Steve serves things with frozen chips – steak and kidney pie, gammon and egg, sausage and beans. That was another reason I wanted the pub as a venue for my party – I knew that I could persuade Steve to let my friend Jane do the catering because he wouldn't want to do it himself for love nor money.

3

Jane wouldn't normally contemplate catering at pubs. She runs a very classy catering company, doing the food for society weddings and posh christenings and swanky business launches. Fortieth birthday parties at local pubs would usually be far beneath her but she had offered to cater for my party as her birthday present to me.

'Are you sure about this?' I asked her when I called round with the good news that Steve had relented and I could have the pub the night of my birthday. 'It's incredibly generous of you. Won't you be losing a fortune doing that for me on a Saturday night?'

'Not really,' Jane reassured me, 'I'll make a few extra canapés every time I do a client gig from now on and freeze them and before long I'll have a freezer-full especially for you. I'll make mini Yorkshire puddings with roast beef, gruyere crostini and baby tomato bruschetta and some of those little sausages with marmalade glaze that you love so much.'

I imagined the faces of some of Steve's regulars turning up for their usual four pints of IPA and instead being offered a glass of white wine and little bits of toasted bread. Foreign food and a girl's drink would have them scurrying down the Royal Oak faster than being excluded from the pub altogether.

'Jane, it all sounds absolutely delicious. I'd be at least a size 24 if I did your job. I'm only sorry the pub won't be as classy as your food.'

'Don't you worry about that,' Jane said, 'I can sort that out no problem. I've got some fairy lights left over from a wedding we did last year where the bride was a bit older than the groom and didn't want any natural light;

4

we'll put those up all over the pub and they'll flicker and twinkle romantically and hide the nicotine stains on the ceilings. And we can go down the flower market and buy some flowers wholesale – I've got loads of plain glass vases we can put them in – and we'll dot them all around, get some lilies so that the place smells nice. Don't worry Anna, I promise I can turn even Steve's pub into a fairy grotto. Just you wait. It'll be perfect.'

We were sitting at her kitchen table, drinking a bottle of Chablis that was chilled exactly right. Cold but not so cold that you couldn't taste the flavour of the wine. That's one of Jane's many skills – she knows how to serve wine at the right temperature. Not only is her white wine always perfectly chilled but her red wine is always velvety smooth and somehow just the right side of warm, slipping lusciously and easily down your throat. I've asked her to share the knack with me dozens of times but she claims she doesn't do anything special, you just put white wine in the fridge and with red wine you open it and leave it on the kitchen counter for a short while before serving. I think that's where I must be going wrong. Any wine that arrives at my house goes directly from shopping bag to glass. Doesn't pass Go. Doesn't collect £200.

You know how sometimes when you've known someone for a long time you stop looking at them? I mean you look at them but you don't really see them. And then all of a sudden you see them again in a different light, as if for the first time. Like a stranger might. That's how I felt that evening, looking at Jane. She was wearing a beautifully tailored, navy wool pinstripe suit with wide-legged trousers, a short fitted jacket and high-heeled boots and she was balancing a slim folder on her knee, scribbling in it as we talked, making a list of the things she was going to organise for my party. Her shoulder-length, honey-blonde hair, glossy and perfectly straight, fell across her face as she worked, and as she absentmindedly hooked a strand behind her ear I suddenly thought: *This is what you do for a living and you are really good at it. You are a really successful business woman, not just my friend who lives down the road who I've known for years and take for granted, and you do this every day and you do it well. You fill every single one of your customers with confidence that you will make their special event absolutely perfect, like you just did to me. Wow.*

Affection and gratitude rushed through me. 'Thanks for this Jane. I really appreciate it.' I reached forward, squeezed her pinstriped knee gently. 'You and Bob will be my guests of honour.'

'Well I'll definitely be there. Can't be sure about Bob. He's usually ready for his bed by 8pm.'

A voice called from the living room.

'Don't listen to her Anna. I wouldn't miss your birthday shindig for the world. I'll have a nap in the afternoon if needs be.'

'Nothing wrong with your ears is there Bob Price?' Jane called back. 'Do you fancy a glass of wine? Anna and I have just about finished in here.'

'Only if you two join me.'

'Is that an invite to your boudoir Mr Price?' I asked.

'Certainly is.'

I waited for Jane to pour a small measure of wine into a half pint glass and plop in a straw and then the

6

two of us went to sit with Bob in what had once been the Prices' living room but which for a little while had acted as Bob's bedroom. Bob was sitting in his favourite armchair, one with a high, straight back and wings. It had once been part of a three-piece suite they'd got when they first moved into the house and it was very out of fashion and a bit grubby in places, but Bob had insisted it was saved from the dump when Jane decided its matching companions had had their day. It was about the only piece of furniture in the room that was not specially adapted and it gave Bob pleasure still to be able to sit in it comfortably.

He smiled at us both, a big, wide welcoming grin that made his eyes crinkle. Bob is still a very handsome man, his olive skin smooth and almost totally unlined, with just the faintest of wrinkles around his eyes and along his forehead. His thick hair, which was dark brown when I first met him, is now mostly iron grey but there is lots of it and the hairdresser who comes to the house is excellent and gives Bob a very short youthful cut which Bob claims makes him look like George Clooney. Jane handed him his wine and I tried not to look away as Bob struggled to hold the glass straight, clamping his lips over the straw and taking a big suck.

'Chablis. A very good one too. Jane must like you a lot Anna. She usually only gives me boring old Chardonnay. You should come round more often.'

'Nothing wrong with your taste buds either is there?' I joked.

'Not a bloody thing. It's just the rest of me that's totally useless,' Bob said without a hint of self pity.

Chapter 2

Bob and Jane moved into our street about a month or so after I had my second son, Niall. He was due the last week of August and I remember clearly how alien my body felt that summer as I waited for him to arrive, stretched and aching and so much more of me than there used to be, hips and belly and breasts bunching around me and slowing me down. The only summer clothes that fitted me were two ugly cotton maternity frocks that my mother had given me and that I'd had no intention of ever wearing. I wore one and washed the other every day. The dresses got thinner and softer with every wash and their faded patterns grew familiar and dear to me. As the school holidays drew to a close, the final precious days, heavy with sunshine and ripe as a peach, slipped away like water through cupped fingers, and I had to accept that my second child was going to be the oldest in his school year and not the youngest.

He finally arrived, eight days late, on the second of September. He did not sleep well and woke often during the night. In the day I was so tired that there was a constant buzzing in my ears and my arms and legs were awkward and clumsy, as if I was wearing layers of thick, padded ski-wear which left no room for my knees or elbows to bend properly. If I sat down my eyes would grow heavy and start to close and then my head would suddenly jerk forward and I'd realise I must have fallen asleep. It could only have been for a few seconds at most, not even that probably, but my inability to stay awake scared me. I was meant to be in charge of two babies. So I stopped sitting down.

Have you ever had a couple of glasses of wine in the afternoon, sitting outside somewhere in the sun, and suddenly felt a great wave of tiredness come over you, a wave so big that you want to lie down on the grass there and then and just let it rush over you, give in to instant sleep? That's how I felt for weeks after Niall arrived. Every day was the same, the same drugged tiredness and the same endless round of feeding and wiping and burping. All of it one long, blurry, milky haze.

The arrival of a new family in our street was a welcome distraction. It wasn't just me. Everyone wanted to see the people who were finally moving into poor old Violet's house. It had taken ever such a long time to sell after she died, due, apparently, to a disagreement between her two daughters-in-law about how much it should fetch. In the end some builder from Cardiff had bought it and there had been several months of dust and loud banging and a succession of rusty skips taking up precious parking space before finally it was back on the market and this time it sold within weeks. No one had liked seeing an empty house in our street, its windows dark and lonely at night, and as soon as the sound of a removal van was heard trundling up the road, my neighbours spilled out of their homes, ready to greet the newcomers. Ours is a friendly street where people look out for each other. This is spin doctor speak for a bunch of nosy buggers who seem to spend more time than is healthy sitting in their front rooms looking out through their nets and clocking what everyone is getting up to. It's not that bad really – not being able to smuggle fancy men into my house unnoticed is a small price to pay for the privilege of neighbours who take in parcels for me and go round my house closing curtains and switching lights on and off when we're away. They probably steam open my post while they're at it but that's the way life is. You've got to take the rough with the smooth.

Following behind the removal van was a Volvo estate, a long clunk of a car that made almost as much noise as the removal van. However curious I was about the new family moving in I promise I'm not a curtain twitcher – but I happened to be in my front window trying to rock Niall off for his afternoon sleep. I watched as the new family got out of their car. Tall dark-haired dad, petite blonde mum with a big curly perm and two boys aged somewhere between about eight and ten, dark like their father. I remember there was a lot of laughing going on and that dad was trying to carry mum over the threshold but she was resisting, only finally giving in when dad got hold of both her arms and her sons grabbed a leg each and all three of them carried her over together. I remember feeling envious of all their energy and thinking that this family looked like a lot of fun. And so they proved to be. An awful lot of fun.

I didn't go round with an apple pie or anything but I did stir myself enough to knock on their door a couple of days later, my two babies stashed neatly in their double push chair.

'Hi, I'm Anna, I live at number 34. Just wanted to welcome you to the street.'

'Lovely to meet you. I'm Jane. Come on in. Have a cup of tea.'

'That's very kind of you but I won't thanks all the same. It's taken me half an hour to get these two into this pram and I can't face getting them out again.'

Jane laughed.

'I remember when my two were small like that. How long between them – two years?'

'Not even that!'

'Isn't it the most wonderful and the most terrible thing you've ever done?'

I smiled at her but tears were pricking at the back of my eyes and she must have been able to see that.

'Here, let me,' and she grabbed hold of the buggy, kicked the brake off with practised ease, and wheeled it round. 'Let's go round the back way and we can have a cup of tea in the garden.'

She manoeuvred my tank of a pram down the side of their house, past a teetering pile of empty cardboard boxes, and into their small back garden. All the houses in our street have tiny gardens – the Victorians obviously didn't care much for outdoor living – but Violet had never been much of a gardener and the builder hadn't bothered at all. Thick, overgrown creepers bulged down both sides of the narrow garden making it even smaller, and a tatty shed took up at least a third of it.

'It's a mess, isn't it?' Jane caught me looking. 'A real shandy van.'

'Not much worse than mine is,' I laughed.

'Well, first things first. I've got a thousand boxes to unpack before I'll be able to tackle out here.'

'That'll take you to Christmas then.'

'At least,' she sighed. 'Right, let's get that tea. Bob! Bob! Come out here and meet our neighbour Anna! Put the kettle on as you go past.'

From inside the kitchen a man's voice called.

'Jane. I can't find the kettle!'

'Neither can I. Use the pan on the stove that we've been using since the day we got here.' She looked at me, lifted her eyes upwards. 'Honestly. Just goes to show how much tea he makes. I put the kettle and the corkscrew in a separate box so I could find them easily the minute we moved in and I haven't seen hide or hair of that box since we left Cardiff.'

The tall man I'd last seen struggling to get his wife over the threshold came out into the garden, wiped his hand on the seat of his trousers and stuck it out towards me.

'Hello Anna. I'm Bob.'

He was the kind of man you looked at twice. Broad shouldered and thick of thigh with a big mop of dark hair and dark brown eyes to match.

'Who are these two then?' he said peering into the pram.

'This one's James – he'll be two in November – and this one's Niall – he's just four weeks old.'

'Duw, good-sized boys for their age you've got there Anna. Make good rugby players one day.'

Jane flicked her husband on the arm. 'Good god Bob Price! Do you ever stop thinking about rugby?'

12

'Only when I'm busy thinking about other things, love,' he said, giving her a big wink, and then went back into the kitchen to make the tea.

I felt comfortable with Bob and Jane right from the beginning. As we sat in their dark, overgrown little garden drinking lukewarm tea, Jane rocked the pram gently and automatically, as if she didn't even know she was doing it. It was lovely not to have to do that for once – just to be able to sit there and drink my tea – and the boys nodded off very shortly.

'Would you like to come in and see the house?' Jane asked. 'Bob will sit out here with these two in case they wake up.'

'Love to,' I said, following her inside.

The builder had transformed the house, knocking Violet's little scullery and dining room into one big kitchen with fitted units and an expanse of terracotta tiled floor, cool and inviting as a Tuscany villa. The two little living rooms had also been knocked into one to make a big airy family living space where Jane's two sons were sitting cross-legged on the floor watching telly.

'Our three-piece suite doesn't arrive till next week,' Jane explained. 'Daniel! Rhys! Say hello to Anna our neighbour.'

'Hello Anna,' they said in unison without looking up from the telly.

Jane sighed. 'Make the most of those babies, Anna, because before you know it this is what they turn into – monosyllabic morons. I'm letting them watch all the telly they want today because they start their new school tomorrow.'

13

Upstairs, thanks to a loft conversion that ran the entire length of the house, the Prices had four bedrooms to my three and two bathrooms.

'Wow. This place is wonderful.'

'Isn't it great?' Jane said proudly. 'The builders might not have been gardeners but they did some great work inside. We just had a ground-floor flat in Cardiff and I can't believe how much more space we've got.'

'Lucky you,' I said jealously. 'Our house is going to feel tiny and horribly old fashioned now that I've seen this.'

'I'm sorry for showing off,' Jane said, 'but I just can't help myself. I'm so chuffed with it.'

'Don't blame you. I would be too.'

Through the open landing window the sound of James wailing floated up.

'Oops, better get back out there and relieve your husband.' I dashed back down the stairs to find Bob pushing the pram with one foot, Niall still fast asleep in it, whilst joggling James up and down on his other leg.

'There you go handsome, here's your mam now,' he said handing me my elder son who by now was no longer crying but looking quizzically up at Bob.

'You're a star, Bob. Thanks so much and thanks for the tea. I'll be on my way now, let you get on with those boxes. I hope you'll be very happy in your new home. It's a fabulous house. Thank you, Jane.'

'You're welcome. You must come again some time. Come round with your husband for dinner one night and Bob'll make his beef in Guinness stew. It's his speciality. By which I mean it's the only thing he knows how to cook.'

14

'That'd be lovely. We'd like that.'

I was newly married back then, the divorce still a long way off, and I remember excitedly telling my husband when he got home from work about the new family that had moved in to our street.

'They sound nice,' he said, trying hard to sound interested.

I didn't bother describing the strong connection I felt with Bob and Jane, right from that very first meeting. It would have sounded silly anyway, like I'd fallen in love at first sight or something, but in a way that's what it was. Friendship at first sight anyway. I knew from the very beginning that Bob and Jane were going to become true friends. Friends that would insist I came down the pub with them on a Saturday night rather than stay at home on my own with the kids, that would pop round at the end of the month with a slab of lasagne, a chocolate roulade and a bottle of wine that were 'left over and a shame to waste', that would tell me without a flicker of the eye that I looked really good two days after having a baby when I patently looked like a beached whale. That would never say they told me so when they so easily could.

About eight years ago Bob started to complain of stiff muscles. Jane just teased him at first, asking him what did he expect? He was in his late thirties and much as she adored him it shouldn't come as a surprise if he didn't have quite the same energy levels as he'd had when they were first married. If he was feeling stiff he should go to the gym a bit more and sample fewer of her canapés. But when his legs started to shake and he couldn't feel down

15

one side any longer Jane realised that it was no laughing matter and insisted he saw their GP. The GP in turn insisted Bob saw a neurologist and finally three months later Bob was diagnosed with MS.

At first, even though we all knew Bob had MS you could barely tell. He just walked a bit more carefully than usual, like it was raining and the pavement was a bit slippy, and he and Jane went on with their lives much as they always had. Bob continued to teach English at Cardiff University and Jane carried on with her catering business. They still came down to Steve's pub on a Saturday night and went on holidays to the same cottage in West Wales they'd been going to since Daniel and Rhys were tiny. They were both so positive after Bob's diagnosis I often forgot that he had MS at all. So, it seemed, did Bob. His career at the University went from strength to strength and he got made a professor. He continued to coach his sons both in their school work and at rugby, and they repaid him by excelling at both. Bob proudly drove them all over South Wales to matches, standing on the sidelines with all the other fathers, weathering the rain and wind with the help of a flask of coffee and an enormous golfing umbrella.

Then, two years ago, Bob suffered a major relapse and in a matter of weeks he needed a stick and then two sticks and then suddenly he couldn't walk by himself at all. His driving licence was taken away from him but Bob just joked that this was perfect timing on his part because Daniel had just passed his test and now he didn't need to buy a car for him. By Christmas last year Bob finally acknowledged that not only did he need a wheelchair but

16

he also needed to accept the University's offer of early retirement on the grounds of ill health. The process had been so gradual and so slow that sometimes I forgot how much Bob had deteriorated until I stopped and thought back on how he used to be, how he was that first day I met him, so tall and handsome. A man so athletic and fit that when he threw a ball around the park with his sons the grace and precision of his movements were a pleasure to watch.

To see him now, his muscles wasted away and his legs no longer working, one hand lying in his lap virtually useless, his one good hand gripping a half-pint glass of Chablis which he had to sip through a straw, was one of the most pitiful things I'd ever seen but I made sure that no pity showed in my face. Because pity was the thing that Bob despised most of all about his illness.

'I don't pity myself so don't you dare do it for me,' he'd say to the people in the pub who would come up to him in his wheelchair and squeeze his hand gently and crease their foreheads and tell him how sorry they were. 'I've had a great life so far and it's going to continue to be great for a long time yet. Just you bloody watch.'

I took my lead on how to react to Bob's illness from Bob and Jane which was to ignore it as far as possible. OK so Bob had to sleep downstairs in the living room and even though I tried to pretend I hadn't seen it tucked away in the corner there was a commode in there so presumably he couldn't get himself to the toilet any more, but Bob and Jane were exactly the same with each other as they had always been. Affectionate, flirty, joky. She still kissed him a lot, touched his arm when she went past, teased him for getting a bit flabby round the middle. His sons, now both over six feet tall themselves, were forever challenging their father on his recollection of the results of old rugby internationals and deriding him mercilessly if he got them wrong. And if those same sons had turned down offers to go to Cambridge to play rugby and opted instead to stay close to home and study at Cardiff no one ever commented on the reason why. So I tried to do the same and be exactly the same around Bob as I'd always been. The girl who made him laugh with funny stories about the things that happened at work and my hopeless love life. Who tried to persuade him to have one pint too many.

It was hard though to ignore how physically reliant Bob was on Jane. Although they still went to Steve's pub on a Saturday night they started staying for one drink only and I knew without being told that this was because Bob refused to let anyone see Jane help him to the toilet. He felt much more comfortable seeing friends in his own home in his battered old chair with wingbacks that helped support his head. Where he had no qualms telling his visitors as he did me that night: 'OK then Anna. Let's be having you. I've got something on Discovery channel I want to watch.'

Jane came to the door to see me off.

'Listen Anna,' she said in a low voice, 'despite what Bob says about coming to your party I wouldn't count on it. He's been having some bad spells of late and I really don't think he'll be up to it. It's a while yet till your birthday and perhaps he'll be feeling a bit better by then but I'm afraid we'll just have to wait and see.

'Oh Jane, I'm sorry,' I said, feeling very ashamed of myself. 'Here I am taking up all your time with something as trivial as my fortieth party and banging on about it all the time while you're—'

I didn't finish my sentence. I couldn't say what I was thinking which was any one of 'watching your husband drink through a straw like a child' or 'wiping your husband's bottom' or 'sleeping on your own'.

Jane kept the conversation light.

'Hey do you mind! Don't go calling parties trivial. They're what my livelihood is all about. So you go ahead. Talk about parties all you like.'

I smiled at her, covered her hand with mine. 'Like I've said lots of times Janey if there is anything I can do, anything at all, just say. I'd like to help.'

Jane sighed.

'Thanks, Anna, and if there was anything you could do I'd take you up on your offer. But there's not. Not for now. The boys call in all the time to visit their dad and to help out; they take him out for a walk and help with bathing and Bob can still do some stuff for himself. We're coping OK. And if that changes I'll let you know.'

'Promise?'

'I promise.'

Chapter 3

I walked the short distance back to my house with a heavy heart. I tried to distract myself from thinking about Bob by recapping in my head the plans I'd made for my party. I'd sorted the food and the venue and the guest list. Now all I had to do was find a DJ who owned a back catalogue of eighties music and work out how I was going to save some money over the next few months to put behind the bar. I wasn't planning on paying for drinks all night or anything but I did want my friends to have at least one drink on me. Hardly extravagant generosity but money was tight in our household and just about every penny I earned was already accounted for. That's what happens when the sweet little babies that could once be fed cheaply and nutritiously on baked beans, broccoli and Shreddies grow up and eat a week's worth of shopping in one meal, while refusing to wear clothes from Primark any more.

Those years of broken sleep, teething and nappies, of children whose faces lit up when they saw me and who, when they were upset, could only be comforted by crawling on my lap and pressing their sweet, snotty faces into my neck, had long gone. My children now had their own existence largely separate from mine and they locked the bathroom door when they were in the shower. Years of first steps, first words, first days at school had somehow tumbled past me and fast forwarded to the point where James was soon to finish his A levels, Niall his GCSEs and even my baby girl Lois had turned nine and thought she was a member of Girls Aloud who should be allowed out in public dressed in little more than her underwear. How had that happened so quickly? I wanted to find the rewind button and go back to the beginning of the film. To watch it all over again, only this time I'd pay more attention.

It was gone 9pm by the time I got home from Jane's house and even though I had left strict instructions to James that Lois should be in bed and asleep before I got back I knew there was no chance of that. She didn't listen to me so she was hardly likely to listen to her brother who, as she continually pointed out, was not the boss of her. As I pushed open our front door, I could hear James at the bottom of the stairs shouting up to Lois to please turn off her TV and go to sleep because Mum would be home any minute and he'd promised he'd have her asleep before she arrived.

James jumped guiltily as I shut the front door behind me.

'Sorry Mum, I did try, honest. You know what she's like.'

'It's OK James. I'll go upstairs and see her now.'

I smiled up at my firstborn. At eighteen he was 6'3" and towering over me with a big shock of tow-coloured hair just like his father's. James has always looked so much like his dad that, try as I might over the years to put that man out of my mind (and I have tried; really rather hard), I've never totally succeeded because so very often when

I look at James I see his father looking straight back at me. James was studying hard for his A levels because he wanted to go to the London School of Economics and I worried that I was an evil mother because in the dark of night I found myself hoping that perhaps he wouldn't get the grades and would end up at the local polytechnic – it was a university now after all – and live at home still. But his AS grades the previous year and his course work had all been excellent and anyway I knew he'd get to London somehow, whatever grades he got, because that's where his girlfriend Amy was studying and he wanted to be with her far more than he wanted to be with us. That's the natural order of life, I know that. Boys grow up. One minute they're round your feet all the time, demanding that you play Lego or read stories, dodging bath time and sulking if you so much as go out for one evening with your friends and you're thinking to yourself can't you give me just one moment's peace, and the next they've got deep voices and hair on their bits and they spend hours in the bathroom washing under their arms and checking out their spots. And not long after that point they get a girlfriend and fall in love for the first time and you realise that you are no longer the most important woman in their lives, and you can have all the peace in the world only now you don't want it quite so much.

My sweet, lanky son smiled at me, relieved at being able to hand responsibility for Lois back to me.

'Over to you then Mum. Niall's on the PlayStation playing Tomb Raider and I'm going to go IMG Amy.'

James strode off to the living room; his red baseball boots making his size 11 feet look even longer and skinnier, like a cartoon character's. I gathered my strength and made my way upstairs for my nightly run-in with Lois and her telly.

She was pretending to be asleep when I got to her bedroom which is one of her favourite devices for avoiding confrontation.

'I know you're not asleep, Lois. The television is still warm.'

'How do you know?' she muttered from the depths of her duvet, 'You didn't even touch it.'

'Didn't need to, did I? You know the rules. It goes off at 8.30pm. If you keep on like this I'll put it in my bedroom instead.'

Lois sat bolt upright at this, ditching all pretence that she was sleepy.

'You can't do that. It was my birthday present. You can't take my birthday present for yourself.'

'Oh yes I can my girl. If you don't keep to what we agreed and turn it off at 8.30pm that's exactly what I'll do.'

Believe me; I struggled long and hard with the dilemma of whether to let Lois have a television in her bedroom. It's against all my natural instincts to allow a child to cut themselves off from the rest of the household and spend their time shut in their room watching the box on their own. When I was a kid we watched telly together as a family or not at all. But times have changed and Lois wore me down eventually.

'All my friends have TVs in their bedrooms. Not just TVs – computers and iPods too – and they've all got mobile phones. All I'm asking for is a poxy telly. It's not fair.'

And even though Lois' tone of voice irked me and I had to resist the urge to tell her yet again that life's not fair and to get used to it, in the end I gave in because I knew she was right, more or less. It wasn't just that her friends all have bedrooms kitted out like entertainment centres that persuaded me. It was that being a single-television household was pretty much like being a single parent. More work with just the one. The boys wanted to play PlayStation, Lois wanted to watch H2O and Hannah Montana and the constant bickering and sniping about whose turn it was for the telly made me feel like I was living in the middle of a war zone. I wasn't woman enough to cope with the collateral damage and eventually one weekend when Lois was in tears because she was missing Swap Shop or whatever kids' Saturday TV is called nowadays, I surrendered. We drove to Argos right there and then and I bought her a little portable, telling her and my conscience it was an early birthday present even though her birthday was a good six weeks off. I ditched my principles, and £79.99 that it had taken me a long time to save, for an easier life.

I did not achieve total ceasefire. Lois and her brothers found plenty of other things to fight about, like whose turn it was to do the dishes and who got to eat the last Tunnock's Caramel Wafer and of course she and I had the nightly argument about turning said portable off but those skirmishes were more easily contained. I still had a few weapons in my armoury – principally the ability to withhold pocket money and to refuse to drive them anywhere – and in that way I was just about able to maintain an uneasy peace.

Chapter 4

Somewhere amongst the Chablis-infused tangle of my dreams that night I came up with a solution to getting my hands on some extra cash for my party. I would go on the game. Truly. That's what I dreamt that night – that I got myself a job as one of those high-class escorts. Actually, it was rather a nice dream. I not only acquired a classy wardrobe to go with my new job but also a rather splendid pair of new legs, long and brown and without a trace of cellulite, and my clients were a very select bunch of men – all handsome and wealthy and good in bed. Not a beer belly or a hairy back in sight. Not even halitosis. Suffice to say I woke up feeling horny and lonely and strapped for cash. Admittedly I regularly woke up feeling one or other of those things although rarely all three at once. Thankfully I had three kids to shout at to get ready for school and four chickens to feed, which meant I didn't have time to loll around in bed feeling sorry for myself.

I got dressed quickly – no time of a morning in our house for showers or make-up – before banging on Lois and Niall's bedroom doors. I went downstairs, put the kettle on and banged on James' door which used to be the door to our dining room before we converted it into a bedroom when James turned 13 and didn't want to share a bedroom with Niall any more because he needed his privacy. That's an euphemism but I'm sure you know what I mean. Then, cup of tea in hand, I stood at the bottom of the stairs for a minute or two, shouting instructions about packed lunches, eating cereal and cleaning teeth, before escaping out to the garden and the chickens.

I got the chickens on a whim. My grandfather's old hen coop was down the bottom of the garden anyway and still in pretty good shape due to my grandfather's serious creosoting habit. I'd always really enjoyed helping him with his chickens and collecting the eggs when I was a kid and I hoped that Lois and even Niall might enjoy it too. They didn't. Niall shouted from the back door on the day the chickens arrived that he was absolutely not interested and never would be and after a couple of weeks of gaily throwing corn about and naming them Aurora, Briar Rose, Belle and Pocahontas, Lois got bored of them too. I re-christened my chickens with the names of famous dead women I'd like to meet, Emmeline (Pankhurst), Marilyn (Monroe) and the Bloomsbury circle sisters Vanessa (Bell) and Virginia (Woolf) – I'm curious to know how those arty love triangles worked in practice – but the new names just didn't stick and so every morning when I slip on my wellies and grab the container of chicken feed it isn't the names of cultural and political female icons that I call out but those of Disney princesses. To make matters worse, Lois is like, you know, so over the princesses by now, and it's just soooo embarrassing for her, you know, when I stand in the garden yelling at Pocahontas to get back in the coop.

We have foxes round here in Stonebridge; sly, fit, country foxes, with tawny red fur and sharp teeth that hunt for their supper – not like those mangy, city foxes that get fat eating take-away leftovers out of bins. It's the fox's job to kill my chickens and it's my job to keep them safe. So far in this particular game of the Circle of Life it's Mr Reynaud *nul points*, Anna *quatre* points but it's always such a relief when all four of my girls come clucking fatly out of the coop of a morning.

While the girls were pecking at their morning corn I checked inside the coop. No eggs again for the fifth day in a row. My chickens had become menopausal in the space of a week. How had that happened? My friend Pippa who is my chicken dealer had told me when she'd first delivered the chickens, then leggy young ladies barely out of yellow fluffiness, that they'd be good layers for at least two years but after three years or so I should consider starting again.

'What does that mean? Start again?' I'd asked.

'What do you think it means, Anna?' she'd said, all matter of fact. 'It means these ones go in the pot and you get new ones. I'll come over and wring their necks for you when the time comes. I'm very good at it – far better than any wall-mounted humane dispatcher. They won't suffer I promise.'

She sounded like some sixty-year-old farmer's wife with ruddy cheeks and white hair and a cabinet full of agricultural show rosettes, not the very recently retired rock chick she is who despite having a smallholding is never seen without her skinny jeans, her black eyeliner or her roll-ups.

'That's horrible, Pippa. Being a chicken seems far too much like a metaphor for being a woman if you ask me.

27

Run out of eggs and you're for the chop. My chickens are going to die happy and of old age.'

'Suit yourself. They live at least eight years you know and stop laying altogether when they're about four. Going to cost you a fortune in chicken feed.'

It was just my luck to have chickens that had packed in egg making when in chicken-year terms they were still barely out of their teens. I was going to have to call Pippa. Perhaps I should feed them a supplement or something. HRT maybe. Anyway I didn't have time to worry any more about my barren chickens. I had to get everyone out of the door, a feat which as usual required me to get slightly hysterical. Lois and I waved the boys off as they set off on their walk to school one way and she and I turned in the other direction to walk to her school. She dragged her feet the whole way.

'Come on, Lois, we're going to be late.'

'*I'm* not going to be late. I'm always there way before everyone else. I hate getting there so early.'

'Well *I'll* be late then. Hurry up.'

So long as I got Lois to school fifteen minutes early I had just enough time to get to work dead on my allotted start time of 9.00am. But this involved precision timing and unfortunately precision timing is not my strong point. You try making a truculent nine-year-old walk faster. I was late for work on a regular basis. It was lucky that I had such an understanding employer.

I was being sarcastic then. When I got to work that morning, all of five minutes late, my employer ever since Lois started full-time school, Frank Mason, Chartered Surveyor and Estate Agent, rolled his eyes and tutted at

28

me, looking at his watch pointedly.

'What was it this time, Anna? Forgotten homework or another defective alarm clock? Right, I'm off to do the first viewing of the day. For which, thanks to you, I'm late.'

I ignored him. Frank liked it when I gave him an excuse to start his day as he meant to carry on. Grumpy. Grumpy was something he'd been pretty much constantly since he got divorced a few years back. I put up with him because I needed the money and anyway being the sole employee of a one-man-band estate agent wasn't that bad. My work was varied, encompassing the duties of assistant estate agent, receptionist, photocopier, tea and coffee maker and she who franks the post, and I liked the location of the office, slap bang in the middle of Stonebridge's high street and within walking distance of my house.

Stonebridge is where I was born and brought up. It's a small market town not far from Cardiff and it's got a really pretty high street, with no shop or office more than two storeys high, except of course for the town hall and the church, which is just how things should be. We've got the usual number of banks and solicitors' offices and chemists but we've also got a trendy little deli, some outrageously expensive designer dress shops, an exclusive jeweller and a fleet of bars, bistros and intimate little restaurants. There are no pound shops on our high street and absolutely definitely no Tesco Express. Ours is the high street that people all over South Wales come to on a first date or to buy an engagement ring or a wedding outfit or to take elderly parents out for a run in the car and a nice spot of lunch. It is a high street whose shop fronts are always impeccably well kept and painted regularly in heritage colours of deep red and bottle green and the odd daring splash of canary yellow and where the shopkeepers have a finely tuned business sense and realise that long-term prosperity depends on maintaining this image of an old-fashioned, picture-postcard market town where time and technology have slowed down just a few notches and where people can still get personal service and stuff that just can't be got at Marks and Sparks.

Of course there's more to Stonebridge than organic smoked salmon and a glass of Sauvignon at the end of a day spent acquiring designer labels. The town is surrounded by lush green countryside, sprinkled here and there with pretty villages but mostly with sheep. Admittedly there are also quite a few whopping detached houses with long drives and indoor swimming pools but they do a pretty good job at nestling in sheltered hollows and hiding behind private forests so they don't spoil the view too much. Drive one way and you hit our beautiful, unspoilt coastline, drive the other and you hit Cardiff which is all theatres, galleries, and the biggest John Lewis outside of London. One of the best things about living in Stonebridge is that it's small enough to know everyone else. That's also one of the worst things about living in Stonebridge.

All of this is good news for the estate agent business. There are always people who want to buy houses in Stonebridge. Frank got to spend most of his working day driving from one gorgeous house to the next in his beloved Jaguar, sleek and predatory like a big cat, rummaging around in the glove box to fish out the sparkling smile he kept stashed away in there especially for the purpose of greeting purchasers and making sales. Making sales was what Frank loved more than anything else in the world because sales equalled commissions and Frank was all about the commissions, that and the task of keeping those commissions safely away from his ex-wife. And while Frank was out and about doing viewings I was the poor sod stuck in the office, dealing with all the customers and answering the phone.

Frank never ever answered the phone, not even his mobile, which he kept switched off most of the time. This meant that a large part of my working day involved fielding the dozens of phone calls he got each day at the office from people who were anxious to get hold of him. These were not just work calls. I could deal with most of those myself – I was really very good at putting house details in the post when someone asked or chasing up solicitors to find out when completion date was going to be. No, these were personal calls. For a man so grumpy, Frank got more personal calls than was feasible.

His ex-wife accounted for at least two calls a day. I don't think she and Frank actually spoke in person ever – they conducted what remained of their relationship through me. This was the most tiresome part of my job because even though Valerie Mason spoke to me almost every single day of the working week, she still talked to me like she was a member of the landed gentry and I was the new chambermaid who'd come in to light the fire in the parlour and wasn't making a very good job of it. Today, like every other working day, I picked up the phone not long after Frank had flounced off to do his first viewing, to hear his ex-wife barking at me.

'Mrs Mason-Wells here, is Mr Mason there?'

When Valerie Mason remarried, she took the opportunity of giving herself a double-barrelled surname again, combining the names of husbands number one and number two. Apparently she had a double-barrelled maiden name and was always incredibly miffed at having given it up to marry Frank. With the excuse of needing to retain the Mason name so that she could share some of her surname with her children she grabbed at the chance of a double-barrelled name again when she married Penry Wells.

'No sorry Valerie, he's out on an appointment at the moment. He's due back at lunchtime.'

I refused to call her Mrs Mason-Wells. Absolutely refused to. The woman was the same age as me and I'd known her for years. Who did she think she was? And I really didn't know why she bothered to ask for him because when Valerie rang even if by some miracle Frank was in the office he always mouthed at me to tell her he was out.

'Then could you give him a message from me, please?'

'Of course.' I resisted the urge to add, 'Why should today be different from any other?'

'Could you tell him that Francesca and Sebastian are home from school this weekend and that I think we should all have a meal together on Saturday night? The four of us and Penry. Could you ask him to ring me to make the necessary arrangements?'

'You mean this Saturday? This weekend?'

'Yes Anna. This Saturday. Could you just give him the message please?'

'Will do.'

As always, she put the phone down on me without saying goodbye.

I leaned back in my chair and blew out a big, deep breath of air. Frank wasn't going to like this. That was an understatement. He was going to hit the roof, for any number of reasons. For a start, I already knew (as the taker of his many messages) that he was being chased by two equally demanding and no doubt equally youthful and desirable divorcees to fix a date for dinner for Saturday night. Divorcees accounted for a very large proportion of Frank's personal calls which I put down to one part big salary and flash car; one part sharp suits; and one part really blue eyes. So blue that for the longest time I thought he must be wearing contact lenses because no one can have eyes that are naturally such a startling shade. It took me years, long after his divorce from Valerie, to pretend one morning when I was handing him a cup of tea that I could see something in the corner of his eye so I could have a proper look but nope, no lenses. Frank's blue eyes are all his own, unless of course you can dye eyes these days. The divorcees that particular month were Sally and Amanda. I had met neither of them but based on the way they spoke to me I favoured Amanda's chances as she was the ruder of the two on the phone and Frank seemed to like rude women – presumably some Pavlovian response to all the years he had spent married to Valerie. Over and above Frank already having a guaranteed hot date, there was the fact that I was pretty certain Francesca

33

and Sebastian had not themselves bothered to tell their father they were coming home from school that weekend. Finally there was the prospect of his spending Saturday night in the company of Penry Wells, owner of a chain of five-star golf resorts and a six-pack stomach (even if said stomach is 55 years old) and the man who had pinched his wife from under Frank's nose when he wasn't looking.

Boy oh boy. I was really looking forward to seeing the look on Frank's face when I gave him this particular message. But for the moment, with him safely out of the office I took the opportunity to make a personal telephone call of my own, without him hovering in the background, listening in and looking at his watch.

Pippa knew the answer to my problem straight away.

'What you need is a cock,' she announced.

'Excuse me?'

'A cock!'

'I thought that's what you'd said. Appealing though that sounds, how does me having sex help my chickens?'

'I don't mean for you, you daft woman. I meant for the chickens. A cockerel. They're probably feeling a bit broody and a man around the place will get them going again in no time. I'll bring one round to spend the weekend with you.'

'Do you think a man around the place will get me going again too?'

'I take it the love life's not improved much then?'

'Dry as the dunes at Merthyr Mawr. You?' Pippa's ten year off/on relationship with a rather famous and very sultry rock guitarist a little younger than her had finally come to an end. He was the one who had wanted to buy the traditional farmhouse with two acres (the drawn-out

34

and complicated purchase of which had led to Pippa and me becoming friends) because he fancied trying his hand at a smallholding and being self sufficient. Unfortunately swiftly after completion he discovered that, as it turned out, he hated physical work/all animals but chickens in particular/shit/the countryside and promptly moved back to London, leaving Pippa in charge of the animals. The time between his weekend visits from London to Stonebridge got longer and longer until finally Pippa realised she was over him already, neatly coinciding with the point at which he stopped visiting altogether.

'Not much better. Not unless you count flirting with your ex-husband and getting him all of a fluster.'

'Why do you do that, Pippa? It's just not fair.'

'I dunno. Because I can I guess. Because he so obviously still fancies the pants off me and that makes me feel good about myself. Because he's the father of my children and when you've had sex with someone as often as the two of us had sex, well, I don't know, you're kind of connected. Forever.'

'Yes OK, I'm with you on that one but don't let's discuss it any more, OK? Makes me feel uncomfortable.'

'That's fine by me. I'll bring the cock round when I get a chance, OK?'

'That would be great, thanks.'

I hung around the office a little longer than I could have got away with but when Frank still wasn't back just after 5.30pm I realised I was not going to be able to deliver Valerie's message in person. Disappointed, I scribbled him a note and left it on his desk before locking up and going home.

Chapter 5

Thursday night is pizza and video night in our house. Actually even we've got a DVD player but DVD night sounds wrong somehow. My kids would like to be able to order pizza from Domino's because Domino's is cool and would make them feel like they live in New York and regularly get down with the boys from the hood. I would like to have the time to stretch my own home-made dough and stew my own home-grown organic tomatoes for the sauce. Life, however, is a series of compromises so I buy a freezer-full of frozen cheese and tomato pizzas whenever they're on offer – thank goodness for buy one get one free – and then they each add ham or pineapple or whatever we've got lurking at the back of the fridge in old margarine pots, even baked beans sometimes, and I shove them in the oven. Then we all squash up on the sofa and eat our pizza and watch a film together. It used to be the kids' favourite evening of all. Now I think they do it to please me more than anything but it does please me and so I'm not about to let them off the emotional hook and say we don't need to do it anymore if they don't want to. I think it's enough of a concession that pizza night has been moved from a Friday to a Thursday at their insistence so that they can do their 'own thing' on Friday nights. Actually I quite like being able to do my own thing on a Friday night too but I would never let on to them about that.

I stopped off at the corner shop on the way and bought a family-size bar of Dairy Milk. I keep meaning to write to Cadbury to tell them that the description 'family size' is frankly misleading because I could eat one that size all by myself, quite easily actually if I ever got the chance. By the time I got in, the pizzas were already cooked, my three children had taken up their usual positions in the living room and were waiting for me to press the play button. Lois was on the sofa, her legs tucked up so that James, sitting on the floor next to her could lean against the back of the sofa. Niall was at the opposite end of the sofa, as far away as humanly possible from Lois. He was going through the darkest, moodiest moments of teenager-hood, which included dying his hair jet black and wearing knee high black leather boots with lots of buckles which I would never have bought him in a million years, not least because I couldn't afford them, but he'd saved up for them himself thanks to that old favourite of getting a paper round. Niall had walked a lot of miles and lugged a lot of papers to buy those boots and thereby qualify as a proper goth, and to have your sister leaning her head on your shoulder just isn't goth-like.

Before she went off to university, Amy often joined us on video night. She'd sit with James on the floor leaning back against his chest, and they'd hold hands all the way through the film. I knew that with Amy away the shine had come off James' life which is why I had also bought at the cornershop a top-up card for his mobile so that he could text her all evening to his heart's content. I wasn't even going to complain when his phone beeped all the way through the film if it was going to cheer him up a bit.

It wasn't just hand-holding that went on between James and Amy. There was also a lot of surreptitious stroking going on but so long as Lois was oblivious to it I didn't say anything to disrupt these few hours of family togetherness. I remembered what it felt like to be his age and wholly obsessed with love and sex although my children like to think they were the product of immaculate conception and that their mother is a born-again virgin. Which, given the amount of action I was seeing, was pretty much the case.

I was just a bit younger than James when I fell in love for the first time. I was still at school with a clutch of good O levels under my belt, studying hard for my A levels and, just like James, hoping to go on to university. I was a good girl. I wore Wrangler drainpipe jeans and V-neck jumpers and my Adidas trainers had laces printed with hearts. I helped my mother with the housework, had a Saturday job in Boots so that I had my own money for riding lessons and was diligently reading my way through the classics section at our local library – George Eliot, Thomas Hardy, D. H. Lawrence – while at the same time secretly reading my mother's considerably more exciting Harold Robbins collection. Then one Saturday Mack walked into Boots and asked me where the Durex were and I lost all interest in horses.

Mack was a biker. He walked into that shop wearing black leather trousers and a big black leather jacket with padded shoulders, as big and scary as Darth Vader, his motorbike helmet slung over his arm. He had thick hair the colour of wet sand. When he came up to the counter and smiled at me I felt like someone had grabbed me hard round the stomach and squeezed all the breath out of my body.

'Can you tell me where I can find the Durex please?'

'Excuse me?' I wasn't embarrassed by his question. A few months of working at Boots had made me quite blasé about all things intimate and requests for pregnancy tests and haemorrhoid creams or even prophylactics didn't make me blush any more. It wasn't that. It was just that I was so dazzled by his beauty I had gone deaf.

'The Durex, love. You know? Dunkeys?'

'Oh, sorry. Right here behind me.'

I moved aside so he could see the range of condoms we had available, which back then was far more limited than today.

'Doesn't matter what type they are. Just so long as they work,' he said with a smirk.

I picked up the red packet, the ones we sold the most of. Mack handed me a five pound note, I put his condoms in a paper bag, gave him his change and he walked back towards the door. Just before he left he turned round again, looked at me and smiled.

'My name's Mack. What's yours?'

'I'm Anna.'

'Hello Anna. Nice to meet you.'

And then he was gone. My legs shook for a good hour afterwards.

That evening my best friend Glynis and I were going

to see the local amateur dramatics society performing *Godspell* in the village hall. See. Told you I was a good girl. But I couldn't concentrate. All I could think about was the incredibly cool, incredibly handsome Mack and every time I thought about him my heart quickened. All I wanted was to see him again.

On the walk home from the performance, Glynis was very dismissive of my newly acquired infatuation.

'You're telling me you've fallen for some bloke who came into the shop and asked you for condoms! You can only have seen him for a couple of minutes and anyway if he's buying condoms he must have a girlfriend.'

'Maybe. Maybe not. Boys come in and buy condoms all the time but some of them are in school with us and I know most of them haven't got girlfriends. They're buying them to put them in their wallets. You know, just in case they get lucky some time in the next three years or however long it takes for condoms to go past their sell-by date. Buying condoms doesn't mean he definitely has a girlfriend.'

'OK, I'll concede that point.' Glynis talked like that all the time. She was planning on doing a law degree when she left school and watched Crown Court on the telly all the time. 'But Anna, be honest, do you really think the kind of boy that buys condoms is the boy for you?'

'You can't call Mack a boy, Glynis. No way. Mack counts as a man.'

She rolled her eyes up to the sky and made that noise that is difficult to write down but sounds like 'hurrumph' if you read it out loud.

'Well I think you're off your head. Anyway, you don't

know who he is or where he lives. He was probably just passing through, his big, fast, black motorbike throbbing between his legs, on his way to Cardiff. To have sex. Lots of sex probably. A whole packet of condoms' worth. So I think you'd better forget about this mysterious Mack and come back to our house with me. Mum and Dad have had one of their dinner parties and they'll be sozzled by now and won't notice how much of their left-over wine we drink.'

I just stared at her in desolation. The prospect that I would never see Mack again was just too awful to bear.

'Anna. Get a grip will you!' and Glynis grabbed hold of my elbow a little more roughly than was necessary and marched me back to her house.

Back then, Glynis and I spent a lot of time at each other's houses. We were the swots at our comprehensive. The girls who didn't smoke in the toilets, didn't wear make-up and crimp our hair like Bananarama or wear our school ties in fat, aggressive knots. The girls who didn't have boyfriends. We were officially not cool. We were OK with that. We were also the girls who intended to do well at our exams and to escape our boring little town and make something of ourselves. So what if we spent a lot of time together because no one else wanted to spend time with us.

Glynis' Mum and Dad – 'call us Eileen and John please' – treated me like a member of their family. I was such a regular visitor that Eileen even bought things especially for me when she went shopping – malt loaf because she knew I liked it and blackcurrant squash even though Glynis preferred lemon barley water which

I hated. Being at Glynis' house was like being in my own home but better if I'm honest because, much as I loved my parents, Glynis' Mum and Dad were much more laid back than mine. Having an older brother who'd already forged a path of small freedoms ahead of us helped. As an only child, I'd had to chop through the jungle undergrowth of adolescence all by myself and it had been a slow process. Glynis had even been allowed to drink wine from when she was about thirteen because Eileen had been on holidays to France and French children are introduced to wine with their meals at an early age, don't you know.

When I started hanging out with Glynis – when we were about 13 and first identified each other as kindred swots, I thought wine was disgusting. Back then, Eileen watered our wine down, which is what children in France get apparently, and frankly I would have preferred lemon barley, but I got used to it after a while. Eventually she stopped watering it down and by the time Glynis and I hit the sixth form we were allowed to drink our wine neat. We would have preferred Blue Moons, a mix of cointreau, blue curaçao and lemonade which Glynis and I had never tasted but which we knew was the height of chic cocktails because the cool girls at school told us this was what they drank when they went to nightclubs in Cardiff, but if wine was all that was on offer we'd take that.

'Just one glass, mind,' Eileen would say, 'don't want to be accused of getting you girls drunk.' But we soon worked out that after one of their dinner parties John and Eileen didn't notice if we topped our glasses up quietly in the kitchen under the guise of helping to clear up and Glynis and I managed to get really quite pissed in this way. But that night after *Godspell* while Eileen and John cranked up the stereo and sang along to Rita Coolidge while they did the dishes I sat glumly at the table, not even able to finish my one official glass of wine. I was just too sick with longing.

'Oh for heaven's sake Anna,' Glynis hissed at me, 'stop looking like your dog's just died.'

'But I can't help it. Sorry. What if I never see him again? I couldn't bear that.'

'If it'll stop you moping I'll ring Ian in the morning. See if he knows anything about your precious Mack.'

I perked up a bit at that. Ian was Glynis' older brother. He was in the RAF and living in Yeovil now but whenever he was home he would meet up with a big group of lads and go drinking in the pubs in the town. Someone he knew would surely know who Mack was.

'Thanks Glyn. Oh thank you.'

I got up and hugged her. She shrugged me off but smiled. 'Pass me your glass then, since you're not going to drink it.'

Glynis snored a lot that night, having managed to snaffle three secret glasses of wine. Even though with Ian living in Yeovil there was now a perfectly good bed going spare down the hall we still slept in the same bed when I stayed over, just like we'd always done. We thought nothing of it, just like we thought nothing of Morecambe and Wise sharing a bed on the telly. I lay in bed next to her, replaying in my head the most important moment in my life so far. The moment that Mack had walked into

43

my life. I imagined what it would feel like if he were to kiss me and this made my belly flutter, deep down inside. Even though I was a good girl, it didn't mean I wasn't awash with hormones the same as all the cool seventeen year olds. If I didn't see him again I would die. Or at least feel like life was not worth living.

When I handed James the phone card I bought him I could tell he was thinking that I was old and past it and that I didn't understand how much he missed Amy. I'd thought exactly the same thing about my own parents when I was his age – that they didn't understand love or passion and absolutely definitely not sex because every teenager thinks, if they think of it at all, that their parents only ever had sex for the purposes of creating them and having achieved that goal never, ever do 'it' again – but I did understand, really I did. I might have been old compared to him but when I reached into my past and pulled out that memory I could feel that aching longing like it was happening right that very minute.

Chapter 6

James

My mother thinks she's hip and cool and mostly she is. OK she makes me want to curl up and die when she sings along in the car to The Feeling or the Arctic Monkeys, bouncing up and down in the driver's seat like she's got worms or something and she's got seriously dodgy taste in clothes – way too many flip flops and love beads and don't get me started on her three-quarter-length jeans – but on the whole she's not bad. Well, she's good really. She watches *Skins* with me and manages (just about) to keep her mouth shut about the evils of drugs and alcohol, she doesn't nag me about getting my hair cut and she leaves me alone most of the time to get on with my work at school. She says she trusts me and that she knows I work hard so there's no need for her to keep checking up on me all the time. She's way more laid back than my friends' parents. But she thinks she understands how I feel about Amy and she just doesn't. Last night was pizza night (which she thinks is this wonderful cutesy family tradition that we all love when actually we're all totally bored with it) and she slips me a mobile top-up card, this little smile on her face, all pleased with herself, as if she's

45

got the solution to all my problems. Like she can kiss me better with a phone card. She hasn't got a bloody clue.

She says she understands how much I miss Amy but then in the same breath tells me to get out with my mates more. Like I can put Amy away in a box and only get her out when I choose to and not think about her the rest of the time. She thinks speaking with Amy on the phone every night is not much different from seeing her every day but it's totally different. I don't just miss Amy. Without her, I feel like someone's ripped a huge hole out of my insides and I never stop thinking about her. Never. From the moment I wake up I'm thinking about her and when I fall asleep at night I'm thinking about her. School is the worst. We used to have our own special corner in the sixth-form lounge, where no one else ever dared sit, and we'd curl up on the sofa there, me and her, and work together side by side. We didn't talk all the time and we never snogged or anything – we just sat together, her arm pressed against mine or her feet curled up next to my bum and we worked. We worked really hard and it was so easy. I felt filled up. Happy. Always calm. And we could both concentrate on our work – we got loads done every day. Amy got two As and a B in her A levels and she says she couldn't have done that without me. That it was being with me that helped her get them. And I thought I was on for good results too but with her away, even though I'm still putting in the hours, nothing seems to stick in my head. It's too jam-packed with Amy in there for anything else to squeeze in. It gets worse the longer she's been away, not better like my mum thinks it should. I can't bear to go into the sixth-form lounge any more because when I see where we used to sit I can almost see Amy, smell her raspberry lip gloss, hear her laugh, feel the weight of her arm against mine and I just can't bear it. I'm like one of those old soldiers who's had amputations but can still feel the chopped-off leg twitching.

I wank constantly. Every morning in the shower. Every night to get me off to sleep. The other day when I was watching telly I did it twice during the adverts. I don't even think of Amy when I do it although it's thinking about her that gives me the hard-on in the first place. Thinking about Amy when I'm pulling on my own cock, wiping the mess up with toilet roll, feels wrong. Dirty. Because with Amy and me it's not dirty at all.

Most of my class managed to ditch their virginity by the end of year 11 at latest. There was a group of us – boys and girls – that used to hang out down by the playing fields in a big gang. We used to call it the Lemon Curry Drinking Parlour. 'See you down the Lemon Curry later?' we'd shout to each other as we got off the bus from school, like it was a real pub or a restaurant or something. But there were no Lemons there or Curry either. Just a bunch of trees that gave a lot of cover so the ground was almost always dry and a little stream that made a nice noise, gurgling and bubbling. In the spring when the nights became lighter and dryer we'd sit around on fallen tree trunks worn shiny by the bums of kids who'd visited the Lemon Curry Drinking Parlour before us and drink cider and play spin the bottle and pass the chewing gum. It wasn't like an orgy or anything – most of our parents had been friends for years and we'd hung out as little kids and played down the park and been herded together in one house to be babysat while our parents went out. And then everyone hit fifteen and the girl whose parents you called Aunty and Uncle and thought of almost as a cousin didn't look like a cousin any more and had suddenly grown tits – big ones, out of nowhere – and we didn't want to go the park any more with a bottle of red pop and kick a football around for hours. We wanted to go down the Lemon Curry Drinking Parlour and play pass the chewing gum so we could kiss all the girls in our group and have them press those brand spanking new tits against us. We were trying each other out for size, seeing who we liked best, although no one admitted that's what we were doing.

We were all pretty much obsessed with sex. Not just the boys. The girls too. All we could think about was tits and mouths and kissing and tongues and our cocks were constantly making tents in our trousers, often when we didn't expect it. I found an old porno mag on the floor of the school bus one afternoon – pretty much intact, only the cover was ripped off – and I stuffed it quickly into my bag, before anyone could see it. I hadn't seen anything like that mag before – my mother and most of the other parents of the kids at school had fixed our home computers so we couldn't access porn on line – and I hid the mag under my mattress. Even though I felt guilty whenever I thought of it and my heart pounded whenever Mum changed my sheets or put clean underwear in my drawer, over the next few months I read that magazine every single night. I knew the names of all the girls – Candy and Bella and Robyn – like they were women I'd actually met. I picked my favourites to wank over, so that the magazine fell open automatically on the pages where the girls I liked best lived.

Somehow I still just about managed to get through my school work. Mum laid down some ground rules as my GCSEs got closer. *I trust you James*, she'd say, *but believe me how you do in these exams will affect how you do for the rest of your life. If you want to make something of yourself you need to put the hours in.* And I thought about how tight money was in our house most of the time and how Mum couldn't afford for me to go skiing with the school and how I'd found her with her head down on the kitchen table breaking her heart about that and how when I put my arm around her and told her it didn't matter, that I didn't care, she held my face between her hands and had looked at me, tears running down her face, saying over and over again *My baby boy, my beautiful baby boy* which made my heart hurt and so I managed to push Candy and Bella and Robyn out of my head some of the time and concentrate on my revision. Lots of nights I didn't go to the Lemon Curry Drinking Parlour at all and then, when the exams were over and I started going again, I found that everyone else had moved on from pass the chewing gum to actually going out with each other properly. The music had stopped and I was the one left without a chair. And then when the GCSE results came out at the end of the summer and I had done OK and most of the rest of the gang had not the Lemon Curry Drinking Parlour closed down for that year and wouldn't reopen again until the following spring when another group of kids hit fifteen.

I met Amy on my second week in year 12. It was really

weird going back to school after such a long holiday and it felt strange finally walking through the double doors of the Year 12 block after all those years of being kept out. I had imagined it would be really cool in there but it turned out to be just a bunch of classrooms same as the rest of the school but with a big scruffy lounge that had knackered sofas to sit around in and get used to the novelty that was free lessons. Our numbers had thinned out a little because some of my year had gone off to college instead to study plumbing or childcare or had joined the army. The gang of boys who had kicked a tennis ball around at the back of the science block every lunchtime for the past two years were all gone and so were some of the girls with big chests and a lot of mascara who used to smoke behind B block. The school system had sifted us and not everyone got through. And the ones that were left behind were more like each other, just like Amy and me.

Going up to year 12 was a bit like going to a brand new school. Kids from the year above us who had disappeared into the year 12 block never to be seen again were suddenly rediscovered. Some pupils re-sitting their A levels and missing in action for years came back on the radar. There was a flurry of activity in those first few months as the older boys picked through the new intake of girls and made their choices. That was the way it worked. Older boys got the new girls. New boys got no one or they could fish in the year 11 pond and spend their lunchtimes back out in the school yard. So, getting my first-ever text from Amy was a big surprise.

Hi, I've forgotten my economics text book but can see

you've got yours. Can I borrow it?

I didn't recognise the number but I texted right back.

Who is this?

A reply came back straight away.

Behind you, sitting in the corner.

I scanned the room. In one corner there were a group of girls chatting, in another a year 13 boy reading. None of them were looking at me. And then I saw her, Amy Morris, her phone in her hand and smiling at me through her long dark fringe. I knew who she was. Most people did. She was captain of both the hockey team and the netball team, always up front in assembly being presented with medals and trophies for something or other.

How did you get this number? I texted again.

I could tell you that but then I'd have to kill you. Are you going to lend me the book or what?

Feeling very nervous, I got up and took the book over to her. She had kicked off her shoes and was sitting with her feet tucked up under her bum. She was wearing black socks and I could see there was a tiny hole in one of them and that her toe nail was poking through. She had very white toenails. 'Here you go,' I said handing it to her. 'I don't need it till 2.30pm so you can keep it till then.'

She took it from me, tucked it under her arm.

'Thanks.'

'Um, you're welcome.' I paused, not certain what the next step was, whether a next step was even what was expected of me. She patted the seat next to her and I sat down quickly and too heavily and that made Amy bounce up a little bit off the sofa.

'Steady on there big boy,' she grinned. 'I'm only five

51

foot three you know.'

I didn't know that although I did know she was small. And a fast runner. On school sports day she always won the 100m race for her house and she was the one who ran the last leg of the relay race. Small and fast I'd known about before, but pretty I hadn't really realised until that day.

'Well, thanks for this,' she said, uncurling her legs and slipping her shoes back on. 'I'll come find you before 2.30pm to give it back.'

'Thanks.'

'See you later then.'

'OK.'

I watched her as she walked away. Amy does a funny little bounce when she walks that makes my heart do a funny little bounce in reply. I was back in the lounge waiting for her way before 2.30pm.

I got Amy right from the beginning. She is clever and serious and really, really pretty. She likes doing well at exams but she loves sport too and plays netball as if her life depends on it and if being good at those two things mean that sometimes she isn't the most popular of people she really couldn't care less. She likes politics and geography and reading and has seen every episode of the *West Wing*. She really liked kissing and touching and later on she really liked sex and she didn't feel bad about any of it.

We did a lot of kissing. Months of it. On her parents' sofa, at home in our front room, up on the mountain where we went for long walks. Moving on from that unfolded naturally. I didn't push her. If anything she pushed me. She was the one who lifted my hand and put it on top of her breast.

'I'm small aren't I?' she said, smiling at me, as we both of us looked down at my hand lying there stiffly on top of her shirt like it wasn't connected to the rest of me. 'I hate my boobs. I wish they were bigger. As big as Suzanne Williams'.'

'Suzanne Williams' tits look like someone has stuffed a pillow under her jumper. Your boobs are just perfect,' I smiled at her.

And she undid the top three buttons of her shirt so I could run my finger under her bra, feel her soft, flat nipples pucker up like lips going in for a kiss as I touched them.

I thought Amy's pubes would feel different from mine. The girls in my porno mag didn't really have any – just a little strip down the middle – and although I knew that Amy wasn't that sort of girl I did imagine that her pubes would be smooth and sort of silky, just like her skin was smoother and silkier than mine. But when I got my hand down her knickers for the first time I was surprised to find that hers were coarse and crinkly just like mine and that she had a lot of them, a puff of dark hair beneath the bright pink cotton of her knickers. My hand stopped for a second and our kiss faltered for a split second so that Amy opened her eyes and looked into mine but I pretended not to notice and just kept smoothing her. I didn't rush things, frightened that if I pushed it too far she'd suddenly pluck my hand out of her pants and stop me so I just kept smoothing, very, very slowly and gently. After a while she reached for me, stroking at the tube of denim at the front of my jeans. I didn't give in to the urgent need I felt to pump against her hand, knowing that this would put her off. For weeks this is what we did, each time moving things ever so slightly forward, me finally dipping my finger gently into the moistness of the cleft beneath the hair, undoing the top few buttons of my jeans so that Amy could get her hand into my boxers, first on the outside, finally underneath the cotton. The first time I felt the heat of her hand against the bare skin of my cock we both of us let out a little gasp.

It's beyond me how my mother can think that speaking to Amy on the phone is the same as touching her, being touched by her.

Chapter 7

The Friday morning after pizza night I was in the office before Frank which is unusual. If I had known he was going to be late I wouldn't have rushed so much, could have made the kids their sandwiches instead of giving them one slice of cold pizza each. They'd all moaned about that, not because they don't like cold pizza – they love it – but the fact that there was only one slice each and they would be starving all day.

'Well you should leave more the night before then, shouldn't you? Here – take a banana and here's 50p each to buy a Twix or something.'

I stopped myself from calculating how many minutes I had to work for Frank Mason to earn that £1.50 because I did that all the time, particularly at the end of the month when money got very tight, and it was really not good for my mental health.

Even more unusually, while I was making my first cup of tea of the day I realised that there was no dirty coffee cup in the sink which meant that Frank hadn't come back to the office after I'd left the night before either. Strange. Frank always called in at the office before going home for the day to pick up his messages. Which meant, oh joy, that he hadn't seen Valerie's message and that I would get to go to the ball after all and witness the reaction. It was sad that my own life as a single mother of three living on a shoestring was so uneventful that the prospect of Frank going off on one with Valerie and me getting a ringside seat was brightening my day no end.

He didn't get in for another 30 minutes and I had just started to get a little worried – if anything happened to Frank I would be out of a job and that would be disastrous – when he turned up.

He avoided my eye when he walked through the door, just scuttled quickly over to his desk, banged his briefcase down and picked up his message list. I noticed that his hair, which has faded from blonde to almost white these days and which he wears a little too long for a man of his age, was still damp. *Must have squeezed in an early-morning shag with one of the divorcees* I thought to myself.

Frank looked up and caught me staring at him. He frowned at me.

'Could you get me a cup of coffee Anna?'

No good morning or nothing. I was buggered if I was going out the back to put the kettle on before he'd read the message from Valerie and miss all the fun.

'Be with you in a minute Frank. Just got to send this email off to Mrs Joseph first.'

He nodded absentmindedly and started to read his messages. I knew when he reached the one from Valerie because he blew air out through his nostrils in a big noisy snort like a horse but he didn't bang his fist on his desk like I'd hoped or jump up from his chair and start swearing about that bloody woman who wasn't married to him anymore and from whom he was not about to start taking instructions again. Instead, he very calmly picked up his briefcase and his message list and said to me, 'Forget the coffee Anna. I haven't got the time now.' He said this with blame in his voice. Blame that was directed at me like if I'd only put the kettle on the second he'd asked me to he could have finished his coffee before he needed to leave, even though the kettle wouldn't even have boiled in that time.

On his way past me he handed me back the message list.

'If any of the women on this list call me again today tell them that I am unavailable this weekend for any engagements as I am away for the weekend.'

'What do you mean, if they call? You know they will. Well maybe not your dates because they won't want to seem over-keen but you know Valerie will ring. What am I supposed to tell her?'

'Exactly what I just told you to say. That I won't be able to join the Mason-Wells family for dinner on Saturday night as I shall be away for the weekend.'

'And what about your kids? What if they ring?'

'If my children ring, tell them I am always delighted to see them but that they need to give me the courtesy and respect of a bit more notice.'

Yeah right. Like I'd be able to get the words courtesy and respect out before Francesca and Sebastian put the phone down on me without saying goodbye just like their mother. Assuming they called of course, which was far from certain.

'OK. Is there anything else you'd like me to do while I'm at it?' *Like stick a broom up my bum and sweep the floor?*

'Yes, there is. As I'm going away, you'll have to come in and cover the office for me tomorrow.'

'But it's Saturday. I'm not contracted to work Saturdays.'

'You're not contracted to turn up for work fifteen minutes late three days out of five either but that doesn't stop you doing it. Look, I'll pay you time and a half.'

'I can only work till 2pm and it'll have to be double time.'

'Work till 3pm and you've got a deal.'

'Done.'

And with that Frank walked out the door.

Now it was my turn to blow out my nose like a horse. Shit. It was one thing to listen to Frank having words with Valerie. It was quite another to be in the firing line for those words myself. This day wasn't turning out to be as much fun as I'd hoped.

And what did Frank mean he was going away for the weekend? Frank never went away for the weekend. All Frank ever did was work. He didn't even go on holiday with Valerie and the kids when they were married, would just go and join them for a night or two on the French Riviera or another equally expensive holiday destination, a tactic which had not worked out well for him because Valerie Mason was not the sort of woman you let get out of your sight for long. Frank hadn't even twigged he should pay more attention even when Penry Wells happened to be holidaying at the exact same destination as his wife and kids three times in the same year.

'Penry, fancy bumping into you! And in Deia/Cannes/ Val d'Isere of all places!'

So I didn't believe for one minute that Frank was away for the weekend.

I logged into his diary from my computer. It took me at least eighteen months to persuade Frank that if we were going to be a competitive business in today's market we needed to get ourselves some computers and a website. He moaned for months about the price of it all – Frank was nothing if not tight – but eventually he gave in, so long as I was the one who sorted it all out and I didn't expect him to learn to type. He never admitted it to me but he found it enormously helpful that I could make appointments for him and that he could ring me up whenever he liked during the day to find out where he was meant to be going next. He even entered his own personal appointments, although he'd been true to his word and hadn't learnt to type so the entries he made tended to be short and badly spelt – dentst, harecut, pesonal trainer – that sort of thing – but I could usually work out what they meant. Frank hadn't twigged on to the fact that in order to keep his diary for him I had to have access privileges to it. His email too, not that there was anything interesting in his emails ever – he didn't even have a private email address and I don't think he'd ever sent an email himself. He got me to do that. So it was an easy matter for me to check Frank's diary and to establish that there was absolutely nothing in it about going away for the weekend. Not a single personal entry. Thought as much. Frank was lying although who could blame him? The prospect of a Saturday night out with your ex, her new husband and two teenagers who didn't seem to like you very much would drive most people to tell fibs.

Before I had completed my little bit of computer sleuthing the phone rang.

'Mason's Chartered Surveyors. How may I help you?'

'Anna, this is Mrs Mason-Wells. Frank has not returned my telephone call. I want to speak with him now.'

'He's not here Valerie. He's going to be out at appointments all day. He did give me a message for you though. He said to tell you he was sorry but unfortunately he can't join you for dinner on Saturday night as he's away for the weekend.'

'What do you mean away? Frank never goes away!'

I didn't have the nerve to tell her that was exactly what I'd thought.

'That's all the message he gave me sorry Valerie.' Actually it was quite a bit more message than he'd given me. Frank hadn't mentioned anything about 'sorry' or 'unfortunately.'

'This is outrageous,' Valerie's voice was tight and angry, 'how dare he turn his back on his children this way. The man's an unfeeling brute. I shall be having a word with my solicitor about this, let me tell you.'

There was a pause. Valerie Mason-Wells was obviously expecting me to comment. I couldn't say what I was thinking which was:

I sincerely hope that if you go to your solicitor and demand an ASBO against your ex-husband because he wasn't available for some dysfunctional extended family dinner on two days' notice that she'll tell you to grow up.

So for once I said nothing and, after a while of breathing down the phone at me in an annoyed manner,

Valerie hung up.

Actually, Valerie's divorce solicitor was no more likely to tell her to grow up than I was. Not because like me she was a bit frightened of Valerie. Far from it. Melanie Farrell LLB is frightened of no one. No, what Melanie would do would be to calmly take Valerie's call and make an appointment for Valerie to come in and see her. Valerie would drive to Melanie's beautiful office – all chrome and glass and long, low cream leather sofas – and one of the secretaries would bring her a cup of green tea and Valerie would moan to Melanie about Frank for an hour. Afterwards, Melanie would write a four-page letter to Valerie, essentially repeating exactly what Valerie had said to her but which would contain precisely three sentences of legal advice to the effect that Valerie would not ultimately be successful in achieving an ASBO against Frank or an increased maintenance order or the reversal of his visitation rights or whatever other unreasonable thing Valerie had requested. And enclosed with the letter would be Melanie's bill for her professional charges in the sum of at least £1,000 plus VAT.

Not that I have any personal experience of Melanie Farrell but you learn a lot about the human condition working in an estate agent's office. An awful lot of the business of buying and selling houses is down to divorce. And in Stonebridge Melanie Farrell is widely acknowledged to be the queen of divorce lawyers. The second an unhappy wife or husband walks through the door of Melanie's office their marriage is well and truly over. Melanie is not concerned about why a marriage is ending or whether it can be fixed and she really doesn't care who unreasonably or adulterously did what to whom. Melanie is all about money not matrimony and what she focuses on is getting the biggest possible divorce settlement for her clients as quickly as possible. Which means there's a steady stream of sad, dazed, divorced people beating a path to our office with big houses to sell and in search of two smaller houses to buy.

You would never guess Melanie's such a ball-breaker from looking at her. She's all of about 5'3" and must weigh seven-stone soaking wet and she's got short blonde hair with caramel highlights cut in that flippy style that Meg Ryan had in *You've got Mail*. I had never seen Melanie wearing trousers and I saw her quite a lot because her office was just down the high street from ours and she was forever trip-trapping her way past our window in her high heels and 10-denier tights, on her way to court to redistribute fortunes. Whenever I saw Melanie walking by it struck me that it was difficult to believe we were both the same breed – she is so utterly different from the 5'9" size 16 woman that is me. Or if we are the same breed Melanie is the miniature version. Yes, that's it. Melanie is like a miniature poodle. One that's just been to the dog beauty salon and had her nails clipped and her fur cut and gets to sit on the owner's sofa, her sharp little teeth gleaming. Me I'm the giant version of poodle, with long curly hair flapping in my eyes and a big red tongue lolloping around in my grinning mouth, knocking small glass objects off side tables with my tail and getting confined to the kitchen for stinky rolling in the park.

Frank used to love Melanie Farrell and all the business she helped create for him. He only ever had praise for

Melanie, until of course Melanie acted for Valerie when she left Frank and it was his turn to be squeezed by the ball-breaker till his pips popped.

Melanie Farrell was not going to be sitting at her desk all day fielding someone else's irate personal telephone calls and looking forward to a Friday evening spent watching *Malcolm in the Middle* and eating chicken nuggets with a nine year old. I was fairly certain that Melanie Farrell's Friday night was going to involve a candlelit wine bar and a bottle of chilled Sancerre and some handsome, sexy, erudite company. Bitch.

Chapter 8

I was even later than usual picking up Lois from after-school club that evening. I was often the last parent to pick up and the carers were usually sweeping the hall and tidying away the final few toys and craft boxes when I got there. But by the time I arrived on this Friday the carers had already locked up and were huddled outside with their coats on, waiting for me and glowering. Lois was chief glowerer, her arms wrapped tight around her and her eyebrows knitted together.

'You're late, Mum,' she hissed at me as I jogged up to her, mouthing sorry with every step I took.

'I'm sorry sweetheart, Frank's been out the office all day and the phone hasn't stopped and then I had trouble setting the alarm.'

'Why can't you be a normal Mummy? Why do you have to work? Can't you just stay at home like Cassie does and drink coffee all day with the other Mums and then be waiting for me at the gates when school finishes. It's just not fair.' She burst into tears which was exactly what I felt like doing too.

'Come on Lois, you know I have to work.' I tried to put my arm around her but she held herself away from me, her little body stiff with resentment. I would not let her guilt me out about this. Could not. I had to work and that was the end of that and it didn't help the situation any if I felt guilty about it. Only of course I did feel guilty. And I hadn't even told her yet I had to work Saturday. Bribery was called for.

'How about we ring Cassie when we get home and see if Emily and Sara want to come over for a sleepover soon? Eh? How about that?'

Lois perked up immediately, yielded a little bit into the cuddle I was trying to give her.

'Can they come over tonight? Can they?'

I always say that Lois is going to be a business woman when she grows up. She always knows exactly when to press home her advantage.

'Um, I don't see why not. They might be busy but we could ask them.'

'They're not busy. Emily already told me at school that their daddy has to work this weekend and they're having some girl time with their mummy.'

I tried not to show outwardly how much I cringed at the phrase 'girl time'.

'Well then in that case perhaps we'd better ask them over another weekend. We wouldn't want to get in the way of their plans now would we?'

'We won't be getting in the way of their plans. We'll be having fun and Cassie always says she loves seeing Emily and Sara have fun. Please Mum – you promised.'

I hadn't promised at all but since I still hadn't broken the news to Lois that I was working the following day I didn't feel the time was right to correct her on that point.

'Oh OK then. I'll give Cassie a ring now and we'll see what she says.'

'Oh thanks Mum. You're totally brilliant.' Lois clapped her hands together excitedly and did a little twirl. My daughter is nothing if not a drama queen.

I very rarely made calls on my mobile because it wasn't really my mobile. It was Frank's. He had given it to me 'in case one of the clients needs to get hold of you out of hours in an emergency'. It beat me what qualified as an emergency for an estate agent – people were hardly likely to ring up at 3am in the morning and demand a viewing. He pored over my bills every month and highlighted numbers with a yellow fluorescent marker pen if he thought I was making too many personal calls so I used it very sparingly. Still, it was handy to have.

Emily answered the phone.

'Hi Emily, this is Anna. Could I have a word with your mum please?'

'Just a minute Anna. I'll go and get her.' Cassie's kids are ever so polite. Mine never go and get me. They just yell.

'Hi sweetie, what can I do for you?' It was a sad reflection on me that every time I rang Cassie she asked me that question but the reality was that when I phoned her I was usually after a favour.

'For once Cassie, ask not what you can do for me but what I can do for you. Lois wants to know whether the girls would like to come for a sleepover. She'd like it if they could come round tonight but it's a bit last minute so if it's not convenient we can do it another time.'

Lois tugged on my arm, glared at me. I ignored her.

'That would have been lovely Anna but the girls are already in their nighties and I don't think it's a good idea for them to get dressed and go out again.' I looked at my watch. It was all of 6.10pm. How early did Cassie get an eight year old and a nine year old ready for bed? And was it normal?

'Never mind. Tomorrow night perhaps?'

'Can't do tomorrow night sorry. We've got the boys staying and I've promised them roast beef and Yorkshire pud and all the trimmings. Listen – what are you and Lois doing right now?'

'Just walking home from after-school club.'

'Then why don't you hurry home, get in that clapped-out old car of yours and drive round here instead? You can have food with me and the girls. Graham's in Norwich tonight giving a lecture and you know what I'm like when he's away, it's all I can do to stop myself getting in the car and driving straight to the Rhondda to stay overnight with my mam and dad but they really don't have room for the three of us. I'm making spaghetti carbonara and there's plenty.'

I hesitated. I'd quite liked being in the position of offering my services to Cassie for once and yet somehow or other we were already back to her offering to do something for me. But spaghetti carbonara sounded so much more appealing than frozen chicken nuggets. Then she delivered the clincher.

'Go on. I've got a lovely bottle of that Oyster Bay you like so much in the fridge. Nice and cold.'

'Go on then. You've twisted my arm. We'll walk home quickly and pick up the car and be with you in twenty minutes.'

I turned to Lois.

'Cassie has invited us over there instead.'

'I know, I could hear her on the phone.'

'Is that OK with you?'

'Course it is Mum. They've got a much better telly than us and Emily and Sara have got on sweets.'

'Is that a new type of chocolate?' I was kidding but Lois didn't notice.

'No Mum. An *on sweet*. Don't you know what that is? It's your very own bathroom in your own bedroom. They're lush. I'd die for one.'

So would I, I thought to myself.

When Lois and I arrived at the house, Niall and his mate Bartley were on the PlayStation thanks very much and yes of course they could make themselves some tea and James was in his bedroom, probably talking to Amy on MSN, but yes Niall would tell him that Lois and I were going over to Cassie's and would not be home till later. Niall could barely conceal his delight that he and Bartley would be left in peace to spend hours crunched up over their consoles without getting nagged about poor posture and square eyes.

Cassie and Graham's house is only about ten minutes' drive away from mine but it is in an altogether different league. If pushed, Cassie will say that she and Graham are 'comfortable' but it would be more accurate to say that they are very nicely off thank you. Graham is an ob/gyn who in addition to working for the NHS also has a thriving private practice which must be very lucrative because Cassie and Graham have the most beautiful house. Five-bedroomed detached in its own extensive grounds and with a mature garden. It doesn't just have en-suite bathrooms. It also has a Bulthaup kitchen, a games room, even one of those fancy twirly underground wine cellars. The place is always spotlessly clean and tidy with fresh flowers in the hallway and clean hand towels in the downstairs toilet.

Their entire lives run in the same, smooth ordered way. Cassie's kids are never late for school and they never forget their PE kit or their clarinets or to bring money for school trips on or before the allotted date in neat little envelopes properly marked with their names and class number just the way her school likes it. They eat nutritious packed lunches of wholemeal pitta bread with tuna and crunchy vegetables and fresh fruit to follow. I've got as much chance of getting my kids to wear wholemeal pitta as I have of making them eat it. Cassie even gets on well with Graham's two boys from his first marriage, Sol and Jethro, who turn up every other weekend absolutely starving and with an enormous kit bag each of dirty washing and Cassie feeds them up and fills those kit bags with clean, pressed clothes. I think Sol and Jethro would move in full time if only their mother would let them. And over and above keeping this whole extended family road show running, Cassie finds time to do voluntary work at the Oxfam shop. She even goes to the gym a couple of times a week although, as Cassie herself says, no one believes she has such a serious Pilates habit on account of her big boobs and her bouncy bum.

'It's because I'm so short,' she says, patting her well-padded arse, 'a couple of inches taller and I'd be a size ten. It's just as well Graham likes my curves. Different from

Pippa. Graham says going to bed with Pippa was like sleeping with an ironing board. Something which Pippa wouldn't know how to use even if she could remember where it's kept.'

Cassie really believes that if you can't say anything nice you shouldn't say anything at all. She sees the good in everyone at all times and she is never ever bitchy or mean. Except, that is, when it comes to Graham's ex-wife, of whom Cassie is fiercely and unreservedly jealous to her very bones and about whom she is bitchy at every possible opportunity. Cassie thinks that Graham is sex on legs and not a tall, skinny bloke with thinning red hair and a truly astounding number of freckles, and she simply can't believe that Pippa is not still secretly in love with him. Even though Pippa walked out on him ten years ago taking Sol and Jethro with her to live with that rather famous rock guitarist.

Yes I am talking about the same Pippa. My chicken dealer. The woman with whom on the previous afternoon I'd been discussing the delivery of a gigolo cockerel for my chickens. The very same woman who just yesterday had told me how much her ex-husband still fancied her. I am friends with both of Graham's wives and, even though they both know that, I really try to keep these friendships separate, like a Venn diagram with me in the cross over bit in the middle and the two of them ringfenced off in separate bubbles. That's not always easy of course. Sol is in the same class at school as Niall, and Pippa will insist on telling me about her flirting exploits with Graham. The thing is, even though Graham thinks Cassie is sex on (little) legs too, I can see from the way he acts around

Pippa that Graham does still fancy her. I guess one of the reasons Graham married Pippa in the first place was because he fancied her and that didn't stop just because she walked out on him.

If I had to choose between them as friends I'd pick Cassie, even though the smug perfection of her life grates on me sometimes. OK, grates on me quite a lot. But Cassie's goal in life is to make the lives of everyone she cares about that much better. It's what she does. That's what she says when she describes how she met Graham, in her very first week of nursing at the Royal Glamorgan Hospital.

'I just knew when I saw him that he was THE ONE,' she says. 'He looked so lost and sad and so drop-dead gorgeous that I just wanted to make it all better for him.'

Graham was lost and sad of course because Pippa had not long skipped out on him. Newly dumped by a posh, skinny, slightly slutty girl from the Vale of Glamorgan he was then chased relentlessly by a plump, cheerful, house-proud Valleys girl. But Cassie did indeed make it all better for him. She cooked him wonderful meals every evening and shagged him stupid every night and when within a few months she became pregnant Graham was delighted to put a ring on her finger. And that's the point at which I came in. I was pregnant with Lois and my midwife recommended that I go to parentcraft classes since, 'it had been quite a long time since I'd last had a baby and things have changed quite a bit', and Cassie and Graham were in my group. Twelve women, all due to give birth within a month of each other, with bellies tight as eggs and eleven worried-looking, hand-holding, bag-packing, back-rubbing men. I was no doubt looking a bit lost and sad myself at that point and it didn't take Cassie long to realise I would be having my baby on my own and so she set out to make things all better for me too. She's been doing the same thing ever since, not just for me but for my kids also.

That night when Cassie opened the door she immediately handed me an enormous glass of Oyster Bay. For Lois there was a beautifully ironed long flowery nightie just like the ones that Emily and Sara were wearing.

'Hello sweethearts, so lovely to see you. Now, Lois, I thought you might like to change into your nightie too so you can get cosy in front of the telly later with Emily and Sara. If you want to have a shower you know where the bathroom is and I've put out a clean towel for you. And you Mrs. You take a big, long drink of this and come with me into the kitchen for a chat.'

Lois dashed off upstairs to make full use of the power shower and fluffy towels, Emily and Sara following close behind so that they could all 'catch up' while Lois got ready.

Cassie's kitchen smelled of hot bread, garlic and French lime candles. She pulled out a chair for me and ushered me to sit down at her enormous family-friendly oak kitchen table, and pushed a bowl of posh crisps towards me. The family cat, a big mackerel tabby called Banjo, jumped on my lap for me to stroke him. He had a make-up sponge in his mouth.

'Oh for heaven's sake Banjo,' Cassie said, wrenching the sponge out of Banjo's mouth. 'Bloody cat has developed a sponge fetish – he can sniff one out within a mile radius. He keeps bringing them home for me like trophies. Other cats bring you half-eaten mice. Banjo brings sponges. Bath sponges, those green scrubbing sponges. The other week he brought home a Vileda sponge mop head. I thought Graham was having me on but no, it was Banjo. Managed to get it through the cat flap and everything.'

I laughed and stroked Banjo who seemed to have forgotten about his sponge and was settling down for a snooze on my lap.

'What a treat this is, you and me getting together on a Friday night,' Cassie said, pouring more crisps into the bowl. 'What sort of a day have you had?'

'Pretty crap actually. Frank announced this morning that I have to work tomorrow. No notice, no explanation. Not even a please.'

'How very rude.' Cassie topped up my glass which despite its size I had done a fairly good job of draining. 'Have you got anyone to look after Lois tomorrow?'

'I was just going to ring my parents see if they could do it for me. Either that or leave her with James and Niall.'

'She can stay here! The girls would love to have her stay over.'

'Oh Cassie that's not the reason we're here. It was me who wanted to invite the girls over to ours for once. I don't want you to think that's why I rang you.'

'And that isn't what I think. But please leave her here. She's absolutely no bother really she isn't. She can share some girl time with us tomorrow and you can fetch her on your way home from work.'

So that's where Lois had got that cringeworthy phrase.

'Are you sure Cassie? She'd be happier here than anywhere else.'

'Absolutely sure. It will be my pleasure.'

Everything all better again.

Chapter 9

I was so determined to find out who Mack was that I bugged Glynis relentlessly to be true to her word and phone her brother.

Today that would be easy. All she would do would be to send a text and he'd send a text back and that would be that. But back then mobile phones hadn't been invented. Or maybe they had but they cost thousands of pounds and only really rich business men in London and New York wandered round brandishing hand sets the size of bricks and lugging shoulder-mounted carry cases for the batteries. For the rest of us, dialling a telephone number still involved putting your finger in a hole and dragging the plastic dial round to zero, and if you wanted to make telephone calls without the risk of your parents overhearing, you had to queue up to use the pay phone on the village green. Wait your turn, tap your foot in annoyance at the woman in front who is keeping her finger on the receiver and avoiding your gaze while trying to conceal the fact that the person on the other end is going to ring her back so the phone call will go on forever because she won't run out of 10ps. Finally you guilt her into hanging up and you heave open the heavy door and step in to be greeted by the tangy smell, peculiar to phone boxes, of cigarette ash, pee and disinfectant. Ring the pay phone at Ian's barracks in Yeovil, line engaged on the first three attempts, eventually get through, wait for ages for another squaddie to go get Ian, panicking that you'll run out of change and that the pips will go before he even gets to the phone.

'Hello?'

'Hi Ian, it's Glynis here.'

'Glynis! What are you doing calling me? Has anything happened? Mum and Dad OK?' (You have to remember that in those days people still used phones strictly for the purposes of disseminating important messages, not to vote people off reality television programmes.)

'They're absolutely fine. Nothing to worry about. What it is, Anna has gone and fallen for some bloke who came in to buy condoms. Ow! Sorry, still nothing to worry about, Anna just pinched me then. Anyway she wants to know who he is. He's called Mack.'

I could hear Ian chortling down the line all the way from Somerset.

'Mack? Mack the Knife? Big bloke, handsome bugger, rides a bike?'

'That's him.'

'Ha ha! Anna's fallen for him has she? You'd better tell her she's in a helluva long queue Glyn. Mack's been out with all the best-looking girls in the Vale of Glamorgan and dumped every single one of them. Anyway, Anna's got no chest so she's got absolutely no chance.'

Glynis was trying to turn her back on me, curling herself round the receiver so I wouldn't hear this bit but phone booths are small. I heard every word and I didn't care.

'Where does he live?' I hissed at Glynis. 'Just ask him where he lives.'

Glynis sighed but did as I asked. 'Do you know where he lives Ian?'

'Haven't a clue. Somewhere out Porthcawl way. Works in a garage I think.'

'That it?'

'That's it I'm afraid.'

'Oh OK then. How are you anyway?'

'I'm fine ta.' Ian laughed again. This was probably the first occasion, in a lifetime of taking each other's presence for granted, that either brother or sister had asked after the other's welfare. 'I'm coming home weekend after next. See you then. Ta ra.'

Glynis put the phone down, managed to put her arm round my shoulders in the cramped phone booth, squeezed me towards her.

'Never mind Annie. I don't think he would have been your type anyway. With any luck you'll never see him again.'

But I did. I saw him the very next Saturday. He came into Boots specially.

I'd spent the few days since the phone call with Ian in a constant state of agitated misery. I hadn't been able to concentrate on my school work, hadn't been able to eat even which was very unlike me. All I could think of was the smiling green eyes and long leather-clad legs of Mack the Knife and the terrible, awful prospect that I would never clap eyes on him again. But at 4.30pm at the end of a long boring day of stacking shelves with shampoo, I looked up from serving paracetemol to Mrs Hughes and there he was, dressed again in his black biker's leathers, every bit as handsome as I remembered him. My entire body hummed like a tuning fork that's just been struck and I just stood there, Mrs Hughes' change sweaty in my hand, staring at him.

'Ahem,' Mrs Hughes said. 'Change please Anna.'

I handed it over wordlessly, still staring at Mack.

'Hello again,' he grinned at me.

I could feel the blush spreading up my face right to the roots of my hair and down to my chest. My little flat chest that gave me no chance.

'Hello,' I managed to say.

'I haven't come in for Durex this time.'

Please let the last lot still be intact in your wallet, I thought to myself. *Please.*

'No?'

'No. This time I need a birthday present for my Nan.'

'Oh, OK,' and then, finally, finding my shop-girl manners, 'Do you have an idea what she might like?'

'Dunno really. I always used to get her bath salts but I don't think she actually uses them.'

'Nobody ever does. They make the bottom of the bath all crunchy.'

'Do they? Anyway, I thought I'd come in here and see if the pretty girl who was working here last week could help me.'

I blushed some more. He did mean me didn't he? Mack the Knife had just called me pretty.

'What about one of these gift sets,' I suggested, efficiently. 'Look, this one's got a little pot of jam in and some biscuits and two little napkin rings. What about that?'

'That'd be lovely. I think she'd really like that.'

I took his money, handed him the gift set in a bag. He didn't rush off.

'Would you come out for a drink with me tonight?'

I know this sounds over dramatic but I almost fainted. Truly I did.

'Umm… I don't know.' I didn't know how to tell Mack the Knife that the only time I ever went to a pub was with my mum and dad when we sat outside in the beer garden and they had half a lager each and I had pop and crisps.

'Don't worry if you've already got plans for this evening. We can do it another time.' He started to leave.

Already got plans? The only plan I had was watching Knight Rider.

'I'd love to. Only I can't stay out very late. I haven't… I haven't asked my parents.'

Mack just smiled.

'Don't worry. We can go straight after you finish here. I can have you home by 7pm if you want. I'll be waiting outside for you just after five. See you then.'

That was how my first-ever date came about. I had to go to the pub wearing my Boots uniform – a very fetching blue-checked nylon overall which that morning I had teamed very sexily with black woolly tights and my flat black school shoes. I couldn't possibly go home to change because my parents would have asked where I was going and I didn't want to tell them and anyway there wasn't time. Mack would be back in less than half an hour. I wasn't even wearing any make up but I did manage to squat down next to the No 17 display before closing time and secretly apply some tester mascara and tester blusher.

A quick squirt of tester Impulse under the armpits of my overall and round my neck and I was ready.

I burst out of the shop door, my heart hammering high in my chest, and there he was. Waiting for me just like he said he would be.

'Hi. Thought we'd go over to the Bear. That OK with you?'

'S'fine,' I managed to say.

Inside the pub was fuggy with smoke and already busy with people who'd just finished work and others who'd just finished shopping. Mack strode up to the bar like he owned the place.

'What do you want to drink?'

My mind went blank. What did I want to drink? The only drinks I could think of were Blue Moon and wine and a frantic scan of the optics behind the bar revealed neither and I was painfully aware that I was only seventeen and not meant to be drinking at all. I swallowed down hard on my rising fear that the man behind the bar might suddenly look at me and my school shoes and ask me how old I was.

'I'll have whatever you're having,' I said, trying to sound all casual, like I went to pubs every day of my life.

Mack looked at me and smiled.

'I don't think you want a pint of bitter really do you? Tell you what – I'll get you half a sweet cider and black. Girls seem to like that.'

Mack led me to a little table tucked away in the corner and I sipped at my drink cautiously. It was nicer than I had expected and I was relieved that 'black' turned out to be nothing more scary than blackcurrant.

'Aren't you going to take your coat off?' Mack asked as he wriggled out of his leather jacket. Underneath he was wearing a white T-shirt and I tried not to stare at his broad chest or the muscles in his arms.

'I think I'll keep it on if you don't mind.' I was trying to conceal the uniform beneath.

'Don't be so soft. Take it off – you'll be boiling if you don't.'

Meekly I did as I was told.

'Nice frock you got on there.'

I flushed with horror but seeing the embarrassment in my eyes Mack took pity on me.

'Don't worry about it. You're pretty enough to be able to carry anything off.'

I took a big gulp of my cider and black. Mack the Knife had just called me pretty. Again. Twice in one day.

I wish I could say that my first ever date went smoothly after that, that the conversation between Mack and me sparkled and that we laughed so hard it was time to go home before we knew it. It didn't. It was awkward at the beginning and it was awkward at the end. A second pint of bitter and a second cider and black were purchased by Mack and I didn't even pretend to offer that I would buy a round. I was far too terrified of going to the bar and anyway I didn't want another drink – I was already feeling light headed after the first. It was confirmed that Mack was from Porthcawl and was working in a garage training to be a mechanic. When I told him I was in the sixth form doing A levels and wanted to go to university Mack looked a bit shocked.

'I thought you worked in that Boots?'

'Only on Saturdays. I'm in school the rest of the time.'

'And do you like it? School I mean, not Boots.'

There was no point trying to be cool and pretending I didn't. My acting skills were not up to that.

'Yes I do. I like studying.'

'Crikey. I hated school. I left as soon as I could – when I was fifteen and three months or whatever it was you had to be. Couldn't wait to leave.'

'Really? No, I like school.'

There was silence for a while after that. Mack had a big swig of his bitter. I took a tiny sip of my cider. Mack looked at his watch. I looked at mine.

'I'd better be going,' I said.

'I'll walk you home.'

'There's no need. It's early and I only live ten minutes walk away.'

'No, come on. It won't take long.'

We didn't speak as we walked. I wasn't sure if it was me or Mack who was setting the pace but it was quite a fair one. Suddenly his hand brushed mine and on the next swing we were somehow holding hands. As his fingers closed over mine he tugged my hand gently, slowed me down.

'Whoa there Anna. I know I said I'd get you home by 7pm but I didn't say we had to jog there.'

I giggled.

'You sound nice when you laugh,' he smiled and right there on the pavement, just down the road from my house, he pulled me towards him and, my fingers still laced in his, he kissed me. He bent his head down towards me and pressed his lips, warm and soft and

82

tasting of bitter, onto mine and then he opened his mouth ever so slightly and ran just the very tip of his tongue along my lower lip. It was the most thrilling thing I had ever experienced.

'OK then Anna. I suppose you'd prefer it if I didn't walk you right to your door so I'll say goodnight here.'

I just nodded at him, speechless from his kiss and rooted to the spot.

Mack the Knife smiled at me one more time, turned and walked away. I watched him go, his helmet slung over one arm, swinging gently. He did not look back.

Chapter 10

Getting ready for work without having to get three kids off to school at the same time was a doddle. I wondered if Glynis, living alone in her fabulous apartment overlooking the Thames with two bathrooms all to herself, appreciated as she got ready to go into work at her hot-shot City law firm the simple pleasure of being able to take a long shower in the morning – a long *hot* shower because no one else has pinched all the water – and the opportunity of a quiet read of the paper over a cup of coffee and a piece of buttery toast? Probably not because that was an everyday occurrence for Glynis and anyway she hadn't eaten butter since 1996 but it seemed to me that if there was only me to get ready in the mornings I could quite enjoy going to work. Okay, maybe that was putting it a bit strong but it did make a nice change leaving the house without having shrieked at anyone. I even resisted the urge to shout up the stairs at the boys as I left to make sure they were out of bed by 11am. What the hell? I was feeling so much at peace with the world, what with going to work with clean hair for once and, safe in the knowledge that even if I was a couple of minutes late for work Frank wouldn't be around to wish me a curt 'good afternoon', they could sleep all day for all I cared.

Saturdays at an estate agents are very different from

weekdays. Saturdays bring out a different sort of clientele, people who regard collecting swathes of sales particulars as a leisure activity. A bit like train spotting but not quite as chilly. Frank had a special name for these people. He called them FWOTS on account of them being a waste of time and he was an expert at being able to spot them as much as ten feet away.

'Black and white particulars Anna,' he'd hiss at me having identified a FWOT coming into the shop. Sales particulars with colour photos are more expensive to produce than black and white ones. FWOTS don't get colour particulars for the simple reason that they have no intention of buying the houses they profess to be interested in. All they want to know is how their houses compare with their neighbours and perhaps pick up some decorating tips while they're at it.

Only the most hardened of FWOTS have the temerity actually to view the houses they have no intention of buying. This is just as well since Saturday is of course an estate agent's busiest day and a quick look at the diary when I arrived at the office showed that this Saturday was going to be no exception. With six viewings booked in before lunchtime I was going to have my work cut out getting round them all on time and would just have to lock up the office for most of the morning. The poor FWOTS were not going to get their particulars fix that day. I was actually rather looking forward to doing the viewings. Despite the fuss I'd made the day before about having to work on a weekend I always enjoyed the opportunity of showing houses. I didn't get to do it very often and even though I regularly complained that I was never going to become a good estate agent if I didn't get to view more houses Frank equally regularly just ignored me.

The first three viewings were to the same couple – Mr and Mrs Robinson – who were relocating to Wales from Bristol because of Mr Robinson's job. I often played a little game with myself at work, imagining how the people I spoke to on the phone would look. I got the Robinsons spot on. Despite being dressed in jeans and a shirt he looked very corporate, as if he'd be much more comfortable wearing his suit, and she was small and petite with lots of long brown hair. Rather too much brown hair, like the weight of it might cause her head to suddenly snap back and topple her over. They greeted me like a long lost relative, like they'd downloaded some sort of 'guide to getting the most out of your estate agent' from the internet which included the tip of being very friendly and making extensive use of your agent's first name so that she likes you and will let you know first when the best properties come on the market. Not that I could do that anyway. Frank always lets the people who have already sold their own homes know first when good properties come on the market.

The first two houses we viewed were not at all what Mr and Mrs Robinson were looking for and although they dutifully let me finish the tours round I could tell from the minute we walked in that they were just being polite and would have preferred not to bother. However the third one was a big hit. It was a modern, detached house on a small close with four bedrooms and a larger-than-average corner plot. It was nowhere near the size of some of the houses on our books but it was still a decent size and because it was partly overlooked by other houses on the close it was on the market at a good price. The Robinsons were obviously very excited but trying desperately to conceal the fact. Possibly another tip from that internet guide is to not show too much enthusiasm in front of your estate agent just in case the asking price suddenly goes up.

I took pity on them.

'Listen, we're a little bit ahead of schedule because we got round the other two quite quickly. As the owners are out how about I go wait for you in the kitchen and you can have another look round on your own?'

Mrs Robinson beamed at me. 'That would be great Anna, thank you.'

'No problem. Take your time and I'll be waiting for you in the kitchen when you're ready.'

On the rare occasions I got to do viewings I always waited in the kitchen. It felt a little less intrusive than sitting in the lounge where the people selling would flop around on the sofa in their pyjamas watching telly and even perhaps having sex. I let the Robinsons scurry back upstairs where they would no doubt have another good poke around, turn on the taps to check the water pressure and then have a whispered conversation about how low they dared to pitch their offer.

The kitchen was a good-sized one with a large window overlooking the garden. We had described it in the particulars as being 'traditional' which meant it was made of reproduction pine and looked dated. I leant on the kitchen counter and looked out over the garden which was very well kept with a long lawn and immaculate flower beds and I was just thinking that I wished I liked gardening and that the garden in our house looked more like this one when out of the corner of my eye I saw a swing of long blonde hair and a swish of pinstripe suit that I recognised. I looked more closely and saw that it was indeed Jane, ringing the bell of one of the other houses in the close. I leaned over to tap on the window and wave at her but something about the way Jane was holding herself, looking over her shoulder in the direction of where my car was parked, made me stop. Instinctively I stepped away a bit from the window, watched as a man opened the door, a man whose face I could not see but who held his arms out open wide to greet her. Jane pushed quickly past him into the house and the door banged shut behind the two of them.

I was still standing staring at that house when the Robinsons came into the kitchen.

Mr Robinson started on his pre-prepared speech. 'We think this house might just be suitable and we are prepared to consider making an offer bearing in mind the age and condition of the property and subject of course to contract and survey.'

'Of course,' I said, my mouth on automatic pilot.

'We'd like to discuss it further tonight at home but we anticipate we will make an offer on Monday morning,' Mr Robinson went on.

'OK,' I said, still not paying much attention to him. My blank expression must have worried Mrs Robinson because she suddenly veered away from the internet guide.

'Anna, I really... I mean we... we really like the house. And we will definitely be making an offer on Monday.'

Mr Robinson stepped hard on Mrs Robinson's toe at this point but she ignored him.

'We really like it.'

'That's good then. Now, if you'll excuse me. I really need to get on with some other viewings.'

'Are you showing this house again today?' Mrs Robinson asked me worriedly as I locked up behind us.

I wasn't but by this stage the Robinsons had started to get on my nerves.

'Yes I am. Three times in fact.'

'We'll be in touch first thing on Monday,' she said hurriedly. Her husband glared at her. 'Possibly even later this afternoon.'

'OK,' I said as I got into my car, motioning for them to get into theirs.

In the nick of time Mr Robinson remembered the internet guide again.

'Thank you so much for you time Anna. Much appreciated Anna.'

I didn't even bother to smile at them as I drove off.

Chapter 11

I had just enough time before my next appointment to get back to the office to pick up the messages on the answer phone and return a few phone calls. I tried hard not to think about Jane and the way she'd stepped into that house; the way that man held out his arms to her. As if she was a regular and welcome visitor.

Finally, even though it was going to make me late for the viewing, I gave up and phoned Glynis. Her mobile number was the only number other than the office and my own home that I knew by heart. Miracle of miracles she answered, but I could tell from the tone of her voice she did not want to be disturbed.

'Hi.'

'Glyn, is that you?'

'Yes of course it's me. Who else is likely to answer my cell?'

'Why do you insist on calling it a cell? We call them mobiles here.'

'It's because I work for so many American clients. It's kind of rubbed off on me.'

'Do you call tights pantyhose?'

'No, but my American clients are all men. We don't discuss pantyhose. Well not much, anyway.'

'Where are you?'

'In the hairdresser's.'

This was no surprise. Glynis went to the hairdresser's twice a week to have her hair washed and blowdried straight. She claimed not to be able to do it right herself. Glynis had become too posh to wash.

'I was just phoning for a chat, see how you are.'

'I can't talk right now. Nando'll be back with the straighteners in a minute. What did you want to chat about?'

'It's just that I'm making a hostile take over bid for M&S and I need you to sort out the legals! A chat Glynis. Just a chat. About nothing. Do you remember the art of chatting? Can you free up some time in your diary to speak to me later this afternoon?'

My irony was lost on Glynis. 'Sure. How would 3pm do?'

'3pm. That's almost the end of the day!'

'It's the best I can do Anna.'

'Fine,' I said huffily. 'I guess it will bloody well have to do.'

'Where are you going to be at 3pm?'

'Locking up the office.'

'You're working on a Saturday?'

'Yes I am. You're not the only one with a job you know!'

'Okay speak to you at three. Got to go. Nando's back,' and she hung up on me.

As I drove very fast to my viewing, I thought about how my life and Glynis' life were so very different. We'd started off in much the same place but over the years she'd walked purposefully one way and I'd drifted another and

91

now the only thing that was the same about our lives was that we were both single, but even then Glynis' reasons for being single were totally different from mine. She was single because she worked so hard that the only men she ever met were the ones she worked for or with. That wasn't to say she hadn't had relationships with those men. She had. Quite a few of them. But most of them had already been married.

'It's not my fault,' she argued in her defence on the rare occasions we discussed it. 'Married men suit me. They don't expect me to cook dinner or wash their socks or be waiting for them when they get home from work. Which is just as well because I won't do any of those things. I just don't have the time for proper relationships... And before you ask me, no, I'm not a lesbian. Just a very hard-working heterosexual.'

There was one bloke she had been keen on. Another married one. His name was Robert but she only ever called him by his surname. Carmichael. She said he was blonde, beautiful and brainy to boot. He had been her boss at the last place she worked and she was smitten with him for 12 months or more, even though he had a wife and a kid. I really thought he might be the one who would leave his wife for her the way Glynis talked about him and the amount of time they spent together but he never did and eventually Glynis claimed it had just fizzled out and she got herself a partnership at an American firm instead. I had no idea what she earned and I would never have embarrassed her by asking, but based on what she sent my kids for Christmas, birthdays and Easter it was a fortune.

But even though Glynis moved in different circles from

me, drank Champagne like it was Lambrusco and applied her razor-sharp mind to getting big commercial deals signed off, she was still my Glynis underneath it all. She could drink Champagne all she liked. I knew better than anyone else who Glynis really was and she knew I knew.

I did my other viewings on autopilot and got back to the office just as soon as I could. At 2.50pm I washed out my coffee cup and shut down the computer. I was just about to start locking up when the office door banged open.

'I'm sorry,' I said without looking up. 'I'm just closing for the day.'

'Don't worry about it. Who'd want to buy a house in this godforsaken place anyway,' Glynis said.

I just stared at her.

'What you looking at?' she asked. 'Come over here and look at me like that.'

I kept staring.

'For pity's sake Anna. Don't look so surprised. You said you wanted a chat. Well here I am for one. Don't just stand there gawping! Finish locking up. I'll wait for you outside.'

I set the office alarm hurriedly. Glynis was waiting for me next to her silver Mercedes CLK 320 soft top, stylishly parked on the double-yellow lines outside the office. She looked even thinner than usual, wearing a chocolate-brown mini skirt and chunky boots, her newly straightened hair black and glossy. I had been feeling quite good about the way I looked that morning but next to Glynis I looked drab and faded. And fat.

'How did you manage to get here so quickly?' I asked.

'Easy. I drove extremely fast.'

'Speeding?'

'Natch.'

'You'll end up losing your licence again.'

'Then I'll sell my car and get taxis everywhere again. Let's go get a glass of wine.'

'Glyn, I can't come for a drink with you right now. I have to go fetch Lois from Cassie's. She's been there since last night and I said I'd fetch her as soon as I finished work. Graham was away last night giving a lecture but he's due back later this afternoon.'

'If Graham's away giving a lecture on fannies then little goody-two-shoes Cassie won't mind helping you out for a little while longer now, will she? It'll give her something else to feel all warm and cosy about inside, being a friend in need and all that.'

'And the boys are at home on their own.'

'It's only 3pm and your boys are 18 and 16. They won't even notice you're not back.' This was harsh but true, yet I still hesitated.

'Oh for heaven's sake Anna!' Glynis fished her minute mobile phone out of her bag and started dialling.

'Hello, James? This is Glynis. Good, thanks. Listen, I'll be calling in to see you in a little while but I'm kidnapping your mother for a bit first. That Ok with you and Niall? Great! See you guys later.'

'Was it OK with them?'

Glynis looked at me piteously. 'What do you think? Right, have you got a number for Saintess Cassie?'

'I'll do it,' I said hurriedly, whipping out my own phone which was three times the size of Glynis', and dialling

94

Cassie's mobile.

'Hi Cassie, it's Anna. Would you be OK to keep Lois till about 5pm? I've got a few more viewings to do yet.'

Glynis smirked at me, mimed stretching her nose out long like Pinocchio's.

'That's great Cassie. Thanks ever so much.'

'There you go, that wasn't so hard was it?' Glynis said, putting her arm round my shoulder and marching me off towards Steve's pub.

'You'll get a parking ticket if you leave your car there you know.'

'I know.'

The pub was deserted. The lunchtime crowd had gone and the evening crowd would not arrive for a few hours yet. It felt naughty to be there in the middle of the afternoon, like playing hooky from school, and a little thrill of pleasure sloshed around in the pit of my stomach.

It was always fun to see the way Steve reacted when Glynis came through his door. The second he cast eyes on her he sucked in his belly and pulled himself up as tall as he could.

'Glynis, how lovely to see you,' he grinned. Glynis leaned over the bar presenting her cheek for a kiss. Shyly Steve obliged. I could tell he held his breath as he did it, just in case he smelled of chip fat or pickled eggs or something.

'Good to see you too Steve,' she smiled back, well aware of the effect she had on him. 'Can we have two glasses of dry white wine please. Large ones.'

'You're terrible you are!' I scolded gently as Glynis sashayed over to our usual table, looking back over her shoulder at Steve as she plonked our wine down. 'You know he's always fancied you and he'll be all of a tizz tonight now.'

'That was the general intention,' she laughed, taking a big swig of her wine. 'This stuff is terrible.'

'Don't act surprised! It always is. And it doesn't matter whether you ask for dry, sweet or medium because as you well know Steve only sells one type of white wine. Terrible.'

'Don't worry. I won't notice after this one.' Glynis took another swig. 'Come on! You know I don't like to drink alone. Get it down you!'

I took a gulp. 'Anyway what's with the big gesture?' I asked. 'You don't normally come tearing down the M4 when I call for a chat.'

'Thanks very much! What happened to the nice to see you Glynis? Or the thanks for making the effort to drive down to see me?'

'Cut the crap Glyn. You know I'm always delighted to see you. But you haven't been home in yonks and you normally give me a bit more notice so I can arrange wall-to-wall babysitters.'

'Actually Anna I haven't been back for more than a year.'

I looked at her, genuinely shocked. 'Never! It doesn't feel that long since I saw you!'

'That's because it's not. You came up to see *Wicked* remember.'

'Oh yes! *Wicked* was great. I really enjoyed it.' Truth was I didn't remember much about *Wicked* at all. Glynis had organised a trip up to London for my birthday, sending me a first-class train ticket in the post (which I'd cashed in for a second class one without telling her) and had met me at Paddington in a cab clutching a bottle of pink Champagne and two glasses. We drank Champagne for the next three hours or so but ate nothing and I ended up sleeping through most of the performance. I had no recollection of the journey back to Glynis' flat afterwards. When I woke up at 6am the next morning still fully dressed and sick to my bones she'd already left for work.

'If it was so great how come you snored all the way through it? We'll have to go again this year so you can actually watch it this time. I'm here my dear because you called me. I've been working round the clock on this huge deal – all-nighters and every weekend for months – and it finally signed on Thursday night so when you called I thought sod it, I'll just get in the car and come down here. It's not as if I have a social life left by now anyway. If I'd stayed in London it would have been a trip to Harvey Nicks for me and a night in with the telly and a bottle of Bolly.'

'Well if you're prepared to argue with the kids for it I can just about stretch to a telly but I'm afraid I'm clean out of Bolly.'

'Who needs Champagne when you can sup Steve's finest pinot grigio! Come on, drink up! I think we've got time for one more before Lois turns into a pumpkin and then I'll take you and the kids out for dinner somewhere. My treat.'

'You haven't seen my boys for a while have you?'

'Nope.'

'Then you have absolutely no idea how much they can eat. Honestly Glynis, they eat half a loaf of bread and butter each just as a starter. I'll cook instead. It'll cost a fortune to take them out.'

'Anna, do you have any idea how much money I was planning on spending at Harvey Nicks this afternoon? The kids can have two starters each. Two main courses if they want! It'll be fun!'

She swigged back the last of her wine and, without her even having to ask, Steve suddenly appeared at our table bearing another two glasses. 'These two are on the house,' he muttered as he set them down.

'So what do you say then Anna? Can your kids come out to play?'

'Well OK if you insist. Thank you. That's very kind of you. The kids will be made up. But I can't drink that glass of wine. I have to go fetch Lois and I'll be over the limit if I have another.'

'Limit schlimit. You go and fetch Lois then and Steve will sit with me for a bit and drink yours won't you Steve?' Glynis looked coyly up at Steve.

'Yeah sure,' Steve drawled, trying not to look as if all his Christmases had come at once.

'See you back at my house in a bit then,' I said. 'See you Steve! Thanks for the wine.' But Steve was already far too busy staring at Glynis to pay any attention to me.

Chapter 12

When I arrived at Cassie's house, feeling more than a little light-headed, Lois complained bitterly about being plucked from the bosom of the sweet-smelling, soft-spoken, all-female company to be had at Cassie's.

'It's not fair Mum, Cassie said I could stay another night if I wanted and have roast beef dinner with Jethro and Sol when they get here and then we were going to watch the *Princess Diaries* in Emily's bedroom and paint our nails and everything.'

'You'll have just as much fun with us tonight, don't worry.'

'No I won't Mum. I absolutely won't. My stinky brothers wouldn't let me watch *Princess Diaries* even if we had the DVD which of course we don't and your nail varnish is all old and sticky and the tops don't come off the bottles any more.'

'Just you wait and see, Lois.'

As I pulled up outside our house Lois spotted Glynis' car immediately.

'Is that a silver sports car?'

'It is.'

'Glynis has a silver sports car doesn't she?'

'She does.'

'Does that mean she's here?'

'She is.'

I thought Lois was going to implode with excitement. Glynis may not come home very often but from time to time she sends impromptu surprise packages to my daughter – Hello Kitty T-shirts, stickers, silver bangles – and as a result Lois loves both Glynis and the postman very much and in that order.

She scurried out of the car and rushed into the house. I followed a few steps behind her in time to see her throwing her arms round Glynis who was sitting cross-legged on the living room floor. The boys were ostensibly teaching her how to play Tomb Raider on the PlayStation but Bartley was clearly more interested in seeing if he could catch a glimpse of her knickers through her crossed legs.

'Hello lovely girl,' Glynis said, trying hard to keep her balance under the force of Lois' hug and prevent Bartley from catching more than just a glimpse of knicker. 'You've grown up too but nowhere near as much as your brothers. Look at these boys! They're proper men now.'

'I'm so glad you're here Glynis. Mum didn't tell me you were coming.'

'Mum didn't know she was coming,' I said curtly.

'You said I'd have just as much fun at home tonight and I didn't believe you but now that Glynis is here it's going to be the best night ever,' Lois exclaimed.

I felt a sudden sharp stab of jealousy which I instantly and guiltily folded away inside me. I love Glynis almost as much as I love my kids but it does bug me that Lois thinks she is so very cool when she hardly ever sees her.

'You bet it's going to be a good night,' Glynis said

ruffling Lois' hair, 'after I've finished being Lara Croft here we're all going to go out for dinner. You too Bartley if you want'

'Yippee!' Lois yelled. Even Niall forgot to be goth and muttered 'Cool.'

'So where would you like to go?'

'There's a new place opened on the High Street,' James suggested. 'It's all done up like an American diner and you can get burgers and smoothies and they've got tiny little juke boxes on every table. It's called Fat Boy Slim.'

'That sounds just the place for us. Do they do ice-cream sundaes? Because I'm not going anywhere where I can't get a Knickerbocker Glory.' Glynis gave up ice cream about the same time as she stopped eating butter so this last bit was for Lois' sake.

'They've got all sorts of ice cream. Me and Amy went there the night before she went to London and she had one with hot chocolate sauce. It was the best.' James voice tailed off slightly at the end of his sentence and a look of longing passed over his face and I knew it wasn't ice cream he was thinking of. Glynis saw it too.

'Right. Fat Boy Slim it is. Here James,' she said, tossing her tiny silver phone towards him. 'Will you go book it for us and then why don't you give Amy a ring? Long as you like.'

'Glynis?' Lois asked, using her best wheedling voice. 'Did you bring any nail varnish with you?'

'Maybe sweetie. I'll go look in my bag after we've finished this bit OK? Right then, Niall, Bartley. If I can manage to open this door I'll get through to the next stage right?'

Fat Boy Slim was a big hit with everyone. We fiddled with the juke box while we ordered burgers which came chargrilled, thick and juicy, with chips that tasted home-made, like the ones my grandmother used to fry in lard in the days before anyone had even heard of obesity. Even Glynis ate some of those. I was proud of myself for managing to resist ordering myself a Knickerbocker Glory but less proud when I finished off the rest of Lois' when her eyes proved bigger than her belly but, alas, mine did not. Afterwards Glynis waved her magic wand a bit more and announced that she and I were going for a few more drinks and that James would put Lois to bed for me.

'Let's not go back to the pub,' Glynis said after we waved them off. 'I think I've had enough flirting with Steve for one day. How about we try one of these trendy new wine bars you tell me Stonebridge has nowadays.'

We walked down the High Street and I led her towards what had been a bank when we were kids but which had now been converted into a very stylish bar.

'Wow!' Glynis said, taking in the brown leather chairs, the swirly brown wallpaper and the oversized chandeliers. 'This wouldn't look out of place in London!'

'You mean London where the streets are paved with gold and where the poor girls of Wales find fame and fortune,' I teased her as we found ourselves a table.

'More like London where the poor girls of Wales get to work an 80-hour week and can't find time to spend their gold,' she muttered, pouring over the wine list.

'Don't give me that! You love it!'

'Not so much actually. We'll have a bottle of the

Sancerre,' she said to the waiter who'd come over to take our order.

'How did you pull off getting the kids to go quietly?' I wondered.

'Told James he could come up to London to stay at my place soon and Amy could come over, promised Niall and Bartley a new PlayStation game and gave my entire nail-varnish stash to Lois. Easy peasy.'

'Easy for you that is. You've got the wherewithal to bribe them and you never have to nag them about homework or tidying their bedrooms.'

'That's because I'm not their mother and you are. It's my job to spoil them once in a while and your job to do the boring stuff I'm afraid.'

'Yes, well, sometimes I think I like the look of your job a whole lot more than mine, thanks very much.'

'You don't mean that,' Glynis said quietly.

'No, trust me, I do! Anyway, what are you going to do with two lovestruck teenagers cluttering up your lovely flat for an entire weekend?'

'Nothing! I'm not going to be there. I've told him to come up when I'm away for the weekend and he and Amy can have the place to themselves.'

'Glynis. He's only eighteen! You can't just leave him and Amy alone all weekend. They'll be—'

'I know. Shagging for Wales! They'll have a wonderful time,' she giggled.

'I don't know if I can allow that Glynis. I'm not certain Amy's parents would approve.'

'Get over yourself Anna. Amy's been away at university for six months. Anyway, don't you remember what you were like at eighteen? How you couldn't wait to get your rocks off with your precious Mack? You didn't give a shit if your parents approved or not. You were in love!'

Glynis rolled her tongue round the word love, stuck an r in the middle so that it came out 'luurrve'. I pulled a face at her.

'James is still my baby boy.'

'Come on Anna! Have you looked at him lately? I can't get over how much he's changed since I saw him last. I hardly recognised him he's gone so handsome and tall! And he's got fabulous hair. Does he have highlights?'

'Don't be so soft. Of course he doesn't. His hair just goes like that in the sun.'

'Well your other son dyes his hair. I thought perhaps it was a family thing. And neither of them could be described as your baby boys any more. You don't honestly think James and Amy are not doing it already do you? And wouldn't you have loved a nice place to go to with Mack, all by yourself for the weekend?'

'Please! Can we not talk any more tonight about Mack or the fact that my firstborn is shagging? OK? Look, here comes our wine. Pour me a huge glass will you?'

I never expected to see Mack again after that first date. When I walked in through our front door, dizzy from cider and black, and my stomach swirling from the excitement of his kiss, I was sure that my parents would be able to tell just from looking at me that something inside me had shifted but they were entirely oblivious. My father raised his hand in greeting from the front room where he was watching the news but without actually looking away from the telly. My mother was busy working her way through a huge mound of ironing in the kitchen and although she did at least look at me, her chief concern, as usual, was to conclude the process of feeding and watering.

'Hello love! You're home a bit later than usual. Your dad and I have already eaten but I've put yours on a plate in the oven.'

'Thanks Mum, that's great. I'll just go upstairs and change and I'll be down in a bit.'

Upstairs in my bedroom, I lay on my bed and with my eyes closed replayed in my head over and over the way it had felt when Mack kissed me. It wasn't as if I'd never been kissed before. Snogging at parties had been the entertainment of choice for most of my class for the past two years and even though Glynis and I were widely held to be a bit boring and swotty we had still managed to get invites to a few of these parties. We suspected we were being used as a front to lull unsuspecting parents into giving permission for the parties to take place – 'Glynis and Anna are coming and they're both real teacher's pets and work all the time so cross my heart hope to die there'll be no trouble and no drink'. Actually there really wasn't much trouble but there was always alcohol, a lethal mix of spirits called Heinous that the boys brought in Soda Stream bottles concealed in their jackets and made up of tiny undetectable nips stolen from every bottle lurking in their parents' drinks cabinets. Fortified by Heinous and lemonade, even Glynis and I had eventually found snogging partners and had sat in the dark in someone's front room, the lips of some boy from our class

105

pressed wetly against ours, fending off wandering hands and worrying about our kissing technique. How wide should we open our mouths we wondered and how often (if at all) were we meant to stick our tongues in – was it a constant flicker in and out like a lizard or should it be left in there lolling loosely at all times? The whole experience was best described as being a bit of a struggle and rather sweaty and damp.

Mack's kiss had been nothing like my previous experiences. He had barely opened his mouth and his lips had been dry and warm, firm against mine. There had been absolutely no flicking, no slug-like lolling, just his breath caught in mine. And then suddenly that small gentle lick of his tongue across my lower lip which had been so thrilling. Every time I thought about that kiss (which I did a lot that night and every night afterwards) that same thrill of excitement swelled up deep inside me.

But I didn't kid myself for one minute that Mack would be remembering it that way. Because when I also replayed in my mind how awkward we had been in each other's company, our stilted, embarrassed, embarrassing conversation, I knew that Mack would not be thinking of me like I was thinking of him. I imagined him leaping on his motorbike the moment he'd left me, riding off to spend the rest of the evening with a much cooler crowd of people, older than me, long since out of school and working. Perhaps one of them would have a flat of their own and there'd be a party going on there, gangs of bikers wearing leathers just like Mack screeching up outside with cans of beer tucked under their arms. Not a Soda Stream bottle in sight. There'd be loud music blaring and lots of women with big boobs wearing sexy high heels and Mack would stand in the kitchen in a white T-shirt, his muscly arms crossed over his big, wide chest, and watch them for a while before choosing which one he wanted for the night. Pour her a cider and black and say as he handed it to her: 'You'll never guess who I had a drink with tonight before coming here? A school girl! Met her in Boots and she looked so sad I asked her out for a drink to try and cheer her up. Poor little thing was wearing her school shoes. Even gave her a kiss goodnight I felt so sorry for her. It'll give her something to remember me by!'

And later he and the sexy girl would go upstairs and he'd crack open his pack of Durex and they'd lie together afterwards and laugh about the naïve little kid who'd been dumb enough to think that Mack might actually have been interested in her.

I dragged myself round school that week, my heart heavy as lead. Now that I knew how kissing was meant to be, I knew that if I couldn't have Mack I would never want to kiss anyone else ever again. Compared to him, all the boys at school, even the ones I had previously considered quite handsome and who I had hoped in vain might pick me some time as a snogging partner, seemed childish and puny. Their narrow little chests and skinny arms, angular and bony under their thin school shirts. Each night I tormented myself by imagining Mack's kiss over and over, running my own tongue over my bottom lip hoping to recreate how his had felt. When I did manage to fall asleep I dreamt not of the kiss but of walking into the pub with Mack wearing my Boots overall and my clumpy school shoes. In the dream everyone in the pub suddenly stopped talking and turned to stare at me, and Mack himself muttered something about forgetting he needed to be somewhere and walked back out the pub leaving me at the bar all myself. This dream was so awful that I would force myself out of sleep to get away from it, swimming up clumsily through layers of unconsciousness, heavy and black like treacle, and when I did manage to reach the surface and wake up, my arms and legs ached as if I had been swimming through mud and I felt awash with shame.

By the time Saturday came round again and I was wearing my Boots overall again for real I was pale and listless, big black circles under my eyes. Usually I could pull the biggest boxes out of the store room and I whirled the price ticket gun round like a cowboy, nailing each box of shampoo or toothpaste with a neat precise price sticker. Boom, boom, boom. Every sticker in exactly the same place on the box, neat and straight, and faster than any of the full-time shop assistants. But today I barely had the energy to pick up the ticket gun.

'What on earth is the matter with you Annie?' The voice of Mr Davies the manager swooped down over my shoulder and shook me out of my lethargy. 'If you can only work at half speed you'll only get paid half pay.'

'I'm sorry Mr Davies. I don't feel myself today.'

Mr Davies looked at me a bit more closely now and his voice became kinder and softer.

'Actually love you don't look too good neither. Do you want to go home?'

I was feeling so low that the kindness in his voice made tears well up behind my eyes.

'I think I'll be OK Mr Davies. I'll just sit here quietly and price these up and I'll feel better in a bit.'

I worked hard on getting back into the swing of the price ticket gun and after a while I managed to hit my usual speed and accuracy. The price tickets slapped down faster and faster onto the boxes and the ticket gun made a loud and satisfying clunk each time it dispensed a price sticker and I repeated in my head over and over 'I am not just a school girl; I am not just a school girl.' I was concentrating so hard on this that it took me a while to realise that someone was standing behind me, watching me.

'What did they do to you, those boxes? Remind me never to fall out with you when you're armed with one of those ticket things will you?'

I looked up and there he was. Mack. I had wanted to see him again so badly that I'd somehow managed to conjure him up. Right out of thin air.

I wanted to hurl myself at him, fling my arms around his neck and push my face into his chest but of course I didn't. My legs had gone all wobbly with excitement but I held it together and just smiled at him.

'Hello again. Are you here for Durex or birthday presents this time?'

He smiled back. 'Neither. I thought perhaps you might like to come out with me again. You didn't give me your telephone number last week so this was the only way I had of getting in touch with you.'

I'd always wondered what swooning felt like when I read about it in books. Now I knew. Inside I was swooning about all over the place but outside I was desperately trying to look cool.

'Yeah, sure, I'll come out with you again.'

'Great. Shall I wait outside for when you finish work?'

'Um, listen. Would you mind if I went home first and got changed out of my uniform?'

'No bother. I'll see you in the pub about 6pm shall I?'

I was gathering confidence by now. 'Do you think we could go to the café this time? Have a cup of coffee?'

Mack looked a bit surprised. 'I guess so, if that's what you'd prefer. Which café?'

'Do you know Rabaiotti's?'

'Is that the one just up by the church?'

I nodded.

'Okay, see you there then.'

When I got home that evening, a bit out of breath from running most of the way so that I would have time to get changed, I didn't tell my parents that I was going out with Mack. I told them I was going to the café with Glynis. I could have told them the truth – I was seventeen after all and girls my age were expected to start going out with boys – but I knew that the sort of boy they had in mind for me was someone from school, a good boy just like I was a good girl, studying hard to go to university and saving up for driving lessons. Not a leather-clad, trainee mechanic biker like Mack. Not that sort of boy at all. So I lied to them. And because they trusted me they didn't notice as I flew back out the door again that I was wearing my favourite jeans and my best blouse, the pink one with little flowers on that I thought made my boobs look bigger, or that I had make-up on. They didn't know that my stomach was churning and that I was all of a fluster.

110

I made myself walk to the café slowly. I didn't want to arrive all sweaty. Even so I could feel the heat rising in my face as I walked in and Mack was already waiting for me, his big frame squeezed into one of the café's high-sided booths and looking as uncomfortable as I imagined I had looked sitting in the pub.

'Hi,' I said shyly.

'Hi. What do you fancy?'

The word 'You' popped into my mouth, rolled around my tongue, sweet and sharp as a sherbet lemon but I managed to swallow it away.

'Frothy coffee please.'

It was what I always ordered when I was with Glynis. Shit! Glynis! I'd have to ring her from the pay phone at the back of the café and tell her where I was or else she could very well ring me at home and blow my cover.

'S'cuse me a minute, just got to make a phone call.' Mack looked at me quizzically but I was panicking a bit now and didn't have time to worry about how he was feeling.

I found a 10p piece in my bag and dialled Glynis' house. Luckily she answered straight away.

'Anna I'm so glad you phoned. I'm so bored here I could die. Want to go out for a walk?'

'I can't. I'm on another date with Mack.'

For once Glynis was lost for words.

'Glynis?'

'Yes, I'm here. Wow! I didn't think he'd come back for more after meeting your Boots overalls.'

'Well he did OK? And now I'm in the café with him but I told my parents I was coming to the café with you so can you not ring me tonight please.'

'Why would I want to ring you tonight? I'm talking to you right now aren't I and you're not in? What would be the point of ringing someone who's not in?'

'Glynis! You know exactly what I'm getting at. If anyone asks I was with you. Got that?'

'O – kay,' she said, her voice rising sarcastically on the last drawn out syllable. 'It's your funeral.' And she hung up on me.

When I got back to the table the coffees had arrived and Mack had sprinkled a thick layer of sugar over the top of his and was eating the crusty froth with a spoon.

'Everything OK? That wasn't your husband was it? I don't have to make a quick exit out the back way or anything do I?'

I laughed and Mack smiled at me.

'Hey, it's not funny. Wouldn't be the first time.'

I was shocked into being blunt. 'Exactly how old are you Mack?'

'I'm 20. Be 21 in a couple of months.'

Just three years older than me. Three years was nothing really. But he seemed so much older than me, so much more experienced. And I knew he wasn't kidding when he said that thing about husbands. There had been women in his past who had been married. Women he had slept with. So what on earth was he doing with a seventeen-year-old virgin like me?

'Sit down will you,' he pushed my coffee towards me, 'yours is getting cold.'

I bounced my bum along the seat of the booth so that I was tucked up against the wall, on the opposite side to

Mack. Mack drank his coffee. I drank mine. Every now and then our knees touched under the table and each time they did I jumped, like his knees were red hot and burning me. Our conversation was every bit as stilted and awkward as it had been in the pub. I felt like all those married women were crowded into the booth with us, sitting on Mack's lap, trailing their fingers over his chest, pushing me out so they could make room to have sex with him.

Suddenly Mack threw some money on the table.

'Do you want to go for a walk down by the river?'

'Sure,' I said and bounced my bum back along the seat and out of the booth.

Outside it was still warm and just starting to get dark, the sky a soft grey-blue colour. It was the end of September. The clocks hadn't gone back yet. Mack and I turned off the high street and made our way to the path that leads to the river. When we were out of sight of most houses he caught hold of my hand in his and laced his fingers through mine like he had when he kissed me. When we hit the river we walked for a while but didn't talk much until we came to a wooden bench, set back a bit from the path. The coarse grass around us was almost as high as our heads. We sat and watched the river, smooth and strong and serene. Eventually he pulled me towards him and kissed me again and all the married women disappeared.

That's how it was with me and Mack. We were at our best when we were kissing. We did in the end get better at talking too but kissing was what we liked to do most of all. Kissing and touching and pressing against each other. After long evenings spent bumping and grinding on that park bench I went home hollow inside and my head aching, hungry for something I would not yet allow myself to have.

So, no, all those years later I was not kidding myself that my eighteen-year-old son and his girlfriend were not having sex.

Chapter 13

I think of myself as being a good drinker. To be a good drinker you've got to first and foremost enjoy drinking and I love drinking so long as it's wine. Not Blue Moons anymore and definitely not cider and black. You also have to be able to drink a lot. Tick for me in that box too. Finally to be a good drinker you have to not get too drunk, too tearful, too maudlin, too affectionate, too aggressive or sick. Usually I tick all these boxes too. Except that is when I drink with Glynis.

Glynis is an excellent drinker. She's had a lot of practice at it over the years and she makes sure she keeps in training. She can drink me under the table and you'd think I'd know that by now. But I don't see her that often and that night after Fat Boy Slim I forgot just how good a drinker she is.

'OK what was it you wanted to have a chat about?' she asked towards the end of the first bottle.

'Oh it was nothing, nothing important anyway, I just wanted a chat.'

'Come on Anna I know you better than that. Something's on your mind. Come on. Out with it.'

So I told Glynis what I had seen, how a stranger had opened the door of his home to Jane and held his arms open so that she could walk into them and how, having seen my car outside, she'd scurried inside in a very familiar way.

'What do you think I should do Glynis?'

'What do you mean, what do I think you should do?'

'Well do I tell Jane what I've seen?'

'Are you out of your mind Anna? You say nothing, absolutely nothing.'

'Are you sure?'

'Yes I'm sure! Honestly, you've been living in this small-minded nosy little town for far too long. What good do you think will come of you saying anything?'

'I don't know Glyn. If she's having an affair that's not right. That's not fair on Bob.'

Glynis stared at me. 'You do know you're doing your holier-than-thou face right now don't you? It's the same face you did at me the whole time I was with Carmichael. Pursing your lips and wrinkling your forehead.' She shuddered. 'Disapproval is such an unattractive look.'

I leaned back in my chair, trying to sweep my face smooth. 'I did not disapprove of you and Carmichael. I worried about you when you were with him that's all which was my job as your friend but this situation is totally different. You're a big girl Glynis – you knew what you were doing with Carmichael and what you were letting yourself in for. But Jane, well Jane's got Bob to think about and Bob is my friend too, every bit as much as Jane is, and he's sick and he needs her and if she's having an affair...well, I just won't know whose side I'm meant to be on.'

'Anna, at the risk of sounding like a lawyer, let's examine the evidence you have here. You saw Jane visiting

116

a house. She visits people at their houses all the time to talk about weddings and christenings and the like doesn't she?'

I nodded.

'And some of those people, her clients, get to really like her don't they and are pleased to see her when she turns up?'

'Well yes, that's true; she's really good with people. You know that.'

'And sometimes these events that Jane is catering for, they're surprise parties aren't they? That the guest of honour is meant to know nothing about?'

'Yes but that wouldn't explain why she looked worried when she saw my car would it?'

'What? Apart from the fact that half of Stonebridge pops into the estate agency to see you every week just to give you the gossip? I put it to you, Anna Lewis, that there could be a totally innocent explanation for what you saw? Do you agree?'

'Well when you put it like that, I suppose so yes. But no! Not really...not when you take into account—'

Glynis cut across me, holding her hand up in front of my face. 'Ladies and gentlemen of the jury. The witness has just acknowledged that there could be an innocent explanation for what she saw. That being the case I have nothing further. Seriously Anna, either all you saw was Jane going to visit some client about work in which case there's nothing to discuss or you saw something more in which case Jane will not want to discuss it. If you really are a friend to them both just keep your trap shut eh? Right! Time for another drink. I'm sure bottles have got

117

smaller since we were young. They empty so much faster nowadays!'

Glynis orders good wine. Expensive wine. It's so much easier to drink than the gut rot I can afford. Just slips down without you noticing it. And she has such a knack with waiters – she can catch their eye in a flash and, hey presto, they appear all of a sudden before your eyes with another bottle. Like the shopkeeper in Mr Benn.

'OK,' Glynis said after filling our glasses yet again, 'enough about the kids and everyone else. How are you doing?'

'Do you know what Glyn? I think I'd like your life. I've had mine for almost forty years now and I'm fed up to the back teeth with it. I'd like to have yours now.'

'No you wouldn't Anna.'

'Believe me I would! Look at you. You look fantastic, got a great job, earn tons and your flat is like something off the telly. I want to be you. Can I?'

'Really Anna you don't want to be me. And anyway you're the one that looks fantastic. You've hardly got any wrinkles.'

'That'll be the fat,' I said, running my hand over my neck. 'Fills them all out. It's the poor woman's botox.'

'Don't talk rubbish. You're not fat. You're just plump.'

'Plump,' I repeated. 'Plump. I like that. Makes me sound like a good juicy plum. I'll settle for plump. What about the crap job and the teeny scruffy house? Can you make me feel better about them too?'

Glynis thought for a while. 'Nothing I can do about the crap job I'm afraid. That's all down to you. Go to college! Get yourself some qualifications! And the reason your house is teeny and scruffy is because it's cram-packed full of your beautiful, funny, lovely, loving kids and if I was you there's no bloody way I'd swap you for my life.'

There was a catch in Glynis' voice when she said this, a hiccup of emotion in the back of her throat that shook me a little out of my drunkenness.

'Don't look at me like that! You don't think I'm not painfully aware that I turned forty this year too and was so busy at work I spent the entire day and night of my birthday at the office. Time is running out for me.'

'You mean to have a baby?'

'Of course I mean a baby. What do women normally mean when they talk about time running out? Soft boiled eggs?'

'I never thought you wanted children. Didn't even cross my mind. I thought what you wanted was a career.'

'Why isn't it possible to have both?'

'Um, absolutely no reason as far as I'm aware. You're the one who always says you can't be taken seriously in the business world if you're a mother.'

'Well I've changed my mind. I've got a career and now I want a baby to go with it.'

I was sobering up fast by now. 'You make a baby sound like the latest handbag from Hermes! The Baby. Made of the softest pink skin and goes with everything in your wardrobe.'

Glynis laughed nastily. 'Don't you know me better than that Annie? I don't want a baby as an accessory. I want a baby because I'm lonely. Do you really think I'm that shallow?'

'Well I think having a baby just because you're lonely is

shallow. Yes.'

'Oh really? Is that what you think? Well tell me Miss Consultant Psychologist all of a sudden why do most people have babies eh? Because they're furthering the human race and breeding the next generation of doctors and bin men? Is that the reason?'

'Well no, of course not. People have babies because they want to bring another person into the world and care for it and love it.'

'Right. And bringing a person into the world because you want to love it is no less shallow than bringing one into the world because you're lonely. You don't think I'm going to put it in the airing cupboard and leave it in there until it gets old enough to play gin rummy and freshen my drink for me do you? Of course I want to bloody well care for it and love it. I'm fucking lonely precisely because I've got no one to care for and love!'

Glynis started to cry, something I've only ever seen her do about five times in our lives. I reached across the table for her hand.

'I'm sorry Glynis. You're absolutely right. I guess everyone has babies for the same shallow, selfish reasons.'

I can never watch anyone cry without crying myself but when Glynis saw the tears welling up in my own eyes she snatched her hand away angrily.

'Don't you start crying now! You know it drives me bonkers when people snivel. There's no need for anyone to cry about this. It's a problem that can be solved just like a problem in business. All I need is some sperm.'

'Don't you need a man for that?' I giggled nervously.

'I haven't got enough time for that.'

'Crikey Glynis. You're only just forty! You've got time yet to meet someone and fall in love and you'll still be young enough to have a baby.'

'That's not what I mean! I know my bits don't go past their sell by date for a couple of years yet. No, what I haven't got time for is a relationship. You know the sort of hours I work Anna. I haven't got time for canoodling in country pubs and romantic weekends away let alone being home in time for dinner. Any bloke in his right mind will have dumped me long before I can even find out if he's shooting live ammunition!'

'You could just walk into a bar and have yourself a one night stand with a total stranger. Shouldn't be too difficult for you. The bloke wouldn't even have to know.'

'And run the risk of getting aids or herpes or some other equally horrible sexually transmitted disease! Do you live in the real world? Anyway, a one-night-stand man won't have the kind of genes I want. I want someone clever and witty and sporty.'

'Well what about a one night stand with one of the lawyers in your firm? They should be clever enough for you. You could probably check out their A level grades on the firm's website.'

'I still can't ask them for a sexual health check can I? And a colleague would be worse than a total stranger. They might have the right sort of genes but I'd have to have some sort of relationship with them afterwards. I'd have to endure eighteen years of some posh bloke from Surrey demanding visitation rights and taking my kid off me as soon as it hits 11 to go to his old boarding school and learn how to be emotionally dysfunctional just like him.'

'Come on Glynis. I bet not all the male lawyers in your firm are posh blokes from Surrey who went to boarding school.'

'Of course they're not. You're missing the point. I don't want a relationship. I don't want a one-night stand either, whether it's with a plumber from Essex or a PPE graduate from Guildford. I just want some sperm and I don't want it to come attached to any man. I want my men to be spermless and my sperm to be manless.'

I looked at her blankly. 'You've lost me now.'

'It's simple Annie. I'm going to get my sperm from somewhere else.'

'Not from a man?'

'Of course from a man, just not from a man I've ever met. I'm going to get some from the internet.'

'You can buy sperm on the internet? Like bidding for it on ebay or something?'

'Well not quite but not far off. You get it from a sperm bank you dummy. You can even specify what sort of academics you want the donor to have, ask for a Harvard MBA even.'

'You mean Harvard graduates are wanking into little pots and sending them over here by DHL?'

Glynis made a face at me. 'Please! It's not referred to as wanking. It's called making a donation.'

I grimaced. 'That's what it's called is it? I'll have to remember that next time I'm washing donations out of my boys' sheets.'

'You're disgusting you know that? Anyway, they've got to go to a clinic to make their donation and then it's screened for disease. Not just AIDS. All sorts –

chlamydia, gonorrhea, a long list of other diseases I've never even heard of – and they've got to answer loads of questions about their health and the health of their blood relatives. It's such a fabulous system it should be compulsory. All men should have to be screened before being allowed to even go on a first date and women should be entitled to have sight of a full sexual health and fertility certificate before even thinking of getting their kit off.'

'You think? It's not exactly romantic is it?'

'And what good did romance ever do you or me? This way Anna I'll get disease-free sperm with good motility—'

'Motility? What on earth is motility?'

'Good swimmers.'

'What sort of bloke puts himself through all that palaver? I would have thought they'd rather die than have someone poking through their man stuff and giving it marks out of ten.'

'Well that's the problem. Not very many men in the UK are willing to be donors any more. When I was at university half the blokes in my year were happy to pop down the local clinic and spend quarter of an hour in a cubicle with some porn for the price of a good night out but it's not like that any more. The law in this country changed a few years ago and donors can't be anonymous any more – the child has the right to know who their father is when they turn 18.'

'So much for manless sperm then.'

'Oh don't worry you can still get it. You just have to go outside the UK that's all. Donors can still be anonymous in America and Scandinavia and lots of other places. I'm happy to travel for treatment to avoid some strange bloke turning up on my doorstep just as I'm about to turn 60 and demanding that my child give him one of his kidneys.'

'You sound like your mind's made up Glyn.'

'It is. I've got to go for a beat the clock check first – where they check your fertility levels, see how many eggs you've got left in your ovarian reserve.'

'Ooh your ovarian reserve. Sounds like an offshore bank account.'

'Stop being flippant, Annie. There's no point even talking about all this sperm donor stuff if I haven't got any eggs to go with it. I'm going for the check next week and provided it's OK I'll be good to go.'

'Seriously though, Glynis, will you be? I mean I can see you've thought through all the mechanics of making a baby without a man but you know being a parent isn't really about you. It's about the baby. How's the baby going to feel? Won't it want to know where it came from, who its father was?'

'You see. There you go again! Disapproving twice in one day. That's why I didn't tell you about this before. I knew you'd make exactly that face at me.'

Glynis glared at me. I took a deep breath and carried on. Real friendship is sometimes about saying out loud the things your friend doesn't want to hear.

'How am I in a position to disapprove? I didn't plan any of my children and for all they have in the way of a father figure I might as well have had a pot of manless sperm delivered by DHL. But at least they know who their dad is, where he lives, what he looks like. He phones them regularly, comes to visit once in a while. What are you going to tell your kid? Sorry I don't know who your father is or where he lives. Not even his name. He's donor number 1656 as far as I'm concerned, the one with good swimmers and no clap. What sort of effect is that going to have on a child?'

'I'm quite confident we'll be able to cross that bridge when we get to it. That's years away. I'll think of something.'

'Those years fly by, Glynis, believe me. Do you remember James when he was a baby? His fat bandy little legs? How he didn't grow any hair till he was at least eighteen months and I was worried he was going to be bald for life? How for his fifth birthday you flew home from a meeting in New York specially so you could be here for his party and we went ten pin bowling and for the first time in your life you actually let someone beat you?'

'Of course I do. Like it was yesterday.'

'It pretty much was yesterday as far as I'm concerned. But that baby, that little boy, is 18 now and as you so graphically reminded me earlier this evening, he's got a girlfriend and is shagging for Wales. That's how quickly years go by Glynis. So don't go into this thinking that you don't have to worry about the future because the future will be here before you know it.'

'You're being melodramatic now. You've had too much to drink.'

'I've had way too much to drink but I am talking total sense. And while I'm on a roll Glynis and you're already

125

annoyed with me anyway, if you haven't got time to wash a man's socks or be home for dinner with him how the hell do you think you're going to find the time to look after a baby?'

'Easy. I'll get a housekeeper.'

'Are you absolutely determined that your kid should be one totally fucked-up individual?'

Glynis looked at me coolly. Despite the amount she had drunk she seemed stone-cold sober.

'Anna sweetheart. We're all totally fucked-up individuals. It just comes down to a question of degree.'

And she picked up her bag and walked out of the bar, leaving me sitting there. I laid my head against the cool damp table. If I'd had the energy I would have cried.

I knew, just as surely as I knew that Niall and Bartley were right that minute still on the PlayStation, Glynis would not come back to the bar. Nor would she stay the night at mine as planned. It's always been her way of dealing with awkward situations. If things are getting difficult or unpleasant she just ups and offs. Takes herself away until things have blown over, before any more words can be said which once out in the open stay lodged between two people and cannot be easily removed, like heavy items of furniture. I wasn't worried that she would be roaming the streets of Stonebridge all night. Even though it was late her parents would be happy to be dragged out of bed for the pleasure of an unexpected visit from their high-flying daughter. Or she would get a taxi into Cardiff and get a room at one of the expensive hotels there, waltz in without so much as a toothbrush, smile knowingly at the concierge who would smile back and think to himself 'There goes a girl and a half'. She'd order the overnight things she needed from room service without even bothering to ask the prices.

I couldn't even worry about Glynis' plans to have a baby. I had something much more immediate to worry about. Glynis had left without paying the bar bill. I had about a tenner in change in my purse and if I was lucky about £15 in my bank account to last me till the end of the month. Was there any chance that the wine Glynis had ordered with such gay abandon had cost less than £8 per bottle? Was there any chance that they even sold a bottle of wine in this place that cost less than £8? It was gone 11pm and the bar staff were already clearing tables and stacking empty glasses up on the bar, looking over at me every now and then as if willing me to ask for the bill so they could finish their shifts and get off home. Eventually our waiter came over to me.

'Shall I clear these glasses away for you madam?' he asked.

'Yes please.' He hovered expectantly.

'Oh and can I have the bill please?'

'Of course, Madam.'

It turned out that a single one of the bottles of wine that Glynis had ordered cost more than all the money I had in the world. I could have done a fortnight's shopping for less than the amount of the bar bill. Panic bubbled up inside me and I could feel heat rising up over my face and chest.

I contemplated doing a runner but only briefly. I lived in this village. Everybody knew who I was. At least one of the bar staff was at school with James and Niall and anyway my hips were too wide to squeeze through the window in the ladies toilet and I had drunk too much to run anywhere. So I went through the motions. I proffered my debit card nonchalantly and while the waiter stuck it in the machine right in front of me I tried to look cool and relaxed, not hug my handbag to my stomach or bite my nails nervously like I wanted to.

Bless him, he tried three times. I think he sussed out the first time my card was refused that the woman with the Gold Card had already left but he kept trying. Finally he admitted defeat.

'I'm sorry Madam payment has been refused on this card. Do you have another we could try?'

I shook my head. 'I'm terribly sorry but my ovarian reserve must be overdrawn. Could I leave my name and address and come back in the morning to pay?'

You know how in the movies when the heroine is faced with that sort of embarrassing situation a handsome stranger comes to her rescue? How the waiter goes away to fetch the manager and then comes back and tells the heroine not to worry because the gentleman in the corner has settled the bill? The heroine looks up in the direction of the corner and then one of two things happens. Either the gentleman in the corner meets her gaze and comes over to say hello and their love story begins or the gentleman in the corner has already left and all the heroine sees is the door of the bar banging shut in the wind and the broad back of her benefactor walking away. Not for good of course. He'll pop up again later in the film. Benefactors always do.

Even though real life is nothing like the movies, my bar bill did get paid for me that night. Just not by a handsome stranger. As the waiter scurried off to tell the manager that I could not pay, Frank suddenly emerged from the very back of the bar. He was wearing dark jeans and an open-necked shirt the colour of cornflowers that even through the depths of my embarrassment I could tell he'd bought because it would make his eyes look even bluer. Handsome enough if you went in for forty-something estate agents but sadly not a stranger but my boss. Frank motioned to the waiter, whispered something in his ear and handed him a credit card. The waiter looked over at me as he took the card, then smiled and winked. It crossed my mind that maybe the waiter thought I was a prostitute and for a second time that night I contemplated doing a runner.

Frank walked over to me. 'Evening Annie,' he said.

I was a bit lost for words so I used someone else's. 'Of all the gin joints in all the towns in all the world, you walk into mine.'

'Is that a really weird way of saying thank you?'

'Um, not really... thanks for sorting that out Frank. Very embarrassing for me. Must be a fault on my card or something.'

'Really do you think? A fault? Or might it be that you've just blown nigh on half a week's wages on two bottles of wine.'

'Gosh Frank, I was feeling embarrassed before. Now in just one sentence you've managed to also make me feel stupid, poor and profligate. Cheers for that.'

'Don't worry. You don't have to pay me back.'

For a second I stared at him in wonder and delight. Just for a second.

'I'll just take it out of this month's wages. Give you a couple of days' credit.'

I wanted to stick pins in his eyes.

'Very kind of you Frank, thank you. Well I'll be off now. Best get back to the kids. Good night and thanks again.'

It was only on the walk home that I remembered Frank's claim to be away for the weekend. If he hadn't lied about that I wouldn't have had to work and if I hadn't worked I wouldn't have seen Jane or had a row with Glynis. In fact, this mess was all Frank's fault.

Chapter 14

I threw up that night, the first time I'd been sick from alcohol for years. It wasn't even a tactical fingers down the throat job. After I'd left my clothes in a big pile on the floor and got into bed without cleaning my teeth I lay there for a while but when I closed my eyes the world was spinning and the minute I opened them again I knew I was going to be sick. I made it to the bathroom in time and even though I was very drunk I do remember hoping that having thrown up what must have been at least a bottle of wine my hangover the next day might not be so bad.

There was no chance of that. It was as bad a hangover as I'd ever had. It started about 3.30am in the morning when I woke up desperately needing both a drink of water and a wee and then once I'd had those two I was unable, despite my banging head, churning stomach and bone-deep tiredness, to get back to sleep properly. Which is how I heard Glynis creeping in at 6am. I wasn't scared it was a burglar or anything. I recognised the sound of her high heels on my laminate floor.

I found my bathrobe and went downstairs to the kitchen. Glynis already had the kettle on, had lit two rings of the gas stove and was warming her hands over the flames.

'Fucking freezing out there!'

'You know where I keep the spare key then?'

'Every bugger in Stonebridge knows where you keep the spare key.'

'Where've you been?'

'Trying to sleep in the back of my car.'

'Really! I thought you'd swan off to Cardiff in a taxi.'

'Tried that. Couldn't get one. And I couldn't face waking Mum and Dad up.'

'You didn't need to sleep in the car you know. Niall and Bartley crashed on the sofa so you could have Niall's bed.'

'I know, Annie. Thanks.'

'I've got a banging head. How about you?'

'Terrible!'

'Kettle's boiled. Shall I make us both a cup of tea?'

'Yes please.' She was so cold her teeth were chattering and she looked blue. I went over to her, wrapped my arms around her.

'You really want one don't you?'

'What? A cup of tea you mean?' She smiled at me feebly.

'A baby.'

She nodded.

'In that case, Glyn, I totally support you. I'll come with you to the clinic if you want. Be with you when you have the baby.'

'Last night you thought my having a baby on my own was a really bad idea and now you want to be my birth partner?'

'I want you to be happy is what I want, and if having a

132

baby is what that takes then I think it's a great idea.'

'Do you think I'll be any good at it? Being a parent that is?'

'Do you think *I'm* any good at it?'

'Of course I do. I think you're a brilliant parent. Seeing you doing it all these years is one of the reasons I want to do it.'

'I'm not a brilliant parent at all, Glynis. But I try to be the best parent I *can* be, working with what I've got. It's what most parents try to do.'

'And it's what I'm going to do too. Although I'd better not get ahead of myself. I have to get pregnant first.'

'You'll get pregnant. Absolutely no doubt about that.'

'How come you're so sure?'

'Because whenever you set your mind to anything you do it. You always have.'

'This is a tad different from passing exams and getting made partner, Anna.'

'And don't I know it. Gosh. What a thought! A baby! It's going to be fun to have a newborn to fuss over again. Nappies and bottles and dummies and sleepless nights.'

'Don't! You'll put me off.'

'As if I could. I already tried that last night and failed.'

I hunted around until I found some paracetamol and we had a couple of those each and then a couple of pieces of toast and whilst I didn't actually feel well I thought I might just be able to get through the day provided I didn't need to leave the house.

'Omigod!' Glynis' hand flew to her mouth. 'I left the bar without paying! I'm sorry! Did you have money on you?'

133

'Not quite enough. Next time we go out girl I'm ordering the wine. You've got more money than sense.'

'I was going to pay, you know that!'

'And I had every intention of letting you pay, don't you worry. Frank bailed me out in the end.'

'Frank! Shit! How embarrassing.'

'Tell me about it! Appears from the back of the bar like a fairy godmother waving a fat wallet. I could have died, Glynis. Really I could. Then he tells me off for wasting money and says he'll deduct it from my wages this month.'

Glynis reached for her bag, tried to shove a wodge of paper money into my hand.

'There's no need. You always pay for everything when you're here. It'll be nice for me to have bought you a glass of wine for once.'

'It wasn't just one glass. It was more like 10. And I know what you earn and what those bottles cost. I was the one being extravagant. Take it please. I really want you to have it. I don't want you eating baked beans all next month just because I flounced out.'

'Well OK then. If you're sure.' I took the money and slipped it gratefully into my own purse. I didn't like to say that without it even baked beans would have been a stretch.

'I don't know about you, Glyn, but I feel like shit. I'm going back to bed for a bit and I suggest you do too or else the kids will be up and you won't get any peace.'

James

Mum and Glynis are talking in the kitchen and they've woken me up. They think they're being quiet but they're not. Mum often forgets that I have to sleep downstairs. Thinks she's tip-toeing around the kitchen when actually she's crashing around in there like a small elephant. It's not even light yet and the two of them are already up and about. Why do old people need so much less sleep? I'd stay in bed on the weekends all day if Mum would let me get away with it. She never does. If I'm not up by eleven she starts hoovering outside my door on purpose.

Glynis being here this weekend has just made me miss Amy even more because Glynis is so much fun and I know Amy would love her. When I called her last night and said Glynis was here and told her about her fancy sports car and going to Fat Boy Slim and paying for everything Amy wanted to know all about her – who she was and what she did – and she seemed surprised that my mum had a lawyer friend who lived in London.

'She sounds like something off *The Apprentice*. Your mum is a secretary isn't she?'

'She's more than just a secretary. She sells houses too.' I felt kind of weird, like I was defending my mum.

'You know what I mean, she didn't go to university or anything.'

'She could have, she was bright enough, but she met my dad and had me instead. And then Niall.'

'But she didn't go did she? So you'll never know if she was bright enough.'

135

'I guess not, no. Doesn't mean she's too thick to have friends who did go to university.'

'I didn't mean she's thick. Sorry. I just didn't know your mum had such high-flying friends.'

'Well she does, Glynis is her best friend. Has been since school. Anyway, thing is Amy, Glynis says we can go stay at her place in London one weekend, one weekend when she's away, and that we can have the place to ourselves.'

'Why would we want to do that? I already live in London. We can stay here.'

'You live in a hall of residence. It's hardly the same thing as having a flat to ourselves. Me having to sneak out to go the toilet, creeping down the hallway wearing your bathrobe. You know pink doesn't suit me.'

'I just don't see the point. All my friends live here too.'

'That's exactly the point Amy. If we go to Glynis' place we can be alone. Just the two of us.'

'But you know I've got netball most weekends.'

'You can still play netball. I'll come and watch.'

'OK, but then usually we all go out for a few drinks afterwards.'

'That'll be OK too. It'll be nice to meet your friends. I'll talk to Glynis tomorrow so we can make a plan.'

'Cool. Listen, James, I've got to go. I'm going out with the girls. Love you.'

'I love you too and I really miss you.'

'Bye then,' she said and hung up.

It was 10.30pm and there I was going to bed when Amy was just about to go out. Amy's got this whole new life going on, full of shiny new people, and here's me stuck at home, doing exactly the same things I always have which was cool when Amy was here but totally stinks without her. Last night when she put the phone down I felt like such a kid. A stupid, lovesick kid. When I feel like that, the only thing that makes me feel better is to think about the good stuff Amy and I did together.

One of my favourite things to think about is the first time Amy and I had sex. Real sex not the everything but sex we'd been doing for months before that. Her parents had gone to a wedding in Wiltshire and were staying over for the night. She didn't tell them I was going over to be with her and they didn't ask. They probably knew exactly what we were going to be doing – probably thought we'd been at it already for months – but they didn't ask. Not like Mum. When I told her I was going to stay at Amy's that night, she looked at me all serious and said,

'You are taking precautions aren't you James?' like precautions were a brand of condom or something.

I ignored her but she wouldn't let it go.

'I'm serious James. I wasn't born yesterday you know. I do remember how these things work. Make sure you take precautions. You don't want to mess things up now.'

Thing is, Amy and I could have been having sex for months but we hadn't. Amy said it had to be special, the first time, and that she didn't want it to be a fumbly, quick thing. She wanted it to happen but she wanted it to mean something. And knowing this weekend was coming up and knowing we were both virgins and there was no danger of either of us catching anything off each other, we'd planned for this weekend and Amy had gone on the pill a month or so beforehand.

I was crapping myself that I wouldn't get it right. I had a wank that afternoon specially, to try to make sure I wouldn't come before she did, and then when I turned up at her house about 6pm with a couple of bottles of Magners and a bar of Dairy Milk and she opened the door I didn't get an immediate hard-on the second I saw her like I usually do and that made me even more nervous. In the living room, she'd closed all the curtains even though it was still light outside, like someone was ill or something, and she'd put the soundtrack to *Love Actually* on which is really cheesy but I let it go.

We opened the Magners, she lit a couple of candles like they do in the films and we drank half a bottle each really quickly.

'Ready?' she asked.

I'd never felt less ready in my life. Me who can get a hard-on if my boxers rub against my cock in the wrong way (or the right way, depending on how you look at it).

We started to snog on the sofa and within a couple of minutes I'd forgotten how nervous I was or that I was worried about getting a hard-on because I had a huge one. When I put my hand up inside her bra it felt silky and sexy and the same when I put my hands down her trousers.

'New knickers and bra,' she said. 'Matching ones specially.'

There was no stopping us then. We wriggled out of our clothes which was strange. I knew her so well, had put my hands all over her so many times, but I'd never seen her actually naked. Her skin was so white, so perfect, and there were little dents round her ankles where her socks had been. Her parents' sofa is leather and it was cold on our bare skin. Somehow I found the right place and I was inside her. She winced a little and I stopped straight away.

'Am I hurting you?' I asked, worried.

'Only a little bit,' she smiled. And then, 'Don't stop you berk!'

Somehow Amy knew what she was doing. She pushed my bum with the flat of her hands, showed me the right way to lie on her, the speed at which to go and she came before I did. How amazing is that? Our first time together. Our first time ever. And we got it right.

Afterwards she waddled off to the bathroom.

'I didn't expect it to be so squelchy,' she said.

'Gee thanks,' I said in my best American accent. But we were both of us really pleased with ourselves.

Afterwards we lay together under this wool blanket her mother usually has folded up on the corner of the sofa. I'd never been able to work out why that blanket was there before then. Amy had her head on my chest and every now and then the two of us sat up and drank some more cider. It was magic.

Snuggled down into my chest, she whispered, 'James I've got something to tell you.'

'You're not pregnant are you?'

'Don't tease me. It's been something I've wanted to tell you for a long time but I couldn't before now.'

'What!' I said, worried by then.

'That's not the first time you've made me come,' she said into my chest.

'You what?'

'You've been making me come for ages. When you

touch me and rub against me. Pretty much every time we've been together actually. I just let it happen. I didn't tell you. I didn't know how to tell you. The first time it happened it was such a huge surprise, a huge, wonderful, lovely surprise, and then I felt guilty because it wasn't happening for you. So now that it has happened for you, I can tell you.'

'Don't worry that's not the first time you've made me come either. Not the first hundredth time even. Although it is the first time that you were in the same room as me at the time.'

Mum says when she feels stressed she thinks about standing on Ogmore beach looking out to the sea and when she's miserable and needs cheering up she thinks about the faces of us lot when we were babies. But I think about Amy and about the two of us that night and how we snuggled up together on that sofa afterwards and sipped cider.

Geez, it's only 6.45am and I'm wide awake and get this! It's all quiet! Mum and Glynis must have gone back to bed. Brilliant. Bloody brilliant. Wake me up and then go back to sleep yourselves, why don't you?

Chapter 15

By 1pm, having refused the bacon sandwiches with brown sauce that the rest of us were stuffing down, Glynis had to leave to drive back to London. Lois made a huge fuss, wrapping herself around Glynis' waist and refusing to let her go.

'I'm coming back, Lois, don't you worry.'

'You say that but you never do, not for ages.'

'No really, this time I'm coming back straight away. Next Friday.'

Both Lois and I looked at her quizzically. Glynis laughed.

'I've decided I'm going to take some time off. Now this big deal I've been working on is over I could do with a break. So I'm going to come home for a whole week, spend some time with Mum and Dad, get over to Yeovil to see Ian and the kids. I need to get back to London to sort some stuff out this week but I'll be back before you know it, Lois, I promise.'

Glynis disentangled herself from Lois, made easier by the fact that Lois had her eye on the last bacon sandwich and needed to move fast if she was going to grab it before Niall did. James had lost all interest in bacon sandwiches. He was looking at Glynis expectantly. She grinned at him.

'Right then, James, I'm going to get a spare set of keys cut especially for you tomorrow so you'd best get on the phone and make a plan with Amy.'

I walked with her to the front door.

'Do you want me to come up to London this week, be with you when you do this ovarian reserve check thing?' I asked.

'God no! It's not going to take very long anyway. No point you being there for that.'

I was relieved. I would have made it somehow if she'd wanted me to be there but it would have taken some juggling both in terms of childcare and bus fare.

'I'm really pleased you're going to be home for a while,' I said, hugging her. 'It'll be good to spend proper time with you again.'

'I'm looking forward to it too,' she said folding herself into her car. 'And to catching up with everybody else, see Jane and Bob too.'

'I'll call Jane, fix something up,' I waved as she drove off.

For the first time since I'd known her, telephoning Jane was not something I was looking forward to. I was going to take Glynis' advice and say nothing about what I'd seen. I wasn't entirely convinced that it was the right thing to do but since I couldn't think of anything better I would say nothing. For the time being at least. I walked back into the kitchen to find a lot of empty plates waiting for me but not one of my three children.

True to his word, Mr Robinson called first thing Monday morning and made an offer on the house I'd shown them.

It was 15 per cent less than the asking price.

'It's not good enough,' I said curtly. 'I'm not even going to bother to put it to the vendors. It will just annoy them. You need to try harder if you really want this house. A number of other people are interested in it.'

I put the phone down. Frank beamed at me. 'Well done Anna! Looks like I've finally managed to teach you a thing or two,' he said smugly.

Ten minutes later Mrs Robinson called back and increased the offer to 5 per cent less than the asking price. When I called the vendors they accepted the offer straight away but I waited two hours before calling the Robinsons back to tell them. I don't know why I was being so mean to them. They were a nice enough couple. But thinking about what I'd seen while showing them round that house put me in a black mood.

Mrs Robinson squealed with delight.

'That's wonderful news, Anna. I'm so happy. Do you think you could arrange for me to look round again one afternoon this week? Measure up for curtains?'

I hesitated. 'Don't you think that's a bit hasty? I mean you'll have to do a survey and everything before the deal goes through.'

'I know, I know, but I love the house so much I just can't wait to get going. Please, Anna.'

I didn't have the energy to say no. Or perhaps, despite my black mood, it was because I wanted to go back to the house too, maybe even more than Mrs Robinson did. Either way on Thursday, a full half hour before my appointment with Mrs Robinson and having parked my car in a little cul-de-sac ten minutes walk away, I was stood at the kitchen window of the house. I knew I was being ridiculous, semi-lurking behind a tall kitchen cabinet like some sort of stalker, but I did not take my eyes off the house opposite. After twenty minutes or so, I saw Jane's car draw up outside. I watched as she got out of the car and rang the doorbell. And this time, with my car safely out of sight, I watched as Jane greeted the man who opened the door to her with a kiss. A full-on, lingering kiss on the mouth. Just as Mrs Robinson rang the doorbell, I watched the curtains in the upstairs bedroom being drawn.

I gave Mrs Robinson free rein with her measuring up.

'You take your time,' I said. 'I've got some paperwork with me. I'll catch up with that in the kitchen.'

My mother could have run up at least two pairs of curtains in the time it took Mrs Robinson to measure up, but the bedroom curtains in the house opposite stayed firmly closed the whole time.

'You managed to get all your paperwork done, then?' Mrs Robinson commented when she and her measuring tape and her voluminous hair finally bounced into the kitchen, pointing at the entirely empty kitchen counter in front of me.

'Pardon? Oh! Oh yes. All done. Better hurry up in here I'm afraid. I've got another appointment I need to get to.'

As I locked up Mrs Robinson asked me if I needed a lift somewhere. 'It's just that I notice you haven't got your car with you,' she said sweetly.

'That's very kind of you but it's parked just round the corner,' I explained. 'It's part of my new fitness regime. Parking ten minutes walk away from wherever I'm going.'

Mrs Robinson's eyes flicked over me and I knew she was thinking that where I was concerned a new fitness regime was certainly no bad thing.

'Well OK then, see you again Anna. Thanks again.'

I should have left then. I knew that. I would be late picking up Lois from after school club yet again if I didn't leave there and then. But I didn't. I loitered at the front door, key and clip board at the ready so it looked like I had just arrived. And a quarter of an hour or so later I saw Jane's car drive past. I lifted my arm and waved and she saw me and after just a moment's hesitation she lifted her arm just a little bit and gave a half-hearted wave back.

Later that evening when Jane telephoned I was not surprised.

'Anna, do you think I could pop round to see you?'

I was relieved she had cut straight to the chase and hadn't wasted any time asking me about work and the kids first.

'Of course, Jane, when were you thinking of?'

'Right now would be good for me.'

'Umm, well I guess so. As long as you don't mind sitting in the kitchen that is. Lois is in bed but James and Niall are here.'

'The kitchen is just fine with me.'

She arrived ten minutes later with a bottle of Chablis, the same wine we'd drunk together when we'd discussed the food for my fortieth birthday, the same wine we'd shared with Bob.

'Thanks,' I said as she handed it to me, 'but I think I'd prefer a cup of tea, what with it being a school night and everything. Do you want one?'

'Sure, whatever.'

I busied myself with the kettle, got two mugs out of the cupboard.

'You saw me didn't you?'

'What today? Of course I did. I waved at you and you waved back.'

'Don't be clever Anna,' Jane snapped. 'I meant you saw me at the house. Not just today. The other day too.'

I turned towards her, leaned my back against the kitchen counter. 'I saw you going into a house twice, that's all I saw,' I replied carefully.

Jane looked at me, tears gathering in her eyes. 'Stop it Anna. Please. I can tell just from the way you're looking at me, from the way you won't open that bloody bottle of wine. You know don't you?'

The kettle was boiling but I ignored it and went to sit down opposite her at my tiny kitchen table.

'I don't know Jane. What is there to know? You tell me.'

'That I've been having sex with someone else!'

'Is that how it's described nowadays? Having sex with someone else? I always thought it was called having an affair.'

'I'm not having an affair!' Jane sounded affronted.

'Oh sorry, forgive me for being stupid! You're having sex but you're not having an affair.'

'No, I'm not. It's not like that Anna. Really it's not. It's… it's well…it's an arrangement. It's just sex. Nothing else.'

Our kitchen is so small I was able to reach over for the bottle of wine and the corkscrew without even getting off my chair. I gestured with my head at the cupboard behind her and Jane got up and reached down two glasses.

'Go on,' I said, as I poured. 'Tell me how this works.'

'His name's Aidan. I met him at a client do. He was a guest. His wife left him recently for someone else and has moved to Birmingham to live with her new man. He's hoping she'll come to her senses eventually and come back to him. The last thing he wants is to make it harder for her to do that by starting a new relationship with someone else so this works for us both.'

'Sorry, Jane, you've lost me now.'

'We have sex a couple of times a week. During the day, when it's convenient for both of us. Not at the weekends. Never overnight. It's just sex.'

'So you keep saying. What exactly does *just sex* involve?'

'Really Anna. I'm sure I don't need to spell it out. I go to his house. We have sex. Sometimes twice. I leave. End of story.'

'So where does Bob fit in with all this *just sex*?'

'For pity's sake Anna. He doesn't fit in. He doesn't fit in at all which is precisely the bloody point.'

I looked at her blankly.

'Let me spell it out Anna. For virtually my entire adult life, Bob only had to see me step out of the shower or bend down to pick something up from the floor and there he'd be, hard as the Opsreys front row, chasing me round the house until he got me into bed. Now I have to hold his dick for him to have a wee. Can you imagine how that feels?'

I thought of all the times I'd seen Bob give Jane that

look. Out in the pub or round their house having dinner. That look which meant the evening would end shortly because Bob had other things on his mind. And then I thought of the commode in the corner of Bob's room.

'Jane, I know your life is tough, but I don't see how that gives you an excuse to cheat on your husband. It can't be right that just because your husband can't have sex any more because – how selfish of him he, he's gone and got MS – that that means you're allowed to go out and sleep with someone else rather than going to Ann Summers like the rest of us? What happened to all that in sickness and in health stuff?'

'Don't forget the bit about until death do us part Anna. I love Bob. I really love him. And I'm never going to leave him, not ever. He's the man of my dreams. He's always been the man of my dreams. So can you imagine what it's like for me to watch him falling apart in front of my eyes? How much strength I need to help him through that? Because it's not easy for him you know having to cope with what's happening to him. He gets frustrated and angry and sometimes he lashes out and he's nasty and the only person he can do that to is me but I am going to hold it together for Bob until the very end. Until the bitter end, Anna. Do you understand? But the only way I'm going to do that without falling apart myself is if someone else holds me from time to time.'

Jane bent her head and I watched as tears plopped down onto the table. I reached across the table, took both Jane's hands in mine.

'I can't begin to imagine what you're going through Jane. Really I can't. But I still don't understand how you can do this to Bob. How you can just nip over to Aidan's to have sex and then go home to Bob as if nothing had changed. How can you do that to him?'

Jane looked at me, wiped the tears from her eyes with the back of her hands.

'The weirdest thing about it is that it's so easy, Anna,' she sniffed. 'I get to Aidan's and it's like I must leave the real Jane waiting in the car or something. He opens the door and I'm someone else altogether. Another Jane. Not me at all. And then when it's over I leave and get in the car and become the old me again and drive home to Bob.'

'And you can do that? Just have quick sex with someone, no talking or touching, just mindless, wordless sex?'

'I didn't say it was quick sex or that there was no touching.'

'You said it was just sex.'

'And that's exactly what it is Anna. Just sex. But that doesn't mean we rut like animals and don't speak to each other. I mean, we don't sit around in the living room having a cup of tea and a digestive and chatting about our day. We go straight upstairs to bed. But he still woos me. He kisses me and rubs me first and strokes my hair. Don't look so disgusted Anna. I'm trying to explain to you that even though it's just sex it's not sordid or anything.'

'And that makes it all all right?'

'No, it does not make it all all right Anna,' Jane said sharply. 'But it makes it easier to understand somehow doesn't it?'

'Not really, no.'

'Look Anna, I've been married to Bob for almost 25

years. He's the only man I ever made love with before Aidan.'

'So it's making love now is it? I thought it was just sex.'

'Oh grow up will you, Anna. I'm trying to explain it to you so just listen will you? The only man I *had sex* with before Aidan was Bob. Bob and I had been young together and had grown older together and he didn't mind my stretch marks or the fact that my boobs were creeping further down towards my waist every day because he'd made the babies that had made me that way. I never thought I'd be able to take my clothes off in front of anyone else. But this other Jane, the one in Aidan's bed, she's still young and carefree and her lips aren't turning into a cat's bottom and she takes her clothes off no problem at all and spends the afternoon having sex and being stroked and told she's beautiful. It's romantic and it's fun and it doesn't mean anything and those couple of afternoons a week of being the other Jane mean I've got the strength and the energy to keep going for Bob.'

'Do you…' I hesitated.

'What?'

'Do you pretend that Aidan is Bob?'

Jane smiled. 'Never. It would be impossible. Aidan is smaller than Bob.'

I lifted an eyebrow.

'Not small in that way. He's slighter, much thinner, and he's got almost no hair on his chest and Bob is hairy as a bear. And anyway, as I keep trying to explain, that woman in Aidan's bed, it's not me. Not really me. I don't think it's really Aidan either. The real Aidan just wants his wife back. It's like we're both in a dream or acting or something.'

'Thing is Jane, it's not a dream is it? And you and Aidan might feel like you're different people when you're holed up in his bedroom having your romantic, loving, sexy afternoons with no strings attached and that it has no bearing on your real lives but I saw the two of you remember? Kissing on his front door step like a pair of teenagers. There must be a real risk that other people will see you too. And then what will you do?'

'I really don't think other people will see us. We only ever go to Aidan's house, we never go out together and we only ever communicate by text. It was a hell of a coincidence that the people across the road were selling their house and that you were showing people round at the very time I was going to visit Aidan.'

'And you trust him, this Aidan, not to say anything to anyone? I mean, if he's stroking your hair and telling you you're beautiful before he fucks you is there a risk he might fall in love with you? Or that you might fall in love with him?'

'There's no risk of any of that, I can assure you. I told him from the very start about Bob's MS and how he would need to be totally discreet and not expect anything more from me. He knows the score and he's fine with that. Anyway Anna, he's young and if he doesn't manage to work things out with his wife he'll meet someone else eventually.'

'What do you mean he's young? You never mentioned he was young. How young is young these days?'

'He's 29.'

'Bloody hell.'

'Exactly.'

I topped up our glasses of wine and took a big gulp of mine.

'You and Bob have been the best of friends to me and there have been times in my life I would not have made it through without you. I used to look at you and feel so sad and jealous that I didn't have what you two had, that I didn't have a husband like Bob – kind and funny and a brilliant dad. So I'm not going to pretend I understand why you're doing what you're doing Jane because I don't. I really don't. What I do understand however is that I love you. And I love Bob. And even though I don't love what you're doing I'm not going to judge you for it because I reckon only someone coping with what you're coping with is in any position whatsoever to judge you.'

'So you won't say anything to Bob?'

'I'm not going to say anything to anyone! I'm going to take a leaf out of your book and pretend that the Jane that sleeps with Aidan is not the same Jane I know. But do yourself a favour eh?'

'What…?'

'Don't kiss him again until you're safely inside his house.'

Jane nodded and smiled at me, a sad, relieved, grateful little smile. I clinked my glass gently against hers and then drained it.

Chapter 16

When Mack first broke the news that one of the customers at the garage had helped set him up with a job on a French campsite and he would be leaving the week I finished my A level exams I thought he was trying to finish with me. I went so cold with fear I thought my heart would stop.

'Why do you want to go to France to work? You've got a good job at the garage, you've got your friends, got me. What more do you want?'

'It's a poxy job, Anna. I spend most of my life on my back lying under cars getting grease in my face. There's more to life than that. And the campsite job is only the start. After that there's the ski resorts for the winter season.'

'But why France?' I gasped. 'You don't even speak French.'

'Just as well you do then.'

It was only then that I realised he was asking me to go with him.

I thought about the place I had lined up at Birmingham University to study history. I thought about Freshers' Week and all the societies I'd join, all the clever history types I'd meet in lectures and tutorials, even though I didn't really know what a tutorial was. I pictured the little room I would have in the hall of residence – the single bed and the desk and the sink in the corner – and my kettle and my mug tree and the framed print of Monet's 'Water Lilies' that I would prop up on my desk to brighten the place up and make it my own. And I realised that I'd spend most of my time lying on that bed, looking at the muted pinks and greens of Monet's famous painting, feeling wretched because I missed Mack so much.

I told Glynis first.

'Are you out of your goddamned, tiny mind?' Glynis had moved on from Crown Court to L A Law by then and was cultivating her American accent. 'We've just finished our exams and you are forecast to get three frigging Bs and to get into Birmingham which for some reason, way beyond me, is the university you've wanted to go to ever since I've known you and now here you are wanting to throw it all away to go live in a tent! Are you hell-bent on messing up your life?'

'No, but I am hell-bent on being with Mack. If he's going to the South of France to work then I'm going too.'

'Go with him for the summer if you really must. Just come back by the end of September. Campsites close then anyway and you'll both be fed up of living out of a rucksack way before then.'

'Maybe,' I shrugged. 'We'll see.'

I didn't mean it. Mack was planning on living out of a rucksack for a very long time and for as long as he was happy doing that, I would be too.

'Well, it's your future,' Glynis said. 'You get to fuck it up if that's what you really want.'

I waited until my exams were over before telling my parents. I knew they wouldn't take it well.

'How could you do this to your father?' my mother shouted at me. 'He's worked his entire life so you could go to university; something that he never got to do. How can you throw it all in his face like this? First love never lasts, Anna! Everybody knows that.'

My father went for a calm, considered approach with underlying blackmail and overtones of bribery.

'Annie, your mother and I can see that you think you love Mack and how exciting living in France sounds but you know it'll kill her if you move abroad. She's barely been able to sleep at the thought of you moving to England let alone continental Europe. Don't do this to her eh love? Tell you what, if you go to Birmingham I'll teach you to drive before you go. How's that?'

Looking back I could have dealt with things better. I could have told them that I really appreciated everything that they'd done for me and that I really loved them both; was proud of being their daughter and grateful to them for always chasing the *bwci bo* out from under my bed when I was little, thanked my mum for pressing my school uniform and my dad for cleaning my school shoes every single Sunday long after I was old enough to do it myself, thanked the two of them for being there at every school concert and presentation, for bringing me endless cups of tea and sandwiches when I was revising and for letting me stick my Kajagoogoo posters up in my bedroom with Sellotape in form 2 when everyone knows Sellotape pulls the pattern off the wall paper. Instead what I said was that I didn't just *think* I loved Mack, that

155

I *knew* I loved him and that I was going to France with him and nothing, absolutely nothing they said, would make me change my mind because they couldn't possibly understand how I felt.

The morning we were leaving for France I set my alarm for 6am. I hadn't told my parents that we were leaving so early. I didn't bother with breakfast or even a cup of tea, just lay on my bed, rucksack at the ready, listening out for Mack's motorbike. I had heard my mother sobbing quietly in the night and the low rumble of my dad's voice trying to reassure her and I was planning on creeping down the stairs and letting myself quietly out of the house before they woke up but as I heard Mack pulling up outside my father opened the door of my bedroom.

'Don't leave without saying goodbye, love,' he said in a sad, quiet voice. 'It'll break your mother's heart.'

When I went into my parents' bedroom my mother was sitting on the edge of the bed, her shoulders hunched up, rocking gently. She had been crying a lot, her eyes swollen and red, and she was twisting a damp, disintegrating tissue between her fingers. As she got up to hug me she started crying again.

'I can't bear to let you go Anna. I really can't. I feel like I'm losing the most precious thing in the world to me, my little girl. But you're going anyway, I know that.' Her words gathered thickly in the back of her throat. 'Just remember one thing will you? Your father and I love you. We always have and we always will. Wherever you are.'

Tears were sliding down my cheeks now. My father came over, gathered me to him in a hard, tight hug. His lips pressed to my hair, he mumbled. 'All you've got to do is call me. Doesn't matter what time of day or night. I'll get straight in the car and come fetch you. Now go. I'll take care of your mother.'

'Are you sure about this?' Mack's voice was muffled inside his helmet. He reached up to wipe my cheek, his glove rough against my skin. I nodded very firmly, put on my own helmet and we drove off.

It took us three days on the motorbike to get down to Languedoc-Roussillon. I was saddle sore and partially deaf when, late in the afternoon, we arrived at the campsite, sprawling on the edge of the Mediterranean Sea. When M. Perez, the campsite owner, showed us the spot where we were to pitch our tent I shuddered to think that this was where Mack and I were going to live for the summer, in a two man tent barely big enough for us to lie down in. But later, after we'd had a couple of cold beers each in the bar and shared a bowl of *frites*, crisp and salty, and were lying side by side in our tent, the flaps unzipped and rolled back to let in the cool, night air, Mack rolled over on to his side and looked down at me.

'This is where I want to be most of all in the world,' he said.

I pulled his face down to mine and kissed him full on the lips. 'And here with you is where I want to be most of all in the world,' I whispered in his ear.

The working day on the campsite started very early. We were up most mornings by 6am. It was already too warm by then to lie in the tent anyway. Mack's first job of the day was cleaning the toilet blocks. This was not a pleasant task. Although there were eight stalls in each of the female and male blocks only one of those eight was a

British toilet. The rest were traditional hole in the floor types. The British campers formed a long patient queue for that one toilet and despite the notice on the door in French and English to please use toilet paper sparingly it soon blocked up.

'It's the toilet paper you British bring with you,' M. Perez explained. 'It's so much thicker than the stuff we use, so very wasteful.'

I was slowly starting to get the hang of his accent. The day we arrived at the campsite I'd just assumed M. Perez was Spanish given his name and the fact that he was small and swarthy with a luxurious moustache and spoke French with a Spanish accent. I'd since learned his family had lived in the area for many generations and that everybody who lived here spoke with the same strong accent, a legacy of the traditional language of the region, Occitan. They used words that didn't feature in my little Collins Gem French dictionary; words that no one in the Language Lab back at school would ever have heard of. Even simple words like vin and pain sounded like 'veng' and 'paing.' I understood about one word in three and got by mostly from watching people's expressions. Mack had no chance. He just smiled a lot and asked me afterwards what people had said.

Even though he wasn't learning much French, Mack had become an accomplished toilet cleaner. He developed a technique of first blasting the toilet block long distance with a hose, giving the offending British toilet a good five minutes blast all to itself before tackling it on a closer range basis. The two of us had quickly switched to using the French toilets on arrival and had developed good leg muscles. Mack cleaned the toilet and shower blocks again at around 4.30pm just before everyone came back from the beach and the evening shower rush started. The rest of his day's work depended on what M. Perez had in mind for him. This could range from maintenance work on the fifteen or so elderly caravans on site that M. Perez rented out to holiday makers, fixing wobbly tables in the restaurant or putting up shelves in the little site supermarket. M. Perez communicated these jobs to Mack by pointing and by picking out the appropriate tools from the tool box. Mack was sufficiently handy to work out what was needed.

Every single thing on that campsite – the supermarket, the bar/restaurant, the launderette – it all belonged to M. Perez. He and his family did most of the work too – his wife cooked in the restaurant, his daughter manned reception all day and then went to join her mother in the restaurant while her brothers served behind the bar. They all worked long hours and never took a day off. They had to if they were going to earn enough in four months to keep them going for the rest of the year.

The campsite was so close to the beach that the tents at the back of the campsite were within 30 seconds' walk of it and the supermarket made a killing out of selling really long, thick tent poles that would actually pin a tent to a pitch of sand instead of pinging out within minutes like the standard ones did. I loved the fact that I could walk from our tent to the beach in a minute, my flip-flops flicking a trail of sand into the small of my back, and spend hours sunbathing and reading and swimming in the sea while I waited for Mack to finish work. It was bliss. For about two weeks. After that I was brown and bored and had finished every book I had brought with me and every book that Mack had brought too. When I asked M. Perez if he might have a job for me too he was unenthusiastic to begin with.

'I can't afford more paid help. If I needed more work done I would tell my children to work harder!'

'I'm not looking to get paid much. I can't sit outside the tent all day waiting for Mack to finish work. We haven't got any chairs anyway. How about I just help on reception for a couple of hours to begin with, see how we get on, and my pay can be an evening meal for Mack and me at the restaurant and a few beers. How's that?'

M. Perez's eyes narrowed. He knew he was onto a winner and that when the English holidaymakers arrived thirsty and tired and frustrated after a long drive on the wrong side of the road they would be pleased to be met by someone who spoke English.

'D'accord. We'll give it a try. But just one beer each and a glass of house wine with your meal.'

'Deal.'

Reception opened from 8am till 1pm and then re-opened from 4pm till 6pm. Danielle, M. Perez's daughter, answered the phones and dealt with the post and faxes that came through. This was 1988; there were no desktop computers and no email. We were busy but in a leisurely, simple way. By 10am the British holidaymakers who had travelled to Toulouse by Motorail started to arrive and I would jump on the battered pushbike I'd been supplied with and lead them to their caravan or to the pitch they had booked for their tents. I would give them my spiel about how to find the beach and the toilet block and describe the restaurant's special that night in glowing terms. Having discovered that a lot of holidaymakers appeared to leave their brains behind at Dover I reminded them that French banks were closed on Saturdays and Sundays just like British ones and to remember to use suntan lotion, warning men especially who were about to break open the sandals or the espadrilles after 12 months of socks and shoes to watch out for the tops of their feet. I'd tell them they could find me on reception if there was anything else I could help with and that if they happened to have any books with them that they had finished could I please borrow them. And then I'd jump on my bike and pedal back to reception.

Danielle, who unlike her father was tall and blonde, shook her head at me pityingly as I arrived back, out of breath and sweaty.

'Why do you work so hard? You are always so helpful, so busy when all you get for your efforts is a *demi pression* and some left-over *moules farcies*.'

I shrugged my shoulders. 'It's fun. I like it. Like making their holidays that little bit better. Anyway, it's something to do while I wait for Mack.'

'Ah yes, your handsome Mack. My mother would have given you dinner every night for nothing, if only Mack had asked. He has made kitchen cupboards that haven't opened properly for years slide open as easily as the legs of a mistress. She is a little in love with him I think. Now, as you are doing so well here, I think I will entrust you to run reception alone and go to Toulouse to do some shopping. *Ciao, bella*.'

I watched her as she walked to her car. There was nothing sweaty or hurried about Danielle. Dressed in a white skirt and small fitted white jacket, oversized sunglasses perched on her head and a tiny white handbag slung over one arm, she folded herself gracefully into her 2CV and drove off, lifting one hand behind her to give me a languid wave goodbye.

Later, when Mack came to reception at 1pm to pick me up to go for a swim, I asked him: 'Do you think Madame Perez is in love with you Mack?'

'Of course she is, AnnPann, I flirt with her, I smile sweetly at her, I fix her dishwasher so she doesn't have to wash up by hand again. But she has a moustache that is almost as big as her husband's so you have nothing to worry about. And she's promised us steak tonight and a good glass of red wine, none of this house rubbish, so I'll be flirting with her again tonight. Right are you ready? Got the Pschitt and the peaches? Let's be off.' And he giggled to himself. A French soft drink whose name sounded like shit never failed to amuse him.

Campsite life suited Mack. His sandy hair had turned blonde in the sun and a daily swim and hours spent walking round a campsite and hosing down toilets had made him leaner and fitter than ever. His skin was smooth and brown. I on the other hand was plagued with mosquito bites that I scratched in my sleep till the tops came off which then hardened and grew a yellow crust. I let him get just in front of me so that I could watch his bum move up and down as he walked.

'Oi! Are you coming to the beach or what Anna?' he grinned at me, knowing exactly what I was looking at.

He reached back, caught hold of my hand, pulled me towards him in one fluid movement so that I was nestled up beside him, his arm tight around me. His skin smelled of sun and sweat.

Chapter 17

Even though I was only working for our supper and Mack's wages were pretty low we made good money that summer. We spent very little and the British holidaymakers tipped me generously. I was surprised the first time a family sought out our tent as they were leaving.

'We've brought you some stuff we've got left over that we don't want to take home with us.'

'Wow this is great,' I said inspecting the Carrefour plastic bag, spotting coffee, tea, some washing powder and best of all a few suncream-stained paperbacks. 'Thanks.'

'And here's a little something to say thank you for all your help.'

A rolled-up note was pushed into my hand by the dad.

'You don't need to do that,' I said, trying to hand it back. 'It's my job.'

'Yeah well, seems you're the one doing all the work and that stuck-up French girl who works with you can't even manage to be civil. I bet she gets paid more than you just because she's French. Please, we'd like you to have it.'

I smiled. 'Well if you're sure.'

'We're positive,' the mum grinned at me. 'You know, I wish I'd done something like this when I was still young enough, had an adventure before this lot came round.' She swatted gently at the heads of her three boys. 'Good on you, Anna!'

If I could have found a way to sell back to M. Perez's supermarket all the washing-up liquid and washing powder we were given, the salt and the oil, we would have made even more money. As it was we took what we needed and placed the other stuff strategically next to the bin, hoping someone else who could make use of it would pick it up.

My brazen begging for books meant that what I read that summer was much like the people who came on holiday to our little corner of Languedoc-Roussillon. A curious mix. Here is where I read Margaret Atwood for the first time, finishing the *Handmaid's Tale* in gulps over three afternoons at the beach. I read Rosie Thomas' *The White Dove* even more quickly, enjoying learning about the Spanish Civil War but enjoying more the love story involving a Welsh miner. I struggled with Simone de Beauvoir's *Second Sex*, wondering why she stuck it out with Sartre when he didn't treat her at all well, giving up halfway through, much like the woman who had left it behind for me had done. I liked that what I read was entirely random, dictated by the tastes of the people who came on holiday and whether they were the type who would give a book away once they had read it.

Our days and our nights fell into an easy pattern. We awoke early and boiled water on our tiny stove for tea and ate stale baguette and jam for breakfast that we dunked into our tea to soften it up. We went to work. We went to the beach and read and swam. We showered and went back to work for a few hours. We had a cold beer in the bar and then went to the restaurant for our dinner. Madame Perez would clap her hands every night when she saw us.

'What treats I have for you tonight, *mes petits.*'

Mack and I ate things that we would never have eaten at home. Rabbit stew and *boudin blanc* and *cassoulet*. We ate green salad after our main course to refresh our palate – lettuce fresh from Madame Perez's own garden, dressed with a light vinegary dressing. Pudding was crème caramel or a fresh pear or my favourite, strawberry sorbet.

'I poach the strawberries ever so gently with a little sugar, then I freeze it, then I break it up a little bit and serve it to you *immediatement.*'

This was not the food Madame Perez was supposed to give us. We were meant to have whatever was left over, bulked out with baguette, but Madame Perez enjoyed cooking for us, ignoring her husband and going off menu to feed us like we were guests in her own home. Each night at the restaurant she expanded our knowledge of food which didn't take much given that Mack and I had been brought up on Smash and Findus Crispy Pancakes. What Mack had said about her moustache wasn't strictly true – she did have a fine down on her top lip but nothing more – she was still slim and her hair was dark which meant Danielle's blonde locks were probably not natural. Perhaps she did fancy Mack but she was nice to me too, explaining in her rapid staccato French what she had cooked for us and why she had chosen this particular wine to go with it.

After our meal, we wandered back to our tent, arm in arm. Most nights we made love. Our bed mats were thin but our tent was pitched on sand. If it was uncomfortable I didn't notice. It was pitch black outside and we never used a torch inside the tent, knowing that it would silhouette our every move to anyone passing by. For the same reason we did not speak much. Tired from our work and the sun and our bellies full we fell asleep, curled up into each other, the moment we were done. It was the happiest I'd ever been.

I saved all our five-franc pieces for our phone calls home. We called once a week every week, as late as we could because French phone boxes are made entirely of glass and before 8pm at night are way too hot inside. We went separately to the phone box, not wanting to listen to the other's difficult conversations with home. Each time my parents shrieked with joy that I had survived another week in that god-awful place you call France but neither of them was very good at chatting on the phone and once we'd established that I was well and they were well my mother would start saying that this must be very expensive and I'd better get off the phone. I had to phone Glynis to find out what was really going on at home; that my parents really missed me – God, even her parents really missed me – and that she hoped I'd finally had enough of all the French bread and frogs legs and round-the-clock sex and would come to my senses soon and get my fat arse back home.

It was Glynis who told me my A level results. She actually phoned reception the day they came in.

'Is that you Anna?' she marvelled, after I'd answered

the phone in French. 'You sounded really good. Really French.'

'I have been here more than two months by now you know. I should hope my French is getting better.'

'Too bad you didn't go there before you sat your French A level exam then. You only got a C in that.'

I was wounded. A C in French. I had been banking on a B, had dared to hope I might even get an A.

'But you got your B in English and you got an A in history so that's the same overall points and school says Birmingham University will take you anyway.'

It seemed surreal, sitting in reception in a French campsite, being told my A level results by Glynis over the phone, her talking to me about going to university when all I was thinking is that Mack would be calling to fetch me in half an hour and we would walk together to the beach and, hot and sticky from our day's work, would dive straight into the clear, cool, sea.

'What did you get, Glyn?' I knew she would want me to ask.

'Three As!' she trilled. 'And a distinction in my special paper. I'm on my way to Jesus College, Anna. I made it to Oxford.'

'That's great, Glynis. I'm really pleased for you. Really really pleased. You deserve it. Well done. Now I've really got to go. I'm getting the evil eye from my boss. Bye for now.'

In fact, Danielle was filing her nails and paying absolutely no attention to me. There was only a month to go till the end of the season and bookings were tailing off. In reality there was not enough work in reception for one of us let alone two. Mack was already talking about the ski resort in Andorra where we would go to work next, how since I spoke fluent French I would pick up Spanish in no time.

Now that Mack had fixed up his ageing fleet of caravans, M. Perez reluctantly gave him Sundays off and I agreed with Danielle that I would do reception on my own on Saturdays if she would do Sundays for me. This was a great outcome for her since Saturdays were still our busiest day and we closed reception on Sundays at 1pm anyway but I didn't mind. This gave Mack and me a whole day together to go off on the motorbike and explore the area, see all the places I'd heard about all summer from the British holidaymakers and never been able to go to because Mack had to work. We went to Toulouse where being in a city again made me feel scared and vulnerable and under dressed in my shorts and flip-flops after so long living in what was basically a field next to a beach. It was noisy and smelly and frantic and we didn't stay long. We drove down to the pretty little town of Collioure and wandered round its cobbled streets before making our way to one of the restaurants on the harbour where we ate langoustine and fresh anchovies looking out across the water. On another Sunday we visited the fortified town of Carcassone with its huge medieval castle and learned how, hundreds of years ago when under siege by the Franks and starving, Lady Carcas had fed all their remaining grain to one pig and then flung the fattened pig over the City walls, causing the Franks to conclude they must have plenty of food in there if they were in a position to throw out a big fat pig, and they gave up

169

on their siege. During these trips I felt I was starting to understand this country in which Mack and I had been living for the past few months – speaking French had become almost second nature, to the point where I had even begun to dream in French and thanks to Madame Perez I could try anything on any menu and enjoy it. Mack and I were starting to belong.

One Saturday, on my own in reception, a phone call came in for Danielle. The man on the other end of the line said he needed to speak to Danielle urgently.

'I'll get her to call you back just as soon as I can,' I said politely.

'I can't wait around,' he said angrily. 'She told me she would be down at the beach. Go and get her for me.'

I quickly locked up reception, got on my bike and pedalled furiously down to the beach to find Danielle. It wasn't difficult. There were very few other people on the beach and it was easy to spot her because she was standing by the edge of the water, slim and brown in a brilliant white bikini which showcased her wonderful big boobs, her long blonde hair held back with a white scarf. She was waving at someone way out in the sea and as I got closer I could hear that she was shouting directions at them about the best way to stand up on a surfboard. The other person followed her instructions and clumsily managed to get up on their feet and stay upright for a few seconds before crashing with the wave on to the beach. Which is when I saw that the person with the surfboard was Mack.

I stumbled over the last few feet of sand towards them. Danielle looked a little startled when she saw me but

Mack just smiled at me, his hair full of sand and sea water dripping from him.

'Hey, babe, coming to join us?'

I frowned at them both. 'There's an urgent phone call for Danielle. It's a man. Said it couldn't wait.'

'That'll be Georges,' she said and she jogged off lightly over the sand towards reception. I noticed how she crossed one arm over her magnificent chest to try to stop it from bouncing and knew without having to look that Mack would be noticing it too. I watched her until she was out of sight, waiting for Mack to say something but he didn't.

'What's going on?' I asked finally.

'Georges is her fancy man,' he said. 'He's married and whenever he gets the chance to phone her she goes running.'

'That's not what I meant.'

'Oh.'

'I meant, how come you're here surfing with Danielle while I'm on reception? I thought you were meant to be working?'

'I'd done everything on old man Perez's list today. Bumped into Danielle and she said she was going surfing and would I like to come too.'

'Really? You just bumped into her?'

'Yes really, I just bumped into her. You're not jealous are you Anna?' He chuckled. He obviously thought that the dread grinding inside me like a cement mixer was funny.

'Is that the first time you've done that?'

'Did I look like I'd been surfing before? I was hopeless.

171

But I loved it, Anna. You've got to try it. It's the best feeling ever.'

'Why didn't you come tell me you were going surfing with her?'

'What and risk being seen by M. Perez? If he knew I'd finished my work, he'd have given me another list. Would have had me down on my hands and knees cleaning those bloody toilets with a toothbrush or something.'

Despite the cold feeling in my stomach, the thought of Mack down on his hands and knees scrubbing at a shitty toilet with a toothbrush made me smile.

He came and pulled me towards him to kiss me. I could taste the salt on his lips. Reaching up beneath my T-shirt, his arm cool and firm against the heat of my skin, he undid my bra with one hand. It never mattered what bra I was wearing. Mack always got them undone with one hand and on the first go.

'You'd best stop there, Mack. You know I'm on reception and if I don't get back soon we'll get no dinner tonight.'

'OK,' he grinned at me cheekily. 'But when you've finished work, why don't we try surfing together eh? I think you'll enjoy it.'

I trudged back across the beach to my bike, doing up my bra as I walked, the sand hot beneath my feet.

Chapter 18

James

Glynis sent me the keys to her flat on Wednesday. They didn't come by post. Some bloke on a motorbike turned up at the front door with a big cardboard envelope and I had to sign for them. My mother was horrified.

'Haven't they got post offices in London?' she said. 'How much must that have cost?'

I asked the bloke on the motorbike how much.

'A courier from London to South Wales for a packet that size? About 50 quid,' he said.

My mother tutted. 'You could have gone up and down to London on the Megabus for a lot less than that and fetched them yourself, James.'

I could have too.

The envelope was packed tight in plastic. I had to cut it open with a pair of scissors. Inside was a note from Glynis, on a thick card with her address printed on the bottom.

Tell your mother I'll be arriving at your house by 5pm on Friday and I'll bring the wine. Flat is yours any time from this Friday till the following Sunday. Also tell your mother that couriers aren't as expensive as she thinks.

'Is it OK if I mitch school and go to London that whole time, Mum? I'll work hard in the day while Amy's at lectures, probably get more done there than I can here.'

There was a funny look on Mum's face and I didn't know if she was going to laugh or cry.

'I don't know James. Your exams are less than two months away.'

I put on my special pleading look, the one that always makes her smile and usually gets me what I want.

'Do you promise you'll do some work as well as…as well as other things?'

'I promise.'

'OK then, write yourself a note for school.'

I've been able to forge my mother's signature perfectly since I was 13 and she knows it too.

And so now it's Friday and here we are, Amy and me, having come up fourteen floors in the lift and I'm fiddling with Glynis' front door key trying to open the door and not having much luck.

'Let me have a go,' Amy says and she takes the key off me and spits on it and then wiggles it gently and the door finally opens.

Glynis' living room is amazing. The walls are bare brick – no wallpaper or paint or anything – and the windows are huge, taller than me even. I go over and look outside and there is the river and lots of sky and bridges and big buildings. I can see boats on the water and tiny people in them like Lego figures.

I turn round and smile at Amy but she does not look as impressed as me. She dumps her bag on the floor and walks off. I follow her.

'What are you doing?' I ask as she goes into Glynis' bedroom.

'I thought she said we were to make ourselves comfortable.'

'She did, but I don't think she meant we should go snooping round in here.'

'She'll never know. Anyway I need a wee.'

Amy pushes open the door of Glynis' en suite, pushes down her knickers and sits on the toilet. Still sitting there, she reaches over and opens the cabinet doors and checks out the rows of pots and bottles.

'It's like Howells' beauty department in here,' she says sniffily.

When she has finished, she flings open the doors of Glynis' wardrobes which are full of clothes, neatly arranged in order of colour, whites through to beige and brown and on to black.

'Just look at all these clothes,' she says. 'All this for just one woman! And look at the makes – Max Mara, Prada, Joseph. The stuff in here cost more than your mother will earn in a lifetime. When there's people in this world starving to death. This is outrageous.'

I don't know why Amy has to bring my mother into it. It feels like she is having a go at Glynis for having too much money and my mother for having too little, all at the same time. I want to tell her to stop but I don't. I don't want to start a row, not before we've got used to each other again. Not before we've even had sex.

'Maybe she bought it all at T K Maxx,' I joke, hoping to make Amy smile, but she just snorts and bangs the wardrobe doors shut as if they have personally offended her.

175

'I'll make us a cup of tea, shall I?' I say.

But Glynis's kitchen just gets Amy going even more.

'She's got Wedgwood mugs! White fucking Wedgwood bone china mugs. What a pretentious cow! And her tea is Lapsang fucking Souchong.'

I think the mugs are nice. All matching and none of them chipped or stained. I think of Glynis, at home with my mother right at that moment, probably drinking tea out of the Barbie mug that Lois got with an Easter egg or the faded commemorative one I got given in scouts when I was ten.

'She's got Glengettie as well as posh tea. Go sit down and I'll bring it over.'

Amy plops herself down on the long, low, cream sofa with silver legs and hugs her knees tight to her chest. I can feel the resentment rising off her like steam and she has a look on her face like she can smell something bad. I hand her a mug and I wonder why it is she's got her knickers in such a twist over Glynis' stuff but I know if I ask her that those twisted knickers will stay firmly on. This is how Amy is when we see each other again after being apart for a while – all prickly and separate from me, like she doesn't know me very well – and then as soon as we've had sex the real Amy comes back to me and everything is OK again. And all I want now is for us to be together like that. It's not the sex I want. Even if I did spend most of my time on the Megabus feeling uncomfortable because I kept getting a hard on at the thought of seeing Amy again. I just want us to be connected again.

I get up and go over to the fridge. A big silver fridge with double doors like you see on American television programmes with a pushy thing for cold water. When I was getting the milk for the tea I had found another note in there from Glynis.

Don't expect to find any food in here but I did buy you some cans of cider.

I crack open a couple of the cans, walk over to Amy, take the mug of tea out of her hand and give her a can of cider instead without saying anything. I don't bother with glasses. They'll probably be crystal or something and just piss Amy off again. I sit down close to her and I say nothing, just drink from my can and watch her drinking from hers. Eventually I put my arm around her and put my can down on the floor and kiss her. She's still holding her can but she opens her mouth to me straight away and we kiss for a long time, slow and wet and cidery, and eventually she puts her can down too. I feel her shoulders relax and her body lean into mine and when we finally stop kissing for a second, I look at her and she doesn't look cross any more. She looks like my Amy. She lets me lead her into Glynis' spare bedroom and to the big bed with white sheets that look really expensive. I push her down gently onto the bed and then straddle her narrow little hips, feeling her tilt them towards me. I kiss her some more and then reach up and pull off my T-shirt before she can say anything about fucking damask or whatever it is these sheets are made of.

Anna

Glynis arrived at my house at 5pm on the dot, bearing two bottles of Sancerre and a bag of kettle chips.

I pointed at her stomach. 'Well?'

'Where are the kids?'

'Frozen in test tubes somewhere overseas apparently.'

'Your kids not mine.'

'One is in London as well you know, probably having rampant teenage sex with Amy right this very second, Niall is at Bartley's house and Lois is in cubs and will get dropped off by one of the other mums at about 8.30pm.'

'A couple of hours' peace and wine for us then. You will be pleased to hear my dear friend that I have the fertility level of a 32-year-old. Still a couple of test results to come back but the Doc said it was all looking good. In fact, he said it was all looking very good indeed.'

'Don't tell me you flirted with your gynaecologist!'

'Just a bit. He was Australian and wearing cowboy boots which, rather surprisingly, looked pretty sexy with a white coat.'

'Possible real life sperm donor?'

'Nah, no chance. He had a wedding ring on. And I went off him anyway when he told me to 'make like a frog' for him to do some of the tests. You have to wonder how those blokes get it up for their wives when they spend so long every day looking where the sun don't shine for their work.'

'Doesn't seem to bother Cassie and Graham any.'

'So you may think. No one knows what goes on behind closed doors.'

'Leave it out Glynis. It just bugs you that Cassie and Graham are so happily married.'

'Bugs you too.'

'A lot less than it bugs you. Anyway, you're going to have to be polite to Cassie and Graham. Jane and Bob have invited everyone round to a family barbecue at theirs next Saturday night, give you a bit of a send off before you have to go back to London.'

Glynis grimaced. 'Great! A whole evening in the company of Little Miss Perfect and the Fanny Doctor. I can't wait.'

'Don't be like that, Glynis. They're looking forward to seeing you.'

'Well I'll just have to take plenty of fizz round and get everyone drunk. I take it since we're having a big family barbecue that you managed to keep your trap shut then?'

'Of course I did. Anyway, I've been back to that house since and seen the guy across the road a few times now. I reckon he's gay because I saw him greeting the milkman in pretty much the same way he greeted Jane. I feel a bit foolish actually for thinking that something was going on.'

'You'd feel a lot more foolish if you hadn't taken my advice and had said something to Jane!'

'Yes well, advising is what you do for a living isn't it Glynis? Right, what's the next step sperm wise?'

'Choosing a donor! I've brought my laptop with me so you open one of those bottles of wine and I'll set it up so we can start cruising the net for daddy.'

I watched, wine glass in hand, while Glynis fiddled with various wires and something called a dongle.

'OK!' she finally announced. 'We're all set up. Let's check out the merchandise.'

We spent the next couple of hours learning about the efficacy of Danish sperm and checking out a long list of donors with code names like Kirk and Lars.

'Look at all this!' I marvelled. 'It's not just their academics these guys have got to list. Poor buggers have got to say what colour eyes and hair they've got, how tall they are and even what they weigh. It's like ordering a Filipina bride out of a mail-order catalogue!'

'No it's not!' Glynis retorted. 'If I choose a donor with the same colour hair and eyes as me then the baby will look more like me.'

'I take it you'll be going for a white man then?'

'Well the baby's not going to look much like me if I don't is it?' she looked at me witheringly.

'I guess not. Pity you can't make sure your baby will turn out good looking while you're at it!'

'But you can. Some of them have got their baby photos on there.'

'You're joking right?'

'Not at all. Take a look'

Sure enough, one in every four or so of the donors listed had been brave enough to attach a baby photograph to his sperm's CV.

'This one, code name Thor, he's got a massive Mexican hat on, you can't see his face at all,' Glynis said, pointing at the screen. 'That's cheating!'

I looked at the photo. Thor was older in his photo than some of the others we'd looked at, maybe five or six. He had skinny little legs and was wearing a hand-knitted red jumper and sturdy sandals with buckles, like the ones from Clarks my boys used to wear when they were that age. The photo looked like it had been taken on holiday somewhere and Thor peeped out from beneath the enormous colourful hat, a big grin on his face. In the picture were two sets of adult feet, a woman's feet in flip flops and a man in sensible sandals, much like his son's. I wondered which of them had taken the photo and whether, later, their son had fallen asleep on a couple of chairs pushed together and they had sat holding hands, watching over him as they finished their drinks.

'How many times can they donate?' I asked

'I'm not certain. I think there's a maximum number of times they can do it. Ten or something.'

'You do realise that your baby will have grandparents out there somewhere. Grandparents who love his father? And half brothers and sisters running around all over the place? Might even fall in love with one of them and get married. How awful would that be?'

'Anna, do I look like the kind of person who does things without researching them properly? Of course I realise that there could be half brothers and sisters. There's a registry for people who want to find their donor siblings or even their sperm donor himself. That's why I'm going to go abroad to have the treatment – so that I can have anonymous sperm and not have to worry about having to tell my kid the truth about where it came from. And if we're in London and the sperm is from Denmark the chances of my kid meeting someone with the same sperm donor father are pretty limited aren't they? I really can't be doing with these women spending hours on the internet trying to find kids with the same sperm donor dad, just so they can work out whether the kids look like each other. It's weird. And don't start on the spiel you gave me last time about people needing to know where they come from. My kid will know exactly where it came from. It will know that it came from me.'

I was glad that Lois arrived home at this point and Glynis closed her computer down. I made a big fuss of Lois, pulling her down onto my lap when she came into the kitchen, squeezing her tight until she wriggled to get away from me.

'How did it go at cubs?' I asked. 'Do you fancy some hot chocolate?'

Lois eyed me suspiciously.

'You feeling OK, Mum? Is anything wrong?'

I wasn't feeling OK at all but I could hardly tell my nine year old that what was wrong was that two of my best friends were embarking on journeys that, try as I might, I just didn't understand and didn't approve of either, and that I was very worried about how it was all going to turn out.

Chapter 19

It had been years since Glynis had spent anything more than a weekend at home in Stonebridge and she was proving high maintenance. She had dinner with her parents twice and spent a day in Yeovil with her brother and his family. She had intended to stay over night down there but by Monday afternoon she was in the office annoying me.

'I couldn't stick it, Annie! You should see it down there. Four kids all wailing and shouting in one tiny little house.'

'Tinier than my house?'

My irony was lost on Glynis. 'Yes, even tinier than yours. And lunch was like feeding time at the zoo! Yoghurt and banana all over the place and I'll tell you something for nothing. There's no such thing as a non-spill cup. I saw plenty of spills.'

'What did you expect? Your brother has four kids under five including a set of twins and they live in army accommodation. Has it put you off babies?'

'I only want one baby, not a braying brood like Ian's got. One will be a lot quieter.'

'Well, it'll be 75 per cent quieter but even one baby makes a lot of noise and a lot of mess.'

'My baby will be different.'

'Don't bank on it.'

'Anyway, I don't have a baby yet so let's go get a drink somewhere.'

'No way, Glynis. I've drunk a month's worth of units since you got home. I'm picking up Lois tonight, on time, or else she says she's phoning Childline, and standing over Niall till he does some work for his GCSEs. You'll have to drink by yourself. Why don't you pop into the pub and see Steve? He'll have a drink with you. It'll make his day.'

'I've already agreed to have a drink with him on Wednesday night.'

'You've agreed to go on a date with Steve? You do know he hasn't even got any O levels let alone an MBA?'

'Hah hah! Very funny! Anyway, it's not a date. He says you go in there every Wednesday with the girls after you've been to the gym. All I said was I'd have a drink with him before you get there.'

'I'd hardly describe the exercise class in the village hall as going to the gym, Glynis.'

'Whatever, he says you all turn up at the pub every Wednesday looking sweaty and laugh your heads off so I thought I'd tag along.'

'They're a nice crowd and they'll be delighted to meet you. Right, I'm going to lock up now. You're welcome to come home and have fish fingers and beans with me and the kids in my tiny house but there's no drinking, OK?'

At this point Frank barged through the office door.

'What's this?' he said gruffly. 'This is an office not a mothers' meeting. Have you got any messages for me?'

I handed him his message list. 'You know Glynis don't you Frank? She's my lawyer friend who lives in London.'

Glynis gave Frank the once over.

'Pleased to meet you Frank.' Glynis smiled at him. 'I've been trying to get Anna here to come for a quick drink with me but she turned me down. Do you want to come for a drink with me?'

Frank looked at me, then quickly back at Glynis.

'Go on! You know you want too,' Glynis teased.

'Um, well OK, sure.'

'Great! Is there anywhere particular you'd recommend we go?'

'There's a good pub down on the coast, around 10 minutes drive away. They do nice food too.'

I knew exactly which pub Frank meant. It was the one he took all his first dates to. A real ale pub tucked away down a country lane from which you could take a romantic stroll down to the beach at Monk Nash and watch the sun set over the sea. Never failed to get him laid, according to Frank.

'That sounds splendid. Shall we be on our way then? Anna's just about to lock up.'

'I'll be with you in three minutes. I've just got to make a quick phone call.' Frank loped off to the back office with a spring in his step, no doubt to hunt down the mouth wash in his desk drawer.

'I warn you, Glynis,' I hissed at her. 'If you say or do anything that means I end up losing this job, me and the kids are coming to live with you.'

'Don't worry,' she grinned mischievously. 'It's just a drink.'

Frank emerged from his office smelling minty fresh. He opened the office door wide and then beckoned Glynis

185

through, doing a little mock bow.

'Ladies first,' he smiled at her.

I made sick faces behind their departing backs but neither of them turned round so didn't see me.

Almost every Wednesday for the past eight years or so my mother and father babysit for me. It started when Lois was about one and my mother announced that I needed to get out once in a while and meet people.

'It'll do you good, Anna, to get out of the house, and anyway your father and I enjoy having the kids all to ourselves for a bit,' she said. 'You could do an evening class. Lots of nice single men go to evening classes.'

Wednesday is Lois' favourite day because it is a day without after-school club. On Wednesdays my dad picks her up from school, arriving at least twenty minutes before school ends 'just in case of traffic' and then waits right by the door so that when the teacher releases the children to a familiar face Lois is the first one out. My dad always has a treat ready for her in the car, a carton of juice or a chocolate biscuit, and she gets to watch whatever telly she wants until James and Niall arrive and it's time for tea. My mother makes a roast dinner on Wednesdays, with roast potatoes and carrots and peas and gravy and for pudding there's always something involving custard, even in the summer.

Wednesday is also a good day for me since it's the one day of the week I don't have to worry about what's for dinner and there are no dishes to do because I just have a bowl of cereal or some toast. It is not however the day I go to evening class because despite my mother's insistence

I had no desire to do more exams, so I ended up going to the exercise class in our village hall instead.

'You're not going to find a man there now are you?' my mother sniffed.

She was right there of course but the classes suit me. They are cheap and there is no membership fee so if I can't go for whatever reason or want to flop in front of the telly instead I don't feel guilty about wasting money. In the village hall there are no wall-length mirrors to highlight lumps and bumps, no mats or weights or bouncy balls. There's just the instructor Andrea, who despite also teaching jazz and tap on a Tuesday and ballet on a Saturday morning to a flock of little girls in pink tutus, remains nicely rounded and non-threatening. Every week she turns up with her battered CD player and strides purposefully to the front of the hall where she leads me and a bunch of other overweight mums wearing leggings and baggy T-shirts through a simple little aerobics routine that hasn't altered much in all the time I've been going. None of us ever seems to lose any weight, probably because, as Steve had pointed out to Glynis, we pile into the pub afterwards and down two halves of lager and a packet of crisps each.

Only this Wednesday it wasn't a bag of cheese and onion that was foremost in my mind as Andrea took us through the cool down routine. What I really wanted was to find out what had gone on between Glynis and Frank in Monk Nash. I hadn't heard from Glynis since she and Frank had sauntered off together on Monday evening, despite having left her a message to call me and texted her three times and although Frank had called into the office a few times to pick up his messages he'd just dashed in and out, barely saying two words to me. There weren't enough appointments in Frank's diary to keep him out of the office for two whole days and I knew from experience that if Glynis wasn't returning calls it was because she was busy. I had a horrible feeling that what she was busy with was Frank and that one way or the other I was going to end up with a pissed-off best friend or a pissed-off boss and I didn't know which was worse.

When I walked through the door of the pub and saw Glynis and Steve tucked away together in a corner, so deep in conversation their heads were almost touching, the odds on a pissed-off boss shortened. They sprang apart as I walked over to their table, looking as guilty as Niall when I catch him going through my handbag looking for loose change.

'Here she is!' Glynis said breezily. 'Come and join us. Do you want a glass of wine?'

'Nah, you're all right. Me and the girls got a kitty going. It's Sian's turn to get them in tonight. Are you coming over to join us?'

'Be there in a sec. I'm just finishing something off with Steve.'

Steve grinned at me. He looked different somehow but I couldn't work out what it was until I went over to join Sian and the other girls at the bar.

'That's the first time I've seen Steve in anything else but a black shirt the whole time I've been coming in here,' Sian said as she handed me my lager.

I looked over again at Steve. That's what it was. He was wearing a long sleeved white shirt with what looked to be a small pattern of flowers in it.

'Suits him actually,' Sian said as she took a big gulp of her lager.

It did suit him. And he looked a bit thinner too. Probably not eaten a single chip since Glynis said she'd have a drink with him. The first time in 20 years that the bloody woman had been in Stonebridge longer than 48 hours and she was on course to break the hearts of the only two single blokes I knew.

I was on my second half of lager by the time Glynis came over to join us. She smiled and nodded at my exercise class buddies.

'This is Glynis, everyone,' I introduced her. 'And this is Sian, Andrea, Karen, Fiona and Jacquie.'

My friends eyed Glynis over the top of their lager glasses, taking in her size eight waist, her 7 For All Mankind jeans and her teeny-weeny, almost transparent cheesecloth shirt which looked like fairtrade organic cotton and could well have been but still probably cost a fortune. In turn, Glynis clocked the Marks and Spencer stretchy leggings and the faded Fat Face sweatshirts, the generous bottoms and the still sweaty faces. If they had been cats they would have hissed at each other.

'Good work out, girls?' Glynis asked politely.

'Great thanks,' Sian replied on behalf of the group. 'Andrea always works us hard.'

Glynis flicked her eyes up and down Sian's curves, just the once. I could tell that in her head she was saying, *'Not hard enough if you ask me.'*

'A good work out is the best thing for busting stress,' Glynis said. 'That's what Anton always says.'

'Who's Anton?' I asked, immediately wishing I hadn't.

'My personal trainer,' Glynis said. 'I see him twice a week. He trains Gwyneth Paltrow when she's in London.'

Sian turned away, towards the bar. 'Anyone for another drink ladies?'

My exercise class huddled together at the bar in big-bummed solidarity, like mountain sheep sticking their rumps out to protect each other against bad weather.

'Let's go sit down shall we?' I said, steering Glynis towards a table in the window before she could piss off my plump friends anymore.

'What's up with that lot?' Glynis asked.

'Nothing that more lager won't cure. Right then girl, what's going on?'

'What do you mean what's going on?'

'You know exactly what I mean. What's going on with Frank?'

'Nothing's going on with Frank! We went for a lovely walk – it's gorgeous down there on the beach at Monk Nash, I can't believe I'd never been before – and then we had a fabulous bottle of Sauvignon, most of which I drank because he was driving, and then he dropped me off at Mum and Dad's.'

'That's it?'

'That's it.'

'You haven't seen him since?'

'Nope. He didn't ask and if he had I would have said no. There was no chemistry there, none at all. I mean he's actually pretty fit...'

'You what?'

'He's pretty fit. He works out doesn't he? And he's got

190

plenty of hair and great suits and he smells really good. But we just weren't interested in each other in that way.'

'What did you talk about?'

'Oh all sorts of things, price of houses down here, price of houses in London, price of houses in other parts of the country. That sort of thing. And you. We talked about you a fair bit.'

I winced, my shoulders crunching up under my ears with tension.

'What did you tell him?' I groaned.

'Just that you were brilliant at your job and that all the clients love you and that you deserve more.'

'What did he say to that?'

'Not much. Just nodded like he agreed with me. Which is when I asked him would he give you the day off on Friday, so that you and I could go into Cardiff for the day and I could spoil you.'

I was horrified.

'Are you telling me that over a drink with my boss you asked him if I could have a day off?'

Glynis nodded proudly.

'What if I don't want Friday off? What if I've got something really important I need to do on Friday?'

'But you don't do you?'

'That's not the point.'

'Stop being such a spoilsport Anna Banana. You and I are going into Cardiff on Friday and we're going to go to a spa and have treatments and massages and then we're going out on the town. My treat, all of it.'

'And what about my children? The ones you haven't dispatched to London for an entire week to play house in your luxury flat?'

'All sorted. My mother is going to baby sit. She's taking Lois to the pictures to some girly film my Dad refuses to see and then she'll take her back to your place and switch off the PlayStation so that Bartley goes home and Niall goes to bed.'

'Oh.'

'Oh come on, Anna. It'll be a great day and you'll love it, you know you will.'

'I suppose so.' Even though I was bristling at the way in which Glynis had infiltrated all aspects of my life behind my back I was already looking forward to Friday immensely.

'So if it wasn't Frank who's been keeping you busy the past few days was it Steve?' I looked over at the bar where the slightly more slimline and considerably more flowery-shirted Steve was making doe eyes at Glynis.

'Don't be daft. Steve's sweet but he's not my type. I've been busy getting our day out organised. Spa days and childcare don't arrange themselves you know.'

Chapter 20

I'd never been to a spa, never even had an official massage. When I told Glynis this in the taxi on the way to Cardiff (when I'd suggested we go by bus she flatly refused, looking at me as if I'd just suggested we jog there naked) it made her hoot with laughter.

'You mean you've never had a massage?'

'Well not one I've paid for. The odd bloke has rubbed my back from time to time.'

'That doesn't count. That kind of rubbing only lasts a few minutes and leads straight on to sex. This kind of rubbing goes on for ages and you don't have to put out at the end of it.'

We pulled up outside the five star hotel overlooking Cardiff Bay where Glynis had booked our spa and she marched in like she went to five star hotels all the time. Because she does. I followed behind her, feeling very uncomfortable, as if one of the smiling, perfectly made-up ladies wearing navy-blue tunics on reception might take one look at me and yank a thumb in the direction of the door. 'Hey you, the one with the fluorescent pink Reebok gym bag from circa 1992. Yes you! Out!'

For Glynis, the fluffy white robes and the towelling slippers, the loungers by the side of the pool and the chilled glasses of water with ice and lemon, were all second nature. She plopped herself down on a lounger with a little sigh and picked up the first of a huge pile of fashion magazines she'd brought with her.

I lay down gingerly on the lounger next to her, carefully tucking my bathrobe between my legs.

'Why have you turned your bathrobe into a nappy?' Glynis asked frostily.

'I don't want that bloke in the pool thinking I'm giving him a Sharon Stone.'

'I told you to wear knickers didn't I?'

'And I am wearing knickers – big ones – which I really don't need to be flashing at anyone from this angle. Trust me it's not a pretty sight. Right, what do we do now?'

'What do you mean, what do we do now? We do nothing until it's time for our treatments. Just lie there, read a magazine and relax for a while.'

Glynis may work really long hours but she is really good at lounging around doing nothing. Spectacularly good at it. Within half an hour of flipping through pages of clothes I would never be able to afford even if by some miracle I lost two stone and could fit into them I found my mind wandering into the terrible mess that is Niall's bedroom. Maybe next weekend I could persuade him to blitz it with me, chuck out all the old toys he never looks at any more – the long-since discarded Top Trump cards and Lego – and borrow my neighbour's VAX machine and give the carpets a clean. If I had any money left at the end of the month I could maybe even give the walls a lick of paint. Then I remembered that right then the only colour paint Niall would even contemplate was black. Just wash the walls down with a bit of Cif then.

'Stop thinking,' Glynis chided from the depths of her *Vogue*.

'I'm not thinking.'

'Yes you are, your foot is tapping. That means you're thinking.'

I immediately stopped tapping my foot. 'No it doesn't. I'm lying here relaxing, just like you. It just doesn't come very naturally to me.'

'Wait until you've had your massage. You'll have no trouble relaxing after that.'

She was right. Glynis had booked us massage treatments that lasted two hours, including a full body massage, head massage and facial. To begin with I felt stiff and awkward and painfully aware that under all those towels I was wearing only my knickers and that a stranger I'd never met before was rubbing oil all over me but, ten minutes in, my body suddenly relaxed and I felt myself float away, rubbed and pressed and kneaded into dreamy oblivion. When I finally emerged, my hair sticking up in greasy spikes I felt as light headed and spacy as if I'd been on the gas and air (which is about the only good thing, other than the baby at the end of it, that there is to say about the process of giving birth). I somehow made it back to my lounger and immediately fell asleep until I was woken by Glynis tapping me smartly on the thigh.

'You're snoring Anna. Anyway, you'd better wake up if you want to have a quick swim before we go have our hair done.'

'Eh? You what?' I said sleepily, checking my cheeks for dribble.

'We've got an appointment at the hotel hairdressers at

6pm. You don't expect me to blow dry my hair myself do you before we go out? You know I'm a hostage to my hair.'

It must have been the drugged-up, loved-up way I felt after the massage but somehow between them Glynis and the hairdresser persuaded me to have my hair cut.

'I don't know,' I said, looking at my shoulder-length shaggy mop in the mirror. 'I've had it like this forever.'

'Precisely,' said Glynis. 'It's time for a change.'

Which is how, an hour later, I found myself sporting a sleek, shiny bob.

'It won't look like that when I do it myself at home,' I said, turning my head and checking my reflection in the mirror from different angles.

'It looks like that tonight and that's all that matters,' Glynis said.

Back in the changing room, Glynis wriggled into a knee-length black shift dress with a pair of high-heeled strappy black sandals. She looked incredible. From my own fluorescent pink bag I fished out a pair of very long suffering black trousers and a sleeveless red top I'd bought in Debenhams a few years ago in which I looked pretty good I thought.

'Hang on a sec,' Glynis said, thrusting a black carrier bag towards me. 'I bought you a present. Why don't you try it on?'

I looked at her in surprise. From the depths of the bag I fished out a bright-red wrap dress.

'It's beautiful Glynis but it'll make me look like a heffalump.'

'No, you won't. Believe me. Wrap dresses look great on

196

everyone, whatever their size. Go on. Try it on.'

I loved it. It swished around my beautifully moisturised and pampered thighs and made my waist look smaller and my boobs look bigger which distracted attention from the size of my arse because there was nothing even a wrap dress could do about that.

'Wow Glynis. Thank you so much. I love it,'

'And it loves you, Anna, it really loves you girl. You look amazing. I bet Mack wouldn't be complaining about the size of your chest nowadays if he copped a look at you in that frock.'

Oh the upside of three kids and an extra two stone, I thought to myself. A pair of tits.

'Right then Anna. Shoulders back, lippy on. We're hitting the town.'

'Where are we going?'

'Central Park Bar and Restaurant in the centre of Cardiff. The word on the street is that it's the place to go if, like us, you're as good looking as the *Sex in the City* girls. Which I think is a polite way of saying it's the place where the older crowd go but hey, who wants to flirt with teenagers anyway and apparently there's a dance floor and a bit of a disco later on. Hurry up. Our taxi will be waiting.'

It had been a long time since I'd been out in Cardiff. When we walked into the babble of noise that was the Central Park Bar I felt something I had not felt for such a long time it took me a while to recognise it. It was anticipation. Nervous, excited, anticipation. Glynis marched up to the long stainless steel bar like she owned the place and the waiter immediately pointed to the last

197

two vacant bar stools and handed us a drinks list.

'What'll it be, ladies?' he grinned at us. 'Cocktails tonight?'

'What a great idea,' Glynis grinned back. 'I'll have a mojito please. What about you, Anna?'

'Margarita,' I said airily. Apart from knowing that margaritas were what they drank on *Sex in the City* I had absolutely no idea what a margarita was.

'Wow, that's strong,' I said when our drinks arrived and I took a sip. 'Two of these and I'll be babbling.'

'I certainly hope so. Babbling is what we're here to do. Hopefully with some of the really nice-looking blokes they've got in here.'

I scanned the room. Now that Glynis had pointed it out there were rather a lot of handsome men around. Smartly dressed in trousers and open-neck shirts, the odd linen jacket here and there. There were no underage drinkers here, just a lot of men and women, aged somewhere between 30 and 50. Quite a lot of grey temples, a fair few bald heads, women showing a bit of cleavage or a bit of leg but not both.

'I don't know Glynis. I'm not very good at babbling.'

'That's because you're out of practice and you've forgotten how to flirt. There's at least four blokes looking in our direction right now and all we've got to do is decide whether we want any of them to come over to talk to us.'

'You can't just order them off the menu like Danish sperm you know.'

'Ha, bloody ha. You know you've managed to go the whole day so far and not make a single sperm joke? I thought it was too good to be true.'

'Sorry, I tried but I couldn't resist it.'

'Well try a bit harder will you. Anyway, you pretty much can order them off the menu. You just have to know how to do it.'

'Easy for you.'

'Easy for you too. Look, I'll show you how. Watch me. You see a bloke you like the look of and you look at him, just once, over your glass like this and then you look down and take a sip of your drink.' Glynis demonstrated a quick upwards flick of the eyes and then a demure look away before glugging down the rest of her mojito.

'And that brings them running?'

'Not just that. I haven't finished yet. Will you just watch and listen. Anyway, after you look away you wait a few seconds and then you look again – like this.' Glynis demonstrated a slighter longer, more soulful gaze. 'If when you look up he's looking back then you smile at him, maybe fiddle with your hair a bit. That's what brings them running.'

'Just like that?'

'Just like that.'

'Don't believe you. Two quick peeks at a fellow and swigging back your drink like a navvy is about as seductive as flannelette pyjamas.'

'Well if you don't believe me it works there's no reason not to give it a try is there? Go on, pick your man.'

'Which man?'

'A man you like the look of, you berk.'

'To be honest Glyn, my eyesight isn't what it used to be. I can't actually see that clearly.'

'Oh for heaven's sake just pick one. Any one'

I looked swiftly around the room. 'OK I found one. He's way over there by the door, tall, dark-haired, wearing a blue shirt.'

'I see him. Handsome.'

'Is he? His face is just a blur to me all the way from here. OK, here goes.'

I looked at the man just as Glynis had shown me, then dropped my gaze. I took a little sip of my drink and looked again. And sure enough the tall man was looking in my general direction.

'He's smiling Anna. Smile back now.'

'Is he? Honestly, I really must get glasses.'

'Just smile, Anna!' I smiled. I ran my hand over my new smooth hair do. I took another sip of my drink. A bigger one this time.

'He's on his way over,' Glynis exclaimed victoriously.

'Well I never!'

We watched as the tall man fought his way nonchalantly through the crowds towards the bar. About ten feet away his face suddenly swung into focus. Really rather good looking.

'Hello ladies, do you mind if I just stand here till I get the barman's attention?'

'Not at all,' Glynis said. 'Be our guest.'

'I'm Ryan, by the way,' he said, looking straight at me. He was even taller close up, probably in his early forties with a nice flat stomach and broad shoulders. I resisted the urge to clap.

'Hi, I'm Anna.'

'And I'm Glynis'

'You don't look like a Glynis,' Ryan said.

'You're not the first person to say that,' Glynis said through gritted teeth. She hates it when people suggest she has an old lady's name. I looked down at the floor to stop myself bursting out laughing. Ryan was wearing good shoes. Black and properly polished. He had enormous feet. All of a sudden an image of what he might look like naked popped into my mind. That's the trouble with getting so little sex. The erotic image is never far from the mind.

'Would you like a drink Anna? You too, of course, Glynis. Same again?'

'Oh no thanks,' I started to say, even though both our glasses were drained down to the last dregs of melting ice but Glynis was quick to cut over me. 'That would be lovely. Thank you.'

'I'll just call my friend over to join us, shall I?'

'Sure, why not,' Glynis shrugged.

Ryan gestured at someone over the door and I watched in disbelief as a man who looked ever so much like Frank pushed his way through the crowd towards us. At the same ten feet point that Ryan had come into focus I realised that this was no looky-likey Frank but the actual real life Frank coming over to join us.

'Did you arrange to meet Frank here without telling me?' I hissed at Glynis.

'I had absolutely no idea he was going to be here, Anna, you've got to believe me.' Glynis said urgently. 'Cross my heart and hope to die!'

Frank looked confused too.

'Do you guys know each other?' Ryan laughed.

'Oh yes, Anna here works for Frank.'

Ryan turned and stared at me. 'You're that Anna? Frank's Anna?'

'Yep I'm that Anna. Frank's assistant estate agent come office manager come tea lady.'

'Well, well, well, Anna.' Frank said. 'Look at you. If you're not spending all your salary on expensive wine you're blowing it on new frocks and haircuts. I must be paying you far too much.'

I smiled a big fat, false smile at him and tried to rise above his snide little comment by turning to speak to Ryan only now Ryan had lost all interest in me and was busily and very pointedly speaking to Glynis.

'Not out with one of the divorcees in hot pursuit this weekend then Frank?'

'Not this weekend, no. Boys' night tonight.'

'How do you know your boy Ryan here, then?' I asked, saying Ryan really loudly in the hope I could draw his attention away from Glynis. By now he was practically sitting on her lap.

'Um, we go to the same gym every now and then.'

Ryan suddenly announced that he and Glynis were going out on the balcony to have a cigarette. I raised an eyebrow at Glynis who had never smoked in her life but she just shrugged and followed Ryan out.

'Shall I order a bottle of wine?' Frank said, easing himself up on to Glynis' bar stool. 'Too many of those cocktails and you'll get indigestion.'

'Go on then,' I said resignedly.

I waited for him to make it clear he was expecting me to pay for my share of the wine and was surprised when he didn't. Then I waited for him to make some bitchy comment about Glynis being ugly or boring because she'd ignored him and gone off with Ryan but he didn't do that either.

Ryan and Glynis were gone for ages. *How long does it take to have a fag for heaven's sake?* I thought to myself. *The exercise class girls can smoke two in the five minutes it takes us to walk over to the pub.* Frank and I sipped our wine nervously. We weren't used to this sort of environment, to being outside the comfort zone of the office, with its sales particulars and ringing phones and demanding customers. I felt very self conscious in my new, clingy, red dress and with my shiny hair and Frank must have been feeling awkward too because all of a sudden and completely out of the blue he turned to me and asked,

'Shall we dance?'

'What do you mean dance?'

'Well there's a dance floor in the back there. I wondered if you'd care to dance with me?'

I was so taken aback I took the hand that Frank was holding out to me and let him lead me to the dance floor and just as we reached it the record suddenly changed and a slow dance came on. I wondered fleetingly if it was a sackable offence to run off and leave your boss on his own in the middle of a dance floor but before I knew it, Frank had put his hand on my waist and pulled me towards him and we were waltzing. Not a full-on head flung back sequins and American tan tights sort of waltz but a gentle, courteous, played down sort of waltz. But a waltz nevertheless.

I could not keep the grin off my face. 'I love waltzing.

My granddad always used to waltz with me.'

'I know.'

'I used to stand on the tops of his feet and he'd waltz me round the living room.'

'I know that too.'

'How do you know?'

'You talk non-stop to the punters about all sorts of rubbish Anna. I hear you rabbiting on sometimes. It's one of the reasons they all like you so much.'

'They do?'

'Yes, they do. Very much.'

'That's nice to hear. He was brilliant my granddad. My gran, too. I live in what used to be their house.'

'I know that too, Anna. Now shut up and dance.'

His hand was firm and strong in the small of my back as he led me round the dance floor and I had to give Frank his due, all those gym sessions I'd seen logged in his diary had paid off. He was strong and sure on his feet, a good dancer who made me feel like I was a good dancer too. The memory of me as a little girl dancing with my grandfather while my gran looked on had made tears prick the backs of my eyes and when a second slower song came on and Frank pulled me closer to him I let my head rest on his shoulder. That's when Glynis tapped me firmly on the shoulder and announced we were leaving.

'What do you mean we're leaving?' I felt dazed, as if I'd suddenly been rudely awakened from sleep.

'Just that we're leaving. I'm really tired and I could murder some curry and chips on the way home.'

'Are you sure?'

'Of course I'm sure. Put her down now Frank. Your

nice, married friend is waiting for you at the bar.'

Reluctantly I followed Anna out. At the door of the bar I turned round to wave goodbye to Frank but he was nowhere to be seen.

'What the hell was that all about, Glynis?' I said as soon as we were outside. 'You teach me how to bag a drop-dead gorgeous bloke and then you whip him right out from under my nose and leave me stranded with my boss. What's going on?'

'Ryan wasn't for you anyway. He swore blind he wasn't married even though there was a glaring white dent in his finger where he'd taken his wedding ring off this evening before coming out. And I came to save you in the end didn't I? Sorry! If I'd realised Frank had carted you off to the dance floor I'd have come and got you sooner.'

'Yes, well you saved me in the end, that's what counts.'

'I've always got your back, babe, you know that.' Glynis spotted a cab and whistled loudly, like they do in New York in the films. Like they don't do at 10.30pm in Cardiff.

'Stonebridge please,' Glynis commanded authoritatively as we climbed in.

'I thought you said you wanted curry and chips?' I said.

'That was just an excuse to get you out of there.'

'I feared as much,' I said disappointedly.

Chapter 21

The campsite closed at the end of September. Mack and I spent another two weeks working side by side with the Perez family putting everything to sleep for the winter. We emptied what little was left on the shelves of the supermarket into Madame Perez's car, we defrosted the freezers and scrubbed everything down. We put bowls of rat poison everywhere. Mack cleaned the stinky toilets for the last time. We wiped down the plastic tables and chairs from outside the tatty caravans and loaded them inside. Finally we took down our faded tent. Over the course of the summer I had acquired two cardboard boxes of other people's paperbacks and another box of stuff that people had given me as presents – a cafetière and four little coffee mugs, a pretty, hand-painted ceramic bowl, a small mirror – I remembered the faces of every single one of the visiting families that had given me these things and was grateful for their thoughtful gifts that had made my time living in a tent more enjoyable.

'We can't take all this stuff with us,' Mack said, as he rolled up the tent. 'There just isn't room on the motorbike sorry. You'll have to chuck it out or give it to Madame Perez.'

He was right. I knew he was right. If we were going to live this life we had to leave light footprints but it still hurt to give away all my precious things to Madame Perez.

Finally, we were packed up and ready to go. The Perez family lined up outside reception to wish us goodbye.

'See you next season maybe,' M. Perez said as he shook our hands. 'There will be a job here for you if you want. For both of you.'

Madame Perez said nothing but smiled and handed me a brown paper bag containing some apples and cheese and a small bottle of wine.

Danielle gave me a huge hug which surprised me initially until I saw the even bigger, lingering hug she gave Mack. When we drove off I watched in the wing mirror of the bike as she stood and waved at our departing backs, long after the rest of the family had gone back to work.

From the campsite we made our way to Andorra as Mack had planned. The ski season didn't begin until December but Mack figured it would be better if we made an early start, got ourselves established and found ourselves somewhere to live. We could hardly live in a tent over the winter. Danielle had given Mack the name of a friend of a friend who ran a small hotel in Andorra and who she said might be able to put us up cheaply for a couple of weeks until we got ourselves settled but when we got to the hotel it was closed down and there was no sign of the friend of the friend or of anyone else. When we asked at the bar across the road, we were told that the hotel had got into financial difficulty and had closed a few weeks previously; it was now up for sale.

I started to panic. 'What do we do now?' I asked Mack.

'What's wrong with you, you silly goose?' Mack laughed, putting his arm round me and kissing the top of my head. 'We've got some money haven't we? And the sun is still shining just about and we're together. We'll get ourselves a nice cold beer and we'll ask around and find somewhere else to stay; we'll take it from there.'

Which is exactly what we did. We checked into a little hotel that the barman recommended and got a great deal for a two-week stay on account of it being between seasons and the place being virtually empty. It was lovely to sleep in a proper bed again with real sheets and to be able to have a bath for the first time in months, even if it did have a seat in it so you couldn't lie down. We slept in and we ate a lot of breakfast so we wouldn't need any lunch and we made love even more than usual. After four months of sex in a tent it was a novelty to have a room with a door that locked and where we could put a light on without fear of an entire campsite being able to see us at it. We had got into a routine at the campsite of having quick, quiet sex, both of us knackered from working all day, but here in Andorra, with no work to do we spent our afternoons having slow, languid, decadent sex. We grinned a lot.

Afterwards, Mack would leave me in bed reading and go out to look for work. Towards the end of the second week he came back to the hotel later than usual, around 8pm, and announced we were going somewhere nice for dinner because he had found a job and somewhere for us to live. He'd been introduced to an English couple who had just bought four ski chalets that needed a lot of maintenance work done to get them ready for the season.

Mack had been to check the chalets out and they needed decorating throughout too and he figured there was enough work to see him through till Christmas. He'd agreed a weekly salary with the couple which wasn't much but which would be enough to feed us and we could live in one of the chalets rent free while the work was being done.

I should have been glad he had a job but I'd enjoyed all the lolling around in bed with Mack and the thought that I would no longer be spending all day with him made me sad.

'When do you start?' I asked grumpily.

'Tomorrow. I've already agreed with Vincent downstairs that we'll move out of here tomorrow evening. Come on then lazy bones! Get your clothes on. We're going to have wine with our dinner tonight and everything.' Mack whipped the sheets from off me and kissed me hard on the lips.

We got on well with the couple who had bought the chalets from the very beginning. Vicky and Chris were in their early thirties, she was from Gateshead originally and he was from Hull but they'd been living in Oxford for many years, both working for Oxford University Press, before making the big decision to jack in their careers and move to Andorra. Vicky was a tall, capable woman with long, strong legs and manly hands, her thin blonde hair tied back in a stringy pony tail. Chris was tall and blonde too, receding slightly at the front. They both wore silver wire spectacles which made them look more like brother and sister than husband and wife.

'Can you imagine those two having sex?' I whispered

to Mack when we were lying in bed on our first night in the chalets.

'I'd really rather not, thanks,' Mack grunted.

There was a ton of work to do on the chalets but as Vicky and Chris had spent virtually every penny they had on buying them there was very little left in the pot to do the repair work that was needed. With the skills he had learned working for M. Perez, Mack fixed leaking roofs and broken window locks, resuscitated wobbly pine bedsteads and wardrobes and breathed new life into knackered dishwashers and elderly washing machines.

The chalets didn't just need repairing. They had previously been owned by another British couple who had arrived in Andorra full of energy and determination just like Vicky and Chris. They had then had three children, including a set of twins, within three years and found they just couldn't cope. Losing money hand over fist, they had decided almost overnight to return home and had sold the chalets exactly as they stood, leaving everything they owned inside – food in the cupboards, toys scattered everywhere – as if they had just popped out to the shops and would be returning at any minute. I couldn't sit around doing nothing while the other three worked so hard so I pitched in with picking through the discarded belongings, putting to one side anything for which there might possibly be some use. In one of the chalets I found at least a hundred sets of white cotton bed sheets and duvet covers and Vicky and I spent days going through them, ripping up the ones with the largest holes for dishcloths, darning smaller holes, then washing and ironing them ready for the first skiing customers. The weather had rapidly got cooler but we hung the sheets out to dry in the weak autumn sunshine, draping them over the balconies of the chalets and on bushes and over deck chairs. We aired the forty single duvets we found in the same way. In the store cupboards we found many months' supplies of jam, sugar, tea and coffee, enormous catering bags of washing powder and rice and pasta and three brown paper sacks of potatoes.

'Eeh, this is marvellous,' exclaimed Vicky in her sing-song Geordie accent. 'We've got to provide breakfast and an evening meal for the skiers every day and this lot is going to be a huge help. No wonder the last lot didn't make any money if they were carrying this much stock!'

I wiped down all the toys I found with warm, soapy, water. I did the same with two high chairs, two cots and a big playpen. I collected together all the plastic plates and bowls and cups scattered around and ran them through the newly functioning dishwasher.

'I'm not certain we're going to have any use for those.' Vicky said. 'These chalets tend to get booked out by big groups of young people.'

'Maybe you should describe one of the chalets as being suitable for families,' I suggested. 'You've got all this stuff anyway, might as well make use of it.'

'Good idea!'

And so in the adverts Vicky placed in the newspapers and magazines back home one of the chalets was designated as 'family friendly' and 'equipped with everything young children need for a stay away from home'.

In the evenings, dirty and tired, the four of us ate

together. Rice and pasta and potatoes mostly, with tinned tomatoes and tuna. Sometimes there were some spicy Merguez sausages for the barbecue or a chicken to roast but not often. Chris did most of the cooking because he enjoyed it and was good at it and could somehow manage to turn wrinkly last season potatoes into delicious gratin potatoes, flavoured with garlic and chicken stock and a thin sprinkling of crunchy Emmental cheese on top. There was always plenty of wine. Chris bought it from a local winemaker in huge plastic containers, like petrol cans. It was rough stuff, often with bits of grape skin floating in it, but it tasted fine after a glass or two. Afterwards we played cards and Vicky and Chris taught Mack and me how to play backgammon. They were both very good at it and Mack and I hardly ever took a game from them, but when Mack and I played against each other we were much more evenly matched.

In what seemed like no time at all the mountains were covered in snow and Mack and I had to go out and buy waterproof coats and thick jumpers and jeans having not brought winter clothes with us. The chalets looked neat and fresh and the furniture and kitchen equipment all worked and was all clean. Our work was done.

'You can work on for a bit if you want,' Vicky offered. 'Help out with making the breakfasts and evening meals and changing the beds. We aren't fully booked yet anyway so there's room for you to stay.'

Once breakfast was done and the kitchens tidied we went skiing. Mack was good at it almost immediately but it took me a lot longer. He hung around with me for a few weeks but once he'd got me to the point where I could ski down simple slopes and stop without falling over I could feel him behind me, longingly staring at the higher slopes, the harder runs.

'Go on,' I finally said. 'You can leave me here and go off on your own.'

He didn't need a second invitation.

Mack would stay on the ski slopes as long as he could but after a few hours I had usually had enough. I'd return to the chalets, take a quick shower and make a sandwich, and then I'd bake four cakes to serve to the skiers with hot chocolate laced with brandy when they finally came down from the slopes around 4.30pm when it started to get dark. I'd never baked anything in my life before then but Vicky showed me how to do it, how simple it was to make fresh, buttery, simple Madeira cake, to flavour it with some cocoa powder for a chocolate version or slice it through the middle and layer it with jam. I enjoyed the ritual of beating the mixture, the smell of baking cake floating through the chalet, the beaming smiles of pleasure on the faces of the skiers as they arrived home, pulling off their ski jackets, blowing onto their frozen fingers, gratefully accepting a warm cup of boozy hot chocolate and a slice of fresh, home-made cake.

Christmas passed almost without us noticing. Skiing didn't stop just because it was Christmas and apart from roast turkey for dinner that day and a few crackers it was just like any other day. Snow, skiing, food, bed. I called my parents from the phone in Vicky and Chris' chalet but they were short with me, hurt that I wasn't home, answering my questions about their well-being with single words. I hung up as soon as I could. I don't think Mack even bothered to ring home.

The chalets got busier and busier and Vicky and Chris could easily have rented out our room but said they couldn't do without us and were happy to lose the business and keep us living there. The family friendly chalet was booked out solid and both Vicky and I made extra money babysitting. I went skiing less and less as I babysat more and more and the pile of money stuffed in the bottom of my rucksack grew steadily. I enjoyed looking after the children. We baked fairy cakes and watched videos on a temperamental VCR that often stopped working mid-way through the film and then I'd have to tell the children how the story turned out.

And then all of a sudden it was the end of March and the ski season was coming to an end. The snow had started to melt, with patches of grass appearing on the lower slopes. I'd lost interest in skiing almost totally but Mack had become obsessive about it, going to higher and higher slopes where there was still good snow to be found. With less work to do looking after the customers Vicky and Chris were able to join him and I'd potter around doing what needed to be done in the chalets and getting the evening meal going, ready for when they got back.

Even though Vicky and Chris had been skiing for years, in just one short season Mack was every bit as good as them.

'You should see him, Anna,' Vicky said one evening when the three of them got back to the chalet, pink-cheeked and bringing with them the scent of cold, clear air off the mountains. 'He's a brilliant skier. Fearless.' I recognised the look on her face. It was the same one

Danielle had when she looked at Mack.

One afternoon when the three of them were out skiing and I was lying on my bed reading, I heard the door of our chalet bang much earlier than I had expected.

'Is that you, Mack?' I got up off the bed. 'Mack?'

But it was Chris who appeared in the doorway.

'Chris, what are you doing here? Has something happened? Is Mack OK?'

'Mack's fine. Just perfect. He and Vicky wanted to carry on skiing for longer. I thought I'd come and see if you fancied an early aperitif.'

I looked at my watch. It was only 3pm.

'Bit early for me. How about a cup of tea instead?'

He moved closer to me, put his hand gently on my arm.

'We could skip the tea if you like.' He nodded, ever so slightly but still very clearly a nod, towards the bed.

I could feel the heat rising in my face, my cheeks burning.

'You should never skip tea,' I said cheerily and rather more loudly than I usually talk. 'Come on, I'll go put the kettle on.'

'Suit yourself,' Chris said nastily. 'You've clearly got higher morals than my wife.'

That night I suggested to Mack that we have an early night instead of drinking wine and playing cards with Chris and Vicky.

'Sure thing lovely girl, you know I always like an early night,' he said winking at me.

After we had made love, I cuddled up under his arm.

'I think it's time for us to move on,' I said. 'The season

215

is pretty much over and Vicky and Chris don't really need us anymore. Are we going to go back to work for Monsieur and Madame Perez again?'

'I thought we might. We know how it works there and it should be easier this summer because of all the hard work we put in last year.'

'That's fine by me. I'll give him a call, suggest we get there in time to help get things ready for the season,' I said.

'OK, but that means we've got a bit of time yet before we have to leave here. We may as well stick around.'

'I thought perhaps we could take our time driving back to the campsite, stop off a few places; have a look around.'

'Great! OK, well I guess we'd better give Chris and Vicky a few days' notice and then we'll push off.'

'Thanks, Mack,' I said, pulling his arm tighter around me and kissing it.

'No problems, babe.'

Chapter 22

That's how we lived, Mack and I, for the next three years. We went from summer seasons at sunny resorts to winter seasons in ski resorts, only going back to Stonebridge once or twice a year for short visits. Our second summer at the Perez campsite was every bit as enjoyable as our first. Danielle had kicked Georges into touch and taken up with a suitably single friend of one of her brothers called Yves. He was tall and good looking and Danielle didn't look at Mack that summer in the same way as she had done the year before but Mack didn't seem to notice. He was far too taken with Yves who was an extremely competent surfer and more than happy to pass on his knowledge to Mack. The two of them and Danielle spent every spare minute left over from work in the sea wrestling with surfboards while I sunned myself on the beach and read.

From there we went on to do a ski season at Chamonix because Mack said the skiing would be better there than in Andorra. In any event, when we left the Andorra chalets, Vicky and Chris had not suggested we come back again next season. Mack appeared not to notice the lack of an invitation but I did. The season went right up until May in Chamonix and we got jobs straight away. I was a chalet girl, baking more cakes and cooking carbohydrate-based evening meals, mostly following the recipes Chris did in Andorra. Lots of garlicky potato gratin and tuna pasta bakes. Mack did maintenance work for three or four different little hotels and chalet owners, negotiating higher rates of pay this time so he could work less and ski more.

After Chamonix we spent a summer in Crete, working and living in a clapped-out youth hostel which tested even Mack's extensive fix-it skills. Try as I might, I struggled to learn any Greek, and found myself continually trying to speak French with a heavy Catalan accent to Greek people who shook their heads and spoke English back to me. The only work I could get was badly paid cleaning work and Mack and I ate a lot of pasta with tomato sauce that summer and most evenings could only buy one big bottle of Amstel beer to split between us. We didn't have a room to ourselves either and had to sleep in shared stuffy dormitories in bunk beds, me on the bottom and Mack on the top. Sex that summer involved furtive trips to the toilets in the middle of the night or sandy encounters on the beach in the dark. Mack didn't seem to mind but I did. I wanted to sleep next to him afterwards, thigh to thigh, ankle to ankle, not slink like thieves in the night back to our bunk beds We celebrated my 20th birthday by walking the Samaria Gorge, getting to Omalos before dawn and walking the 16km route to arrive at the village of Agia Roumeli where we splashed out on barbecued lamb with chips and a Greek salad with big chunks of creamy feta cheese before getting the boat to Hora Sfakion and from there the bus back to the hostel.

It had been impossible to save any money working in

Crete and we could not afford to go home to Stonebridge before the start of the ski season. Instead we went straight back to Chamonix making the long journey by motorbike and ferry, arriving back there much thinner than we had been when we left. We were both of us delighted to have the privacy of a room to ourselves again and to be able to have sex whenever we wanted.

It was towards the end of that season in Chamonix that I found out I was pregnant. It was a huge shock to us both.

'How the hell did that happen?' Mack said when I told him, his head in his hands.

'How do you think it happened?'

'I thought you were on the pill.'

'I was! This isn't my fault you know. I didn't get pregnant on purpose!'

'I know that Anna. I know you wouldn't do that.'

'What do we do now Mack?'

'I think that's up to you, babe. Do you want to have a baby?'

'I don't know. I haven't ever thought about it. Not really. Do you?'

'Not really. Not now.'

'OK, well I guess I'll have to sort something out then won't I?'

Only I didn't sort anything out. When it came down to it, even though I didn't want a baby at that particular moment of my life, actually doing anything to get rid of it was beyond me. Each night I lay awake, Mack fast asleep by the side of me, and gave myself a talking to about the two of us being young and having our whole lives ahead of us and how having a baby would put the kibosh on all that but when I did finally fall asleep I dreamed I was giving birth to a tiny baby, smaller than a doll, while standing in a bath tub and then when the baby started to slip down through the plug hole I tried desperately to stop it from swirling away from me, frantically grabbing at its miniature hands. I woke up from these dreams with my face wet with tears and feeling sad and empty.

For the first few weeks Mack nagged me gently, asking if I'd made an appointment with the doctor yet and that I didn't have much time left. When I replied that I hadn't he asked me whether I wanted him to make the appointment but I shook my head. Eventually, one evening when we were both lying in bed, he propped himself up on one elbow and looked down at me.

'You're not going to make an appointment are you?'

I shook my head, tears forming in the corners of my eyes and running down my face, gathering damply at the back of my neck.

'So we're going to have a baby then.'

'Well, I'm having a baby at least.'

'No Anna, *we're* having a baby. It'll be a beautiful baby. Now stop crying. There's nothing to cry about.' He put his arms round me and snuggled in close to me and held me until I finally fell asleep and for the first time in weeks I slept through all night without dreaming and I didn't wake up crying. And about two weeks after that I told Mack that it was time to go home.

'We don't need to be in Wales to have a baby Anna. I can earn enough money for us all out here. All three of us. I want us to carry on living like we have been. I don't

220

see why things have to change just because we're having a baby.'

But they did have to change. For three years I'd done whatever it was that Mack had wanted and had been happy to do it. More than happy. But as soon as the decision had been made to keep the baby, some sort of homing radar suddenly activated in my brain. I wanted to go home to Stonebridge, to a place that didn't need exploring because it had long since been explored and was familiar and comfortable and safe. Where I would know better how to look after a child because I'd been one there myself and where my parents would be nearby to help me.

I thought my parents would hit the roof when I told them I was pregnant but my mother was delighted.

'It's not as if you're a teenager is it? I suppose 20 is young to be pregnant these days but you'll be 21 by the time it's born. And of course you'll get married before then.'

'Will we?'

'But of course. I can't have a grandchild of mine being born out of wedlock. I'll talk to Mack's mother and we'll get it organised. Nothing fancy. It'll have to be register office, of course, and just a small reception. And what good luck your father and I have not been able to sell Nana's house. You and Mack and the baby can live there.'

My grandmother had died when Mack and I were in Greece, very suddenly, from cancer of the stomach. She was already buried by the time I phoned home and was told she'd died and even though I felt bad about missing her funeral and not saying goodbye I was glad I'd never seen my lovely Nana get sick and then die. Far away from Wales it was easy to pretend that Nana had not died at all and was still cheerily pottering away in her little terraced house, wearing one of her blue flowery house coats and cleaning up crumbs in the kitchen with the rusty little carpet cleaner she'd had for as long as I could remember and which was, according to Nana, far more efficient than any noisy old Hoover. It was impossible to imagine me and Mack living in that house. Using that carpet cleaner. Having a baby.

When I look back at that time, the speed at which everything happened amazes me. One minute we were in Chamonix, me puking my guts out every morning and cooking high calorie meals for skiers every evening and Mack fixing boilers and going off skiing as often as he could and the next we were married, back home in Wales living in Nana's house, with Mack back at his old job in the garage and me washing down walls and wiping out cupboards while I finished growing a baby. And the thing that strikes me most when I look back at that time is that I don't remember Mack getting much of a say in any of it.

Having the baby hurt far more than I expected. I had always known it was going to hurt – there was a girl at primary school called Lisa Darnley whose father was a doctor and at playtime she used to urge us girls to hook our index fingers into the corners of our mouths and pull hard. We did as she instructed until we winced with pain, and she would then declare triumphantly that her father had told her that's how much it hurt to have a baby. But it turned out that Lisa Darnley and her father (who might have been a doctor but who was after all a man at the end of the day) were way off the mark.

My mother had reassured me that yes it did hurt a bit but the pain didn't last for long and it was all worth it because you had a baby at the end of it and that helped you forget the pain. My mother's friends all said much the same thing. I had to rely on my mother for information because I knew nobody my own age that was stupid enough to have got pregnant and I had no access to more up-to-date experiences against which to verify the accuracy of my mother's information. It was only about the time I was begging for an epidural and turning round and round on the hospital bed on all fours like a dog in its basket in a vain effort to escape the pain of another contraction, while Mack looked on with horror and terror in his face, that it dawned on me the women of my mother's generation had taken some sort of secret vow not to tell their daughters the truth about child birth. Maybe they feared this might somehow dissuade them from procreating and thereby bring about the end of the human race. Since then, cable television and entire channels devoted to broadcasting women giving birth on camera have come along and crushed this conspiracy. For the record and if you don't know already from personal experience, having a baby hurts. A lot.

My mother was right, of course. The baby at the end of it did make it all worthwhile. James' safe arrival into the world made the rest of my entire life worthwhile.

Chapter 23

James

This has got to be the worst fucking week of my life. Honestly, it's been shit. Well, not all of it. The first part was OK. Better than OK. It was good. Once Amy and I had had sex things were normal again. It was like she'd forgotten who I was, stuck up here in London all this time without me, forgotten who she is even, but then once we'd done it, it was like she found me again. She stopped having a go at Glynis' apartment and Glynis' expensive things and went back to being Amy. We drank cider and shagged till we fell asleep and then woke up early Saturday morning starving hungry but still managed another quick one before we got up.

We had a shower together. That was the first time we'd done that. It was the bomb. Glynis' shower is huge – plenty of room for two – the water comes pounding out really hard, and her shower gel is grapefruit and smells good enough to eat. I could have stayed in there longer but Amy wouldn't.

'Do you have any idea how much water these power showers waste?' she said. I didn't bother answering because I didn't want her to start on the Glynis bashing again.

We went all over London that day. Amy seems to know this city like the back of her hand. We bought travel cards which meant we could hop on any bus or any tube and go wherever we wanted. We stopped in a shop and bought a couple of croissants and a take-away milky coffee each for breakfast, and we ate those waiting for the bus to take us to Covent Garden. I thought it was wonderful there – lots of different shops and restaurants and buskers singing opera, which sounded amazing, and some ripped guy painted silver top-to-toe and pretending to be a gladiator or something and to chop people's heads off when they dropped money in his tin. It was rammed there, tons of people milling around, gawping at everything.

'It's terribly touristy isn't it?' said Amy.

'I like it, but then I suppose I'm a tourist aren't I?'

'Well I'm not. Come on. I'll show you somewhere else.'

We went to Trafalgar Square and the National Gallery and then all the way down to Buckingham Palace which looked a bit like a prison to me. Like the Queen was being kept inside against her will by all those bars, rather than all us tourists being kept out. We went and sat in a park for a while and had a hot dog. The sun was shining and I couldn't get over how many other people were in the park – whole families with pushchairs and kids and dogs even, couples on rugs lying close together or kissing, people sitting cross-legged on their own, reading books or the paper.

'It's because only really rich people in London have gardens,' Amy explained seeing me look around. 'If you want to sit out in the sun in London you have to go to the park.'

I thought about how on sunny days when Lois was a baby Mum would drag the paddling pool around our titchy garden, following the sun. Lois would sit in the pool giggling and me and Mum and Niall would sit on the grass, our legs hooked over the edge of the pool to paddle. That made me feel kind of sad for all the Londoners who couldn't do that.

Afterwards we got the bus back to Glynis' flat and had a pint of cider in a little pub just round the corner. We would have liked to have had another one because it was fun sitting there just the two of us, watching people come and go, but it was way too expensive so we walked to a Tesco Metro not far away and bought some crisps and two ready-made lasagnes and a bar of Dairy Milk and more cider. Back at Glynis' we ate and drank and watched DVDs on Glynis' monster telly and then went to bed to shag some more. It was ace.

By Sunday morning, though, Amy seemed to have had enough sex. She pushed my hand away when I reached for her and said she was going to have a shower. I could tell from the way she said it that she wanted to have a shower on her own. When she came back into the bedroom, which I noticed was quite a while despite her telling me off yesterday about wasting water, she told me to get a move on because she wanted to get out and about not hang around Glynis' flat all day, like I'd actually suggested we hang around Glynis' flat all day which I hadn't.

'I want to go to Columbia Road flower market,' she said.

'OK cool,' I said even though I had absolutely no

interest in flowers whatsoever and we had no money to buy any anyway.

Actually, even though it was in East London and took ages to get to on the bus, Columbia Road flower market did turn out to be pretty cool. Again it was rammed but London seems to be rammed wherever you go and loads of people pushed past each other to get down one little narrow street lined with flower stalls. They were carrying huge yellow bags full of potted plants and lugging massive armfuls of flowers and everyone seemed to be in a hurry to buy as much as they could as quickly as they could.

'What's the big rush?' I asked Amy.

'It's only open on a Sunday and then only till lunchtime.'

Behind the flower sellers were little shops selling all sorts of quirky stuff that my mum would have loved – pink cake tins and mugs with birds on them, and knackered looking antique furniture. We walked round a corner and there was a big, old-fashioned pub and next door a bread shop and loads of people drinking coffee and listening to some bloke play the violin. A really sad tune that made me feel sorry, even though I wasn't sorry about anything and was feeling over the moon to be in London with Amy with another whole week to go before I had to go home.

I had my first bagel in Columbia Road market, filled with egg and bacon, which Amy said was a bit ironic given that it was Jewish people who invented bagels and they don't eat bacon and don't mix meat with dairy. I always thought Americans invented bagels but I didn't say anything because Amy seemed to like being the one who did the telling in London and I was happy for her to do that, and anyway the bagel was delicious. We stayed until the very end and watched the flower stalls pack up and all the people drain away so that suddenly the place was almost empty.

'Last few bunches of anemones a pound. Just a pound,' one flower seller shouted so I dashed over and bought a bunch for Amy. They were bright purple and pink with black spiky middles and they looked to me like they had friendly faces. Amy reached up with her hand and stroked my cheek when I gave them to her and then smiled at me and that felt just as good as having sex with her.

We walked all the way home from Columbia Road because Amy said she fancied a long walk and even though it took us almost two hours and my feet hurt by the time we got back it was a great way to see London. We walked through the City bit where all the bankers and lawyers and accountants work and then past Saint Paul's Cathedral and worked our way down onto the wibbly-wobbly bridge and walked over it. We walked past the Tate Modern and the South Bank and the London Eye and finally on to Glynis' flat. We stopped in at Tesco again and I bought stuff to make pasta with cheese sauce which is one of the things my mum has taught me and Niall to make. It's good and it's cheap and according to my mother boys who can cook impress women. We had enough money to buy a bottle of white wine to go with it. A *Sunday Times* had been pushed under Glynis' door when we got in and Amy read the paper and sipped her wine while I cooked pasta on Glynis' fearsome, shiny, five-burner cooker and I felt like we were a real grown-up couple.

But on Monday Amy had to go to lectures again and had netball practice afterwards, so she didn't get to Glynis' place until after 9pm by which time I was going off my head with loneliness all the way up fourteen floors on my own. She was late the next couple of nights too, saying she had work to do she could only do in the library or that there was a speaker coming to the students' union that she wanted to hear and no I wouldn't be able to come along because you needed a students' pass to get in and I didn't have one. Even though we had sex every night, I was so fed up I thought about going home – even the chaos in our house was better than swotting on my own all day in Glynis' bright white tower. I went out for a walk every day and although there were tons of people about nobody seemed to know anybody and everyone just hurried past each other all buttoned up and silent. I suppose I could have gone somewhere a bit further than just the park near Glynis' flat but I didn't have much money and wanted to save what I had for when I was with Amy and anyway I had studying to do.

Finally, I asked her straight out if she would prefer to go back to her hall of residence.

'Of course not! Why do you say that James? Because I've had to go to lectures and not been able to just bunk off for a week like you? I am at university you know. It's more important than just school.'

That's how I'd felt all week. That Amy's life was more important than mine. More relevant.

'It's just that you don't seem very happy to be with me. Like you'd prefer to be somewhere else. You haven't introduced me to any of your friends or anything and I feel a bit left out.'

'Don't be so childish James. I haven't left you out. I've just been doing what I always do here. Look – if you feel like that why don't we go to the student union disco tomorrow night? There's one every Thursday and a crowd of people I know go so it's usually a laugh. I know the people on the door so I should be able to get you in even though you don't have a student pass. How about that? Will that make you happier?'

I nodded. It was going to make me happier. Being with Amy always made me happy.

Only now we're at the frigging disco and it's probably the crappiest night of my life. Amy doesn't just know a crowd of people who come to this disco. She knows every bugger here. She's flitting around chatting to people having left me at the bar hugging a plastic pint glass of warm cider, like she's forgotten I'm even here. She's not drinking cider tonight. She's drinking vodka and tonic. I've never even seen her have a vodka and tonic before but she says she drinks it all the time here. I feel like adding, 'all the time you're here without me,' but don't because I don't really know what I mean by that.

There's one bloke that Amy seems to be talking to more than most. He's tall and he's got black hair in a sort of feathery style round his face which makes him look very girly if you ask me. He's wearing a white, round-neck cotton shirt undone so you can see all the hairs on his chest and Diesel jeans and I can see he's got some sort of silver-and-blue bangles round his wrists. This boy Amy returns to over and over when she's chatting with her friends.

Finally, I've had enough. I throw back the rest of my pint and go over to him.

'Hello, I'm James. Amy's boyfriend.'

'Hello James. I'm Inigo.' Inigo? What kind of name is that? Did his parents think he was going to be a film star or something?

I see Amy looking over at the two of us and I think I can see worry in her eyes.

'It's good to meet you,' Inigo says. 'Amy talks a lot about you.'

'She hasn't said anything to me about you.'

I see something flicker in his eyes. I think it's disappointment.

Despite the rockstar look he's affecting, Inigo has a very posh accent. For some reason this makes me step up my Welsh accent. Like I want to show him that Amy and me are from the same place. That we've known each other a very long time. Way longer than Inigo has known her.

Amy bustles over at this point. 'I was just about to introduce you two but I see you've already done it for me. Inigo is in my hall of residence,' she explains. 'He's in his final year, doing English.'

'English eh?' I don't know what else to say. What I'd like to say is, 'You lay so much as a finger on my girlfriend you arsehole and I'll fucking kill you,' but I know this is the wrong thing to say and anyway not true. I haven't been in a fight since Niall and I used to scrap on the living-room floor when we were in primary school.

'Right then,' Amy says, all false and bright. 'I see your drink is empty James. Let's go get you another one shall we?' She steers me towards the bar and from the corner of my eye I see her mouthing something at Inigo. 'Thank you,' is what I think she says.

Amy buys us more drinks but doesn't say anything to me. Nor does she introduce me to any of her other friends. The music gets louder and she asks me if I will dance with her. I don't really like dancing but Amy loves it and I'm usually very glad to be dancing with her. I follow her on to the dance floor but I'm really not in the mood and just stand there shuffling around a bit, not grinning at her like I usually do when I watch her dance. I know I look stupid and sulky but I just can't help myself. It seems to me that whenever I do look at Amy she is searching the room for Inigo. When her eyes find him she looks at him quickly and then back at me.

I'm buggered if I'm going to be the one who suggests we go home. I can just imagine what Amy will say to that. Something about school kids like me not being able to cut the pace. So I stick it out till the bitter end. Drinking lots of warm cider. Inigo fucks off around 11pm I see him standing at the door. He lifts his hand and waves at Amy before he disappears.

It's quite a long way on the tube from the student union to Glynis' flat. I find I've drunk so much that I daren't look in the same place for long and have to keep moving my eyes around because the world is spinning a bit and I'm pretty certain that if this tube journey isn't over soon I am going to puke which would be a marvellous end to a marvellous night. I want to ask Amy about Inigo but I daren't and anyway I'm too drunk. The minute we get into the flat I collapse onto the bed still wearing my jeans. I wake up about 3am feeling like shit. Amy isn't in the bed next me. I find a note next to the kettle. *You were snoring and I have to get up early tomorrow anyway for lectures so I've gone back to the halls of residence. See you tomorrow. I'll call you later.*

No kiss or nothing.

Chapter 24

It's always a problem when one member of a couple is so much better-looking than the other. Mack knew it and I knew it and so did everyone else who saw us together. I knew that when women looked at Mack and me, beautiful women like Danielle and even ordinary women like Vicky, what they were thinking to themselves was: *'She did rather well for herself didn't she?'* Mack knew it too but it didn't matter. Mack liked the fact that we were different. He liked that I could speak French and had a go at speaking Spanish when we were in Andorra; that I was a swotty type who wasn't much good at surfing and skiing but read a lot instead. He liked the fact that I loved him enough not to go to university so I could be with him. He loved it that I ached for him physically and never ever turned down the opportunity of sex with him. That nothing made me happier than making him happy.

I didn't love him any the less after James had arrived. It was just that I had less time for him. It was hard to believe how much effort went into looking after such a tiny human being. The feeding and the burping and the getting up in the middle of the night. And then of course James was so beautiful. Such a wonderful baby. The best baby in the world. Mack was working really long hours in the garage to make as much money as he could for us and sometimes by the time he got in both James and I were already fast asleep. It wasn't that I didn't want to have sex with him any more; it was just that I wasn't awake when Mack was. And that when I *was* awake Mack wasn't. Mack wasn't what you'd call a hands-on dad. He loved James and was fiercely proud of him but when it came to feeding him I was the one with the boobs. And nappies are such fiddly things aren't they? So much easier for women to deal with.

Having always had such tiny boobs, it was as much a surprise to me as it was to Mack that breast-feeding gave me what Mack described as a phenomenal rack. Trouble was it wasn't much good to either of us. I had huge tits but they didn't belong to me and they certainly didn't belong to Mack. They belonged exclusively to James. I couldn't bear it when Mack tried to touch them. I couldn't bear it when my arms so much as brushed against them. They were no longer a fun part of sex but rather a pair of feeding bottles. Constantly filling, constantly aching feeding bottles. I felt like anyone looking at me would be able to see that these huge throbbing boobs were not really mine, had appeared down the front of my shirt like alien flesh, the sole purpose of which was to feed my ever-hungry son.

'You mean to say the tit fairy finally came but that the tits are out of bounds?' Mack was teasing but it was true. The tits were well and truly out of bounds.

We still managed to have sex, of course. By the time James was six weeks old Mack was climbing the walls. He practically chased me round the house and, actually, once I'd got over the awkward feeling of having sex again

I really rather enjoyed it.

'How was it?' I asked worriedly afterwards. 'Did it feel, you know, different?'

'It was lovely, babe,' Mack replied contentedly. 'How do you mean different?'

'You know what I mean. Was it…baggy in there?'

'It was just perfect.'

And even though we didn't have sex quite as often as we used to, we still had sex a lot. It was a way of being together again, of being the carefree young people we had been in Languedoc-Roussillon and Andorra and Crete. A way of being together that was just the two of us. That had nothing to do with James or his two sets of doting grandparents or a boring job in a garage or a little old-fashioned house in my home town that didn't have a Hoover and still smelled like Nana.

Which is how I got pregnant again just before James turned one.

'You've got to be kidding me?' Mack was so shocked when I told him that all the colour drained out of his face.

'I wish I was,' I said, tears gathering thickly in the back of my throat.

'How did that happen?'

'Exactly the same way it happened the first time!'

'But how did you let it happen, Anna?'

'What do you mean how did I let it happen? How did *you* let it happen? I thought you were being careful.'

'I was being careful. I got off at Grangetown. I never took the train the whole way to Cardiff. And anyway you were still breast-feeding. The blokes in the garage say you

236

can't get pregnant when you're breast-feeding.'

'That's one of the biggest old wives tales' going. And since when have you been taking contraceptive advice from the boys in the garage?'

'But James is still a baby. He'll still be a baby when the other one comes. He'll still be in nappies for heaven's sake.'

'Well I guess you'd better learn to change them then. I can't change two nappies at once.'

The second pregnancy wiped me out. I couldn't believe how tired I was. Sometimes when James woke in the night I didn't hear him. It wasn't his crying that woke me but Mack tapping me on the leg.

'James is crying.'

'You go to him then.'

'I've got to be up at 6am to go to work!'

I was so tired all the time I didn't notice how unhappy Mack had become. How he worked longer and longer hours at the garage. How when he came home he didn't want to eat what I'd left out for him. Boiled potatoes and chicken kiev. Sausages and spaghetti. Food as fuel cooked as quickly as possible; nothing like the lovely meals that Madame Perez had cooked for us or the tasty, filling things I'd made for the skiers in the chalets.

One night when the second baby was already a week overdue James' crying woke me up. Bloated with baby, I struggled to get out of bed, wobbling myself to the end of the bed and heaving myself up. I scooped James out of his cot and went downstairs to the kitchen to warm his bottle and found Mack sitting at the table. He was crying.

'Omigod! What's wrong? You haven't lost your job have

you?' And then immediately. 'Don't worry if you have. We'll manage. My mum and dad will help us out till you find another.'

Mack shook his head, tears dripping down his face. I'd never, not once, seen him cry before. Even when James had been born he hadn't cried. He'd punched the air like they do in adventure movies and shouted 'Yipee-ki-aye-ay motherfucker,' which hadn't gone down too well with the midwives, but he hadn't cried.

'What is it then? What's the matter? Are you sick?'

Mack shook his head again. 'I'm not sick. Or maybe I am. I can't do this anymore Anna. I just can't do it.'

'You mean work at the garage? Give it up then. You can set up as a handyman. People always need handymen. Or you could re-train. Do something else you'd like more. We'll manage Mack. I know you hate the garage. We'll find you something else.'

'It's not just the garage Anna. It's this.' He swept his arm around in a big circular gesture, taking in our little kitchen, still decorated with the wallpaper my nana had put up in the early seventies with its little orange pattern of a cup and a saucer and what looked like a tomato sauce bottle; me jiggling James on my hip with a big baby belly wearing a tatty dressing gown. 'It's all of this. I can't do it anymore.'

'You mean me? Me and James and the new baby? You can't do *us* anymore?'

Mack nodded and dropped his head in shame. 'I'm sorry Anna, but this isn't what I wanted out of life. I wasn't planning on ever coming back to Stonebridge. On this being married with two kids malarkey. I was going to work in America and New Zealand and Australia and Hong Kong. I was going to see the world. This is just no fun.'

'You ought to try being pregnant or breast-feeding for two years straight. That's hardly a barrel of laughs either…' I smiled at Mack, trying to signal to him that I was making a joke but he didn't smile back.

'You deserve better than this Anna.'

'Oh no you don't! Don't go down the "it's not you it's me" road. I won't stand for it.'

'But it *is* me, not you.'

'Mack Lewis. Listen to me just for five minutes will you. I know this isn't what you bargained for. It isn't what I bargained for either. I'm only 23 years old. You're only 26. We were travellers you and me. Free spirits. Living on love and cheap wine and peaches. And it was brilliant. The best time of my life. The best time ever before James came along and made life even better. I know it's a big change. I know it kills you to work in that garage again. But we can get through this you and me. We're going to have another baby any minute. And a year after that things will have settled down a bit and we can make a plan. We can go work abroad again if you want. I can be a chalet girl again, offer babysitting for other mums, like I did in Andorra. We can have a life a lot like the one we used to have. It's just there'll be four of us not two.'

'Do you think? Do you really think that?'

'Absolutely. We'll get a camper van and live in that and travel all round Europe. You and me and our two kids. It'll be a huge adventure. Can we go back to bed now?'

With tears still glinting in his eyes Mack got up and

put his arms around me and James. As I turned my face
to kiss him my waters broke.

Chapter 25

Mack was very determined to make it up to me for what he'd said the night Niall was born. We didn't talk much about it. To begin with we were just too knackered to talk about anything at all. I'd thought one baby was tiring but juggling two seemed more than was humanly possible. Later, when we'd got ourselves into more of a routine, I tried to ask him a few times how he was feeling but he refused to discuss it. He worked hard at the garage but came home in time to put the boys to bed most nights and he was very careful with me, stroking and smoothing me for a very long time before we made love. Within a few weeks of giving birth I got myself down to the family planning clinic and went back on the pill. Neither of us wanted to have another child.

It was me who pointed out to Mack that it was possible to surf in Wales. He would need a wetsuit but there were quite a few good surfing spots within easy travelling distance of Stonebridge – places like Southerndown and Ogmore. Just because he was stuck in Wales didn't mean he couldn't do one of the things he loved most in the world.

'I love you and the boys most in the world,' he said quickly.

'I know that Mack and we love you. Enough to give

you a bit of time every week to do something by yourself.'

And so on Sundays Mack was out of bed even before the boys, in rain or shine. He'd ride his motorbike to the garage where he kept his board and borrow the owner's van and go surfing. He was always back by 2pm, salty, sandy and content.

The rest of the weekend he worked hard on our house and soon it started to look like the home of a young couple not that of a little old lady. He took out the pink bathroom my nana had had since before I was born and put in a modern white one with shiny taps and an overhead shower. I was sorry to see the old bathroom go. When I was a little girl I'd loved its pinkness and the matching dolly with a knitted skirt under which my nan had hidden the spare toilet roll – it had been familiar and cosy, a bit like my nana – but it was old fashioned and the lino which had once been pink to match the bath tub had turned brown over the years and was curling in the corners like ham left uncovered in the fridge. I knew Mack was right when he said a new one would be much better. He stripped off the tomato-sauce bottle wallpaper in the kitchen and painted the walls a faint yellow colour called Hint of Lemon, humming Procol Harum's 'Whiter Shade of Pale' as he worked. In the boys' tiny little bedrooms he put up blue wallpaper with big red space rockets. They loved it. Finally one Friday he came home a bit later than usual, driving the garage owner's van with a brand new double bed for us and a pine headboard.

As soon as the boys were in bed, he pulled me towards him and kissed me, soft at first and then harder. 'Wanna skip the light fandango in our new bed?' he asked.

Afterwards, just as we were both dropping off, he said, 'That's better. I never felt comfortable having sex in the bed your nana must have had sex in at some point.'

'Oi!' I said, kicking at his ankle gently. 'Nanas don't have sex. Everyone knows that.'

Of course my grandmother had had sex. My mother was proof of that but also in amongst all my nana's stuff that I'd cleared out – the jars of old buttons and string and the drawers stuffed full of saved tin foil and greaseproof paper because my nana had lived through the Second World War and never ever threw anything out – I'd found a bunch of old black and white photos of her and my grandfather, from the days when they went ballroom dancing together, back long ago in the days when it was my gran who danced with my granddad, not me. In these photos the two of them were young and beautiful and even though they smiled shyly at the camera you could tell that this was a couple that had plenty of sex.

I was happy living in my grandparents' little house. Very happy. The work Mack had done had made it much more comfortable and more ours, but it still carried the imprint of my grandparents' love and that was a good feeling. A safe feeling. I framed some of those old black and white photos and hung them in our hallway. Whenever we could afford it I bought us something we needed. A set of new sheets or some lovely thick towels. Mack built some bookshelves for the hundreds of books I seemed to have acquired.

'Where did all these books come from?' he asked as he helped me stack them on my new bookshelves.

'Charity shops mostly.'

'Have you read them all?'

'Most of them, yes.'

'Then why keep them? Why not just give them back to the charity shop.'

'I like having them around. Like knowing I could read them again if I wanted to.'

'OK, if that's what you want.'

It was what I wanted. I liked the fact that I didn't have to throw out my stuff anymore at the end of every season; that I could keep all my pretty things and put them out on show in my clean comfortable home, even if everything did have to be out of toddler reach. We were putting down roots, making a family life. Before I knew it James had started nursery school, just until 11.45am every day but it made life so much easier, and next year he'd be full time and Niall would go to nursery school and then perhaps I could think about getting myself a job. I felt like I was finally getting on top of things. That my life was in control.

It was about this time that Mack suggested we really could do with having some transport of our own and perhaps we should buy that camper van I'd talked about.

'The boys are getting a bit older now. We can start getting out and about a bit as a family. I'll be able to start teaching James to surf before too long.'

'He's only three Mack!'

'He can walk can't he? If he can walk he can learn to surf.'

'And anyway I can't drive!'

'I'll teach you. You'll get the hang of it in no time. And won't it be nice being able to drive to the supermarket rather than having to get the bus with a pram?'

'How will we be able to afford it?'

'We've done most of what we need to do on the house now so we should be able to manage OK. And we can get a cheap one that needs work doing and I can do it up.'

Within a week he drove home in a rust bucket of a navy-blue camper van. Smoke was billowing out of the engine when he pulled up outside the house.

'You found one that quick?'

'Had my eye on it for a while.'

Mack divided his weekend into three. Some time for surfing, some time for me and the boys and some time for the camper van. It seemed to me that he took the whole thing apart, covered it in grease and then put it back together again but once he'd done that, the engine didn't smoke anymore. It wasn't the easiest thing to learn to drive on, as my dad pointed out more than once, but Mack was patient and, once I'd got going, I really wanted to learn. I passed my test first time round – mostly I think because the driving instructor was amused that I was taking my test in a camper van.

'First time for everything!' he said as he climbed up into the van next to me. Even though my emergency stop wasn't what you'd call speedy because the camper van didn't really do speedy he just smiled at me.

'You followed the instruction. That's what counts.'

We went all over in that camper van. To begin with we just tagged along with Mack when he went to Southerndown or Ogmore. When it was fine the boys and I sat on the beach and made sandcastles and ate picnics while Mack surfed. Then we started to go further afield, to the Gower, where there was better surfing to be had at beautiful beaches like Llangennith and Rhossili. We camped overnight and had chips for tea. The boys were in their element, all three of them.

Mack had to send away to get James his first wetsuit. Nowadays you can pick up wetsuits for children at the supermarket, but not back then. I fretted anxiously the first few times Mack took him out. He was so tiny still, so susceptible to drowning. I stood at the water's edge, holding tight onto Niall's hand, who, desperate to get out into the water and join his father and brother, tried hard to wriggle his damp little hand out of mine. I need not have worried. James had inherited his father's ability to do pretty much anything he tried to do and a year or so later Niall proved that he could too.

I should have known really. After all, it was me who had suggested it all those years ago, the night Niall was born. I was the one who had said we could do it – could live the sort of life we used to. And perhaps Mack would have let things carry on as they were if I hadn't started to look for a job in earnest, trawling through the papers looking for jobs that I could do with no qualifications beyond A levels.

'Teaching assistant. I reckon I could be a teaching assistant don't you Mack? I've been assisting teaching right here at home for five years. I'm pretty good at it by now.' We were sitting at our kitchen table, sharing a can of lager. The boys were in bed, the dishes were done and the floor swept and the house was calm and quiet.

'If you feel the boys are old enough for you to go to work Anna, don't you think it's time for us to go off again?'

'What do you mean?' I really didn't know what he was talking about.

'Go back travelling again, like you said we would. The four of us and the camper van. We could get in touch with M. Perez. I bet he'd have us back for a summer. They'd love to have you back on reception again. The boys could learn French. How cool would that be! Our kids would be bilingual.'

'They're already learning to be bilingual. They're learning Welsh at school.'

'I can't speak Welsh.'

'You can't speak French either.'

'Come on Anna! You know what I mean. How amazing a life would it be for two little boys to travel around, learning different languages, having different experiences. They're great little surfers already. Imagine what they'd be like surfing somewhere where the sun shines.'

'What about school?'

'We'll put them in school wherever we pitch up. They'll love it. Somewhere different every six months or so. Bet they'll take to skiing like they took to surfing.'

I pictured my sons swooping down snowy mountain sides, shouting at each other in French, laughing proudly as they snow-ploughed neatly to a stop. I smiled.

'We couldn't live in a camper van in a ski resort.'

'Of course we couldn't. But I've been thinking. Maybe we could sell this place? What do you think? We could buy our own little chalet out in Andorra. Just one. Use

247

all the lessons we learned working for Vicky and Chris and set up our own business. You and me working together. And then when the season is over we'll go off in the camper van the four of us – I guess we'll need a tent too, it'll get a bit cramped with the four of us and won't exactly be good for our sex life – and go wherever we want. Italy – I've always really wanted to go to Italy and southern Spain, maybe even down to Gibraltar. It'll be the most amazing life.'

It was the first time I had heard Mack talk so excitedly for a long time. I pictured the four of us travelling around in the camper van, all brown as berries, gabbling away in whatever language we fancied, poring over maps as we decided where we would go live next.

'This is what you've been waiting for isn't it Mack? This is the moment you've been waiting for since Niall was born?'

'Yes! Well no, you make it sound like life hasn't been good in the meantime. It has been good Anna. Really good. I love you. I love the boys. This is where I've wanted to be. With you and with them while they were little and needed all this.' He gestured round the kitchen, at the fridge and the cupboards, the boys' shoes lined up by the door ready for school the next morning, their lunch boxes on the counter, ready for me to fill them with sandwiches.

'But now they're old enough and you are seriously talking about getting a job. It's time for us to do what we've always wanted to do. This place will be easy to sell now we've worked so hard on it.'

'You were the one who did all the work Mack.'

'No I didn't. You're the one who made it all pretty and

248

homely, with pictures and cushions and stuff. It'll sell it in no time and with that money behind us we can go wherever we want.'

'There's just one little problem with that plan Mack.'

'Our parents will be fine. They'll get used to the idea, don't you worry.'

'We don't own this house Mack.'

He looked shocked. 'We don't own it?'

'No, we never have. My nana left the house to my mother. It's in my mother's name.'

'But she transferred it to you right? When we moved in?'

'No, she didn't. She meant to. She always said she would. But she hasn't.'

'But we must have some sort of rights? We've been living in it all this time. Doing it up, spending money on it? It must be ours by now.'

'We didn't pay anything for it. We live here rent free. I don't see how just because we've done it up that means we own it.'

'If you talk to your mum I'm sure she'll give it to you.'

'What so I can sell it and take the money and run away with her grandsons? I don't think so Mack.'

His disappointment lasted only seconds. 'Well I guess we won't be able to go into the chalet business then. But we can still get jobs out there, jobs with accommodation, there's nothing stopping us going anyway.'

'I guess not.'

'Brilliant. Because I don't think I could stick it for much longer round here Anna. The garage is doing my head in. No air, no light. I feel like I can't breathe in there. Like my lungs are closing down on me. And Stonebridge is so small and boring. We don't need stuff you and me. All these books and ornaments and pictures. All we need is each other. You and me and the boys. I'll get us another can of lager shall I? Seeing as we're celebrating.'

We shared another can of lager and then we went to bed. We made love and I could feel a lightness about Mack, a joy and a freedom so great it oozed out of the pores of his skin. He fell asleep straight away and I held on tight to his hand, the way I used to hold Niall's hand when he watched his father and brother surfing.

Chapter 26

I didn't go with Mack. I couldn't. I loved the sound of the life that he was describing – the places we'd see, the things we'd do, the tastes and the smells and the sounds. I loved seeing his face when he talked about that life. The Mack who lived in a camper van – with nothing more than a few pots and pans and a sleeping bag – that was the real Mack. The real live Mack. The one who had been living with us in my nana's little house was not the real Mack. He was just a shadow of the real man.

Me I needed to stay in Stonebridge. I needed somewhere safe and clean for my boys, a place where there was running water and a fridge and towels and beds made up with sheets. A place where they went to school with the same kids for years on end and I got to know the parents of those kids, where they had grandparents nearby and cubs and a library. Where I could frame the annual school photo of the boys and put it on the mantelpiece. I needed the boring, samey, dull routine of it all. Without it I would be the one who was only a shadow of my real self.

Nobody understood why I let Mack go. Nobody understood either how he *could* go. How could he leave us, his family? Because he loved us. Everybody said that. He really did love us. And I loved him. I really really loved him. That's what made it possible to tell him that I couldn't go with him and that the boys wouldn't be going either but that he could go if that's what he wanted. With my blessing. And that he could come home and visit his sons whenever he wanted and that I wouldn't hate him or say bad things about him or make it difficult for him to visit. Not ever. I made it easy for Mack to go because I knew that if he didn't he would suffocate. That I was going to lose him whatever I did.

Being all grown up and mature about the situation didn't stop me falling apart. I missed him so much in the beginning that there were days when I could barely get out of bed.

'Go after him love,' my mum said to me one morning when she called round to find me curled on the sofa sobbing. 'You can't live like this. No one can. If being without him makes you this unhappy you've got to go join him.'

'Never thought I'd hear you say anything like that Mum,' I sniffed. 'You made enough fuss when it was just me living away, can't imagine what state you'd be in if I took your grandsons away from you.'

'Well my girl, that's love for you. I'd rather be unhappy myself than have you unhappy. I let you go with him before; I can do it again.'

Sometimes I thought I would go. In the middle of the night, so sad and lonely I hurt, I vowed I would leave first thing in the morning. When Mack phoned like he did every couple of days after he first left and begged me to join him I even started packing a few times. But I couldn't bring myself to rip the three of us away from the safe, ordered, secure life we had in Stonebridge to wander round Europe in a camper van. Mack was a rolling stone. I understood that. I'd lived that life with Mack and I'd loved every second of it because he loved it so much and I loved him. But I was a mother now and things were different. I needed to gather moss for my boys and even though I could barely believe it myself, that need was stronger than my love for Mack.

I would not have got through that time without my friends and family. Bob and Jane were incredible, delivering a plated-up dinner for me every couple of days because they knew that otherwise I would probably only eat toast, taking the boys out to the park to give me a break, calling round on a Saturday night with a couple of pizzas and a bottle of red wine, their own two boys in tow, claiming to be at a loose end. Mack's parents and my parents were great too. They had never got on that well before but Mack's leaving had brought them together in a united front. They were going to see me through this if it killed them.

Even though Glynis was busting her gut to make partner at her law firm she came home as often as she could. She and Bob and Jane had some sort of visiting rota worked out between them. Once or twice she got the train back to Wales mid week, arriving in Stonebridge after 8pm with a big bag of paperbacks she'd bought for me at the W H Smith in the station and a wine bottle tucked under her arm.

'Get the glasses out, girl,' she'd announce when I opened the door to her. Glynis has always believed that wine is pretty much the answer to all ills. I'd have a glass of wine and she'd have three and she'd tell me funny stories about life as a female lawyer in London – how she'd gone to meet a bunch of clients and when she walked into the room they asked her when the lawyer would be arriving; how one male client in his fifties had told her boss that he knew he was being old fashioned but he'd actually rather have a man dealing with his case if it was all the same to him.

'Doesn't that make you furious?' I'd ask. 'Having to work in such a sexist environment.'

'Not really,' Glynis laughed. 'I'm never going to be able to change the attitudes of people like that. They're too long in the tooth. I'll just have to wait for all the old bigots to die before I can become managing partner.'

The main reason I got through it was James and Niall. I had to hold it together for them. At first they missed Mack and asked about him all the time, cried for him at night, but they got used to being without him very quickly. The rest of their lives went on exactly as they had done before, it was just their father that was missing, and since he'd been at work a lot of the time they were awake they were used to not seeing him. They had me, their grandparents, their bedroom and their toys. They managed without their dad.

Eventually Glynis insisted I got divorced. I played about as much part in organising that as I did my wedding.

'I don't even do divorce work but I do know that you need to get this sorted out straight away. You can't have him traipsing round the world having the time of his life and then turning up like a bad penny years later with three other wives in tow and demanding you hand over the kids or the house. If you're cutting him loose Anna, cut him loose good and proper.'

Glynis set me up with some family solicitor friend of hers from law college who dealt with all the paperwork without me having to even meet her or pay her. Some forms for me to sign, some forms sent to Mack care of M. Perez for him to sign and we were done. I was divorced, I owned the entire contents of our home and I had full custody of my children. Two weeks after the divorce was finalised my mother transferred my nana's house into my sole name.

'I didn't forget to do it before now you know. It was just that I could feel it in my water that he wouldn't stick around for ever,' she said, although not unkindly.

To begin with Mack came home to visit the boys about three times a year. He'd come for up to a week at a time, at the end of the summer season and the end of the ski season and for a few days at Christmas too. Officially he stayed with his mother but most of the time he spent with me and the boys. I didn't want us to be the kind of divorced parents that their children only ever see together for the time it takes to drop off or pick up their offspring. My aim in life was that when the boys were grown up they would be able to say 'Yeah my mum and dad were divorced but they were cool. They could still hang out together, no problem.' And so when Mack came home we spent time together as a family – went to the pictures, ate fish and chips out of the paper sitting round the kitchen table and of course we went surfing. Niall and James loved going surfing with their father and I loved watching them surf. It was easy actually to be together the four of us. Mack could be gone for months but the second he was back the boys just budged over a bit and made room for him and were not in the least resentful of his long absences. I worked hard at being resentful of him but truth was I was every bit as happy as the boys to see him again.

I never admitted it to my parents or to Glynis and Bob and Jane – I barely admitted it to myself – but Mack and I always had sex together in those early years when he came home. A lot of sex. I knew I shouldn't. I knew that Mack had made his choice in life and that I should make mine but I just couldn't. Every time I opened the door and saw him there all I wanted was to run my hands along the breadth of his shoulders and down across his tight arse and then trail them across the front of his jeans. On his first visit home after we'd put the boys to bed he'd held out his hand and I'd taken it and he'd led me upstairs to our big pine bed and that's what we did every time he came home after that. It was pathetic really only it didn't feel pathetic at the time. It just felt natural and normal and unbelievably good. I didn't ask questions and Mack said very little about what he got up to when he wasn't with us which was most of the time. I knew there'd be other women – possibly a lot of women – but I really didn't care. When he was home I just wanted to pretend that we were a proper family and Mack wanted to pretend that we were too.

The year that James turned 9 and Niall was going to be eight Mack came home for the entire six-week school holiday. I couldn't believe that he was skipping the summer camping season but he said he needed a rest and wanted to spend a chunk of time with his sons. I was glad to have him around for so long. We pretended that he slept on the sofa throughout that summer but I don't think anyone believed us. I let myself hope that perhaps finally he was done with the travelling bug and that he might come home for good but at the very end of the holidays a few days before the boys were due back at school Mack announced that he was moving to Hawaii.

'It's one of the world's best surf spots and I'm going to set up a surf shop. It doesn't take much money – couple of boards, few extra wetsuits.'

Divorced or not, I was still devastated. Mack saw the look on my face.

'Don't look like that Anna. That's why I came home this time for such a long time. So you and the boys would learn to love me again properly. Enough to want to come with me.'

I was so shocked that I couldn't say anything for a while.

'You want us to come with you?'

'Of course I do. It's what I've always wanted. To be with the three of you. Just not all cooped up here in grey, rainy, boring Stonebridge.'

'Oh.'

'Is that all you've got to say? Don't you want to be with me Anna? I love you so very much. You know that don't you?'

I did know that. I didn't think anyone else knew it or could begin to understand the relationship that Mack and I had had for so long now but I did.

'If I say no is there some other woman you'll be asking instead?'

Mack smiled. 'I'm not going to pretend that I haven't slept with other people when we've been apart. But nobody that mattered Anna. Nobody that I wanted to be with forever. Nobody like you. You have no idea just how pretty you are, Anna, which is probably one of the most attractive things about you. You used to flip-flop around that campsite in your scruffy shorts and T shirt without realizing that all the dads with the Volvos and the 2.4 children had their tongues lolling out when you walked past. We might be divorced on paper but as far as I'm concerned you are my wife Anna and you always will be. What do you say, eh? Come with me. You and the boys come with me and we'll live near the beach in Hawaii and we'll surf every single day for the rest of our lives.'

I think he knew all along I wouldn't go. I didn't even need to tell him out loud. All I needed was to look at him.

'OK then, Anna. I understand. Once I'm in Hawaii it'll be a lot more difficult for me to get here. I won't be able to visit you and the boys as often from there. And I think that perhaps we both need to stop this thing you and I have got going on, for both our sakes. Do you agree?'

I still didn't say anything, just nodded at him, knowing that if I opened my mouth I would howl.

'I'll leave tomorrow then. No point stringing it out. I was going to stick around a few more weeks, help you and the boys pack up but it seems like that won't be necessary.'

I started to cry then, tears spilling down my cheeks. He

came over to me and held me tight and we stood together like that for a while. When finally I moved away a little, he looked down at me and kissed me. A gentle kiss, at first, that got harder.

'So lovely girl. How about it? Shall you and me skip the light fandango together one last time before I go. For old time's sake?' He reached up beneath my shirt and undid my bra in one go and that made me smile and then I took the hand he was holding out to me and followed him upstairs to bed.

Even though I cried all the way through, that was some of the best sex that Mack and I ever had which is saying something because we never ever had bad sex, not once. The second time we made love he cried too and then finally we fell asleep in each other's arms. When I woke up he was already gone and I was pregnant with Lois.

Chapter 27

James

I know that note from Amy means I should wait patiently for her to call me. Sleep off my bad head and scrub the nasty taste out of my mouth and wait for her to call. Only I can't. I can't hang around here all day waiting for her to phone me. I'll go off my head.

So I get myself another tube pass thing and I find my way to Amy's college. It's not that hard really. London seems big and confusing if all you do is follow someone around who already knows their way but actually all you need is one of those tube maps. Not exactly rocket science but I'm still pretty chuffed with myself when I walk through the doors of Amy's college. I'm all ready with some story for the bouncers on the gate about how I've lost my student pass, the one Amy said I would need to get in, only there aren't any bouncers and nobody pays a blind bit of notice to me as I walk in.

It's a big place this university. Lots of corridors and passageways and it's a jumble of new buildings and old buildings that don't really go together very well. Like someone decided one day that this was a good place for a university and just joined together a bunch of buildings that happened to be lying around with a couple of connecting corridors. Anyway, I walk around in there for ages trying not to look suspicious and mostly getting lost. There are students everywhere – all colours, all sizes – and they're all on their way somewhere, threading their way through this maze of corridors, like a colony of ants. I feel horribly empty and lonely because I'm not a member of this colony and I don't know anyone. I don't belong here. But the person I belong with, she does belong here, and I've got to find her. Got to tell her I'm sorry – sorry for being such a tit, for being rude to her new friend, for getting drunk, for snoring. This apology is building up in my chest and I've just got to get it out of me. I know I'll feel better then.

I traipse through different bars and cafes and finally I get in a lift and go to the fifth-floor bar. It's got amazing views over the river and for a while I just look out of the window. I don't see Amy straight away. She's tucked into a corner and she doesn't see me either. She doesn't see me because she's too busy being kissed by Inigo. She's got her feet up on a glass table and there's a drink in front of her – what looks like a vodka even though it's only just after lunch – and he's holding the back of her head with one hand and she's flopped into him like she's drugged or something.

I feel like I've turned to lead, that if I tried to walk I'd be like one of the monsters in Transformers or something, like the whole floor would shudder with every heavy step I take. For some reason I think about the boys from the Lemon Curry Drinking Parlour and what they would have done if they'd found someone else kissing their girlfriend, down there under the leaves with the little stream babbling past. I know they would have punched him. Punched him really hard. Would have rammed Inigo's poncy little bracelets down his throat. But instead I stay there, my leaden feet rooted to the spot, and I just stare. I stare and stare until they stop kissing and take a swig of their drinks and smile and laugh at each other and then finally Amy sees me.

She has the decency to look gutted. Gutted and guilty and a bit frightened. Inigo just smiles at me in what I swear is a smug kind of way and my legs stop feeling like lead and I feel this anger rising in me, red hot lava that makes my cheeks hot and my fists curl in tight, all by themselves.

Amy rushes over to me.

'James, we need to talk. Let's go downstairs.'

I say nothing and somehow she manoeuvres me into a lift and then all of a sudden we're down at ground level and she's marching me away from the university down towards the river to some dusty little triangle of a park with a few benches, surrounded with iron railings. There's a tramp asleep on one of the benches and all the others are surrounded with fag ends, from all the people in the offices round about who slope down here to smoke secretly like junkies.

We sit down on a bench as far away as possible from the tramp.

'I'm sorry, James. I'm really sorry. I didn't mean you to find out this way.'

It's only then that the penny finally drops. Amy isn't going to beg my forgiveness for being kissed by Inigo. She isn't going to tell me it was a one off – that she was mad at me for being rude to him or for getting drunk and that she doesn't know what came over her, she's really sorry and it'll never happen again – Amy is going to dump me. She is going to dump me for some posh kid with flyaway hair who wears bracelets.

'Why did you let me come up here this week, Amy? When you were with Inigo already?' It kills me to have to say his stupid name out loud.

She says nothing so I squeeze her knee. I do it hard. I know it will hurt.

'I didn't know.'

'What do you mean you didn't know? You didn't know you were with him?'

'I didn't know which one of you I wanted.'

'Do you know now?'

'Yes.'

'And?'

She looks at me, cocks her head slightly to one side, screws her mouth up in a way which could be pity but which could just as easily be contempt.

'Say it Amy. Say it out loud. You owe me that much.'

'Inigo. It's Inigo I want.' And then, like she hasn't already spelled it out loud and clear. 'It's not you, James.'

'So why fuck me all week like it was me you wanted. Why fuck me at all?'

'You make me sound like a slag!'

'And you're not?'

'No I'm not James. Whenever I'm with you again I get confused. I go back to being the person I was before I came to London and that person, that other person, she

263

loves James. But the person I am here? Well...' Amy drops her head. 'Well she's not certain that she loves Inigo yet but she is certain that she doesn't love you like she used to.'

'But you do love me?'

'Of course I love you. You are my first love. Part of me will always love you.'

'If you love me and you're not certain you love Inigo then we can still make it work, can't we? You and me. The two of us together.' I catch hold of her hands, try to pull her towards me, but she pulls away.

'You need to understand something James. You and I are over. Last night, when I finally saw the two of you together, in the same room at the same place, that's when I knew that it was well and truly over. I don't want to be some sort of two-timing cow, James. That's not what I'm about. I've been unfair to you and I've been unfair to Inigo and like I've said already, I've made my choice. It's him I want.'

'Did you go to his place after you left me last night? Have sex with him?'

'There's no point in even answering that question James. What good is it going to do anyone?'

'I don't care if it's not going to do me any good, Amy. I need to know the answer.'

'In that case, yes. Yes I did.'

'And how do we compare, Inigo and me? Which one of us is better?'

'It's not a case of being better James. It's just different.'

'So you're binning me just for different sex?'

'It's not about the sex James. '

264

'What is it about, then?'

'James why are you torturing yourself like this? Why are you torturing me like this?'

Amy starts to cry and the tramp wakes up, looks over at us briefly, then closes his eyes again.

'I'm not trying to torture anyone. I'm just trying to understand. I love you. You say you love me. I don't understand why you're ending it for some posh knobhead who doesn't know you like I do.'

'He knows me in a different way James and that's the point. He knows a different Amy. A grown-up one. And I like the way I feel when I'm with him but when I'm with you what I feel is responsible. Guilty for leaving you back in school when I came up here. You're on the phone to me constantly, texting and ringing, and I don't want that anymore. I want the life I've got here.'

'So that's it. You're chucking everything that we had away. Just like that.'

'It's not just like that. I've been struggling with this for a while now. And anyway, what we had James was first love. First loves never last. Everyone knows that. They're special and everything but they always come to an end.'

'Is that what you lot in there tell yourselves when you're busy dumping your girlfriends and boyfriends from home? Is that what Inigo tells you?'

'Inigo had a girlfriend back home for a long time. They made it all the way to the second year but then it ended. It's what happens. I'm sorry James. Really I am. I didn't mean to hurt you. I'm going back to college now – I've got a lecture. I'll see you around Stonebridge some time, OK?'

'What about your stuff back at Glynis' flat. Don't you need to come round to pick it up?'

'I took everything with me last night, James.'

And now she's gone and it's just me and the tramp left in the park and I want to curl up on my bench just like he has on his and go to sleep too.

I sit there for a long time. A very long time. By 5pm the park starts to fill up. The working day is ending and people are cutting through this little park to get to the tube. Other people are stopping for a while for a coffee or a can of coke or another fag before facing the journey home. The tramp picks himself up and moves off somewhere quieter. I know I need to get off my arse too and go somewhere. Anywhere. I can't sit here all night. But I just haven't got the energy. If I got a move on I could get the Megabus home, be back in Stonebridge before midnight. Could sleep in my own bed. But then I'd have to tell my mother what's happened and I can't do that. Not yet. I need to get things straight in my own head before I can face my mother. Because right now if I see my mother, if she holds out her arms to me and calls me her lovely boy, I'll cry.

I walk out of the park and join the rush of commuters and students and tourists disappearing down the hole of Temple tube station.

Chapter 28

Glynis' mother Eileen was surprised to see me back so early from my night out with Glynis in Cardiff.

'You're never back already? I didn't expect you until the small hours, thought I'd be fast asleep on your sofa long before you got home. Niall hasn't long been in bed himself. What's wrong? Didn't you have a good time?'

'We had a great time thanks Eileen, it's just that we're getting on a bit now Glynis and me. We can't take the pace any more. Come on now, time to go. Glynis has got the taxi running outside to take you home and you don't even want to begin to know how much the fare is already.'

Eileen scurried off to join her daughter in the waiting taxi. I waved them both good night and went upstairs to bed, but even though I was very tired I could not get off to sleep. I kept thinking about Frank asking me to dance. Fancy that! Frank was capable of being nice. Frank had never knowingly been nice to me ever before. And what a good dancer he was too. That was a turn up and a half for the books. When I finally drifted off it was to a long dream of Frank and me dancing at the Central Park Bar until they called last orders when my beautiful new red dress suddenly transformed into my old Boots uniform.

Niall was not at all happy at my going out again the

next day.

'But I don't want to go to Gran and Granddad's,' he whined. 'I'm not a baby like Lois.'

'Less of the baby please, young man,' Lois said, unperturbed.

'You see? You see what I have to put up with from her? Why can't I stay home? I'm old enough to look after myself.'

'Because if I leave you here by yourself, you'll be on the PlayStation all day with Bartley and not do any work for your GCSEs. Granddad is going to set you one of his tests.'

'Might as well shoot me now,' Niall groaned, hanging his head in his hands.

'You'll enjoy it once you're there,' I soothed. 'And Gran's cooking Sunday lunch for us all tomorrow, roast potatoes, Yorkshire puds, the lot.' I used the fleeting appeasement the promise of gravy provided to steer them both into the car and drive them over to my parents.

When Jane throws a party, Jane throws a party. She'd said it was just going to be a little barbecue but by the time I got there, early as instructed, Jane was in full corporate event catering mode. A barbecue round my house involves a few sausages and some burgers. At Jane's it involves marinating and lots of different fancy salads in wooden bowls and home-made bread rolls.

'Jesus, Jane, is one of us getting married and you didn't tell me?'

'Very funny Anna. If something's not worth doing properly it's not worth doing at all. Now take this through

268

to Bob will you – he's been shouting at me to fetch him a glass of wine this past half an hour.' She handed me one of Bob's half-pint glasses of wine complete with straw and I knocked gently on his door.

'About bloody time! What's a bloke got to do around here nowadays to get a drink! Have I got to get up and walk or perform some other kind of miracle! Oh, sorry Anna, I thought you were Jane. I wouldn't have been quite as rude to you.'

'Don't hold back on my account.' I handed him his glass and he took a big sip.

'That's better! Whose ruddy idea was this barbecue anyway? Totally cut across my Saturday morning. She's been up since 6am running the Hoover over and banging away in the kitchen like a banshee.'

'Nothing to do with me Bob. One hundred per cent Jane's idea. Don't go blaming me.'

'I'm only kidding. I'm looking forward to it. It's nice to have an excuse to get everyone round. Daniel and Rhys are coming too with their blonde girlfriends – I wouldn't admit this to either of them but I can't actually tell which of those girls is which and I haven't seen Graham and Cassie for ages. And you know how I love to tease Glynis.'

'Oh I know, I know.' Bob and Glynis' runs in were legendary, ranging from Glynis' betrayal of Aneurin Bevan by getting private medical insurance to the veniality of the British judiciary. They loved nothing better than getting stuck into a good ding-dong and using really long words.

'Where is she anyway?' Bob asked. 'Isn't La Femme

Glynis required to turn up early for kitchen duties like you are?'

'She's on her way, don't worry.'

I went back to in the kitchen but Jane dispatched me to the garage to fetch wine glasses. I say garage but no car has ever been kept in there because Jane uses the space for her catering business. There are three huge chest freezers in there and two fridges. Open storage cupboards line the walls, some packed with industrial quantities of tinned tomatoes, olive oil, pasta and rice in tall glass jars; others stacked with giant saucepans, baking trays, boxes of glasses and china. Jane buys odd plates in junk shops and at car boot sales, it doesn't matter what pattern so long as the plates are bone china and beautiful, and one of her trademarks is serving her lovely food on lovely plates that don't match. I would never tell Jane but these solo plates make me feel kind of sad – I wonder what happened to their mates, whether they were once part of a wedding service perhaps, a big matching crowd that over the years got dropped or developed cracks until finally the last surviving pieces were no longer wanted and given to the charity shop.

I collected two plastic boxes of wine glasses and took them into the kitchen to polish them. Jane insists on wine glasses being polished. I think this is a total waste of time since they're about to get all greasy and lipsticky anyway but I do things Jane's way so long as there is Jane's food at the end of it. I had worked my way methodically through an entire box and one big glass of white wine before Glynis arrived, as always with a swagger and a bottle in each hand.

'Stop drinking the flat stuff. Let's get busy with the fizzy,' she announced.

There is no better sound in the world than the pop of a Champagne cork. Glynis insisted on taking a glass through to Bob and without even needing to be told she poured it into a half-pint glass to take it through to him. I could hear the two of them in there laughing while I polished another dozen glasses. Somehow she persuaded him to get in his wheelchair and come out to the kitchen to observe the polishing.

'This looks marvellous Jane,' Glynis said, pinching a big lump of feta and a black olive out of one of the wooden bowls and popping them in her mouth. 'Delicious! Shall I take you for a spin in the garden Mr Price?'

And off they went, leaving Jane and me to pile marinated lamb chops, home-made burgers and skewers of organic chicken onto trays.

'The others should be arriving any minute now, Anna. Will you listen out for the doorbell while I nip upstairs to get changed?'

'No problem.'

The doorbell rang a few minutes later but when I opened the door it wasn't who I was expecting. It was a man, tall and fair haired, wearing a blue, open-necked shirt and a charcoal grey suit. He was carrying a big bag of ice over his shoulder.

'Hi. Jane asked me to bring over some ice so here it is.'

'OK, great.' I reached out to take the ice from him.

'I'll drop it into the kitchen for you. It's quite heavy. Is Jane around?' and with that he somehow managed to squeeze past me. I followed him into the kitchen and watched as he placed the bag of ice on the draining board.

'Ooh Champagne!' he said. 'I love Champagne.'

I had no idea who he was and was not about to offer him a glass. 'Jane's just getting changed. Shall I tell her who's here?'

'Just a friend doing a favour,' he said mysteriously, staring out the garden at where Bob and Glynis were sitting, chatting animatedly. Somehow Bob and Glynis sensed they were being watched. They looked up, stared at the bloke for a while, but then when they didn't recognise him went back to their conversation. It looked as if Bob was giving Glynis a good listening to.

'I guess that's Bob out there is it?' he asked.

I noticed that he had very delicate, fine-boned hands and was wearing a chunky, expensive-looking silver watch that looked far too heavy for his wrists. Like he'd borrowed his dad's or something.

'Not many other men who live here use a wheelchair. I'll see you out shall I?' I said pointedly.

Reluctantly he made his way to the door. He hovered for a while at the bottom of the stairs.

'Look, do you need to see Jane before you go?' I asked

'I'll catch up with her another time. Just let her know I delivered the ice as asked will you?'

As I opened the door to let him out, Cassie and Graham were arriving. Cassie was carrying an enormous strawberry pavlova and Graham was laden down with a box of lager and two bottles of wine.

'Quick. Let me through before I drop our dessert!' Cassie giggled. By the time they were in the house the man had disappeared.

I poured Champagne for Cassie and Graham and told them to go out to the garden to join Bob and Glynis. I told them I would come out in a bit, that I was waiting for Daniel and Rhys to arrive, but really I wanted to ask Jane about the iceman. She finally came back down, in a waft of Nina Ricci's L'Air du Temps, her favourite perfume, and looking lovely in a cream linen pair of trousers and a pink T-shirt. I waited for a while before saying anything.

'Oh good, Cassie's made one of her legendary pavlovas. I was hoping she would.'

'Pavlova's not the only thing you got a delivery of. Some nice guy arrived with a bag of ice. Said you'd asked him to deliver it.'

Jane froze, just for a few seconds, but she definitely froze.

'They're brilliant those delivery men,' she said casually. 'Always helping me out at short notice.' She lifted her Champagne glass to her lips and drank deeply.

'Jane, I've never seen anyone who looked less like a delivery man. Who was it?'

'Just one of my suppliers.'

'Oh is that what Aidan does for you now is it Jane? Supplies you?' Jane's phone suddenly pinged loudly, notifying her of the arrival of a text.

'Did he leave the ice on the doorstep like I asked him to?'

'No Jane he did not. He breezed in here like he owned the place and had a good long look at Bob while he was at it. What the hell were you thinking of? Asking him to come to your house? Do you actually want to get caught? Is that it?'

'Of course not! I didn't ask him to come in! I just asked him to pick up some ice for me and leave it outside. I'm not that stupid!'

'You seem pretty damn stupid to me Jane. Because it's really not the done thing asking your secret lover to drop off stuff for a party he's not invited to. For heaven's sake your sons could have been here.'

'Well they're not here are they? They're late as always. I'll be more careful in future I promise.'

'You'd bloody better be.' I grabbed my drink and went out to the garden to join the others. When I looked over at the kitchen Jane was still standing at the window, phone in hand, texting furiously.

'Just look at my wife,' Bob grinned. 'She's like a teenager with that thing. I hardly ever see her without it in her hand. I've told her she'll get tennis elbow in her thumbs at this rate.'

I couldn't help myself. 'Yes,' I said. 'She's exactly like a teenager.'

Glynis looked at me, one eyebrow raised. I deliberately misinterpreted the gesture and topped up her glass. I topped Bob's up too.

'That's my girl!' Bob said appreciatively. 'Jane doesn't let me drink too much nowadays. She can't cope with the extra toilet duties.'

It's hard to get into the swing of a party when you feel angry. I tried to calm down, tried to enjoy the company of my friends and the lovely salads and wonderful pavlova but I could barely swallow I was that worked up. I could not believe that Jane could have taken such a risk. I was glad when Daniel and Rhys finally arrived with their girlfriends and the babble of noise reached a level where my own silence could go unnoticed. Jane carried on as if nothing had happened, pushing her chair up close to Bob and resting one arm on the back of his wheelchair, quietly cutting up his food for him, laughing with him as their sons told stories of their recent victories on the rugby field. Cassie got tipsy and started making her sex eyes at Graham which meant that those two would be sloping off any second to make the most of the fact that the girls were at Cassie's mum's overnight and the boys were with Pippa. I caught Glynis' eye and pinched my ear, the secret sign we had agreed on at school to let the other know when we'd had enough of the snogging parties and wanted to go home. She made her way over to me.

'Not surprised you want to go home,' she whispered to me. 'What with Mrs Perfect there acting like a porn star!'

'Leave her alone Glyn, she's only having fun. I'm a bit tired actually and I haven't got my drinking head on. Do you want to come back to the house with me to have a cup of tea?'

Glynis looked a bit sheepish. 'Actually, I've agreed to pop into the pub and say goodbye to Steve.'

'Is there something you're not telling me, Glynis?'

'No of course not. Fat barmen are not my type. I got bounced into it rather.'

'Well don't go then!'

'I said I would. I don't want to let him down.'

'You don't want to lead him on either!'

'I lead everybody on you know that. It's my modus

operandi! Anyway, I'm going back to London tomorrow morning first thing and I won't be back again for ages so he'll get the message there's nothing doing between us.'

'OK you know best. Let's leave together then. I hate all that business of saying goodbye at the end of a party.'

We thanked Jane and Bob, said goodbye to everyone and left. Glynis walked me the couple of hundred yards to my own house.

'Who was that bloke in the kitchen earlier on? Looked pretty drop-dead gorgeous. Have you got yourself a fancy man in the past few days you haven't told me about?'

'No such luck. It was some bloke from Threshers that Jane had sweet-talked into delivering some ice for her.'

'Pity. He looked like he had promise.'

'You think?'

'Yes I did. I like that nerdy intelligent blondie boy look. Sort of Milky Bar Kid all grown up.'

'Yeah well, sorry to disappoint you, he was just the Ice Delivery Kid. OK, bugger off now. Time for you to lift the fat barman's hopes only to dash them to the ground. It's been good having you home Glynis. I hope my son hasn't trashed your place while you've been here. Come home again soon eh and keep me in the loop on the sperm donor front.'

'Ciao bella.'

We hugged briefly and then I watched from my doorstep as she walked off in the direction of the pub. I wished my kids were home. All three of them.

Chapter 29

James

It's Sunday. I haven't slept and I feel like shit. My first exam is in just over a month and I need to get out of Glynis' flat and get myself to Victoria and get on the bus but I just can't face it. It's like I'm paralysed with sadness. Amy has dumped me for someone else and I couldn't give a fuck anymore about getting my A levels and getting to university because the whole point of getting to university was to be with Amy and she doesn't want to be with me anymore. She wants to be with some posh fucker with a girly name who wears bangles. And I roll over onto my side and somehow I fall asleep. I wake up when I hear the door of the flat banging. For one wonderful second I think it must be Amy, come back to tell me how she'd made a terrible mistake and actually it was me she wanted after all but the next thing I know Glynis is standing at the end of the bed.

'James! I thought you'd be long gone by now. Your mother is expecting you home today.'

She doesn't look pleased to see me. I look at her and she looks at me and I start to cry. I start to fucking cry! I'm eighteen years old and I start to blub like a baby in front of my mother's best friend.

She rushes over and sits on the edge of the bed and puts her arms around me. I'm conscious that I'm naked under the duvet and that her thigh is pressing up against my cock and that I need a pee and I've got a huge morning glory. I wiggle myself a few centimeters further back from the edge of the bed.

'What's the matter James? What's happened? You can tell me anything you know that don't you? I won't tell your mother, I promise.'

And I start to cry even harder and I tell her how Amy has dumped me and how fucking sad I feel. She strokes my hair and squeezes my shoulders and just lets me cry. I'm embarrassed but at the same time the crying feels good. Like I'm getting stuff off my chest. Off my heart. Eventually I stop crying and lie still and Glynis stops patting my hair.

'Feeling a bit better?' she asks.

I nod. 'A bit.'

'Well let's make you feel a whole lot better shall we? You go hop in the shower because, no offence, you smell a bit funky, and I'll just pop out to the shop.'

By the time she's back I'm out of the shower and dressed. I feel really foolish, like a big stupid kid. I thought she must have gone out to buy chocolate biscuits or something which is what my mother would have done but she's carrying two plastic bags full of booze. She sets them on her kitchen counter and winks at me.

'It's like 11am in the morning Glynis!' Suddenly I feel like she's the kid and I'm the grown up.

'It's actually gone two. The perfect time for someone

with a broken heart to get bladdered.'

'I need to go home. Mum will be worried about me.'

'No you don't. I rang her while I was out. Said you and Amy had tickets to go to some gig somewhere and that you'd be back tomorrow sometime.'

'Was she pissed off?'

'A bit. She'll get over it.'

'So you didn't tell her what had happened?'

'I think you'd better tell her that. When you're good and ready. Right. What will it be? A can of Bow or some wine?'

'A can of Bow please.'

She hands me one and takes one for herself even though I know she drinks wine not cider and then wanders over to her stereo and flips through her pile of CDs.

'Rock music is the best for broken hearts,' she says and cranks it up real loud. So loud it feels like the Kings of Leon are performing for us right there in the middle of the living room. It's 'Sex is on Fire' and it makes me smile.

'What are you smiling about?' she asks. 'We haven't even started on the process of healing by drinking yet.'

'Lois. She thinks this song is called 'Socks is on fire'. She says that now when she's accusing someone of lying. You know, 'Liar, liar, your socks is on fire.'

And Glynis smiles too and starts playing air guitar. When my mother does that I could die of embarrassment but Glynis doesn't look too bad. She looks pretty good actually. The two of us sing along loudly to the chorus. 'Oh oh, your socks is on fire' we sing.

Later, she teaches me drinking games. I know most of

them already but I pretend she's teaching me something new and the two of us sit there in her living room playing Fuzzy Duck and left hand drinking. I'm way better at it than her and she gets much more drunk than I do, especially after she insists we drink Blue Moons, some disgusting sweet drink that she claims used to be my Mum's favourite. I guess we're both pretty pissed because later on we play more air guitar, together this time. When a slow song comes on we do a slow dance together. She smells really good, like lemon and lime, and she feels tiny in my arms, smaller even than Amy, and I forget she's my mum's friend and I hold her tight. And she holds me tight right back.

Anna

The morning after Bob and Jane's barbecue I was awake by 7am. I'd gone to bed feeling lonely to my bones and I woke up feeling exactly the same way. I was forever moaning about the noise my kids made – the blaring TV, the arguing and bickering and never ending banging around – but I didn't like the quiet when they weren't there and I wished I hadn't accepted my mother's offer to keep Niall and Lois until after lunch. I couldn't remember the last time I'd been entirely on my own in the house. It made me feel sad and single and old and even though heaven knows my saggy skin would have thanked me for the lie in, I put on my thickest bathrobe, the chenille one that reaches from my neck to my toes and which my children say makes me look like a teddy bear – a fat teddy bear, and went downstairs to make myself a cup of tea. As I waited for the kettle to boil I made a shopping list. My children would all be back home by that evening and I decided I would make sausages and buttery mash and beans for tea and that we would eat it off our laps watching reality TV together and that made me feel happy again.

But first I needed to go to Bob and Jane's to help clear up as I'd promised Jane I would. It was barely 8am when I knocked gently on the door but I knew Jane would be long since up and champing at the bit to get her house back in order. When she didn't come to the door I knocked again a bit harder and the door swung open gently. Jane must have left it unlocked so I could let myself in. I walked into the kitchen expecting to find the coffee machine bubbling and the dishwasher already running but the blinds were closed and it was still dark.

Wow, I thought to myself. *Jane's not up yet. What do I do now – put the kettle on or come back later?*

And then I saw that Bob was asleep in the kitchen, sitting awkwardly in his wheelchair, his head lolling at an uncomfortable angle. For one horrible moment I thought he might be dead but then I heard him snoring gently. I crept over to the window and opened the blinds slowly. As the morning sun filtered into the kitchen, Bob began to stir.

'Jane? Is that you?'

'No Bob, it's me Anna. Come to help clear up. Are you OK?'

'Not really, no.' He gestured at his lap and I saw that

he had wet himself.

'OK, nothing to worry about. I'll go get Jane out of bed.'

'She's not here Anna. She's gone.'

'What do you mean she's gone?'

'She's with her lover.'

'Oh.'

'You knew about him then? I thought you must. You weren't yourself yesterday. That was one of the things that made me do it. That and that young chap staring at me from the kitchen like I was the enemy.'

'Do what Bob?' I was trying to keep calm, to speak slowly in a low voice, but inside I was panicking.

'Check her phone of course. Her precious mobile phone. She left it on the table when she went to wave the boys off.'

'Oh,' I said again, helplessly.

'Do you know what those messages were all about Anna?' I shook my head, even though I had had a fairly good idea.

'Betrayal, that's what they were about. Cold-hearted cunning betrayal. The things he was going to do to her and the things she was going to do to him. The sorts of things she used to do for me once. Before I became a big lump of useless flesh like a deadweight round her neck, dragging her down.'

I went over to him, bent down and put my arms around his neck, ignoring the strong smell of stale urine.

'Don't do this to yourself, Bob. Please.'

He pushed me away with his good hand, the one that still retained some of his former strength.

'Yes well she won't be reading those filthy messages again. I threw her bastard phone into the washing up bowl, drowned the evil thing. You should have said something to me, Anna. You knew about it. You should have told me.'

'Jane loves you, Bob, she really loves you. That's why I didn't say anything. I'm sorry.'

'It's not you that should be apologising, Anna.' It was Jane, standing at the kitchen door.

'What the fuck are you doing back?' Bob hissed at her, angrily. 'I told you to get the hell out.'

'Bob, don't be like that. We need to talk.'

'I'll leave you two alone,' I said, grabbing my bag quickly.

'You stay right there, Anna,' Bob jabbed his finger towards me. 'I want you to hear what I have to say.'

I looked at Jane. She nodded silently. I put my bag down.

'In 24 years of marriage all I have ever done is love you and fancy you, Jane. I've never even so much as looked at another woman and it's not as if I didn't have plenty of offers you know, over the years. All I ever wanted was you. You're the only woman I have wanted to sleep with since the day I met you. And if it had been you that had ended up in this wheelchair instead of me that would not have changed.'

Jane began to cry quietly. 'Bob, I'm sorry, I—'

'Let me finish, Jane. Give me that much respect at least. We've always had a wonderful sex life, you and me, and that has been a joy throughout our marriage, one of the things that made us strong. The fact that that part of our life is over has been a huge loss for me and I knew you felt that loss too. I understood that. I did. But I thought we were bigger than that, that you and me were about so much more than just sex. Our sons, this house, all those years we shared together—'

Jane hurled herself to her knees in front of the wheelchair, sobbing. 'I'm sorry Bob, please forgive me. I don't know what I was thinking. I was weak and pathetic and stupid and I'm sorry. I love you, I always have, I'll stop and never do it again and we can carry on like we always were.' She tried to take hold of his hands but he pushed her away as he had done me.

'But that's where you're wrong Jane. We can't just carry on. Because you've just pissed on everything we had together, just like I've pissed in my pants sitting here all night thinking this through. What we had together, what we had left together, wasn't enough for you. Not precious enough.'

'But it was, Bob, it is. You and me, that's what's important to me. What I want. Aidan was just, was just…'

'Just what Jane?'

'Just a distraction. You're the man I love, Bob, believe me. You're the one I want to be with, take care of, live with. Aidan means nothing to me.'

'The messages on your phone would indicate that he means rather a lot to you. That you mean rather a lot to each other.'

'That was just sex, Bob, not real life. Not like you and me. You and me are the real thing.'

'And that's what I thought Jane. That's what I've

thought for 24 years. But we're not the real thing are we? Not any more? Because you've slept with someone else. You've pressed your skin against someone else's skin and let somebody else other than me make you come. It's over, Jane. If you had fucked someone else when I was able-bodied I would have ended it and I'm not about to act differently just because I'm disabled. It's your feelings that have changed, not mine, and I will not accept second best.'

'Don't do this, Bob, please, I beg you. I love you. I always have. I would never have done this before you got ill, would never have done this to you.'

'I know that, Jane. I know that if I wasn't in this wheelchair you wouldn't have betrayed me. That's the bit that hurts the most and that's why I'm ending it. I'm setting you free, you slut. Now please, just go.'

'But you need help, you need to get out of those wet things and have something to eat. Please, Bob. Let me take care of you.'

'Jane, I'm done with this conversation. I'm done with you. Just get out will you? Anna will help me, won't you Anna?'

He looked over at me. 'Yes, yes, of course I will,' I said quickly.

Jane got to her feet, sobs wracking her body. I went with her to the front door. 'I'll sort out Bob, tidy up a bit in here, then I'll give you a call shall I?'

She nodded silently. I was about to ask her where she was going to be later but when she opened the door I saw a car parked a little way up the street. Aidan was sitting in the driver's seat looking anxious. The second he spotted

Jane coming out of the house he jumped out of the car, opened the passenger-seat door wide open for her. He was wearing jeans and a pale green T-shirt with some sort of motif on it and looked even younger than he had done the day before. I didn't even bother to watch Jane get into the car, just closed the front door quietly behind me and went to get a bowl of warm water and some flannels to clean Bob up.

Chapter 30

Between us, somehow, Bob and I managed to get him out of the wheelchair and onto his bed. I managed to keep looking straight ahead at the wall as I hoiked down his trousers and underpants and while Bob wiped himself with the flannels that I handed to him but when it came to helping him thread his feet through the legs of a clean pair of track pants it was impossible to do so without catching sight of his nakedness.

'I can take it from here thanks, Anna,' he said, curtly.

I left him to it and came back ten minutes later with a cup of tea and some toast but he was already asleep or pretending to be. For the next hour I worked hard in the kitchen, loading the dishwasher, piling a lot of empty wine bottles into Jane's recycling boxes and stacking them neatly in the utility room. I threw Bob's wet clothes and the dirty flannels into the washing machine and even though it wasn't even half full I set it going. *The environment will forgive me, this once,* I thought. That's when I spotted Jane's mobile phone and realised I would not be able to call her later after all. I fished it out of the washing-up bowl and tried to turn it on, but not surprisingly after its night in Davy Jones' locker it did not work. I slipped it in my handbag anyway. I wiped down the surfaces and threw soggy salad and greasy, congealed pork chops and lamb kebabs into a black bag and put it out the back, ready for the bin men. I wiped down Bob's wheelchair with a warm, soapy cloth and wheeled it quietly into his room for when he needed it later. Everything was shipshape. Everything was ruined. I closed the door behind me and since I had no other way of contacting Jane, I got in my car and drove to Aidan's house.

He wasn't surprised to see me.

'She's sleeping,' he said sullenly, opening his front door just a crack.

'So? Wake her up. I need to talk to her.'

'I'll get her to call you later, when she wakes up.'

'I need to talk to her now.' In a move I'd seen used to great effect on *The Bill*, I jammed my foot in the crack of the door and started shouting Jane's name. She came to the door quickly, fully dressed, obviously having not slept at all.

'Jane, can I just talk to you for a minute? In private? Please?'

Aidan grimaced at me but I ignored him. He stepped aside and let an ashen-faced, trembling Jane go past before shutting the door.

'What a fucking mess,' I said.

'A total fucking mess,' she repeated, weakly.

'What are you going to do, Jane?'

'I don't think that's any of your business, Anna.'

'Isn't it, Jane? Because I think it is. Because I'm the one who's just changed your husband like he was a baby and put him to bed. It's my business Jane because you made it my business.'

'I did nothing of the sort. That was all down to you. If you hadn't acted all strange after Aidan dropped off the ice, if you and Glynis hadn't made it your mission to pour as much Champagne down Bob as you possibly could, he would never have thought to look at my phone and then none of this would have happened.'

I hadn't hit anyone in the longest time. Not since I was about 12 and slapped Helen Davies in the mouth during Scripture class for suggesting I had bad breath, resulting in a lot of detention and huge amounts of shame. But I really wanted to slap Jane then. I could feel red heat and anger rising to a boil in my stomach and I wanted to slap her very hard across the mouth and hurt her as much as I could but I didn't. Just.

'Don't you dare lay this one at my door! Don't you dare! If you hadn't been so stupid as to ask Aidan to fetch ice for the barbecue, hadn't left your phone on the table, hadn't taken up with him in the first place – that's when none of this would have happened. Crikey Jane! You need to face up to what you've done. Take responsibility for it.'

Jane hung her head. She looked wretched. I think she would have preferred it if I had slapped her. She looked like she wanted to slap herself.

'I've really fucked up, haven't I?'

'Uh huh. But the question now is what happens next. Because Bob can't stay in that house on his own. He can't look after himself and I can only do so much to help out you know? I'm picking the kids up in an hour or so. You're going to have to work something out.'

'But you heard Bob, he's not going to forgive me. Never.'

'Never is a long time Jane. People make mistakes all the time. The people that love them forgive them those mistakes. That's how life works. But if you really want to make things right with Bob you are going to have to fight for him. Very hard. Very hard indeed.'

Jane started to cry. 'That's what I want, Anna, to make things right. To make things go back the way they were before. To be Bob's wife. That's all I want and I'm willing to fight for him, very hard like you say. If I'm going to make things right with Bob the first thing I have to do is finish it with Aidan.'

'I'll be off then and let you get on with that.' I reached into my handbag and handed Jane her phone.

'You're going to need a new one I think. Ring me if there's anything I can do or if you need me to help Bob.'

Wordlessly, she took the dead phone from me and went back into Aidan's house.

I didn't hear from Jane or Bob for the next three days which was just as well as I was busy coping with James. When I got home from work on Monday I burst into his bedroom all ready to give him a hard time about missing another day of school for the sake of a gig and for being such a coward and getting Glynis to ring me rather than doing it himself, to find him sorting through his bedroom, throwing stuff into a big black bag. I took one look at his face and I knew straightaway what had happened. James has never been able to hide anything from me. I held out my arms and he hugged me once, very hard, and then turned back to sorting his stuff.

'My poor baby. What happened?'

'Got dumped Mum. For someone older and richer and more interesting that she'd been two-timing me with for a while.'

'I'm so sorry, love. So very sorry. What a little bitch.'

'Please don't start slagging Amy off Mum. I couldn't take it. It's over. There it is. I need to deal with that. It really won't help if you start telling me how you never liked her anyway.'

I opened my mouth to say something then closed it again suddenly like a trout.

'So now I'm going to put all the stuff she ever gave me and all the photos of her and me into this black bag, and then I'm going to put it up in the loft and forget about it for a while. That OK with you?'

'Of course.' The loft was jam packed with rubbish already but I was fairly certain we could squeeze one more bin bag up there. I watched as James added a bright green toy dragon to the shirts and hoodies and books already in the black plastic bag.

'Do you want any help with that?' I asked.

'No Mum, I don't.'

'What can I do to help?'

'Nothing, there's nothing you can do.'

He was right of course but it didn't stop me fussing over him, making him his favourite meals, buying him chocolate and touching his arm all the time until he started to bat me away, like he would an annoying fly. He spent ages locked away in his bedroom and when I asked him what he was doing he told me he was studying because it was even more important now that he did well in his exams because he was buggered if he was going to do less well than Amy had. I couldn't say fairer than that so I left him to it but my heart ached for my little boy.

That's not to say it didn't ache for Bob and Jane too. It did. It even ached a bit for Aidan who, from our limited contact, appeared to really care for Jane but I figured he'd get over it soon enough. As far as Bob and Jane were concerned my plan of action was to do nothing, wait to hear from them, and then, when I did, act as if nothing had happened.

But that proved not to be possible. Wednesday lunchtime Jane came into the estate agency.

'Have you got time for a chat, Anna?' She looked ten years older than she had when I saw her last, her skin grey and her eyes small and puffy from crying. Frank was out and even though I knew I'd be in trouble if he came back to find the place locked up, I grabbed my keys.

'Let's go sit by the river shall we? It's quiet and peaceful down there.'

We walked in silence down to the riverbank until we got to the bench were Mack and I had spent so much time snogging. I thought to myself as I sat down that when I died someone should get an inscription done on this bench. *In memory of Anna Lewis, 1970 to 2050, who spent many long happy hours on this bench.*

I waited for Jane to speak. Eventually she did.

'I did what you said, Anna. I fought for him; I fought for him really hard. But there's no point. He won't have me back, Anna. Not under any circumstances. It's over.'

It was not what I'd been hoping to hear. What I'd hoped for was a request to say nothing to anybody about what happened, to come round for dinner some time soon and be the same way I'd always been, that we could all carry on as if nothing had changed.

'He'll come round eventually, I'm sure. Give him some time Jane. It's going to take a while.'

'He's not going to come round, Anna. He's told Daniel and Rhys what's happened and neither of them is talking to me either. They've got Bob into a respite care home for the time being. He says he couldn't possibly live under the same roof as me.'

'That's what he says now. He'll change his mind.'

'No he won't, Anna.' Jane's tone of voice was short and harsh, like a parent telling a child not to touch the oven door because it's hot. 'It gets worse. I've already had a letter from Melanie Farrell, starting divorce proceedings for adultery.'

I was fighting back tears at this point. I couldn't believe what I was hearing. How final things sounded. 'That's madness. It's way too soon for either of you to be making decisions like that. Isn't there something you can do? Counselling or marriage guidance or something?'

'I've suggested all that, so have social services. He won't listen.'

'You seem very calm.'

'I'm cried out, Anna. I've cried and I've begged and I've pleaded and I've cried some more. Believe me, I'm not calm. I'm just physically and emotionally knackered.'

'What about Aidan?'

'What about him? I cut him dead. He was upset but he took it pretty well. It's too late to save my marriage but I am hoping I can salvage some sort of relationship with my sons. Even though at the moment they both say they don't want anything to do with me because I cheated on their dad with someone closer in age to them than to me.' Jane smiled ruefully. 'Nothing like having your life whipped away from under your feet for making you act sensibly eh?'

'I guess not. Is there anything I can do?'

'Will you be there for Bob? I'm not suggesting you try to talk him out of it or anything. I don't think there's any point or else I would have asked you before now. But will you call on him; help him if he needs anything? I'm worried about him.'

'Of course I will. That's if it's OK with you? You know how these things are. People usually have to choose whether they side with the woman or the man.'

'I hope it won't come to that.'

'It won't. Look, I'd better get back to the office before Frank gets back. Do you want to come round tonight? Or any other night? You know there's always a welcome for you at my house.'

'I know that thanks, Anna, but I need to be on my own right now. What was it you said I needed to do? Face up to what I had done and take responsibility for it? Well I'm doing that right now and it's better I do it on my own.'

Chapter 31

The next few weeks were tough. James spent the whole time holed up in his bedroom, studying until the early hours. He was hardly sleeping or eating and had big bags under his eyes. Even though his A levels were just a couple of weeks away and I should have been glad he was working so hard, I was sick with worry for him. The way he was working just wasn't normal. I wished Niall was working even a tenth as much. I'd taken the PlayStation off him and hidden it in my desk at work, and put a total embargo on Bartley coming round, in the hope this would make him study a bit more but nothing seemed to be working.

When I wasn't worrying about my sons and their lack or excess of studying, I was worrying about Bob and Jane. I tried to arrange to visit Bob but when I rang the hospice I was told that Bob didn't want to see me, not for the moment at least, and Jane had gone into organisational overdrive. She was getting the house ready to put on the market and she spent every minute she wasn't catering cleaning and tidying and weeding and scrubbing so that it would be more desirable to potential purchasers.

'Why are you doing this Jane?' I asked when I called round to check on her which I did most evenings. 'This is your home. You love this house. Bob loves this house.

Don't you think it would be better for both of you not to rush into things, wait a bit until everyone's calmed down?'

'It's Bob that's in the rush, not me. Melanie Farrell says he wants the divorce finalised as soon as possible and this place sold quickly so that he can get a proper place to live. I'm hoping that if I do what he wants maybe Daniel and Rhys will speak to me again.'

Jane's sons had been steadfast in their refusal to have anything to do with their mother. Neither of them would take her calls and when she called round to see them they had shut the door in her face. Daniel's girlfriend had called Jane in the end and said she should just back off for a while – that the boys were very hurt and angry and were supporting their father and that Jane should just stop pestering them.

'They'll get over this,' I tried to reassure her. 'You're their mother. They know how much you love them and they love you. It's just going to take some time, that's all.'

'I hope so Anna. I really hope so. And in the meantime getting this place ready to sell is keeping me busy and I really need to keep busy right now because if I stop to think I just fall apart.'

'Have you thought about keeping the house on yourself? Buying Bob out? You've got a good business, make decent money. Could you afford that?'

'You of all people Anna know how high house prices have got round here. This house is worth twenty times what Bob and I paid for it. I can't afford to buy him out. I wish I could but I can't. The best thing now is to sell and sell quickly.'

I knew that was not going to be a problem. Jane had insisted that Frank deal with the sale. I would have preferred it if Jane had used another estate agent but she was adamant.

'I'm instructing Frank on condition that you are the one that does the viewings. I want it to be you showing people round, not some stranger.'

Frank didn't seem to mind Jane's stipulation.

'That's fine. You know that house anyway, you'll be able to do the sales spiel better than me and that'll get it sold that much quicker. I'll get a nice little fee out of that one.'

You're a tight bastard, I thought to myself, *even if you do dance like a dream.* Neither of us had so much as mentioned our random night out together since.

'One other thing, Anna. Make sure Jane gets herself a good solicitor,' Frank said, not unkindly. 'A really good one. Or else Melanie will have her for breakfast.'

I hated to think that Melanie Farrell knew the whole sad story. When I saw her now, trotting down the high street on her Jimmy Choos I wanted to shoulder barge her skinny little arse to the floor. And of course Jane was refusing to get legal advice. She was convinced that not putting up a fight and giving Bob everything he wanted was the way to redeem herself in the eyes of her sons. He wanted a quick sale and a quick sale was what he was going to get. Bob and Jane's house was within walking distance of the high street, beautifully presented and of the highest decorative order, in the catchment area for the good schools of Stonebridge and competitively priced. That's what Frank's particulars said and for once it was all true. Dozens of people had shown interest and there had been one or two viewings a day. I hated showing people round and did it with little enthusiasm but people loved the house anyway. I knew we would have an offer at the asking price within the month.

I tried to prepare Jane. 'What are you going to do when the house is sold Jane? Where will you live?'

'I'll rent somewhere I guess. Shouldn't be too difficult.'

'There's not that many good rentals come up round here you know? People mostly buy in Stonebridge.'

'I really don't care where I live Anna.' She really didn't. I was fairly certain that she was going to give Bob every penny of equity in the house and would end up living in some nasty, tatty rented flat with no money, just to punish herself even further.

'You've got your business to think about Jane. You need somewhere where you can cook, with big freezers like you have now at home. I mean, some landlords might not be willing for you to run a business from a rented property.'

'Then I'll only do small jobs for a while, no weddings or buffets. None of it matters any more anyway.'

I had no option but to bring in the big guns and call Glynis. She was not amused.

'You mean to say this all happened after the barbecue and you're only now telling me?'

'Well I was hoping nothing would come of it and they'd patch things up and I wouldn't have to tell you but Frank says Jane needs a good lawyer to combat Melanie Farrell and I reckon you'll be able to—'

'Whoa! Back up there a bit. Frank says Jane needs a good lawyer? Frank says? You mean Frank knew about 'my friends getting divorced before I did?'

'Well he knows they've separated. He doesn't know why or anything.'

'So I'm the one you phone when you suspect Jane of having an affair but then when you turn out to be right you tell Frank but not me?'

'It wasn't like that Glynis! Jane was putting the house on the market. Frank had to know.'

'Just because he whisks you off to the dance floor to save you the embarrassment of watching the bloke you fancied trying to cop off with me does not mean he's your best friend all of a sudden.'

'You can be a childish bitch sometimes you can Glynis. Frank is not my best friend all of a sudden. Are you going to help Jane or what?'

'Shit! What was she thinking of? The stupid cow – the first rule of adultery is not getting caught out. And what's Bob playing at, getting all high and mighty over Jane doing something with someone else that he can't do with her any more anyway. Christ – he didn't throw her out because she went for a walk every now and then with you did he?'

'I don't think sex is quite the same as going for an evening stroll.'

'Who says it isn't Anna? It's just something that people do together every now and then. Like going to the pictures or out for dinner. I've had sex with lots of married men, really very good sex, and then they've gone back home to their wives and stayed very happily married, thank you very much. What the eye doesn't see, the heart doesn't grieve over. Jane should have been more careful and then she could have had her Milky Bar kid and eaten him.'

'Glynis, do you know any good divorce lawyers or don't you?'

'You know I do. Sorted you out didn't I? I know divorce lawyers that'll have Melanie Farrell's guts for garters.'

'Could you send me their names please? So I can tell Jane?'

'I'll tell her myself. I'm going to come home this weekend and talk some sense into her, get her to stop the sackcloth and ashes routine and start taking control of her life. Can I come straight to you when I arrive Friday night?'

'Of course you can but are you sure Glynis? You were only home a few weeks ago. You could just give Jane a talking to over the phone. Or have you got an ulterior motive for visiting? A barman to visit perhaps?'

'Don't you so much as breathe a whisper to Steve that I'm coming back,' Glynis hissed at me. 'He's been calling and texting me non stop and it's only after total radio silence from me that he's finally getting the message I'm just not interested.'

Poor bar steward, I thought, as I put the phone down.

I told James that Glynis was coming to visit on Friday and that it was his turn to be turfed out of his room because Niall had obliged last time.

'Whatever,' he said. I'd expected him to kick up a fuss but he even tidied his room and put the Hoover over.

'It's only Glynis you know. Not Cheryl Cole coming to stay,' I muttered.

He didn't even go out on Friday night.

'Aren't you going out with your mates? You've done more than enough work this week. You deserve a night out.'

'Nah! Can't be bothered. Thought I'd stay in with you.'

I was seriously worried about him. Since Amy had dumped him all he'd done was work and mope and now he didn't even want to go out on a Friday night like any normal teenager but hang around the house with his mother. I wondered whether perhaps I should take him to the doctor's. Perhaps he wasn't just sad about Amy. Perhaps it was more serious than that and his sadness had crossed over into depression.

James

I'm trying really hard not to show Mum how excited I am about Glynis coming. I mean, I've always been happy enough to see her whenever she's been here before but things are different now. Very different. Glynis isn't just my mum's friend any more but Mum is never going to understand that.

I've still been feeling really bummed about what happened with Amy. She's texted me a few times, asking if I'm OK, which I think is a bloody cheek. She breaks my heart then wants to know if I'm feeling OK, probably because she's spending all day having sex with bangle boy and doesn't want to let feeling guilty about me spoil her fun. I haven't texted her back. She can sod off.

What I am going to do though is get better A level grades than she did. I know that's not much in the way of revenge but I know Amy. It'll piss her off if I do better than she did. After she told me about Inigo, I could easily have just given up. A levels, going to university, all of that seemed pretty pointless. But what Glynis said made total sense. Glynis said that throwing the towel in would be letting Amy win, letting Inigo win, and that what I needed to do was channel all the time I used to spend thinking about Amy and online with Amy and on the phone with Amy into my work. That way I was bound to do better than she did. So that's what I'm doing. The exams are not far away now, just a few weeks. I can keep this up that long.

Hasn't stopped me thinking about sex, of course. But now when I'm wanking I don't think about Amy or any of the girls in my porno mag. I think about Glynis. How she smells. How she looks when she plays air guitar and how her hair whips around her head. How small and light she is. What she looks like when she's sleeping.

Only when she arrives Glynis acts like nothing has changed. She waves her hand at me, asks how I'm bearing up? How's the studying going? And then she goes off to the kitchen with Mum and they close the door behind them. I can hear them talking away in there, yackety yak yak like they always do. I wait for a bit then go in and pretend I want a cup of tea. Mum tells me she'll make it for me and to go make myself comfy on the sofa in the living room and then Glynis says not to worry, she can't stay overnight with us anyway and comes out with some story that she's got to stay with her parents because

302

she's taking her mother shoe shopping first thing in the morning so there's no need for me to sleep on the sofa. Like I was planning on sleeping on the sofa anyway.

Anna

'So, how is everyone coping?' Glynis asked as soon as the kitchen door was safely shut.

'Not so well if I'm honest. Jane is up till midnight every night scrubbing her bathroom tiles, James is a long streak of misery who studies too hard, Niall doesn't seem to be studying at all and Bob refuses to talk to anyone.'

'And what about you?'

'I'm worn out with worrying about them all.'

'Well that's not going to do anyone any good is it? You need to think about yourself from time to time. How are your birthday party plans going?'

'Oh, I'm going to cancel that. It doesn't seem right to have a party now after all that's happened.'

'What do you mean, all that's happened? An eighteen year old getting dumped? Forty somethings getting divorced? A few exams that will all be over before your party? That's life Anna. Life is what has happened. And your life is turning forty and we need to celebrate that. Big style. None of the people you are worrying about are going to thank you for cancelling your party so do yourself a favour and don't.'

'Well, Jane was going to cater for me. She's not going to want to do that now is she?'

'Who says? She'll probably be glad of something else to do rather than being on her hands and knees with Mr Muscle. And even if she doesn't want to cater, so what? I'll drive down to Culverhouse Cross on the morning of your party and buy up Marks and Spencer's entire stock of sandwiches and Scotch eggs. Nobody's going to care about the food. Everyone just needs a chance to let their hair down. You most of all.'

'You do know it's at Steve's pub don't you? I thought you were avoiding him.'

'I am. But only for a bit. He's stopped texting me now anyway. I'll be able to flirt with him again by the time of your party without him thinking I'm applying for the vacancy of wife.'

'Well, I'll think about it. It would be nice to have something to look forward to I must say. I could wear the red dress you bought me.'

'Yes, wear that. It'll distract Steve's attention. All the men's attention come to think of it,' she grinned.

'Gosh Glynis you've been here a full ten minutes and haven't demanded wine yet. And you need to tell me how you're getting on with the sperm donor thing. Do you want white or red?'

'Do you know what? I'm quite tired. It was a long drive home tonight. Friday nights getting out of London are hell. I'm going to push off to Mum and Dad's if that's OK with you.'

'Of course. You go. You can fill me in on Thor and his wriggly mates tomorrow. See you at 1pm at Jane's? Is that what we agreed?'

'Yep, see you there. Good night Anna Banana.'

Glynis rapped loudly on James' door on her way out but didn't open it, just shouted out to him, 'Keep on truckin' in there,' and then she was gone.

Chapter 32

Subtlety is not Glynis' strong point. As soon as Jane opened the door she was off,

'Really sorry to hear about you and Bob. You were my favourite married couple, by a very long way. Still, you're getting yourself a solicitor, like it or not. Here are her details. I've told her you'll be getting in contact on Monday and I've negotiated a 15 per cent discount on her fees. Are you still going to cater Anna's party for her because she says she's thinking of cancelling it?'

'Come in Glynis. Nice to see you Glynis. Why don't you mind your own bloody business Glynis.'

'That's my girl,' Glynis said. 'Got a bit of your fighting spirit back, that's what we like to see. First step to getting up off the door mat. So you fucked some young hottie? So what? Shit happens. People cheat on people for lot less reason than you had, Jane. For absolutely no reason at all.'

Jane sighed. 'Glynis, I know you're being nice, trying to let me off the hook, but actually I regret what I did. It came at far too high a price. I miss Bob so much I could die and I don't miss Aidan at all – not one iota – and I truly cannot believe what possessed me to throw my entire life away to "fuck some young hottie" as you so eloquently put it. I will phone this solicitor of yours

I promise, but only because Melanie Farrell is insisting I take legal advice too and that I'm slowing things down by not doing so, and yes of course I'm still going to cater for your birthday party Anna – what do you think's been keeping me going in the evenings these past few weeks? You'd better have a lot of guests because I've got a lot of food in those freezers of mine.'

I went up to Jane and put my arms around her. 'I'd like to apologise for our mutual friend. She likes to tell it how it is even if we'd prefer not to hear it.'

'That's OK. Believe me, no one can make me feel any worse than I feel already.'

'So, what have you made us for lunch?' Glynis asked. 'I'm starving.'

'Come on through, girls. I've got a fresh herb and onion tart to start, served with a green side salad and a walnut-oil dressing, followed by baked salmon, carrots and mange tout and to finish home-made honey ice cream served with home-made shortbread biscuits.'

'Have I ever told you how much I love you?' Glynis said as we followed Jane through to the kitchen. 'I mean, really love you?'

James

Glynis didn't come back with Mum after the lunch with Jane.

'Glynis not with you?' I asked when she got back, keeping my voice light, like I didn't care.

'No, she had to go straight back to London. She got a call to go work on some super urgent trillion dollar deal or something.'

'Pity.'

'Yes. But I'm helping Niall study tonight so it's just as well really.'

I texted Glynis, three or four times, told her there was something I needed to discuss with her. Eventually, hours later, she texted me back.

I love you too Jimmy Boy, you and Niall and Lois. You're like family. Call you later in the week, in work right now.

In the end, because I didn't know what else to do, I sat down at my computer and emailed my dad and for the first time since I was a little boy I asked him for his advice.

Anna

I was sitting at my desk on Monday morning, just about to get started on sending off all the particulars that people had asked for at the weekend, when the offer came in on Jane's house. It was for the full asking price, cash buyer, looking for a speedy completion.

'Are you sure?' I asked Frank.

'Of course I'm bloody sure. I never get it wrong where cash buyers are in the question. SSTC. Job done.'

I phoned Jane to break the news to her but she already knew. 'Frank called me a few minutes ago. It's OK. I'm pleased. Really I am. It's what Bob wants.'

'Shall I start keeping an eye out for good rentals?'

'That would be a great help, thank you.'

I spent the whole of that afternoon trawling through the internet and ringing up rental agencies but found absolutely nothing that would come close to suiting Jane. Annoyingly, Frank was in the office all afternoon and every time he got up to go to the toilet or the photocopier or fetch something from the filing cabinet I quickly minimised the websites I was looking at and pretended to be typing up particulars.

'Are you looking for somewhere for Jane to live on my time Anna?'

'Of course I'm not. I'm typing up poxy sales particulars for you.'

'Good. Because you'd be wasting my time. The buyer for Jane's house called me earlier. They're a property company and this is an investment purchase. They've asked me if I can help them find a tenant. They want a pretty steep rent of course – that house is in great decorative order – but I think I know someone who might be interested.'

He grinned at me, a cheeky, little boy.

'Off you go then. Get yourself round there and tell her the good news. £1000 a month rent mind, plus a month's bond.'

I grabbed my bag and was out the door before he could change his mind.

'You're kidding me?' Jane could not believe what I was telling her. 'Bob gets his money but I still get to live in my house.'

'Yep!'

There were tears in Jane's eyes. 'Will you say thank you to Frank for me Jane. That's the best thing that's happened to me for weeks. Tell him I'll bake him a cake. Lots of cakes.'

Chapter 33

We got through the exams. It was the most stressful two weeks of my entire life but we got through them. About ten days before the first exam, panic set in for Niall and he started to study frantically, at the same pace as James. Lois and I crept around the house as quietly as we possibly could, keeping the telly turned down low and talking to each other in whispers. At regular intervals we dispensed tea and caramel wafers and omelettes to the boys because the week that Pippa's cockerel had stayed over had proved very effective and my chickens were back to full productivity.

Late on the night before the first exam, when everyone was already in bed, Niall came into my room.

'What's wrong, sweetheart?'

'I can't do it Mum. I messed up. I wish I was clever like James but I'm not. And I've left it all too late and now I'm so nervous I can't sleep.'

I patted the space on the bed and Niall flopped down next to me. I smoothed his back and stroked his hair, his spiky, funeral black hair. I noticed his blonde roots were coming through but I didn't say anything.

'It'll be fine,' I soothed him. 'Don't you worry, you'll do great, all you've got to do is take deep breaths and keep calm and concentrate on what you do know, not what you don't, it'll be fine, don't you worry, there, there, my lovely boy—'

He fell asleep quickly, snuggled up tight to me. I was awake long before he was, when it was just getting light and the birds had started to sing. I lay and watched my boy sleep. My baby boy was right there, next to me, in there with all the black hair, the acne, and the beginnings of a moustache. At 6.30am I nudged him gently. He opened his eyes,

'Morning, Mummy.'

He hadn't called me Mummy since he went to secondary school. Love made my chest tight, like a balloon filled with water, fit to burst.

James was focused throughout his exams by which I mean incommunicative. I'd always boasted to the exercise class girls that I had a teenager who spoke in whole sentences not grunts but I would have been glad of even a grunt. When I asked him how it had gone, all he did was hold out his hand and turn it slightly from left to right, indicating that it had been so-so. *Couci-couça*, as they said in France. Niall was not much better. 'It was cool Mum, better than I thought.' Each night the boys shovelled down their dinner in silence and disappeared into their rooms to study some more. Lois and I did jigsaw puzzles and threaded beads onto friendship bracelets and watched *High School Musical* and *Mamma Mia*. My stomach was in knots for the entire fortnight and my face ached from frowning so much, from clenching my neck muscles with the tension of it all. I was pretty useless at work, forever checking my watch. Had the exam started by now? Had it finished? How had it gone? For once, Frank cut me some slack – no snidey comments about my productivity or my concentration levels. He even bought me lunch one day. He came back from an appointment and slid a greasy paper bag towards me. There was a corned beef pasty inside, still warm from the oven.

'Thanks Frank!' I said. 'These are my favourites.'

'I know that.'

'I usually like—'

He put his hand in his pocket and fished out a small sachet.

'…brown sauce with a pasty.'

Finally it was over. The exams were done and the whole house breathed a big sigh of relief and sagged onto the sofa. I fetched the PlayStation home from work and Bartley came round. I wished for James' sake that Amy might too but he had barely mentioned her name since that day he'd got home from London.

'Are you going out to celebrate with your mates?' I asked him.

'At the weekend. Some of them have got a few more exams yet.'

'You'll have to think what to do with this lovely long holiday you've got, make the most of your time off before you go to university.'

'I'm working on it, Mum.'

With the exams over it was not long till my birthday party. I wished I'd never started on it. It was proving to be a lot of hassle. People phoning me constantly and asking what the dress code was and what did I want for a present and was there going to be food or should they eat before they came? Jane popping in every two minutes with mini shepherd's pies and wee chicken kievs for me to say which one I liked best, my parents nagging me not to have the music too loud and telling me they thought it best they didn't stay till the end but took Lois home around 10pm as she'd be tired.

'Lois can outlast everyone else there put together,' I laughed. 'Don't you worry about Lois.'

And in the midst of all this, one evening after I'd got home from work and changed into my comfy leggings and an oversized grey T-shirt and was about to cook fish fingers and oven chips for Lois because the boys were out and that was her favourite, there was a knock on the door and there was Mack. When I saw him I felt that I'd just been slapped across the face with a big meaty fish, a tuna or something. Smacked in the gob by a skipjack.

'Hi Anna, are you going to invite me in?'

Wordlessly I stepped aside and he walked past me to be met by the human cannon ball that was Lois, bowling herself in free fall towards him. 'My daddy,' she shouted. 'My daddy.'

When I did the pregnancy test that confirmed I was having Lois I wasn't surprised at all. I sort of knew, even as we were making love that last time that Mack and I were making another baby. I didn't tell him I was pregnant for months, made sure he was settled in his new life in Hawaii, only told him in the end because his mother threatened she'd tell him if I didn't. When I did finally telephone him I knew that he'd offer to come home straight away, knew that he'd tell me he loved me and wanted to look after me and the boys and the new baby but I made it very clear from the outset that was not an option. We already had two kids when we split up and I didn't see why a new one should make any difference to that decision. I was a single parent of two, I could manage a third. And I did.

Mack had stayed in Hawaii for a while but had soon moved on again, setting up his surf shop on the beach in whichever of the world's best surf spots he fancied next – the Gold Coast of Australia, Bali, Costa Rica and California. I bought a big map of the world and the kids and I pinned up on it the postcards he sent from all the beautiful places he visited on his travels. He sent a lot of postcards but not much money. About five years ago he returned to Hawaii where he'd been living ever since. He only managed the trip to Stonebridge every couple of years. On his last visit he'd brought his Californian girlfriend Tei with him (another surfer, tall, skinny, blonde but gratifyingly sun damaged I'd noticed from the photos Mack emailed to the kids) but I'd engineered to be up in London visiting Glynis, leaving the kids with his mother for him to collect so it had been four years or more since I'd set eyes on him in the flesh. The kids and he Skyped each other most weekends but I kept well away whenever I heard that burbling sound coming from the computer which meant he was calling them. I'd walk past and yell hello at the computer while the three of them were huddled round it. 'Mum says hello, Dad,' one of them would tell him. Then a few seconds later another one would shout out, 'Dad says hello back, Mum.' It was much better for me to keep contact with Mack to the bare minimum wherever possible.

But now here he was, in my house, rolling around in

the hallway with our daughter. Even though Lois and Mack have never lived together she loves him every bit as much as the boys do – more if anything. I tried not to notice but the lucky sod was ageing well. His hair was so bleached by the sun I couldn't tell if he'd gone grey or not but he had the same flat stomach and tight little bum. I felt my insides lift up a few floors, like they always did whenever I saw Mack. Hell, whenever I thought about him.

'Hi,' I smiled at him when he and Lois had done wrestling.

'Hi yourself.'

'What are you doing here?'

'I've come for a visit! Didn't James tell you I was coming? We arranged it a few weeks back.'

'He didn't say anything to me.'

'He didn't say anything to me either!' Lois said, hugging Mack tight. 'It's the best surprise ever!'

'Tei not with you this time?'

'Nope, she went back to California. A couple of months ago now.'

I waited for him to tell me more but he didn't. 'Do you want a cup of tea?' I asked, not knowing what else to say.

'Lois says she's having fish fingers. Any chance of a fish-finger sandwich?'

I abandoned the idea of oven chips, made them a sandwich each and left them to it in the kitchen to go sit in the living room. It was good for Lois to have a little bit of time alone with her dad before the boys came home and it got even louder and more chaotic. I could not for the life of me work out why James had not mentioned to me that Mack was coming. What was James playing at? He hadn't talked much to me about Amy, not talked much to me about anything for quite a while. Was that it? Was that why Mack was home because James had confided in him how unhappy he was?

Suddenly Mack flopped himself down on the sofa next to me. So close I could almost smell him or at least could remember what he smelled like. Sun and salt and soap and man skin. I really wished I wasn't wearing leggings and had washed my hair.

'Penny for them Anna?'

'Worth way more than that. Where's Lois?'

'Upstairs trying on the T-shirts I brought for her. Are you OK with me being here?'

'Yes of course I am. I just wasn't expecting to see you, that's all.'

'You didn't think I'd let your fortieth birthday party go by without making an appearance did you?'

'Is that why you're here? You didn't seriously come all this way just to gate-crash my fortieth birthday and flirt with all my friends did you?'

'Of course I didn't. Fun though the party's going to be, especially the flirting bit, I came because of the kids of course. Where are the boys anyway?'

'Out somewhere.'

'Out where?'

'I don't know. Did your mother know where you were every second of the day at this age?'

'She didn't know where I was for a single second of the day at this age. Got any beer in?'

'In the fridge.'

I followed him into the kitchen. It bugged me how comfortable he was in this house, how natural it felt to have him here. And it excited me too. Because, annoying though this was, when I was round Mack I felt just like I used to feel, all those years ago when he showed up at Boots. He could still make me swoon.

Mack popped open the can and poured one half into a glass which he handed to me and kept the rest of the can for himself.

'James told me about Bob and Jane splitting up. I was really sorry to hear that.'

'We all are. It's devastating. Jane's in a total mess about it.'

'Yes well, that's what happens when you fuck around on people.'

'James told you that? I didn't know James knew what had happened!'

'He didn't tell me. Bob did.'

'Bob's been in touch with you?'

'I emailed him after James told me. I'm going to go visit him later this week, see how he is.'

'He's agreed to see you? He won't let any of us go visit him.'

'I haven't told him I'm going.'

'Yeah well, good luck with that,' I said sullenly. 'I'm sure he'll want to chat with friends who've just landed from Hawaii rather than the ones that live here all the time. Assuming it was Hawaii you landed from or have you moved on again?'

'No, still in Hawaii.'

Lois burst into the room, wearing a T-shirt with the

words Mack's Surf Shack emblazoned on the front and with a string of pink and yellow fabric flowers round her neck.

'How do I look, Dad?'

'Like the surf princess you are.'

And then the boys were home and more wrestling ensued and high fives and whoops of joy and T-shirt distribution and for the first time in months I heard James laugh and I felt like my family were home.

Chapter 34

Mack announced he wanted to take the kids off to Llangennith camping for a couple of nights and teach Lois to surf.

'She's meant to be at school,' I grumbled half-heartedly.

'She's nine and it's the end of term! What exactly are they doing at school right now? Colouring in?'

'Watching DVDs mostly,' Lois advised us.

'So, conscientious Mummy, do you think watching DVDs is better for her than spending time with her big brothers and her dad learning to surf on one of the finest beaches in the Gower and sleeping under canvas?' Mack cocked his head to one side and grinned at me.

'OK, you can take her. Take the lot of them. Tell me – don't you ever get sick of it? Surfing I mean?'

'Nope! When you're tired of surfing you're tired of life. Come with us, Anna. It'll be fun. We're going to surf all day and then have a barbecue in the sand dunes, make a camp fire and watch the sun go down.'

It sounded lovely, really lovely. But I knew I couldn't possibly go. It was way too dangerous for me to be round Mack for that length of time.

'No thanks surf dude Dad, I've got to go to work.'

So there I was, a week off my fortieth birthday and all on my ownsome lonesome in the house again. *Better get used to it,* I thought glumly, *James will be off to London in October and then Niall will go in two years and before I know it it'll be Lois' turn to leave.*

I tried to phone Glynis, not only because I was lonely but also to warn her that Mack was back and would be making an appearance at my party but I only ever got her voicemail. I did get a text from her sent just after 4am one morning *Knee deep in a deal and not got time to answer my phone. I will make it back for your party tho.* I wondered whether she was on her way to work or on her way back when she sent it.

Frank teased me rotten when he caught me on the Surf Cam website checking out the waves on Llangennith beach.

'You're not going to be able to spot your children on that you know.'

'I know. I just wanted to see how big the waves are. Mack had better be keeping a good eye on Lois.'

'He will be. If he was in the habit of getting kids drowned I don't imagine he'd still be in business teaching surfing.'

'I suppose you're right.'

'Look, we're about done for the day here. How about I buy you a glass of wine?'

I must have looked shocked. 'I'm only suggesting a quick drink after work,' he said, sounding a little put out. 'You don't have to come if you don't want to.'

'It's just that we've never been out for a drink after work before.'

'That's because you're usually rushing out of the door at 5.30pm sharp to attend to some domestic crisis.'

'Well, OK then. I don't much fancy going back to an empty house just yet.'

'Come on, get your stuff and we'll go.'

We walked over to the wine bar, the one where Glynis and I had first discussed her madcap decision to have a baby on her own. I wondered if she was reconsidering that now, given that she worked so hard she didn't even have time to answer her phone.

Frank ordered a good bottle of Chablis and we sat at the table in the back, the same spot from where he had emerged that night to pay the bill and save me from having to do a runner. I suddenly realised with glee that he'd never actually got round to deducting that from my wages.

'So Anna, how's things?'

'Oh, OK I suppose – for someone who's old, fat, divorced and lonely.'

'Snap.'

'You're not fat,' I said and then winced when I realised I had effectively agreed with him that he was however old, divorced and lonely. To take away the sting of what I had said, I carried on. 'In fact, based on how you dance you may very well have a six-pack hidden away under that shirt. Or a three-pack anyway.'

He smiled and smoothed the front of his shirt absentmindedly. 'You're not fat either. Just curvy.'

'Yes, well, us fat-bottomed girls we make the rockin' world go round you know.'

Frank didn't comment after that so I changed the subject hurriedly. 'Um, Valerie's not been on the phone much lately.'

'Actually I've been phoning her instead. I worked out a little while ago that so long as I phone her regularly, around 8am, she and Penry are having breakfast and doing Sudoku together and she doesn't actually want to chat much.'

'That's great,' I chuckled. 'Saves me having to take irate messages from her.'

'That's what I thought.'

'And are things OK with your kids?'

'They're much better these days. I've been picking them up on a Saturday afternoon from that ruinously expensive boarding school that Valerie insists they go to and taking them out somewhere to eat before driving them home to Valerie and Penry for the rest of the weekend. You know how teenagers are. They don't really want to spend that much time with their parents anyway. They'd rather be with their mates, hanging around shopping centres drinking cider and smoking.'

I looked at him quizzically over my glass of Chablis. 'I can't quite picture Sebastian and Francesca hanging around shopping centres.'

'You're right. They go to pool parties and polo matches and hang around there instead to drink cider and smoke.'

'Well your new arrangements must be working for you because you certainly seem—'

Frank finished my sentence for me. 'Less grumpy, maybe?'

'More cheerful, let's say. Your glamorous divorcees must be pissed off with you though, not being around on Saturdays. They haven't been calling much lately either.'

'No they haven't, you're right.'

'You can bring one with you to my birthday party if you want. You'd be very welcome. Jane's catered for the five thousand and the more ex-wives and ex-husbands there are there the better. Won't make me feel so weird about having my own there.'

'OK, well I'll have to have a think about which woman I'd like to spend the evening of your party with.'

'You do that. I'd better be off. I promised Jane I'd call in quickly tonight. We've got final menu details to discuss apparently.'

'See you tomorrow then. And Anna?'

'Yes?'

'Make it bright and early for once will you. You've no excuse to be late with the kids away.'

I grimaced at him. 'Bright and early it'll be.'

Walking home, I realised that I'd really rather enjoyed my drink with Frank and the opportunity, just for an hour, to be distracted from worrying about my children or my friends or the fact that I was very nearly forty years old.

Mack called me from Llangennith to ask if it was OK if he and the kids stayed a few days more, right up until the Saturday of my birthday. I wanted to say no, that I hated them being away, even hated the fact that the house stayed miraculously clean and tidy and there was milk in the fridge, but I could hear all three of them in the background while he was on the phone *Please Mum please the surf is awesome* so I agreed. Seconds after I put the phone down Mack texted me a photo of the four of them sitting on the beach, cwtched up close, Mack's arm stretched out in front of him holding his phone far enough away so they could all get in the photo. My ex-husband and my children looked tanned and happy and healthy and absolutely gorgeous. I wished then that I had gone with them, to sit on the sand and look out to the sea with the sun on my back, but knew that if I had gone it would have been impossible to resist Mack. The joy that rises from him when he surfs and the smell of salt air and the sun on his skin would have been my undoing. Keeping safely away from Mack was just about worth the prospect of waking up on my own on the morning of my fortieth birthday.

I thought I'd have trouble getting to sleep the night before my birthday but actually I fell asleep straight away and didn't wake until 8am when I heard my phone pinging downstairs with a text. It was another photo from Mack, this time of the number forty made up of smooth round pebbles arranged on the sand. Before I could begin to feel lonely there was a knock at the front door and I opened it to find a glorious sunny day and Mack and the kids shouting 'Happy birthday' at me. Lois was holding a big bunch of fortieth birthday balloons and Mack was proudly clutching the ear of a bright orange Space Hopper.

'You didn't think I'd leave you with an empty house on your birthday morning did you?' Mack grinned, holding me tight and kissing my cheek. 'We've brought eggs and orange juice and Champagne – the real stuff, not Asti Spumante – and James and I are going to make you a birthday breakfast. But first you've got to try out your Space Hopper.'

Turned out that riding a Space Hopper is much like riding a bike. You never forget how. And it gets surprisingly easier after the second glass of Bucks Fizz.

Chapter 35

At lunchtime Mack gathered up our children and their party outfits and took them over to his mother's.

'I thought you'd like to be able to get ready for your big night in peace,' he explained.

'How long have you known me Mack Lewis?'

'A lifetime.'

'And how long does it usually take me to get ready?'

'Ten minutes or so.'

'So how come now that I've turned forty it suddenly takes me five hours? I could fit in a little light plastic surgery in that time!'

'You know what I mean Anna. You can have a long bath, do your hair, all that sort of stuff, without fussing over the rest of us.'

Even though I'd missed them so much while they were away, I was rather glad that I didn't need to share the bathroom with the children. Even more glad that Mack's mother would give them lunch and that I didn't have to worry about food for them all or washing up after. So I took a long bath and shaved my legs and put a conditioning mask on my hair and then lay on the bed on a towel and moisturised everywhere I could reach and then I must have fallen asleep because someone was at the front door knocking loudly and it sounded like they'd already been knocking for quite some time.

'Here she is! The birthday girl!' my mother said when I opened the door. 'Happy birthday, sweetheart,' my father said, hugging me.

'We thought we'd drop in quickly before the party to give you your present, just me and your father quietly,' my mother said, handing me a small jewellery box.

Inside were my grandmother's ruby drop earrings. 'Oh Mum, I can't take these. Gran left these to you. You look lovely in them. As lovely as she used to.'

'I want you to have them, Anna,' my mother said briskly. 'Your grandmother would have wanted you to have them too. It's not every day that my little girl turns forty you know. You need something special to wear tonight.'

'Thanks Mum,' I said, trying not to cry. 'I'll cherish them.'

'Here's something else that arrived for you, love,' my dad said, handing me a box. 'It's not from us. There was a delivery man at the door when we got here. Rather too pleased he was if you ask me to deliver it to us rather than you. We could have been anyone knocking on your door. Jehovah's witnesses even.'

Inside the box was a single, large, deep-red flower, its petals so velvety and fresh I was surprised when I touched it to find that it was silk.

'Gosh, isn't that pretty,' my mother said. 'I think it's a peony. Is there a card with it?' my mother asked. 'Did the delivery man give you a card to go with it, Eric?'

'Did you see the delivery man hand me a card, Doreen? No? There you are then. No card.'

I double-checked inside the box. Nothing. 'Must be from Glynis,' I said. 'Can't think of anyone else who'd send me something like this.'

'Look Anna, there's a clip attached to it. You'll be able to wear it in your hair tonight.'

'Me Mum? I'm not the flower-in-my-hair type.'

'Not usually no, but this will look lovely with your red dress and with Gran's earrings. Just try it will you?'

'I don't know, it's a bit girly for me.'

I turned the flower in my hands. It really was very pretty.

'Wear it Anna, it'll look lovely.' My dad squeezed my hand before he and my mother clattered back out of the door.

Jane was true to her promise. She did manage to make Steve's pub look like a fairy grotto for my birthday party. Dozens of strings of fairy lights twinkled from the rafters, the ugly brown tables had been transformed by dazzling white linen tablecloths with tea lights flickering gently in glass holders. Big vases of white lilies scented the air. A small army of waiters and waitresses, wearing crisply ironed black shirts and trousers and starched white aprons were polishing glasses and arranging gorgeous food on silver trays ready for when the guests arrived in half an hour or so.

I made my way to the pub's kitchen where Jane was busy loading bruschetta into Steve's barely used ovens.

'You look lovely Anna,' she said as she kissed me on the cheek, holding her floury hands well away from my red dress. 'Happy birthday.'

'Thank you Jane, I've been for a walk through the pretty forest and put make-up on and everything. What do you think of the flower though? Too much?'

'It looks fabulous Anna. Just perfect with that dress, which is gorgeous.'

I did a little twirl. 'Isn't it just? I love it. Glynis bought it for me.'

'Where is Glynis anyway? I thought she'd arrive with you.'

'She'll be here later I guess. She's been working silly hours lately and I've not been able to speak with her.'

'Have you seen her surprise?'

'No. What surprise?'

'Come over here and see.' Jane took me by the hand and led me over to the bar.

Arranged on the bar were dozens of bottles of wine, red wine lined up in rows and white wine in big silver buckets full of ice. Steve was standing guard over the bottles, grinning. He was back wearing his black dart-player shirts but had obviously been keeping off the chips – he looked considerably thinner than he had the last time I saw him.

'They're from Glynis,' he said. 'You said you wanted everyone to have a drink on you. Being Glynis she thinks that means a minimum of three glasses of wine each.'

'Wow – that's brilliant.'

'That's not everything,' Jane said excitedly. 'Wait till you see the garden!'

I looked at Steve, confusedly. 'This place has a garden?'

'Well it does now. Come see.'

I followed Steve out through a door that in all the years I'd been coming to the pub I had never once before seen open. It led to a walled garden with roses and hydrangeas and fuchsia bushes all strung with paper lanterns but most of the garden was taken up by an enormous teepee tent.

Steve prodded me. 'Go inside and have a look.'

The teepee was lit by Moroccan-style lanterns hanging from the ceiling. There were brightly coloured rugs on the floor and low round tables with more tea lights and cushions to sit on. Pinned to the ceiling of the teepee were dozens of paper butterflies.

'Do you like it?' Steve asked.

'It's the most amazing thing I've ever seen.' I could feel tears tickling the back of my throat it was so beautiful. 'How? I mean…has this always been here and you just never shared it with us customers?'

'Are you kidding! All that was out here before last week were a load of beer crates and the rubbish bins. Glynis organised it all. Bunch of blokes turn up in a van with someone else's garden and a tent and abracadabra there's a casbah in my back yard. That woman blows me away, she does.'

'She is coming tonight isn't she?'

'She'll be here, don't you worry. Now come on, time for you to come back inside and greet your guests.'

Mack and the kids were the first to arrive. Lois rushed over to me and hugged me tight.

'You look beautiful, Mum. Pretty as a princess. Can I have those earrings when you die?'

'Yes you can, Lois. And you look wonderful yourself.'

She did. So did Mack. No man had the right to look so bloody sexy wearing only jeans and a white T-shirt. Mack leant over and whispered in my ear.

'Boy, Anna, you look amazing. You certainly know how to make a man regret some of his choices in life.' Then he kissed me, not on my cheek but full on the lips.

'Yeuch,' Niall groaned. 'That's gross.'

Other guests started to arrive now – Cassie and Graham and the girls, my parents, Mack's parents, the exercise class girls. Pippa arrived with Sol and Jethro and even though she and I had agreed that she would just drop the boys off and not stick around for long I noticed that she'd accepted a glass of wine from Steve and was leaning on the bar sipping it incredibly slowly. I knew Pippa being there was going to wind Cassie up but I was having such a good time I didn't care. The next hour or so was a blur of people kissing me and hugging me and piling cards and birthday presents on the end of the bar. I really did feel like a princess and every time I led someone out to the garden and saw the wonder on their faces as they took in the teepee and my guests sitting on cushions eating Jane's delicious food by lantern light I felt like clapping. The only thing that wasn't perfect about my party was the fact that Glynis wasn't there yet.

And then, when Glynis finally did arrive she was not alone. She was pushing Bob in his wheelchair.

'Omigosh, omigosh,' I babbled rushing over to them. 'Am I glad to see the two of you. On so many different levels.'

'Told you I wouldn't miss your birthday shindig for the world, didn't I?' Bob said.

I looked up, searching around the room for Jane, but I could not see her and then there she was coming out of the kitchen, proudly carrying an enormous chocolate cake on a silver tray, ablaze with extra long birthday candles. 'Hap—' she started and then everyone joined in with singing happy birthday and hip hip hurrah to me.

'Come on, Anna, blow the candles out and make a wish,' she said. Suddenly Lois, who can never resist the opportunity to blow out birthday candles, was at my side and together she and I blew out the candles. And when they were all out and Jane was no longer dazzled by the light of forty candles, that's when she finally saw that Bob was there. Her hand flew to her throat and she was shaking, but Bob smiled at her and she managed a wobbly smile back.

'Wheel me out to have a look at this tent thing will you, Jane?' Bob said and when Jane took the handles of his wheelchair he reached back with his good hand and squeezed her fingers.

'How on earth did you manage that?' I asked Glynis.

'Nothing to do with me. It's all down to your ex-husband. Apparently Mack went to see Bob this afternoon and persuaded him to come. All I had to do was go fetch him from that hospice place where he's been living and bring him here.'

I looked over at the little dance floor in the corner of the pub, where Mack was swinging Lois around. He winked at me.

'This has got to be one of the best days of my life! You're a star Glynis – the best friend ever – and thank you so much for organising the garden and all the wine. It's amazing. I love it. I love it all. I wore the flower see?' I swung round so she could see where I had looped two strands of my hair together at the back and fastened it with the flower.

'Yeah well, it's because you're worth it,' she said, flinging her hair around flamboyantly like they do in the shampoo ads on telly. 'But the flower's not from me. Why did you think it was?'

'It was delivered to my house but without a card. I thought you must have sent it because it's the exact same colour as my dress.'

'You must have a secret admirer, Anna! Right, I need to speak with Steve a second. Back in a bit. Looks like you're wanted on the dance floor anyway.'

Mack and Lois were waving at me, motioning to me to join them. As I watched my daughter show off her girl band moves to her father and me, every now and then holding both our hands and grinning at us from ear to ear, I felt a familiar feeling of regret catch in my throat. I had often wondered over the years, usually in the dark of night when one of the kids was ill or upset, whether life would have been better for me and my children if I had been willing to lead the footloose and fancy free life that Mack had asked me to. A life without baggage or roots. One that could be packed away overnight, ready to move in a moment to a different destination. A life without Christmas decorations in the attic or school photos on the mantelpiece or kitchen drawers full of string and pens and odd buttons but with a husband and a father. I would never know if that life would have been better but I did know that the life I had chosen, more than twenty years ago when I was pregnant with James, was the only life I could have lived.

I was shaken from my thoughts by Jane calling my name from the edge of the dance floor. I looked at Lois and pointed to indicate that I was going to join Bob and Jane. She just nodded and turned her full dancing attention to her father. Jane wheeled Bob into the little kitchen and I followed them in there.

'Hi, you two,' I said nervously. 'How's it going?'

'Well!' Jane said, clasping her hands together. 'We've got a long way to go. A very long way yet. But Bob's agreed to come home.'

'That's brilliant! The best birthday present I could have had.'

'Don't go getting too excited, Anna,' Bob smiled. 'Like Jane says, we've got a long way to go. But I've had time to think at the hospice and then that ex-husband of yours comes barging in today and gives it to me straight between the eyes about love being so much more than one betrayal and how I shouldn't make Jane's mistakes worse by making bigger mistakes of my own. And he's right. So we're going to work at things. And I got a catheter fitted while I was at the hospice that is going to help us both to live more normally and get out a bit more and other stuff too if you know what I mean, and well, together I reckon we can get through this.'

I hugged Jane and then bent to kiss Bob on the cheek.

'I'm really glad for you both. So very glad.'

'Us too,' Jane smiled. 'OK, Bob and I are going to make a move now. It's been a big evening for us both. The girls will carry on serving until the food is finished and then tidy up.'

'OK, OK, you go. And thanks again for doing the food

Jane. It's been the most amazing party, thanks to you.'

'It's been my pleasure, Anna. And my saviour too actually. If I hadn't had your party to think about I think I would have gone totally out of my mind.'

'And I'll tell Frank when I see him next that the house is off the market. He's going to be miffed as hell at not getting his commission!'

'It's not just commission he's not getting,' Bob said. 'I did some research online at Companies House about the property company that was buying the house. It was Frank's company.'

I was shocked. 'The opportunistic pig! How could he try to benefit from other people's misfortunes like that!'

'That's not what he was doing Anna. He offered full asking price even though he told Jane he was inflating the price and to expect offers at 20 per cent less and the rent he was going to charge her was about £500 a month off the going rate for a house like ours. He wasn't trying to benefit himself at all.'

For a good few minutes after Bob and Jane left I was speechless. Not something that happens very often.

Chapter 36

I should have known it was a mistake letting Pippa stay. From her vantage point at the bar she kept glancing over at Graham. I knew she was only doing it to annoy Cassie but it had worked even better than Pippa could have hoped. For every tiny sip of her one glass of wine that Pippa had taken, Cassie must have taken an enormous gulp from a series of glasses. It wasn't until I saw that Cassie had dragged a very uncomfortable-looking Graham out on the dance floor that I realised just how pissed she was. She was wriggling in front of Graham in what she clearly intended to be a seductive way but which actually looked like she'd got a wasp in her knickers. Graham tried hard to keep his eyes fixed on Cassie but every now and then his eyes flicked nervously over to Pippa.

I went over and joined Pippa at the bar. 'I thought we'd agreed you wouldn't stick around tonight?' I hissed at her.

'Can't a girl have a glass of wine with her friend on her birthday?'

'Not really, no. You're just trying to cause trouble.'

'But it's such fun, Anna, and so easy! Besides seeing Graham look at me like that, well it gets a girl going again, just like my cockerel did your chickens,' and then she winked, very slowly and deliberately at Graham.

Just as Pippa had intended, Cassie saw the wink. And to my horror she started marching straight over to Pippa. I suddenly discovered a pressing need to check how much more wine we might need for the night and quickly moved down the bar a few feet to speak to Steve who was totally ignoring me and was watching intently as the scene in front of him unfurled.

'Oi, you...' Cassie shouted.

Pippa pretended not to have seen her.

'I'm talking to you, you skinny cow. Don't you ever wink at my husband again. Ever! Because it's big tits he likes these days.' With this Cassie lifted up her top to demonstrate to Pippa just how very magnificent her tits were, beautifully levered into a cleavage of wondrous proportions by a Rigby and Peller black and pink lacy bra. 'So don't bother winking until you've got a pair like these.'

Just about every bloke in that pub was staring at Cassie's chest and waiting with baited breath hoping she would punch Pippa in the mouth and a full-on girl fight would ensue but it didn't. Because a much louder kerfuffle suddenly kicked off somewhere else and everyone's attention immediately switched to that. Including mine. Because this kerfuffle was between James and Glynis.

He was shouting at her really loudly, his face so twisted with anger and pain, that I hardly recognised my own son. And even though my instinct was to rush over to them and stop whatever it was they were arguing over I somehow found my feet rooted to the floor as I listened to them.

'Pregnant? How can you be pregnant?' James was

338

shouting. 'I thought you said it was a one-night stand! You're not planning on actually having the baby are you?'

Glynis nodded, tried to pat James' arm, but he snatched it away.

'Are you off your fucking head?'

'I've never been more certain about anything in my life,' Glynis said, firmly.

'You've gone and ruined it all now.'

Somehow I managed to move my feet, walk across to James and Glynis. 'What's going on?' I asked. 'Are you OK, James?'

'No, I'm not OK. I'm totally fucked up. She's screwed everything up by getting pregnant and I'm definitely going to go live in Hawaii now.'

Mack came over at that point and grabbed James' elbow and marched him away, leaving me staring at Glynis.

'What the hell is going on, Glynis?' There was a whooshing noise in my head, like when you hold a seashell up to your ear.

'Let's go outside where it's quieter. I'll tell you everything there.'

She led me outside, not to the teepee tent where my guests were tucking into chocolate cake, but to the wooden bench out the front of the pub where the smokers go for a cigarette. There were fag ends everywhere and it smelled like a damp ashtray. I shivered, even though it was a warm night. The whooshing in my head grew to a thumping noise.

'How can you be pregnant already? I thought you had to go off to some clinic in Scandinavia first.'

339

'It wasn't donor sperm Anna. Well, I suppose it was in a way.'

She looked at me and suddenly a terrifying, horrifying realisation dawned on me.

'The father of this baby? It's not, well it's not, I mean... have you brought me out here to tell me that James, my eighteen-year-old son, is the father of your baby?' I could barely get the words out.

'Don't be so bloody soft. Of course he's not.'

Relief flooded through me. 'Thank you God. Thank you so much. I swear I'll never take your name in vain ever again. Hang on a minute though. Why is James so upset then? Why does he mind so much that you're pregnant?'

'I'm afraid that's down to a lack of judgement on my part. That afternoon, after Bob and Jane's party, when I got back to London he was still in my flat. Amy had dumped him and he was devastated so I got him drunk. Actually, I got me more drunk than I got him. And we slow danced a bit, well more than a bit, and I knew he was attracted to me but I just ignored it—'

'And? And what happened Glynis?' I was angry now, could feel heat rising in my face.

'And then I must have passed out because the next thing I knew it was the morning and I was lying in my bed and James was next to me.'

'And did you? Had you?'

'Of course not, Anna. I might not have actually ever changed his nappies but I saw you do it plenty of times. Do you really think I'd sleep with James? I woke up with my clothes on.'

'So? It's perfectly possible to have sex with your clothes on Glynis. I'm sure you've done it plenty of times. Over your office desk, no doubt.'

'I was wearing my knickers and my tights Anna. Or pantyhose, if you prefer. Not even I can have sex wearing tights! I can assure you I did not have sex with your son. Even more importantly I didn't *want* to have sex with your son. He's like family to me Anna. All your kids are. I did flirt with him a bit, I've got to admit that, but it was only to try to cheer him up. Only now he thinks he's in love with me and that we're going to live happily ever after.'

'You stupid, irresponsible bitch.'

'I know Anna, but I was trying to help, really I was. And I think this thing with me, well, it's just a displacement of how he feels about Amy. It's not really about me at all. And that means he'll get over it soon enough.'

'He better bloody had, Glynis. Because believe me, if you've screwed with my kid's head I'll never forgive you.'

'Fair enough.'

'So who is the father then? If it's not my son?'

'Who do you think it is?'

'I've no fucking clue! Are you back with Carmichael? Is it his? Or is there some new married bloke at work you've been getting it on with recently? How pregnant are you anyway?'

'Only seven weeks. It's Steve, Anna. The father is Steve.'

'Steve the barman? Steve in there? I thought you said nothing happened between you.'

'Well I lied. It was only once, the night after the barbecue actually. That was one eventful weekend for everyone.'

'And this is another one Glynis. Only this one happens to be my fortieth birthday.'

'I know, I know. I'm sorry. I wasn't going to say anything tonight. I was going to tell you later. But James cornered me back there and I thought if I told him I was pregnant he'd go off me pretty quick and we'd avoid a scene. Got that one wrong.'

'And what does Steve make of all this?'

'He's sickeningly proud about it. Says he wants to marry me, the lot.'

'And what about you?'

'What do you think Anna? Of course I don't want to marry Steve and live above a pub, have my hair smelling of chip fat from noon to night. No chance. But he's a decent bloke. He'll be a good dad. And at least this way my kid will know what his dad looks like, where he comes from, all that stuff you were spouting off about.'

'So how are you going to work things out? Work? Baby? Steve? All that?'

'I've no idea. I'm only just coming to terms with the fact that I'm pregnant by anyone other than a Viking in a syringe. Who knows? Maybe I'll come back to Stonebridge, get a job in a law firm in Cardiff. They do have law firms in Cardiff don't they?'

'I believe so yes. And running water and electricity too.'

'Or maybe I'll stay in London, get a nanny, one from Wales so my baby doesn't get a Cockney accent, and Steve can come up to visit whenever he wants. I don't know. It's way too early to make decisions yet. I'll just have to take it step by step. But I've got my mum and dad to help and Steve now I guess. And you. Do I still have you?'

'Of course you've got me. I'm still tamping mad with you, Glynis, but you know I'll do everything I can to help you. Congratulations.'

'Thanks, Anna.' We hugged then, just a little one.

'One last thing, Glynis…'

'Yes.'

'What was all that about going to Hawaii.'

'That I have no idea about. You'll have to ask James. Or Mack.'

Back inside the pub, it didn't take me long to spot Mack and James. They were standing at the bar, not talking, miserably staring down at a couple of pints.

'OK, Glynis has told me what happened between you and her James. I've got all that. She was way out of order getting you both drunk like that but she assures me nothing actually happened between you two. Is that correct?'

James nodded.

'So what's this about going to Hawaii then?'

'Well, Dad and me have been talking—'

'Oh, your dad and you have been talking, have you? You've not been talking to me.'

'Keep your hair on Mum. Dad and me have been talking. I've been thinking, well, that maybe I'll have done well enough in my exams to have a shot at going to Oxford, like Glynis did. I didn't apply before, didn't

343

think I'd make it and anyway I wanted to be with Amy. Only now I'd like to give it a go.'

'So where does Hawaii come into all of this?'

'Three As don't get you into Oxford these days Mum. You need to show that you've done other things, had lots of other experiences. So what Dad and I have been discussing is me taking a year out, going to Hawaii and living with him and working in the Surf Shack and applying to Oxford from there. Dad says there's a kids' club thing he's involved with that I could volunteer at too, Oxford would love that.'

I took a deep breath. 'James, go find your sister. Make sure she's all right.'

'She's fine, Mum. I can see her from here. She's making Granddad do the Macarena.'

'Well go do it too,' I said sternly. James stomped off and I turned to Mack.

'How many times are you intent on breaking my heart, Mack?'

'What do you mean?'

'You know damn well what I mean. How could you take my firstborn away from me? How could you?'

'Whoa, now hang on, Anna, that isn't fair. James is eighteen years of age and he was the one who reached out to me, asking for my help, told me all about Amy and this thing with Glynis and how he didn't know what to do with himself. All I did was try to suggest some alternatives. I am not taking him away from you. He was leaving home in October anyway.'

'Yes to go to university in London. That's not the other side of the world like Hawaii is.'

'Come on Anna. Whether it was London or Hawaii you wouldn't have seen that much of him once he'd left home. You know that.'

'That's not the point. He'd be on the same time zone, I could get on a train to London to see him if I wanted, even if it was just for a cup of tea, take Niall and Lois with me. I won't be able to do that if he's in Hawaii now will I?' I started to cry. Of all the things that had happened that night, this was the one that finally brought me to tears.

'Well why don't you come too?'

'What do you mean?'

'You know what I mean, Anna. Why don't you come too? You and Lois and Niall. Lois and Niall can go into the American school system, they'll have a blast. You can all live with me, I've got plenty of space, and I'll finally get to teach you to surf Anna. You don't have to come for good – just for the year with James if you want. It'll be like a year out for all the family. And if you like it, if the kids like it, perhaps you'll consider giving me another chance and staying on afterwards. All of us, together. What do you say, Anna.'

'I can't believe you're asking me this again, Mack.'

'It's not the same question, Anna. I'm done with the travelling. That's why Tei and I split up – she wanted to take off again and I didn't. Not any more. I'm too old for that now, Anna. I want to stay in Hawaii, where the sun shines and the beaches are golden and the surf is good, where I have a home and a decent business these days. I've finally grown up, Anna. And I'd like to share being a grown-up with my family – with you and the kids. Will

345

you think about it at least?'

'I don't know. Maybe. Seems like a spur-of-the-moment invitation to me.'

'Well it's not. I was going to ask you properly, just not tonight. Tonight was meant to be your night for showing off your pretty face in your pretty dress. But then James kind of brought things forward a bit. You can even bring your books with you if you want. We'll ship them over.'

'All of them?'

'All of them. I'm brilliant at building shelves.'

He smiled at me and I thought about kissing him and Mack thought I was going to kiss him too and turned his face towards me and did his deep stare at me, the one that always leads to hot sex in my experience of him, only I didn't kiss him. Because that was the point at which I saw Frank sauntering in, fashionably late and with Melanie Farrell. Melanie bloody Farrell. I was incandescent with rage. How could he bring her as his guest? Her of all people? Who'd taken him to the cleaners when Valerie divorced him and had been poised to do exactly the same thing to Jane. Who the bloody hell did he think he was?

I left Mack standing at the bar and marched up to Frank.

'How could you? How could you bring that woman to my party?'

'What woman?'

'You know which woman I mean. The bloodsucking, ballbreaking one.'

'She didn't come with me! I came on my own. I just met her on the way in. Said she was hoping to track down some wonderful bloke she'd met at the hospice when she was in a meeting with Bob.'

When I looked again Melanie Farrell was making a beeline straight for Mack.

Chapter 37

'Er, has it been a good party then?' Frank asked, moving into my line of vision to block the evil looks I was giving Mack and Melanie.

'It's been emotional.'

'What do you mean?'

'How much time have you got?'

'Plenty. Can I just grab myself a drink first?'

'Don't worry, I'm not going to bore you with the detail. Go ahead. Plenty of wine, courtesy of Glynis. I'll have one too please.'

Seconds later, Frank was back with two glasses of wine. 'Here you go. Good stuff actually, not Steve's usual rubbish. Bravo Glynis.'

I took a sip and looked around. My party was in full swing. There were lots of people on the dance floor including my parents with Lois and most of the exercise class girls who were, without realising it, all doing one of our aerobics routines. Graham was standing over Cassie making her drink water while rubbing her back. Niall and Bartley were lurking in the shadows, surreptitiously passing a bottle of beer between them and James was sitting with Sol and Jethro, all three of them sullenly watching the dancing with a look of teenage disgust on their faces. Glynis and Steve were sitting quietly together at one of the tables. I noticed she was drinking Coke. Boy was her life going to change. And then of course there was Mack and Melanie, now deep in conversation. Mack saw me looking and just shrugged and rolled his eyes at me over Melanie's petite, perfect head. I wondered if he was in the process of asking her to go live with him in Hawaii too. Maybe he was thinking of setting up a commune?

'Do you want to dance?' Frank asked.

'I'm not really in the mood.'

'Don't be daft. This is your birthday party. You've got to dance at your birthday party. Come on, step on my old size nines and I'll take you round.'

I let him lead me on to the dance floor for the second time ever and even though it wasn't really waltz music he pulled me firmly towards him in a ballroom hold. There was absolutely no doubt that Frank was a brilliant dancer. I could feel the muscles in his shoulders through the thin material of his shirt, a pale purple one that suited him.

'If I was as good a dancer as you, I'd go dancing every single night.'

'Who says I don't? The flower in your hair looks nice. It goes really well with the dress. Even better than I thought it would.'

'The flower came from you? Gosh thanks, Frank. It's really pretty. That was very thoughtful of you.'

'You're very welcome. So, go on then, tell me all about the emotional stuff that's been going on tonight.'

'Well Bob and Jane are going to give it another go so the house is off the market.'

Frank didn't miss a step. 'You're joking right? I'm going to lose my commission?'

'You're going to lose a whole lot more apparently. Like a good-sized house in great decorative order with a sitting tenant.'

'Oh.'

'Oh, indeed. What was all that about? You weren't doing something nice for a change were you Frank?'

'Not really, it was a good investment.'

'Not really, at a rent lower than market price.'

'Well whatever, it's off the market now.'

'And then Cassie flashed her tits at Pippa and keep it under your hat but Glynis is having a baby with Steve, and James is going to live in Hawaii with his dad and Mack has asked me and Lois and Niall to come too.'

This time Frank did miss a step. He stopped dancing and pushed me away from him.

'This time you'd really better be kidding.'

'Sorry, Frank, I didn't think you were that interested in Glynis.'

'It's not Glynis I'm interested in! It's you!'

'Pardon me?'

'You heard me. You're the fat-bottomed girl that makes my rockin' world go round.'

'Um, well thanks for the compliment, I guess. But you're my boss! And you're usually rather mean to me.'

'Not really, I let you get away with murder most of the time.'

'How long?'

'You mean how long have you been making my rockin' world go round? You're just fishing for more compliments now.'

'Just a bit.'

'Pretty much since I first heard you chattering away to clients on the phone, all smiley and pleased to talk to them or maybe it was the first time you turned up late for work, pink-cheeked and beautiful and full of pathetic excuses or maybe, come to think of it, it was when you insisted I spent a fortune on that computer system and then started spying on me – sorry – organising my diary.'

'But that's a long time!'

'A very long time. But I was trying to ignore how I felt. It doesn't do to screw the crew apparently.'

'Who said anything about screwing!'

'It's just a saying Anna. All I'm saying is that I was trying to be professional, a good, respectable, respectful employer. But when I saw you that night in the wine bar, after Glynis stormed off and you didn't have the money to pay, I knew that all I wanted in the world was to be with you, take care of you. And screw you, of course, if I'm honest. And the night we met in town – which was a set up on my part by the way, I knew if I told Glynis that Central Park was the in place to go that you two would end up there – but it all backfired and you fancied Ryan, I felt physically sick at the thought of you being with someone else. Thank God Ryan worked out who you were and stopped flirting with you or else I would have had to punch him or something and he's way bigger than me.'

I grinned. 'So that's what all that was about! Look Frank I'm very flattered and everything and more than a little worried for my job but I can't cope with this right now. My head is spinning. Two of my best friends in the world have got back together tonight, another one has announced she's pregnant, James has told me he wants to

351

go live in Hawaii and Mack has asked the rest of us to go too. It's just too much to take in, all on one night.'

'I'm sorry, Anna. I wasn't going to say anything.'

'How many more people are going to say that to me tonight?'

'But I wasn't. I was just going to come here, ask you to dance, go home again. Nothing heavy! I was planning a long, slow campaign. Lots of dancing and corned beef pasties. Only if you're thinking of going to live in Hawaii I haven't got time for that. Are you Anna? Are you thinking of going?'

'Yes! No! I don't know. Maybe.'

'Do you love Mack?'

'Yes of course I do. I've loved him forever. My life wouldn't make sense if I didn't love Mack. *I* wouldn't make sense if I didn't love him. Mack is part of me, I'm part of him. That's how it's always been.'

Frank sighed. 'Then you should go to Hawaii and be with him.'

'Really?'

'Yes, really.' Then he pulled me towards him again, cupped my face gently in both his hands and kissed me on the lips, a slow, soft, kiss. And then he walked out.

The thing about being forty is that I don't feel that much different from the way I felt at twenty. Really I don't. I still like the same food I liked when I was twenty and I still have the same lefty views, more or less. OK, admittedly a bit less nowadays. I still drink too much of a Saturday evening and I still feel when I'm with my parents that they're the grown-ups really. Even though

I've got kids of my own now, I'm still the me I was when I was twenty.

And that being the case I didn't go to Hawaii. I didn't even need to think about it very long. A big part of me wanted to go. The part of me that loves Mack and always will. The part of me that wanted to learn to surf and sit in the sun every day and feel the sand between my toes. The part of me that never wants to let go of James, not ever.

But a bigger part of me needed to stay in Stonebridge. I wanted Niall and Lois to go to the same schools they were already at, to have the same friends and to live in the same house as they'd always done. To be near my parents and Mack's parents too. To be rooted here, safe in Wales, part of this community, even if it is a bit boring and nosy from time to time. I needed all that too because this is my home and it's where I belong.

James went to Hawaii of course. It was time for him to go. He was ready to leave home, to leave Stonebridge just like I'd been ready at his age. It seemed fitting that he should leave with Mack, just like I had.

'Are you sure you won't come too, Anna?' Mack had asked. 'I'd really like you to.'

'I know you would. And that counts for a lot Mack, an awful lot. But I can't.' There would always be a long line of Melanie Farrells making a beeline towards Mack to keep him company. Mack was never going to be lonely, not ever.

I miss James terribly. I feel his absence constantly. I finally understand how my parents felt when I left home all those years ago. But I am getting used to it. Now when Mack Skypes Lois and Niall I do sit in front of the computer, so we can all talk together as a family. James looks fantastic – he's filled out from all that surfing and his hair is white blond. He's working hard for his dad but also goes out a lot. He tells me there's no particular girlfriend but that there are plenty of girls and I like it that way. I don't want him to fall in love out there and not go to Oxford because of course he did get his three As and Niall did pretty well at his GCSEs too, better than he'd expected anyway. I've agreed with Mack that Niall and Lois can go over to Hawaii for a long holiday next summer. They can't wait. I'm dreading it but the lure of long days surfing in sunshine works wonders for encouraging Niall to study for his AS levels.

Bob and Jane are doing great. Daniel and Rhys forgave their mother as soon as they were sure that Bob had and everything is back to normal there. Normal is of course a relative concept for Bob and Jane – the biggest hurdle is yet to come but at least they're facing it together and hopefully it will be many years off yet.

Glynis' baby is due in four weeks. She's fat as butter and she waddles when she walks. It's great. She's sold her flat in London and bought a big house in Stonebridge with a granny flat attached. She says she'll apply for jobs with Cardiff law firms when the baby is about six months old and install a live-in nanny in the granny flat. She and Steve get on really well. I don't know if they'll make a go of it as a couple ever but they will definitely make a go of it as parents. I also think Steve will be applying for that nanny job when Glynis is ready.

Pippa has finally stopped flirting with Graham. Not because of the tit-flashing though. She was at a farmer's market a couple of months ago selling eggs and she met – wait for it – a farmer. He's quite fat actually and bald but he thinks Pippa's the most beautiful woman he ever set eyes on and the two of them are having an absolute whale of a time together. Non-stop amazing sex apparently, way better than the rock star who was so beautiful he didn't feel he had to try very hard, says Pippa. Cassie is still convinced that Pippa is out to get Graham back but that just makes her love Graham all the more and he's not complaining about that.

And Frank and me? We dance every chance we get, thanks for asking. In my living room mostly, with Niall shouting at us to get out the way of the television and with Lois standing on Frank's feet as he teaches her to waltz.

More from Honno to enjoy...

Back Home by Bethan Darwin

Ellie is broken hearted and so decamps home. Tea
and sympathy from grandad Trevor helps, as does the
distracting and hunky Gabriel, then a visitor turns
Trevor's world upside down...

*"A modern woman's romantic confession, alongside a
cleverly unfolding story of long-buried family secrets"*
Abigail Bosanko

*"Lively, fresh and warm-hearted – an easy-going and
enjoyable read"*
NiaWyn, author of *Blue Sky July*

9781906784034
£7.99

Sweets from Morocco by Jo Verity

Gordon has to go... Tessa and Lewis decide that
something must be done when the arrival of baby
Gordon threatens their, so far, perfect childhood.
A bittersweet story of sibling love and rivalry.

"A richly detailed and absorbing narrative journey"
Andrew Cowan

*"A ripping yarn and pitch perfect evocation of
childhood and sibling relationships"*
Daily Telegraph

9781906784003
£7.99

The War Before Mine by Caroline Ross

A brief wartime romance leaves Rosie heartbroken
and pregnant, not knowing if Philip – on a suicide
mission designed to stop the Nazi invasion – is alive
or dead.

"A versatile and senstive chronicler of the world at war"
Sunday Telegraph

"Complex and engaging" – Western Mail

9781870206976
£6.99

Hector's Talent for Miracles by Kitty Harri

Hector, his mother and grandmother live quietly in a small Spanish town but when Mair arrives on a mission to find her lost grandfather their meeting has explosive results, and all their lives are revealed as fragile constructions forged in the fire of a vicious conflict...

"An intelligent and sympathetic exploration of the lasting damage done to survivors of war."
Planet Magazine

9781870206815
£6.99

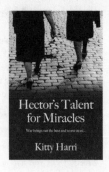

Salt Blue by Gillian Morgan

Life is made of memories, sweet and sour: Stella's journey from seaside Wales to upstate New York, from child to woman, set in the late fifties. A first novel of tangible sensual pleasures, *Salt Blue* paints a striking picture of life in a largely forgotten era...

9781906784157
£8.99

Freshers by Joanna Davies

Sex, drugs and rock'n'roll amidst the ivory towers in the early 90s...what it's like to leave home and find a whole new world waiting, one that is frequently unkind to the unwary and inexperienced.

"A riot of a novel full of the ardour of college days – but not for the fainthearted!"
Caryl Lewis

9781906784140
£7.99

Cut on the Bias: Stories about women and the clothes they wear
Edited by Stephanie Tillotson
An anthology of short fiction that explores the
intensely personal relationships women have with
what they wear.

*"From haute couture to granny-knit, there's plenty to
please in all shapes and sizes"*
www.thebookbag.co.uk

9781906784133
£7.99

ABOUT HONNO

Honno Welsh Women's Press was set up in 1986 by a group of women who felt strongly that women in Wales needed wider opportunities to see their writing in print and to become involved in the publishing process. Our aim is to develop the writing talents of women in Wales, give them new and exciting opportunities to see their work published and often to give them their first 'break' as a writer.

Honno is registered as a community co-operative. Any profit that Honno makes is invested in the publishing programme. Women from Wales and around the world have expressed their support for Honno. Each supporter has a vote at the Annual General Meeting.

To receive further information about forthcoming publications, or become a supporter, please write to Honno at the address below, or visit our website: www.honno.co.uk

Honno
Unit 14, Creative Units
Aberystwyth Arts Centre
Penglais Campus
Aberystwyth
Ceredigion
SY23 3GL

All Honno titles can be ordered online at
www.honno.co.uk
or by sending a cheque to Honno.
Free p&p to all UK addresses